HIDEAWAY

Also by Nicole Lundrigan

The Substitute
The Widow Tree
Glass Boys
The Seary Line
Thaw
Unraveling Arva

HIDEAWAY

NICOLE
LUNDRIGAN

VIKING

VIKING
an imprint of Penguin Canada, a division of Penguin Random House Canada Limited

Canada • USA • UK • Ireland • Australia • New Zealand • India • South Africa • China

First published 2019

www.penguinrandomhouse.ca

Library and Archives Canada Cataloguing in Publication

Title: Hideaway / by Nicole Lundrigan.
Names: Lundrigan, Nicole, author.
Identifiers: Canadiana (print) 20190043679 |
Canadiana (ebook) 20190047488 | ISBN 9780735237810
(softcover) | ISBN 9780735237827 (PDF)
Classification: LCC PS8573.U5436 H53 2019 | DDC C813/.6—dc23

Cover design: Terri Nimmo
Book design: Jennifer Lum
Cover image: IPGGutenbergUKLtd/Getty Images

Printed and bound in Canada

10 9 8 7 6 5 4 3 2 1

For my guy, Miro.
And for Miro's guy, Robert.

I thought how unpleasant it is to be locked out; and I thought how it is worse perhaps to be locked in.

VIRGINIA WOOLF, *A ROOM OF ONE'S OWN*

When he strikes, the surface opens up and lets him in. He drops down and down through the cold folds of water. Knees bent, his legs float forward, pale arms waving. Light from the full moon cuts through the blackness. Above, the outline of a figure leans over the boat, watching him sink. The oar still gripped in both hands.

He gasps, stomach and lungs filling with water. Twigs scrape across his spine, stringy plants slip through his fingers. He sinks deeper. The moon dims until it is just a thumbprint in a starless sky.

His mind goes blank. The water presses on him. He is shrinking and shrinking into the darkness, and any moment he will disappear.

PART ONE

ROWAN

I could tell by her face. She knew what I'd done. The school counselor had said he wouldn't tell Gloria, but one glance at my mother and I was sure she'd gotten a phone call. When I walked down Pinchkiss Circle she was standing in front of our house holding a hammer and a piece of wood. As I got closer, I could see she'd painted a single misspelled word right in the middle of it.

THEIF.

I wasn't expecting that.

The whole meeting with the counselor had been no big deal. That was what I'd thought, anyway. He wanted to talk about the change in my "family structure," which meant Telly walking out on me and my little sister last month. Gloria had tried to hide it, but once our neighbor Mrs. Spooner noticed Telly's truck was gone all the time, everyone soon found out. "Rowan, I know school's almost over," the counselor had said, "but I want to end on a positive. You've been upset, that's clear, but some people do really constructive things with their anger."

I didn't know what he meant. Was I supposed to build something? Tear something down?

Then he asked if I had "good buddies to lean on."

I shook my head.

"Boys to pal around with?"

I shook my head again. The fact was, I didn't have a single friend. Besides Darrell, an older kid who lived a few houses up from us on the circle. Sometimes he'd invite me over for a soda, or to see his motorcycle.

The counselor leaned forward, put his elbows on his desk. He was wearing a skinny purple tie. It matched the purple frame on his glasses. "What about the future? What do you dream about?"

"At night?" I asked. I didn't mention how he'd just ended three of the last four sentences in prepositions. That would really bug Mrs. Spooner. She was also my language arts teacher.

"No, in general. What are your aspirations?"

I told him I wanted to fix my skin. Maybe that would help me find some "good buddies to lean on." People were afraid I was contagious. Even the teachers never came too close. Well, besides Mrs. Spooner. The only person who actually liked my spots was Maisy. Ever since she was little she'd thought there was a map growing out through me. That I was the key to some treasure. Sometimes when Gloria said mean things, I'd find a tiny note on torn paper under my pillow. "You ar beeutifell." Even though it was weird for Maisy to say that to her brother, I kept every one.

"What other things? What makes you happy, Rowan?"

I didn't tell him my idea of getting on a train and going back to find Gran. Which was impossible now, because Gran was dead. Instead I told the counselor about my dream of hitting a home run. Having that bat in my hands, swinging it as hard as I could, and striking the fat round ball out of the park. The crowd always leapt up from the stands and screamed and roared.

"Do you imagine that a lot?" he said.

"Yeah. I do. All the time."

"Maybe we should start a team in September. Get uniforms. I could coach."

I stared down at my hands. There was a neat white island over the bottom part of my thumb.

"The school might fund it."

"Still," I said. He thought I was worried about money. "I don't think it'd work."

"Why not?"

I shrugged. I didn't mention that in my dream I was the only one on the team. And I certainly didn't mention that when I looked down at the bat it was often a blur of red. Bits of bone and broken teeth. Sometimes in my imagination the ball was just a ball, but most times it was a head. Sound of a melon smashing as the swinging bat tore it straight off. My stomach filling up with satisfaction.

Mrs. Spooner always told me I had a creative mind.

"Well," the counselor said, "at least you've got a supportive mom. Even with your dad gone, she's on your side. We've got to count our blessings, right?"

"Yeah." I nodded and smiled. "I'm pretty lucky. You won't tell her about what I took, right?"

"Stole, you mean."

"Stole," I whispered.

"I'll have to think about it, Rowan. Leave it with me."

I'd thought that meant he wouldn't call. But as I got closer to home, Gloria was staring at me. One foot up on the steps leading to the front porch. Maisy was nowhere to be seen. She'd already walked home from school with her friend Shar. She could be out playing, or she could be hiding away. She was like that, vanishing at the first sign of trouble.

"Get over here," Gloria said.

I dragged my feet.

"I'm at the end of my rope with you. Do you know that? The very end of it." She spoke in a low growl. Gloria never yelled outside.

I looked down at my sneakers. They were covered in a fine film of dust from our driveway. "Sorry," I said.

"Sorry? Sorry? That's all you got to say? I've never been so ashamed. Grabbing chocolate bars out of some teacher's purse? Like you don't get enough to eat at home? And everyone nosing around in our business. That woman, that, that Mrs. Spooner, and now some school counselor calling me. Talking about Telly running off. Because nothing ever went wrong in their perfect lives."

"I said I was sorry, Gloria."

"Oh, buddy boy. You're going to be sorry."

I expected her to walk up our driveway and stop at the bottom of Pinchkiss Circle. I thought she'd make me stand beside the rain gutter so our neighbors could see the sign. But instead she went in the opposite direction. She strode across the fresh green grass and stepped into the woods.

As I followed behind her I noticed Maisy, tucked into the furthest corner of the deck that was built off the side of our house. Our dog, Chicken, was snoring beside her. She watched me with her blue eyes, her round face frowning. I knew what she was thinking. *Don't go. Don't go in there.* I waved, made a weak attempt at a cartwheel to make her smile. Then I ran to catch up with Gloria.

When I entered the woods, my heart sped up a bit. I called out, "Isn't this the wrong way, Gloria?" As far back as I could remember, Maisy and I had called our parents by their first names. Gloria said it was modern, progressive. Our mother was always Gloria. And our dad was always Telly.

She ignored my question, just kept marching forward, her new blond hair bouncing, the sign jammed into her armpit. I had to rush to keep up. One of Gloria's steps was two of mine. We went further and further into the woods.

"This is just dumb!" I yelled. "Someone's supposed to see me, aren't they?"

She snickered, said over her shoulder, "You know, lots of wolves live in here." Her voice was cheerful.

I laughed. "I'm thirteen, Gloria. That dumb stuff doesn't scare me anymore."

She swept past branches and stomped over mossy logs. Gloria had thick legs. "Telly almost caught one once. Enormous ugly thing. Fur all stuck down. They like to hunt when it's dark."

"So?" I said.

"Green eyes show up first. Then you hear them sniffing and scratching."

"Oh." A squirt of sickness shot through my guts. Around me the shadows were long and narrow.

After a lot of walking, Gloria stopped. The trees had grown thicker and the ground was spongy under my feet. She turned in a slow circle, then lifted the sign. Dug a nail from her pocket and fixed it to a trunk. Three hard slams with the hammer. "Stand there," she said.

"There?"

"That's what I said, didn't I? Under your sign."

I didn't understand why we were in the woods. Weeks ago, Gloria told us about a girl she saw outside the front door of Stafford's department store. Apparently, the kid had taken a baby soother because her brother was crying. As punishment, her mother taped construction paper to her T-shirt with a message that read, "Do not trust me. I rob stuff." I thought Gloria was going to do the same thing. So the neighbors could gawk. "This doesn't make sense. Nobody lives in here."

"How do you know?"

"Because it's just trees, Gloria. And squirrels."

She looked me right in the eye. "Wait and see, mister," she said. "No-*body* don't mean no-*thing*. Try not to breathe when you hear one of them. They'll smell you a mile away."

Then she left me standing under the sign. She wound her way back through the trees, and I could hear her humming a tune. The notes of her music vanished just seconds before she did.

I stood there, waiting. My stomach groaned. It had to be dinnertime by now. Gloria was probably cooking noodles or heating up a can of soup. Any moment, she'd be back. She'd find me exactly where I was and realize I wasn't bothered one bit. And who'd win then? Wolves? What a joke.

But she never appeared. Water from the swampy ground seeped through my sneakers. My feet itched but I didn't reach down to scratch. I kept leaning against the tree as the afternoon passed and the light changed. I had to pee, badly, but I knew any second she'd be there. Each time I heard a branch snap or leaves rustle I'd squint in her direction, but I didn't see her. Gradually color seeped away. Shadows expanded and consumed the ground. I watched. Soon, she'd return. The woods turned grayer and grayer. Soon. Then, in a single long breath, all my eyes could see was black.

Realization made my skin turn cold. She wasn't coming back for me. She'd left me for the night. Why would I ever have believed she'd stick me out in the road with that sign? She'd never purposely give the neighbors something to talk about. Not Gloria. She didn't want me to feel embarrassed about grabbing a few chocolate bars. She wanted me to feel afraid.

And she'd succeeded. In the pitch black, I was too scared to twitch. To breathe. To think. I had no idea which way was east or west, or how I'd get home. I patted the gnarly bark of the trunk behind me. Reached up to feel my THEIF sign, just in case I'd accidentally gotten turned around. My heart clacked loudly, but my ears strained to identify every sound. Plants uncurling, insects crawling, small animals under the dead layer of leaves. Burrowing toward me. So much noise inside the silence.

The darkness grew darker.

Then the unmistakable sound of footsteps. Something creeping. Crunching. Grunting. Or whispering. I couldn't tell.

I saw a thin beam of white light cutting through the trees. Flickering as it bobbed left to right. Not from the way Gloria had walked home, but from deeper inside the woods. I stared at the light without blinking. It was getting closer and closer. What was coming? Anything could live in these woods at night. Wolves or killers or aliens with leathery blue skin and split tongues. Behind the glow I could see a shadow. A massive shape. A lumbering boulder. It moved closer and closer and my heart slapped so loudly my whole head was flooded.

Please be Gloria. Please be Gloria wearing an enormous coat. Or Telly. Please, please be my father.

"Gloria? Is that you?" I heard grumbling. "Gloria? I'm sorry. I'm really sorry." My throat constricted. I croaked, "Gloria? Telly? Telly!"

No response.

The light bobbed along until the beam reached my feet, slid up my legs. Shone straight into my eyes. I squinted, tried to yell "Leave me alone." But nothing came out.

Panting, then. A quiet clicking. An animal's wet mouth opening and closing.

"I am not a Gloria." A grown man's raspy voice. I couldn't see him. "And I am, am, urh, not a Telly."

Pee spilled down my leg, a burst of warmth. I shook my head. Fast. I wanted to run, but outside the circle of light was thick tar. I pressed my back into the tree. The ripples of bark cut into my shoulder blades.

Then he flashed the light on the sign above my head.

"But you're a thief." He mumbled something, then said, "Whoever created your signage has difficulty with, urh, proper letter arrangement."

I clamped a hand over my gaping mouth, teeth stabbing my palm. I sucked air through my fingers.

The voice continued speaking in a flat, mechanical way. "Juvenile delinquent in the system. Once he's in, it's very, very, urh, difficult to get out." The flashlight moved over my jeans and sweatshirt. "What sort of offender?"

A mousy squeak popped from behind my fingers. He aimed the light directly in my eyes. I tried to twist away.

"What did you steal?" Louder this time.

I lowered my hand. "Chocolate."

"Petty theft. Confession."

"Just from my teacher."

"*Just from my teacher*. Urh. Doesn't matter." He kept grunting as he spoke, as though he had to force his words over a hurdle.

"Were you influenced? Coerced? Workers find all kinds of ways in. Through your electricity." The sound of nails scraping bristles. Was there a wolf there, too? Crouched next to him?

"I—I don't know." What did he mean, *workers*? How were they finding their way in? I wanted to cry.

He started grumbling. "She wants to change your sign to HUNGRY, but I have no markers." There was a woman with him? "But she's, urh, a lenient judge. I have a candy bar, though. Here somewhere." A thump then, and he dropped his flashlight. The glare crossed his bearded face and I jumped. Dark shiny eyes. Stained skin. Scraggly curls were growing down over his ears, his face. Metal balls were caught in his hair and beard. He was patting the pockets of an oversized coat.

"Take this," he said.

I heard paper ripping and a sweet smell threaded toward me. Before I even thought, my fingers reached for it. Could've been poison, but I chewed it down.

He picked up the flashlight. Angled the beam away from my face just as a warm, wet sensation moved over my hand. I yelled out, and then realized it was a dog's tongue.

"Girl," the man said, and he laughed. "Get back here."

"It's okay," I whispered. My mouth was still full of sugar and my heart had slowed. Strangely, I didn't feel so afraid anymore. If this man was going to stab me or strangle me or shoot me in the head, he'd probably have done it already. Not given me chocolate.

The man laughed again. It was a good-natured laugh. "Dot thinks you're going to get indigestion."

Who's Dot? I wanted to ask. The woman must be standing behind him. Hidden in the darkness and watching me. Or maybe he was crazy and thought his dog was talking to him? He didn't sound crazy, though, wasn't slurring his words or swearing and spitting. He sounded smart, like a doctor or a businessman. But a weird one.

I licked caramel off my back teeth, then pushed "Thank you" out of my mouth. I don't think he heard me.

The dog stuck its muzzle in the wet crotch of my jeans. I lifted up my knee.

"I don't know. Who expects to see a tiny boy standing in woods in the middle of the night? Under some misspelled sign. Where is his, his, his, urh, mother? Maybe he's not there. He's not there."

The light was slicing through the air, across the trees. I wanted to tell him I was there. I was right there in front of him. And I wasn't a tiny boy. I was a teenager and I couldn't help it if I was shortest in my grade. But he was talking fast, and there was panic behind his words.

I was getting afraid again. Even wondering if I was the one imagining everything. Petrified inside the woods and making up a person to keep me company. But if I *was* doing that, wouldn't I imagine someone *normal*? Someone *nice*? Would my tongue feel bulbs of sugar stuck on my back teeth?

I heard him breathing in and out. Slowly. "Calm down. Calm down. Girl?" The dog yipped. Then his voice, clear and loud, came directly at my face. "You soiled yourself."

My heart smacked against my rib cage again. "An accident."

"You're not in trouble." Soft now. "It doesn't matter if you're there or not. We still have to be ourselves, right?"

"What?" I didn't understand. My legs were shaking and the skin behind my soaked jeans stung.

"You can come with us, if you want. Girl and I have something of a home. No one's going to hurt you."

I looked up at my sign. *THEIF*. I looked into the black all around me. Green eyes could appear at any second.

"Well?" he said.

I shuffled my feet. Ever since I could remember, Gloria had told me not to talk to strangers. She explained that the only people I could trust were my family. "And Gran, too," I'd said once when I was little, but Gloria shook her head. "Just me and Telly. Nobody outside this house wants to protect you. Under this roof is the only place you're actually safe. Repeat what I just said." And I did. She'd smiled, said "I'm telling you, Rowan, other people are just going to hurt you or take from you or disappoint you."

I thought about the school counselor ratting me out that afternoon. That was a disappointment. But Mrs. Spooner had never done anything wrong. Not really. Gloria called her a no-good gossip because she'd told people about Telly, but why would I care about that? She'd always been nice to me, even though Gloria couldn't stand her. And was Gloria protecting me now? Leaving me out in the woods at night? I wasn't completely sure if she was or she wasn't. Maybe I didn't understand what she was trying to do. She was always saying that. I was too young to know. Too young to realize. Perhaps this was a test I needed to pass.

"No one's going to force you either, Magic Boy." *Magic Boy.* "That's for sure. You may remain with your sign. It is your legal right to do so, urh, but it may not be your obligation."

There was so much confusion swirling around inside my head, but everything in my heart was telling me to stay with the man. I didn't want this peculiar person and his dog to wander away and leave me alone. So as he left I hung a few feet back, taking bowlegged steps so my thighs wouldn't rub on my jeans. Walking ahead of me, he chattered to invisible people. Often laughing. I couldn't hear what they were saying. Occasionally he turned and pointed the light on the ground, warned me of a fallen branch or a rock. "Don't want you getting hurt, do we?" For some reason I can't explain, I believed him.

"Where are we going?"

"Not far, urh. I have a camp. Clean and warm. Under the bridge. Do you know where that is?"

"Yes," I said. It was an old stone bridge that was no longer used. I'd been there a couple of times with Darrell. But that was a long time ago. We'd caught a bucket full of tadpoles, and I brought some of them home. Maisy watched them for hours, skittering around, until Gloria found the bucket and dumped it on the grass.

We reached Slowrun Creek and walked along the edge of it. I could hear the water rushing over stones, and in the glow from the man's flashlight, it glittered. The faint odor of smoke hung in the air as we came closer. When we arrived underneath the bridge, I saw the remains of a fire. He poked the embers with a long stick, put broken branches on top. Soon enough the fire crackled and I could see blankets lifted up on sticks, a make-shift tent. There was a large backpack and a neat pile of garbage off to the side. The dog sniffed all around the perimeter, then settled in, sucking on a stuffed toy. I think it was a squirrel.

The man clapped his hands together. "There's heat coming off that now. If you want to stand closer. Dry off. Or you can wash your trousers in the, the, urh, water and hang them up. With soap."

"I'll stand," I said. No way was I taking my pants off. I edged nearer to the flames.

"You won't smell acceptable, but it is your choice."

The man went to his backpack and came back with an orange. Peeled it and tossed the rind into the fire. Then he cracked it open, ate a section, and handed half to me. I took it.

"Do you have a real home?" Maybe because I'd stopped shivering and had food in my stomach, I felt safe enough to ask questions.

His eyes narrowed. "This is real. It doesn't change much day to day, so I know it's real."

"I mean like a house."

"Of course. Urh. But it's not a good place to stay."

"Why not?"

His head jerked up. "Why not? Wait, Stan. Wait."

"Stan?"

"Scans," he said. He ate another piece of the orange. Juice glistened on his beard. He tapped the corners of his mouth with his finger in an almost delicate way. "Beams in the attic had trackers. I let birds loose but they couldn't dig them out." He scratched his beard, tugged at a handful and twisted it in his fingers. "Saying too much? Okay, okay. Full stop."

"What's your name, mister?"

His eyes darted left and right and he whispered, "Which one, which one? You're always mumbling. Henry."

"Henry?"

He laughed as though that was the funniest thing to say. "No, no." Then he nodded. "That's good." He looked at me and said, "Carl."

"Carl?"

"Yes, just Carl."

"I'm Ro—"

He waved his hands. "Don't tell me. They might be listening." He pointed upward. "Metal and concrete block the worst of it. But."

"Okay," I said. Maybe if I thought about it later, I'd know what he meant.

My jeans were finally getting dry, and I crouched down. Carl placed an itchy blanket over my shoulders. My head dropped to my knees, the sharp stench of dried pee coming up from between my legs. I closed my eyes. My arms and legs were like weights pushing into the sandy ground. Then behind me, I heard soft footsteps. I lifted my head. A familiar voice. Telly! How had my dad found me? I was so tired I could barely keep my eyes open, but I felt his hand move down over my back.

"Thank you, sir," he said to Carl, and shook his hand. "Thanks mightily for looking after my boy. I've got him now." He clutched my hand like I was a toddler and I drifted up and followed behind, full of relief. His red truck was idling in among the trees. I wondered how he'd managed to drive it in there. He tugged open the door, put a towel down on the passenger seat. "Let's get you home and cleaned up," he said.

"Home?"

"My home. After what Gloria did, you think I'd ever let you go back there? She'll just have to accept it whether she likes it or not." We drove through empty streets and pulled up to a house on a hill. His place was bright and clean and smelled of oranges. I changed into flannel pajamas, and Telly put another log on a fire. Water from a fish tank gurgled. A lady I didn't recognize hugged me. "It's nice to finally meet you," she said, and pointed to a large brown dog. "Don't mind her. That's just Girl."

"Her name's Girl, too?"

"Sure, it's a common name," she said. I felt the dog's paws on my chest, wetness gliding over my cheek, my eyelids. Telly came closer, and nudged me. "Hey, buddy. What trouble should we get up to today?"

I startled awake. Telly and that lady and his perfect house evaporated. The dog was licking my face and the man, Carl, was tapping me gently on the shoulder. The fire was out. The creek tumbled along. Frogs burped, and some birds were chirping. Morning had arrived. The light was hazy gray. I stretched and the blanket fell away. My neck and back were sore and stiff, but I was all right. I was okay.

"Sun's coming up," Carl said. "Shouldn't you get back to your sign, Magic Boy?"

"I guess so." I liked that he called me *Magic Boy*. I'd just survived an entire night in the woods with a stranger. That made me kind of a magic boy in my mind.

"You don't want to miss your ride." He lifted his hand and shook it. "No. I'm serious, Dot." He sounded irritated. "You can't just decide to keep one. He's not a sweater or a stone." He closed his eyes, shook his head.

I understood what he was arguing about. What the invisible woman in his head wanted. My mind flew toward a cottony *what if*? This man was eccentric but friendly. He had a cozy shelter and blankets and food and a fire. I'd managed to stay one night. Why couldn't I stay another? It would be the best adventure. He didn't mind me hanging around, and besides, no one would miss me.

That wasn't true; Maisy would miss me. Her pale face was probably watching the woods right now. I stood up.

"Do you know the way?"

"Sure," I said. Orange and pink light filtered through the trees.

I asked one last question. "Are there any wolves in these woods?"

"Wolves?" His laughter sounded like it came from deep within him. As though he had a wonderful and endless supply of it. "No."

"None?"

"Not a single one," he said. "Urh. Not for a hundred years."

"Oh," I said. "Oh."

I was back beneath the sign for only five minutes when I heard Gloria clomping through the woods. I'd know her heavy foot anywhere.

"I hope you learned your lesson" was all she said.

MAISY

"Were you scared in the woods?"

The rain was stopped, but all the water was still gushing around. Rowan said we could look in the ditches around the circle. That was fun. Sometimes good stuff came floating by.

"No, I wasn't scared."

"Not a bit?"

"No, Turtle. Not one bit."

He always called me that. *Turtle*. He said I hid inside my shell too much.

"You want to know what Gloria said?"

"Not really. But tell me."

"She said if you acted like a wolf, you got to live like a wolf."

Rowan laughed, and he curled his fingers up and grrr-ed real loud. I jumped.

"That's funny," he said. "It's just a dumb lie to frighten you."

"It's not," I said. Gloria never told lies. There were wolves in the woods. I never saw none, but she said when they're hungry they come right into our backyard looking for children. She told me never to trust a wolf. Not all of them had fur and pointy ears. A wolf could look like anybody.

We walked around our circle. The water in the ditch was dirty brown and I used a stick to stir it.

"Well, did you see any?"

"No, Maisy. And no aliens or murderers or anything stupid like that. Nothing but a few possums, maybe. Birds, sleeping. I kind of liked it."

"You did?"

"Yeah. I didn't have to listen to Gloria complain about Telly."

I tried to keep my laugh in, but it came out. After Telly drove off, Gloria was always mad about him. She really wanted him to come home. She said she wasn't going to get a wink of rest until our family was right back like it was.

"How about we go up to the top of the circle," Rowan said. "That's where the best stuff floats down. And Shar's not there."

Shar was my best friend. She lived with Darrell and his mom, Aunt Erma, who was not really my aunt, but Gloria told me to call her that. Shar's mom was not a good mom, so Shar couldn't stay with her. But she always went to visit every summer after school was over. But this year she left today. Shar said her mom was extra excited to see her.

We walked by Shar's house. Darrell was outside, and he was working on a motorcycle. He was always doing that. He was wearing a T-shirt with a skull on it and shorts that had lots of threads sticking off the bottom.

"Hey," Rowan said.

"Hey guys," Darrell said back.

My face got warm right away. I looked at my rubber boots. They were green with frog eyes near where the toes were. Gloria got them from Stafford's and they were way too big. I didn't like them, but I couldn't tell Gloria. I was afraid the frogs would get dirt in their eyes when I walked. I didn't wear them for a long time, and Gloria said she was going to put my frog boots outside for the wolves to eat if I didn't start.

"Something broken?" Rowan said.

"Nah. Just fine tuning. You want to see?"

"Sure, but later. I'm looking after Maisy. Last month after it rained she found a plastic duck in the ditch. Now she always wants to look."

We found more than a plastic duck. I wanted to tell Darrell, but I didn't. We also found a pink rubber thing that looked like a long submarine, but Gloria screamed when I carried it home.

"You guys doing anything neat this summer?"

I looked at Darrell. "Last night, Rowan slept in the—"

Rowan stomped right on the frog's nose holes and said, "In the attic. Hung a hammock from the rafters."

"Cool, that's real cool."

Then Rowan grabbed my arm and dragged me up the circle away from

Darrell. I took a tissue out of my pocket and cleaned my boots. "Why'd you do that for? You almost squished my toes."

"You can't say shit like that, Maisy."

"What?"

"Tell people Gloria stuck me out in the woods."

"But it's Darrell."

"Doesn't matter."

"Oh."

"Do you want Gloria getting in trouble?"

I shook my head.

"People coming to take you away because she's a crap mother?"

"Like with Shar?"

"Yeah, like with Shar. But we don't have an Aunt Erma, do we?"

"Sure we do. We know Aunt Erma."

"You don't get it. Just keep your mouth shut."

I closed my mouth and nodded.

Then I looked into the ditch and saw something. It floated out of the big metal tube that went right under Mrs. Spooner's driveway. There was hair and eyes and no body. It bobbed up and down. A doll's head.

"Rowan! Catch it, Rowan! Save her!" He stuck out a stick and caught her. He held her up and water dripped out of her hair and her neck. "She needs to get washed."

Mrs. Spooner must've heard me yelling because she opened her door and called out, "What did you kids find?"

"A head! We got a head."

"A head? Not a real one, I hope!"

"No, no!" I laughed big. "Just a doll."

"Let me take a peek," she said. She waved at us.

I took the wet head off the top of the stick and ran to Mrs. Spooner.

"Well, that is a nice surprise to start off the summer."

"Rowan saved her from the wolves."

"What wolves, sweetheart?"

I looked at Rowan. He was standing behind me and he was frowning bad. "Nothing," I said. "I was just telling a joke." I had to know what to say and what to hold inside. There was always so much to remember.

"She's like me, Mrs. Spooner. Big imagination."

"Oh, yes, of course," Mrs. Spooner said. When she smiled there were tons of lines all over her face. She looked like crumpled-up paper. "I understand. Should we get this little lady cleaned up?"

"Yup!"

Me and Rowan went inside, and I sat on a chair in the kitchen. All the walls had blue flowers on them and there were tons of pictures of Mr. Spooner. There was a brown box on the wall over the table full of spoons. That was really funny. I poked Rowan, but he frowned again and said, "Don't be rude."

Mrs. Spooner turned on warm water and Rowan washed the doll in the sink. He used soap to clean her hair back to yellow and he used his finger to dig out dirt and leaves that filled up her brain.

"Here," Mrs. Spooner said. "Why don't you use a sock to make a proper body? It was Mr. Spooner's, but I'm sure he won't mind."

Mr. Spooner was in the cemetery now. There was a grassy spot right next to him someday for Mrs. Spooner, but she told me once she wasn't in a rush.

"I've got some stale oats you can use to stuff it," she said. "Plump that girl up."

Rowan filled her body up to the top. Mrs. Spooner gave him a needle and a thread, and he stuck out his tongue and pushed the needle through the sock and then through the tiny holes on the bottom of the doll's neck.

"I love her," I said when he gave her to me. "I love her so much. Her name's Jenny. I won't lose her. I promise I won't."

"Well that's a relief," Rowan said. "Because you've lost every single doll you've ever had. Good thing they're not real."

Mrs. Spooner laughed. "She'll be just fine, won't you, Maisy?"

"Yup! Thank you, Mrs. Spooner."

"My pleasure," she said. "Helping out my two favorite neighbors."

I put my frog boots back on and Rowan held my hand and we went outside. Gloria was just getting off the bus at the top of the circle. She was gone all day working at Stafford's. Sometimes she helps people pay and sometimes she puts clothes on clothes hangers. She waved at me, and I ran over. I cradled Jenny in my arms. She was fat and heavy with the oatmeal. One of her eyes didn't close right, so she looked half sleepy, but that was okay.

"What's that thing?"

"Jenny. Rowan and me got her before she drowned in the ditch. Mrs. Spooner gave us a sock because Jenny lost her body somewhere away. And Mrs. Spooner got spoons on her wall."

"Mrs. Spooner?"

"Yup." I could smell the flower soap from Jenny's hair.

"I don't want you going in there."

"Where?"

"To that woman's place."

"To her house?"

"Nowhere near her. Unless you're stuck in her classroom or at the library. Other than that, you steer clear."

"But she's nice," I said.

"I told you I hate that word. *Nice*."

My middle started to feel funny and my mouth got fuzz in it. Like the television when nothing was on.

Gloria nipped my arm. "Listen, Bids," she said. "You don't know her. She could be anybody. You don't know what she's really after. Maybe she'd love a little girl all for herself. Is that what you'd like?"

"No."

"I can't hear you. Is that what you want?"

"No," I said louder.

"Well you best remember that next time you find yourself in some weird old lady's kitchen. You hear me?"

"Yes," I said.

"I'm trying to keep you safe, Bids. You think everyone is decent and good, and that's not true at all, darling. That's your mind making stuff up."

I looked down at Jenny's new body, and I tiptoed the rest of the way home. The frogs on my feet already had too much dirt in their eyes. I think they were probably crying.

MAISY

When I got home I put Jenny right in the middle of the kitchen table. I wouldn't lose her there. Gloria started buzzing around like crazy. She scrubbed out the toilet and she vacuumed up the carpet. She gave me a rag and some blue water, and I sprayed Chicken's drool off the walls. Then she mixed eggs and butter and cherries and flour and other stuff and put it in the oven and out came a cake. She even did icing. That was Telly's number one favorite.

"Telly's going to be there, Bids. Front row, I bet. And then he'll come back for a slice, won't he?"

I nodded.

"Yes, he will. He'll see what he's been missing."

I followed her upstairs and she pulled on a red dress that went low on her front. There was a lot coming out the top. Her mouth was red too. She smiled at herself and rubbed at her teeth with her finger. Then she brushed her hair. It used to be brown but now it was yellow.

"You got your costume in the bag? You're going to be amazing," she said. "Do you know when I was your age, I was quite the actress myself? My teacher even thought I should go out for auditions. Real auditions. But my mother pooh-poohed it all. Never saw my talent. Not like I see yours, sweetheart. As a child, I mean, you really don't stand a chance without someone in your court."

Gloria kept talking and talking and the more words she said, the more my middle knotted up. When we walked to the school, Rowan put his arm around me and said, "You're going to be great, Turtle."

"Now, you," Gloria said to Rowan when we were almost there. "You better act sharp when you see your dad. You understand me?"

Rowan frowned and shook his head. But he said, "Yeah."

Everything next went fast. We got to the school and I went to my classroom and my teacher helped me get changed. I was the mother flower sprite. She put pink circles on my cheeks. Then I was waiting and then the curtain came up and there was no spit in my mouth, and then two hands were on my back pushing me on the stage. I looked out at everybody. A lot of people looked back. I could see Telly right next to Gloria. They were in the front like she said. Even with the lights burning my eyes, I could see her waving and grinning and pointing and clapping her hands. I tried to swallow but nothing went down my throat.

"Go, Maisy," someone said. "Go!"

I wiggled around the kid tulips and bumped them on their heads to help them grow. Then the sun danced over but he went to the wrong place. I tripped on my ribbons and the tulips all giggled. The sun tapped his foot because I had to say something. I looked out at Gloria. She kept sticking her thumb up. My heart was racing like crazy. I couldn't remember what I was supposed to say. Something about saying goodbye to spring or hello to summer. I'd practiced and practiced, and my teacher told me when we practiced all together "You're ready!" but I wasn't ready. The sun stared at me with his spike paper thing around his head. I looked out at the front row and Gloria's thumb was gone. Telly was nodding his head, but Gloria's smile fell off her face. I blinked. All the tulips laughed louder and louder. The people watching the show were laughing too. There was a lot of roaring in my ears. The sun stuck his elbow in my neck. One of his paper spikes poked in my eye. "Outta my way, stupid." I got out of his way. I put a hand over my hurt eye. I held my breath. Everyone in their chairs made an *aww* sound.

After it was all over, Gloria and Telly and Rowan all came to the classroom to pick me up. Telly gave me a giant hug and said, "You did an amazing job, Bids. I was so proud." I wiped my nose real hard. Then he got down on one knee. "Now, you listen to me. Don't you feel one bit bad about yourself. Every single actress you see in movies had stage fright. Forgot a line or two. It's part of learning."

"Really?" I said. I couldn't stop looking at his teeth. They were white like a camera flash.

"Absolutely," he said back. "In fact, if you didn't have it, I'd say you weren't a serious actress at all. Feeling nervous, having a few good slip-ups, that's par for the course. How do you think you grow?"

He hugged me again, and the bad pain in my middle went away.

"And you're coming back for cake, Telly," Gloria said. She stood in front of me. "I insist. Maisy and me made cherry and chocolate."

His voice turned strange then. Not nice no more. "Can't."

"What?"

"We got something on, Glow."

"We?"

"Yep. Can't manage it."

"You got to be kidding me. Now's the time to celebrate your daughter's achievements."

"And I will. Just not tonight. You understand don't you, Bids?"

"It's okay," I said.

"*It's okay*," Gloria said in a silly way.

Rowan tapped his shoulder. "But I got to talk to you, Telly. I really got to talk to you about stuff."

"Can't tonight, Row. Sorry about that. But we will. We'll catch up soon. Once I get some things figured out. You got my word."

Rowan shoved his hands in his pockets. "Sure. Whatever."

"I said you got my word. That means you got my word."

We walked home behind Gloria. She was talking the whole way. "*It's okay, it's okay*." I think she was pretending she was me. "What a disaster," she said when we reached the circle. "What an awful, awful embarrassment. I was so ashamed."

I couldn't keep the tears inside no more. They just slipped out. They were really wet and quiet. Rowan squeezed my hand until it hurt. He whispered inside my ear, "You were the best sprite I ever saw, Turtle. You banged those tulips on the head like a hired hit man. That sun was so lame. What a loser in a crap costume. No wonder you didn't want to say anything."

When we got home Gloria went to the kitchen and called out, "Rowan, sweetheart." Then, "Chicken." She never said my name. I waited on the bottom stair. I waited a long time thinking she might call me. That was how I knew she disappeared me. She did that sometimes. Mostly it was Rowan, but tonight it was me. She couldn't see me no more. Gloria's heart was all locked up because only one of us was allowed in at a time.

I heard them cutting the cake. "I'm going to give you an extra big piece, my darling." Rowan was her darling. "I'm not hungry," he said. "I don't want cake." And then she said, "Nonsense, Row. After sitting through that display of garbage, you need a treat."

I went to my bedroom and waited and waited until Gloria closed her door. Then I waited another long time before I sneaked downstairs to find Jenny. I was afraid I'd lose her. I could see the cake under a glass bowl. Some moon was coming through the window and making it look extra special. I wouldn't touch it though. She'd know.

Then I felt something strange under my feet. Like dirt. I looked down and I didn't know at first. Something was all over the kitchen floor. It was Mrs. Spooner's oatmeal.

"You don't have much luck with dolls, do you, Turtle?"

My arms jumped up. I didn't know Rowan was behind me.

"She was on the table when I went upstairs. Chicken must have gotten hungry."

"Yeah." I swallowed.

"Made a real mess, hey? Probably wishing he didn't now, though. I bet it gave him bad dreams."

He was in the corner snoring. He wasn't having bad dreams at all.

Rowan found Jenny under one of Chicken's back legs. Her hair was a big drooly mess and her body was all ripped up. Her face was covered in bites and slime from Chicken's mouth. Rowan broke the string so the sock came off her neck. He stepped on the garbage can and the lid flipped up and in went the sock.

More tears came out of my eyes. Even though I knew I shouldn't let them go, I couldn't stop.

"It's okay. Don't be sad. I'll even clean up."

He gave me Jenny and I wiped the drool on my nightgown.

"And don't mind what Gloria said. She's just angry about Telly."

"She's mad at me."

"No, she's not. I'm telling you the truth. If Telly came over, you wouldn't be able to wipe the smile off her face." He punched my arm. But not hard. "You all right?"

I sniffed and said, "I didn't like Jenny's heart being stuck inside Mr. Spooner's dead sock anyway."

"Then it's good she's just a head, Turtle. Who needs a heart?"

ROWAN

Mrs. Spooner always encouraged me to write things down so I'd feel better. She said the smartest people in the world did that as a way to "get in touch with their feelings." So the day after Maisy's concert, the day after Telly turned his back on me in the school hallway, I took a pen and some sheets of paper and I wrote down exactly what happened that night with Gloria. The thrill of sneaking chocolate bars, the misspelled sign, the wolves, the bathroom accident, the smoky camp under the bridge, Carl and Girl. And the others who seemed to reside up inside Carl's head. I changed Gloria to an angry stepfather and me into a nine-year-old boy named Freddy. School was now closed for the summer, so I brought it to Mrs. Spooner at the library. She volunteered there most days, slipping books back onto the shelves, but when she saw me she stopped what she was doing. I gave her my story and she started to read it immediately. I wandered through the stacks, skimmed a short story and two comic books, and then she appeared clutching my story to her chest.

"I know I don't have to grade you, but I couldn't resist."

She handed me the pages and I unfolded them. A++!! in red pen across the top of the first sheet. Then a bunch of comments scrawled up and down the sides. She said she'd never read anything so well written by someone my age. "The fear is palpable! A modern-day fairy tale! Goes to show kindness lurks in the most unlikely of places!"

"You don't have to say all that," I said.

"I meant every word, Rowan. It's just nice to write it down, and you can go back and reread it. If you're ever doubting your skills."

"Thanks. I mean it, really."

"Have your mom and dad read it yet?"

"No, you know. She's busy with work and all, and not much of a reader, and well—"

"Oh, yes. That's right. Your dad. He's away lately, isn't he? But I'm sure he'd love it, Rowan. He really would."

"It's hard to reach him." I'd called him six times at the garage the day before, and Telly's boss kept saying he was occupied. Finally he told me not to call again, said I was getting worse than my mother.

"Well, why don't you pop out there and surprise him? He's got to take a lunch break, right? And the bus passes right by his garage out on Wendell's Road."

I scratched at the white spot underneath my eye. "I mean. I could, right? I could do that."

"Of course you could. He's your dad, and he loves you." She clasped her hands together. "Now, a quick question. Would you mind if I took a copy of your story and submitted it to a contest for young writers? The theme this year is suspense, and you've certainly demonstrated an aptitude for it."

"Sure," I said. "But don't get your hopes up, Mrs. Spooner."

"Too late. Already up." She took the papers from my hand and rushed away to the library office.

I waited for her by the glass front doors. A man was coming across the parking lot with a little boy and a bagful of books. I opened the door for them, and as they walked past my stomach knotted up. I didn't know why the thought of seeing Telly made me so nervous.

Mrs. Spooner rushed toward me. "Sorry, sorry. Lineup at the photocopier." She gave me back my story, then turned her wrist and tapped her watch. "And that bus leaves in seven minutes, Rowan. If you want to catch it to see your dad."

The brakes on the bus groaned to a halt near Telly's work. I walked up the aisle, slapping the back of the seats, and stepped down onto the asphalt. Heat rippled up around my legs. My mouth tasted sour. What if this wasn't a good surprise? What if he didn't want to see me? Of course he'd want to see me. Even Mrs. Spooner said so.

One of the garage doors was wide open, and I slipped in as quietly as I could. I wanted to see his face light up. Telly was standing near a car. There was a lady there, too. She leaned against another car drinking from a can and wearing peachy-colored clothes, like a nurse might wear. Her hair was the same color as Gloria's now that Gloria had dyed it. Telly said something I couldn't hear, and she tossed her head back and laughed. I edged closer.

"So about those weeks in October, Theodore." *Theodore?* "I can't take the first, but the second and third would work."

"Should be good for me. Just need to lock it down."

"Dad's friend has this cottage we can use. Three hours north near Ranton Lake. It's gorgeous. Mountains are right there."

"Fishing?"

"Of course, Theo. Would I suggest it if the lake wasn't full of fish?"

Telly was grinning a whole lot and his teeth shone right out of his mouth.

A thread of excitement wound around my chest. What if Maisy and I went with them? No reason we couldn't. Telly always promised to take me fishing one day, and this would be a chance to teach me how to cast and reel in. Clean whatever I caught. I could build a fire with sticks and bark, and we could roast marshmallows and sing dumb songs. Maybe Telly would even teach me how to tie flies or fix a motor on an old boat. He could do that. If he wanted.

"Aw, Dian. How'd I get so lucky?"

Dian.

She touched Telly's face in this soft way, and when I reached up to touch my own cheek, I bumped a metal trolley. A bunch of wrenches clattered to the ground. Dian flinched, and soda sprayed out of her can.

"Rowan," Telly snarled.

"Well, break's over for me, I guess!" she said, patting droplets off her shirt. "See you tonight, Theo. And firm up your dates for our trip, okay?" As she slid past me, she smiled. Sort of. Her mouth started in that direction, but then it turned down. Maybe she saw the island over my eye, or the beginning of a new white blotch beside my mouth. Like a pale moth had settled there and didn't want to move.

"You can't come 'round here like this. Just showing up." Telly yanked a greasy cloth out of the front pocket of his overalls, started scrubbing at his palms. "Boss says you been calling, too. You and Gloria, coming at me non-stop." He threw the cloth down on a bench. "She send you here?"

"What?"

"Trying to sucker me in. Get me back there with that look on your face?"

"No, Telly. No."

"Well, what do you think you're doing?"

"I—I just wanted to see you." My words a pathetic croak.

He put his blackened hands up. "I can't hear it. I can't hear it right now. This is my work. Your mother's already bugging the hell out of me. Sure half the time the phone rings, it's her. Then all this sneaking around, leaving crazy notes on my truck."

"Notes?"

"Dragging your sister in here, too. Parading her around."

"I want to talk to you about her. She's worse, Telly. She made me—"

He took two steps toward me. Unfriendly steps. "You want to see me, you got to get it arranged. Proper, like. Through the channels. I'm done with her, you got that?"

"What channels? Through Gloria?"

"I don't know. You got to figure it out."

I picked up the wrenches. Placed them back on the trolley. "But Gloria said you don't go to the phone when she calls."

"Yeah, well, she knows right where I am. Every single day I'm at the same old spot."

"So she should come out here?"

Telly took a breath and blew it out. "Listen, buddy. Listen." A second breath, deeper and slower. "Things are real messed up right now. I mean, she's trying every angle. I shouldn't be getting frustrated at you." He put his hand on my shoulder, leaned his head down closer. "You're my boy, right? But I just don't know which way to turn."

I stared down at the wrenches. Blinked fast.

"If your mother doesn't stop I'm going to get myself fired. And then where will I be? But I'll get it all straightened out. You don't got to worry about it. You understand?"

"Yes," I said. But I didn't.

"Dian's a good woman, Row, but you know, I need to make sure things are strong before I bring you and your sister into it. We're talking about getting a bigger place. We are. But it all takes time. You got to trust me."

One by one I lined up the wrenches, wanting to tell him that none of what he said made sense. If he wanted to take us, he could. But he hadn't called once. Hadn't come over once since he left. He wouldn't even let me say a single word.

"I'm not mad at you, Row. I'm not. Just keep your little visit to yourself. Can you do that?"

"Yeah."

"Promise me, Row. It'll only complicate things. And I don't want to hear from her about it."

"Okay," I said. I rubbed my eyes hard. Then I turned and walked away. Went to the bus stop. Waited in the sunshine for over an hour until the next bus arrived. Then another hour of inhaling exhaust, trying not to vomit as the bus bounced and jerked and drove all over before it reached Little Sliding. Stopped at the very top of Pinchkiss Circle.

I spent the whole bus ride deciding about Telly. Over and over in my head I heard him say "You're my boy, right?" But if I was his boy, why had he upped and left? Why didn't he come and get Maisy and me? It took me a while, but I finally figured it out. I was the same as those old ladies he used to brag about to Gloria. They came into the garage with their not-so-broken cars. Had no clue about engines and carburetors, about brake pads or the cost of replacement parts. He would fix stuff that didn't need fixing or break something just enough so they'd drive a couple of weeks and come right back again. Every now and again he'd lift up the hood, pour oil on the inside, then point at the dripping underneath. A fresh black stain spreading on top of all the other black stains. Smooth words slid out of Telly's mouth, right into their brains. And they believed him.

Telly had fooled me, too. I was just another con. Another stupid scam. But that was the last time.

When I got back to the circle, Darrell was in his driveway again. He waved at me and said, "Hey, Row. Got the motor purring. Want to listen?"

I didn't even answer. I marched past him and went straight into the woods.

ROWAN

Stomping through the trees, I kicked every stick and root and rock I passed. Eventually I reached the bridge. The creek was gurgling along. It smelled of damp cement and dog and fried egg. Insects buzzed and leaves shivered. When my eyes adjusted, I saw the circle for the fire. A finger of smoke wiggling up. I saw a mess of twigs that looked like a nest. I saw a folded blanket. I saw a mound of wrappers and cans off to the side. And after I'd stood in the middle of the camp for several minutes, I saw Carl. He and Girl lumbered out of the bushes.

"Heard you coming a mile away," he said and cleared his throat. There were more shards of metal worked into his bushy beard. "Thought you might've been the Workers."

He had mentioned workers before. Were there people repairing the bridge? "What workers? Why are there workers out here?"

"Not much sun finds its way, urh. Always stays pleasant. And cool. It's a fine place to live."

"Oh." Girl came over and licked my hand. A bird was cheeping up above. "Yeah, yeah. I can see that."

He stared at me for a minute without moving. I shifted my feet.

"Anyway," I said. I started to feel wobbly inside. Carl kept twisting strands of his beard in his blackened fingers. Tugging and releasing the loose hairs. There were some patchy spots. "Um. I was just walking through."

"No, I don't think so, Stan. Urh. I don't think that's it. He doesn't have a two. They always have a number two. That's the key. The piece of, urh, irrefutable evidence. The rules never change. They're rules."

I wiped my sweating hands on my T-shirt and took a deep step backward. "I just wanted to say—" I swallowed. "Um, thanks for, you know."

"For what, Magic Boy?" He twisted and tugged. Twisted and tugged.

Magic Boy. He remembered me. "For helping me out the other night. Sharing your orange and all."

He lifted both his hands and shook them. Like an angry preacher. "I don't need reminding for every single, single, single, urh, thing. I don't. You hear me?" He bellowed out that last part. It echoed off the underside of the bridge. Girl lowered her head, pawed at Carl's pant leg.

My throat went dry and I glanced behind me. It was a mistake coming here. I could run. I took another step back. "I'm sorry. I didn't mean—"

"Your mother taught you nice manners, Magic Boy, but rational truth professed, you helped me out. Guided me out of a perpetual conundrum, you see?"

His voice had flipped to soft and friendly.

"I didn't. Um. Carl."

"You did, then. I was stuck in a time spot, really tight, and the temporal shift wouldn't budge. Dark for about three days before you showed up, urh, and fixed it."

I shook my head. "I don't understand."

"The government," he said. "Can give you the worst charley horses. They have your nerves all mapped out. Strategic defense and all. Control your mind."

"Oh. I didn't know." Was that even possible?

"Every single one of us. Your mom might've called them growing pains, but that's a falsehood, Magic Boy. A bold-faced lie. It's neural stretching." Twist and yank, twist and yank. Scattered hairs tumbled down from his fingers.

"That doesn't sound so great. You a doctor?" Even though he looked about as much like a doctor as Girl did, he sounded like he knew what he was talking about.

"No," he laughed. "Could've been but all those doctor types were a proliferation of arrogance, urh. I stayed on the legal side of things. Graduated top of my, urh, class."

"Yeah. Okay."

"Yeah, yeah. I'll say. I'll say it. Don't worry, though, Magic Boy, about your nerves. Not much you can do about it. Dot says no point in getting stressed. Solid structures can conceal." He smacked the concrete wall with his open hand. It was clean except someone had spray-painted the word *Almost* up near the top. Maybe Carl? Almost what, though?

He smacked the wall again, and I jumped.

"You understand?"

"Sure," I said. I didn't understand at all. I stepped back again. "Sure." I was close to the rocky slope now.

He started laughing again. "Is the condition that, urh, led to your signpost still applicable?"

"What sign?"

"Your T-H-E-I-F sign." He winced as he said it, as if he hated misspelling the word.

"I'm no thief, Carl. Not really."

"I'm no thief, Carl." A piece of metal fell out of his beard and he bent, plucked it up, fixed it back in place. "I meant, are you hungry?"

I one-shoulder shrugged.

"I have another orange. All that acid dissolves your metals."

"What do you mean by acid?"

"Vitamin C. It's beneficial. Structures and metals are excellent blockers. Metals and structures. Solid, solid, urh, solid. Prevent government infiltration."

He smiled then, and his teeth were not what I expected. They weren't cramped together or missing or sharpened or full of brown decay. They were white and neatly organized in his mouth. They were perfect. Not *Telly* perfect, but fairly close.

"Would you care for some?"

"Um." I wasn't sure. Maybe he was harmless after all? He did look after his dog, didn't he? And Girl seemed healthy enough. Then I said, "If you want to share."

"I always want to share," he replied.

He sat down on a rock, and without thinking too much I walked over and sat down beside him. After he'd peeled the orange and thrown the rinds on the dead fire, he cracked it and handed me half.

"Thanks," I said.

"You're welcome, Magic Boy."

I sucked on a segment. It was sour but good. "Do you live here all the time?" I asked.

"I do. I'm going to live here for the rest of my life. Until they reclaim me." He looked me up and down then, scratched the knots of hair on his head.

"What about your mom and dad. Don't they miss you?"

"My mom, urh. She doesn't exist. Just a ghost now." He tapped his head and shuddered. "Just a ghost."

"Oh," I said. That was a strange way for him to say his mother was dead. "And your dad?"

"Never had one. I just came to be. Spontaneous generation, I suspect, though it's not notarized. No stamp, urh, no stamp on me. You, Magic Boy?"

I ran my thumb over the white spot on my other hand. "I don't really have a dad either," I said. "Not much of one anyway."

"Did you make him a ghost?"

"Make him? No. Sometimes I wish it though."

"Urh. Difficulties."

"Yeah." And then, because Carl was listening, I told him everything that had happened with Telly. How Gloria was always picking at him, but he never seemed to mind. Until this lady came into his work, needing her belts replaced. She was a dental hygienist at the clinic that opened across the road from the garage. After Telly fixed her car, she entered him into this smile contest they were running. Somehow Telly won, and they fixed his teeth, scraped off the gunk, took out chipped ones, glued on fake ones. He had a plastic and metal thing he clipped in when he slept, even though Gloria called him Tin-Mouth Telly.

Everything changed after that. He shaved off his enormous mustache. Grinned like a hissing cat. I barely even recognized him. He looked like he should be inside the television instead of gawking at it. And then I noticed how his nails got cleaner and he trimmed the hair out of his nostrils and there was more space between his words. When Gloria took little swipes at him he started clapping back, a little here and there. She didn't like it.

"Sure, you treat Chicken better than you treat me," Telly said once.

"That's 'cause I don't like dogs." She laughed. If that was a joke, Telly didn't find it funny.

One night at dinner he started to describe a book he was reading. About a man who made this fortune and built a house to get a girl's attention. "Daisy's her name."

"Daisy?" Gloria replied. "Daisy who? Who's Daisy?"

"The girl in the book, Glow. Aren't you listening? This guy improves himself hoping she'll fall in love with him."

She put down her fork. "What's wrong with you? You never read a book your whole life."

"So? Does that mean I can't change? Better myself?"

"Change why? You think someone else'd put up with you?"

It turned out someone else would. Telly left the next weekend. Took most of his stuff in garbage bags. Some of his beloved guns from the basement in a couple of totes. Piled it all in the bed of his truck. "Going where I'm wanted!" he yelled.

"You'll be back!" Gloria screamed as he drove off. "Begging me. Hands and knees, Telly. Hands and knees. You're nothing without me."

After his truck disappeared, Maisy and I just stood there watching the cloud of dust fall back to the ground. Gloria bumped past me, said, "Too bad he didn't throw *you* in a garbage bag. Toss you on top of the rest." Maisy started to gasp, trying to hold her crying inside.

"And he hasn't called once or come around since," I told Carl.

"Urh," Carl said. "Real difficulties." He pinched the metal beads in his beard. "The molars. That caused the fluctuation. I never realized there was so much power in teeth. Electrical impulses in the roots, I suppose."

"I went to see him today. Took the bus all the way out to his garage. He was there with that lady. Dian. And he kicked me out. Right on my ass."

"Right on my ass. Urh, the two of them. They could be Workers, Magic Boy. You've got to protect your mind. Avoid being encapsulated. Monitor the beams."

I picked up a pebble and threw it into the creek. "Yeah, you're right, Carl. I'm not going to think about it. Not believe any more of his shit."

"Good, good," he said. "Critical analysis." He dug around inside his coat and pulled out a deck of cards. On the back they had a picture of a woman in a flowing dress.

"Do you want to play a hand?" I asked. "Poker? I'm not very good though. And I don't have money."

"No, Magic Boy. Don't, don't, don't, urh, play with these."

"Missing some, then?"

"No."

"Oh, okay." I was confused.

Then Carl said, "Tomorrow's on them. In, urh, hypothetical analogies. Divide and divide and divide until the single option remains. They belong to my mother." He snapped the cards slowly in his hands.

"The ghost?" I didn't want to ask him how she became that way.

"Urh," he said.

"Did your mom teach you?"

"Urh," he said again.

Carl dug out a handkerchief from one of his pockets and laid it on a rock. He shuffled the cards and then held the deck toward me. "Tap with your pointer finger," he said. "Three times."

After I tapped the deck he fanned out the cards, turning five of them over slowly on the handkerchief. He tugged at his beard. Hard. "Oh, oh. I never, urh, saw that before."

I went closer. All five cards were black. A row of spades.

"What does it say? Am I going to be famous? Have an enormous boat in the ocean somewhere?"

"It doesn't mean a thing, Magic Boy."

"Come on, Carl. What's my future?"

"Not right, not right." He grabbed up the cards. He pushed them back into the deck and put a red elastic around them. Then he hid them inside a pocket. "I haven't got that knack. Too many responsive guidelines. Infinite manifestations." He picked up a bottle of soda and twisted the cap. Foam rolled out on his hand. "You're fine. You're perfectly fine." He took a long swallow from the bottle.

I was disappointed, but I didn't let it show. Not like it meant anything anyway. They were just cards.

"I should get home, Carl. I got stuff to do."

"Sure, sure, sure. You can visit me anytime."

"I can?" This surprised me. It made me feel warm on the inside. "You don't mind?"

"You don't mind?" He had this habit of repeating what I said, but I don't think he was mocking me. "You're one of them, I know," he said. Soda dripped off the hairs of his beard. "But you're not like the others. You're not a Worker. It's nice to see you out here, urh. I like that. I do."

I had no idea what he meant, but I liked it, too. Having a secret place to go. Even though he was peculiar, I had the feeling he was also kind and dependable. People could be more than one thing at the same time.

MAISY

Since school was done, Rowan's been keeping a secret. I could tell because lots of days he was sneaking off into the woods and never asked me to come along. Not once. Last summer he always let me go with him. Well, mostly. But now when I asked him where he went he just said, "Nowhere, Turtle. I'm right here." That was a big lie. He was playing at something, and he wasn't letting me join his game. I didn't like it. Not one bit.

I thought he was gone again that afternoon, but then a bird smacked the window and I heard him yelp. He ran right down the stairs and out into the yard. I ran after him. Together we hunted in the grass until we found a robin. When Rowan picked it up its head wobbled around like a marble.

"Why did it make itself dead?" I asked him.

"Because it didn't see the glass. Just its reflection. And trees and leaves and outdoor stuff."

"Bad," I said.

I got a shovel from the shed and I dug a hole near the side of the house. There was a broken plastic thing on the wall above where I was digging. Rowan said it was a vent that "snakes right down into the basement bathroom." I didn't know much about our basement, only that it had guns. Lots of guns. Telly took most of them when he left, but there were still a bunch, Gloria said. We weren't ever allowed to go down there.

"Should we say something?"

"Like what?"

"That we hope it likes heaven? That it gets better?" I imagined the bird with a little white collar around its neck. Gloria had one of those last year because a man bumped into the side of Telly's truck. Not a big bump, but Gloria got really, really hurt. Sometimes she still limped when we were outside. That man had to give her money.

Rowan squinted his eyes in the sunlight. "Won't make any difference, Turtle." Then he said, "No one's listening."

I didn't like that. How did he know?

After he dropped the bird in the hole, I scooped the dirt. Rowan pushed down on the spot with his bare foot. He wasn't wearing a shirt, so I could see the white spots on his back. It looked like when Gloria spilled that cleaning stuff all over Telly's clothes. Accidentally. I never told Gloria, but I thought my brother's skin was like a special map. I spied on him whenever I could. I was waiting for his islands to grow because I knew someday a tiny *x* would show up and it would tell us where we had to go. Just me and Rowan. And Gloria, of course. I'd never leave her behind. Maybe Telly. I didn't decide yet about him.

I rinsed off the dirt with the hose. The water was hot. Then I went and sat on the steps of the front porch. Nails were poking out of the boards, but I knew just where to sit so I wouldn't get stuck. Rowan plunked down next to me without even looking. He didn't care about getting a nail in his rear end.

Gloria was painting the front door of our house. It used to be angry red and she was making it look like sunshine. But she wasn't a neat worker. The paint was on her T-shirt and the porch and on the screen and even on Chicken's fur. He was yipping in his sleep and didn't mind.

"So? What do you think?" Glorai said.

"It's nice," I said.

"Nice?"

"Super duper?"

"That's better."

"Do you think Telly'll love it?"

My hands turned sweaty. "Is he coming home?"

She didn't answer me. She just started growling. I saw spit pop out of her mouth. Paint went all over. I knew she was making a mess because she was in a big knot ever since Telly went away. Once after he left we took the bus out to his garage. I snuck a secret love note under his windshield wiper. Then me and Gloria hid in the bushes and we saw this lady who had yellow hair. She walked over to the garage and went inside and her laughing came right out through the big open door. That made Gloria mad. She threw rocks at Telly's truck and they bounced off the roof. On the way home she kept asking me, "Do you think she's pretty?" I shook my head, but we got off the bus early and went into a store and Gloria bought a box of stuff so she could make her hair yellow too.

Gloria squatted down and painted the bottom of the door. I read the label on the can and the paint was called "Happy, Happy." I nudged Rowan and pointed at the name. Maybe things would be better. Maybe the new door would make Gloria smile. Maybe Telly would come back after all, driving in slow and careful with no dust this time. Then we would all be happy, happy.

Gloria threw the brush into the can and went inside. I don't think she was mad at me no more about the school concert because I called Telly at his garage, just like she said, and I did a good job. He got on the phone this time and I told him I missed him bad. He said he missed me too and he was sad we weren't together and that he'd see me soon. That made Gloria real excited.

When she came out of the house she only had two lemonades. She gave one to me and said, "No sharing."

Rowan didn't get one because Gloria didn't see him no more. She looked right through him. That was partly Chicken's fault, to tell the truth. When he was hungry, he was Gloria's dog, because she was the only one allowed to feed him and sometimes she forgot. But when he was full, he belonged to Rowan. Gloria didn't like that. She called Chicken a "sneaky double dealer."

No one was allowed to feed Chicken. Only Gloria. But last night, Rowan picked some fries off his plate and dropped them on the floor. Chicken was right there because he was half starved. Gloria probably heard the pat, pat of the potato dropping. Or she saw Chicken licking his chops a million times. Or she could've read my mind, like she does sometimes. She caught him. She always caught him. She grabbed Rowan's fries and she threw the whole plate in the garbage. Then she disappeared him. She made Rowan vanish right out of her sight.

Sometimes he was disappeared for just a day. Sometimes she couldn't see him for a whole month. Once she told me the problem started when his two front teeth came in. She found it hard to look at teeth that were so huge and crooked and stuck out funny because "He just wasn't cute no more."

Gloria gulped her lemonade. "You know it's not easy taking care of two kids by myself," she said. "You get that, right, Maisy? I'm not perfect, but I'm doing my best."

I nodded.

"Takes everything I got to juggle work and keep the house and put food on the table and clothes on your back. Trying to make it look decent."

"I really like the door," I said. "It's a good color."

"Isn't it, though? I've got a natural skill for that, Bids. Everyone says it. And Telly'll see all I got done when he comes home. See how much effort I put in."

Rowan grabbed my glass and crunched up all the ice. Gloria saw. "You didn't hear me?" she said. "No sharing."

"Sorry," I whispered. I took the glass back from Rowan and put it on the step. Then I got up and went back to the bird grave. I wanted to see in case a feather or a claw or orange beak scritched up through the dirt. Maybe the bird would come alive again. But Rowan's footprint looked just the same. That made me feel sad. The robin's mom should have told it not to trust the window. Like Gloria told me not to trust Mrs. Spooner. Or to watch out for wolves in the woods. If that robin had a better mom, it would still be flying or making a nest or eating worms.

Rowan walked past me to the clothesline that went between the house and the shed. He was wearing his sneakers now, and he yanked a T-shirt off the line and put that on. Then he yanked some other stuff off too. I think it was Telly's clothes. Gloria kept washing his work stuff over and over and hanging it out even though it never got dirty no more. Even though everyone knew Telly wasn't even home.

"Tell your brother he can take all the clothes off the line. Fold them proper," Gloria yelled. Then I heard the screen door slam. She must've gone inside.

I opened my mouth but Rowan said, "I heard her already."

He pulled underwear and pajamas off the line. Clothespins popped and fell in the grass. He rolled up the clothes and threw them in the basket. He was mad, I could tell. I knew he was going fast so he could sneak away, just like he'd been doing. He thought he was going to leave me behind again. But this time I had a better idea. I was going to follow him.

I went in the front door to get my shoes. Gloria was yelling more. From the hallway I could see the phone on the wall in the kitchen. It was wiggling and she had the cord yanked tight. I stopped to listen.

"No, not a chance!" she hollered. "That was your choice. One hundred percent your fault. As always."

Then she got quiet for a second.

"No, you listen to me, darling."

I knew *darling* didn't mean *darling*.

"Me the problem?" She snorted. "You got real mental troubles, you know that? Everything you say is twisted." Then she said, "It's about time. But you better not leave them hanging. You messed around long enough." Her words went warm and sweet. "Telly, these kids need a father. They've really been suffering. Especially the boy." She puffed out air. "For a while? Of course, sweetheart. I understand what you're saying. We all love you, Telly. We do. I'll see you then."

She put down the phone. Then she saw me standing in the hallway. "Maisy. Why do you got that face on?"

"What face?"

She rolled up her eyes all white and stuck out her tongue. "It's not very becoming."

"I don't," I said. I touched my cheek. "I don't look like that."

"You think I'm making it up?" Her eyebrows jumped up high. "Calling me a liar, are we?"

I shook my head. Fast. Fireflies zoomed around.

"You're actually calling your mother a liar. Gloria's a big fat liar. Bends over backwards for everyone, but she'll screw you over. That's what you're saying."

My heart started knocking on my neck, like there was a woodpecker hiding in there. Tak-tak-tak. Tears came in my eyes, but I blinked them away. "I'm sorry, Gloria."

"Well, I don't got time to deal with your sorrys right now. You just better look smart at dinner. Your father'll be here."

I nodded, but cold air ran up my insides. Telly was coming back. With his black garbage bags and his extra guns. Would that other lady start calling us all the time? Or showing up to throw rocks at our house? Would she leave love notes under the mat on our front step?

"Now get out from under my feet." Gloria put an apron on over her head. She patted her hair. "Everything's got to be just exactly perfect for his welcome home."

When I went outside, Rowan was already gone. The laundry was balled up inside the basket in a big mess. I ran behind the house and around to the other side with the deck. He was there, almost to the woods. He had an armload of clothes and with his other hand he smacked a red cap against his leg and put it on his head. He went past Telly's potato garden without no potatoes this year. Then he disappeared behind some trees.

Gloria wouldn't like it, but I had to follow him now. Not just to know his secret, but I had to tell him Telly was coming home. Rowan would know if that was good or bad.

I went the same way as Rowan as fast as I could. In the woods the air was full of buzzing and cracking like the leaves were growing in the patches of sun that got in. I saw Rowan's red ball cap up ahead. I stayed real quiet going behind him. I climbed under and over fallen trees. The moss was soft on my knees but slippery on my shoes. Rowan was whistling a song. I never heard it before. It was weird and lonely and it made me feel empty in my middle.

We walked forever before we reached a bridge. I never been in the woods this far before, but I kept my eyes wide open and watched all over. I didn't see no wolves like Gloria said I would. Rowan started going fast. When he got to the bridge, he pushed through the bushes and then I couldn't see him no more.

I crawled closer and hid behind some branches. I heard Rowan laughing. When I peeked through the leaves, I saw what he was hiding. A scary man was sitting on the rocks near a fire. He had knots in his hair. There were shiny things in his beard. His face and his hands looked grimy and he wore way too much stuff for summer. He was smoking a cigarette. A skinny brown dog was next to him and it had its head on the man's leg.

Rowan had been disappearing to go see a dirty troll and a dog. My heart started banging. Gloria was not going to like that.

The troll called out, "Hey, Magic Boy. Back again?" He knew Rowan. He even had a funny name for him.

"I brought you some shirts. They're good shirts, but no one needs them anymore."

Telly was coming home. I had to tell Rowan. Telly might need his shirts. He might be angry Rowan stole them off the line.

He handed the armload over to the man, and the man got a big smile. He held one out. "I'm Carl," the man said. "But I can be a Telly too."

"You don't want to be a Telly," Rowan said. "Tellys suck."

"Okay, okay," he laughed. "Thanks, Magic Boy. I'll only, urh, be a Telly if Workers come." He put the shirts down and then he pushed a wiener on a stick and stuck it in the fire.

A twig cracked under my shoe and I held my breath. The dog jumped up fast and ran over to my hiding spot. I tried to be as small as I could, but it started barking. When I peeked again, the troll was looking right at me. His eyes were tiny. Then he clapped his leg and the dog went back to him.

"Urh," he said. It sounded like someone punched him in the middle. "A little fawn is tracking you. Can she be trusted?"

Rowan shook his head when he saw me. "Shit, Maisy. Why'd you go trailing me?" I looked down at my shoes. They were wet and had moss stuck to them. Then he said to the troll, "Sure, Carl. That's my sister. I'd trust her with my life." That made me feel better. But the troll still looked like he did bad things.

Rowan stomped over and grabbed my hand and pulled me out of the bushes. "Did Gloria send you after me?" He was angry.

"No," I whispered. There was no sun under the bridge and it smelled bad.

"Then why are you on my heels?"

"I thought, I thought." My throat started to hurt. "Last summer Gloria said you weren't allowed to leave me out. She said that a bunch of times. And now you're leaving me out every day."

"I just want some time on my own. And that was a whole year ago."

"Still," I said. What difference did that make?

Then he said I could never ever tell Gloria about the troll. "Absolutely no way." I had to promise. He made me swear on Telly's grave. "But Telly's not dead," I said, and Rowan told me to just pretend he was. So I swore on Telly's grave. Future grave, same as Mrs. Spooner.

"Never mind, Magic Boy," the troll said. "Why don't you two take a seat on these fine chairs?" He waved his hand next to the fire.

I tugged Rowan's T-shirt. There were no fine chairs. No chairs at all.

The wiener was bubbled up, and the man tugged it off with his huge fingers and cracked it in two. Steam came out. He offered half to me. I tugged harder on Rowan's T-shirt.

"We're good, Carl," he said.

"We're good, Carl," the troll said back. Then he gave it to the brown dog. The dog swallowed it in one gulp.

"We should go," I whispered to Rowan. "We shouldn't be here."

The troll turned his head to the side, whispered, "No, no. Not everyone. You can't believe that." Then he laughed, but it was a scary laugh. "It's concentric reasoning."

I opened my mouth, but air just sat in front of my face.

"Relax, Turtle," Rowan said. "So he rambles a bit. Not like it's hurting anyone. Carl's my friend."

"Carl's my friend," the troll repeated. He had his head down and his face inside the front of his coat. "Carl's my friend, Turtle. Carl's my friend." The dog barked and scritched the troll's leg.

"For sure," Rowan said, a bit louder this time. "We're friends, Carl."

Rowan liked saying that. I could just tell.

Then the troll lifted his giant head and looked at us. "Who's Carl? Nobody knows Carl."

I yanked even harder on Rowan's T-shirt.

"I thought—" he said.

The troll mumbled into his hand and laughed again. He pulled some cards out of his coat pocket. He smeared them all around on the ground and then put them back into a pile.

"Little Fawn! Your future awaits."

"Rowan," I whispered. That troll was crazy. I yanked Rowan's T-shirt as hard as I could, but he smacked my hand away.

"Stop it, Maisy. If you're such a wimp, then go home out of it."

"I'm not a wimp." That was a lie.

The troll held the deck out to me. "You have to tap it three times. With your pointer finger."

I shook my head.

"Don't you want me to see, Little Fawn? What's going to happen to you?"

"Come on, Maisy. Don't be like that. It's just a game. And Carl's trying to be nice."

"Carl's trying to be nice."

I didn't like how he kept saying Rowan's words. Why didn't he have his own?

I took a tiny step closer so Rowan wouldn't think I was scared. I tapped the deck. The troll smiled, and then he flipped some of the cards over on the ground.

"You are quiet," he said. "Urh. You are not brave, but one day you will be brave. Very brave." I took another step closer and got down to see the cards. They were old. Some of the corners were torn off. "But—" He tapped the third card. "But. But. Urh. Two paths here. Two paths. One will seem warm and familiar. One will be thick and dark. You need to go in, or, or, or, urh, come out."

Rowan poked me with his elbow and said to the troll, "I told you she was a turtle."

Then he laughed and scritched his beard. I could hear his fingernails. "Love," he said. "Only love is on the other side."

"Maisy's got a boyfriend," Rowan sang. "Probably Darrell."

"Stop it," I said. I went a little closer. The troll smelled like Chicken that time he rolled in rotted squirrel. Then he took something shiny from another pocket and unfolded it. It looked like one of those grocery store pie plates made of soft metal. He tore a piece off, and reached his hand out and touched my hair. My middle was shaking, but I stayed still. I would be brave. He picked up some of my hair. I closed my eyes waiting for him to yank it. But he said, "There." When I opened my eyes I felt around in my hair. I lifted some of it and saw a piece of silver was pinched there.

"Protection." He tapped my nose and laughed until he coughed. "The Workers are always listening, Little Fawn. But you'll be safe now. Don't lose it though. Otherwise, I, I, I, urh, don't know. Terrible stuff. Terrible, terrible stuff is coming."

I touched the metal. It was cold and had sharp parts. *Terrible stuff was coming.* I remembered then that Telly was moving back. Maybe Telly was the terrible stuff.

"Rowan. Gloria said—"

"Shush, Maisy. Carl, can you try mine again?"

"Magic Boy."

"Yeah," Rowan said. "Let's see what's happening for me."

The troll smeared the cards out again. Then he picked them up in a pile and Rowan tapped on them. He turned some over, but before he said anything he grabbed them up again. I saw they were all black, though. They were all upside-down shovels.

"Broken," the troll said. "The cards are broken."

Rowan looked sad because he didn't get his future. He didn't get a metal thing neither. Not like me. I wonder if it was because his hair was the wrong color. Gloria said my hair was spring chick, but Rowan's hair was muck.

I stomped my foot. "I'm leaving." I was getting cold in the shade and flies kept landing on me.

"Fine," Rowan said. "I've got to get her home, Carl. I'll see you later, though, okay? Bye, Girl!" The dog ran over and licked at Rowan's hand.

The troll tugged on his beard. "Don't worry. We'll get it all evaluated. You're not going, going, going, urh, away. Don't listen to everything you see. Those wave particles are from the Workers. Not you, Magic Boy. That's what I told Stan."

"Who's Stan?" I whispered.

"Never mind, Turtle. It doesn't matter."

"It does too," I said, but Rowan didn't say nothing else.

We walked through the bushes near the side of the bridge. In the leaves, a bird sang the same song over and over. After we'd been going for a while I said, "I don't like him, Rowan. He smells. And he got garbage stuck on his face."

"It's just metal. Besides, you've got metal now too. Who cares?"

I touched the shiny twist in my hair again. "You shouldn't go there."

"Why would you say that?"

"Because he doesn't got a house. Because he's a secret. Because he's not good."

Rowan broke off a stick and threw it. "Not good because he offered you food? Or played cards with you? Or gave you a lucky thing?"

"I—I don't know. His clothes are bad. Gloria says we got to stay away from people like that. He likes you, Rowan. I can tell he does. I think he might be a wolf."

"He's not a wolf. Wolves don't even exist. Not that kind, anyway."

"They do too."

"Not around here they don't."

"Well, it could be catchy. His kind of sick."

"Don't be a moron, Maisy. Just because he thinks differently doesn't mean he's not okay. That he's not good inside."

"You don't know him one bit." I squished up my eyes so he'd know I was mad. "Gloria said you're not supposed to talk to strangers."

"Some stranger. I've been there tons of times."

"He's bad and he's dumb. Giving that dog half the wiener." I wondered why Girl didn't run away when her stomach was full. She just curled into the troll. "The big half, too."

Rowan let out a sigh. He shook his head back and forth. "That's not dumb, Turtle. That's just another way he's being nice."

I kept walking. After Rowan said that, I didn't know what to think about the troll—Carl—in my head. Maybe that *was* being nice. But I still didn't like him hiding under the bridge. I didn't like that Rowan and Carl got sparkles in their faces when they saw each other. Even that dog looked at Rowan like it just found a pile of meat bones.

When we got out of the woods the sun was already going down behind the house. Rowan said, "Shit. What the hell is that doing here?" He pointed at the driveway. I looked. A red truck. Not a speck of dust on it. I forgot all about Telly coming back.

That cold snaky feeling rushed right back into my middle. *Terrible stuff. Terrible stuff is coming.* I touched the metal thing in my hair one more time. Telly was already waiting inside.

MAISY

"Oh, my darlings," Gloria said when we walked through the happy, happy yellow door. Her eyes were crinkly, and she was wearing a new blue dress. It was tied tight around her middle. I saw the tag up under her arm stuck on with a safety pin.

"Where were you two?" Telly was standing there. His hands were in his pockets. "Off having an adventure?"

"No," I said. "Me and Rowan. We just went, um . . ." I saw Rowan's eyes get small then. He didn't need to do that. I wasn't going to say nothing about Carl. "We were looking for butterflies. I like butterflies a lot. Their wings are pretty. But you're not supposed to touch them because it hurts. That's what Mrs. Spooner said."

"Again with Mrs. Spooner, Maisy? What did I tell you?"

"I wasn't." I swallowed. My story wasn't coming out right.

Then Rowan said, "She did a lesson with them. On bugs. That's all. I was trying to show her some stuff."

"Isn't that nice," Telly said. "You watching after your little sister. Teaching her about all the wildlife around. Respecting it."

"Yeah, sure. Whatever." Rowan wiggled out of his sneakers and kicked them into a corner.

"It's true, Row. I wish I had a big brother growing up."

Then Gloria tugged my hair. But not hard. "You got something snarled up in there?"

I covered Carl's lucky gift with my hand. "It's a decoration."

Gloria laughed. "Like a crow she is, Telly. I swear. Always dragging home junk." Then she whispered, "Pick it out, Bids. In the garbage right now."

I went to the kitchen and stepped to make the garbage lid flip up. I tugged the metal from my hair, but I didn't throw it in. When Gloria turned around I squished it small and hid it in my pocket.

"Good girl," Gloria said. Then she put a hand on Rowan's shoulder. He rolled his shoulder away. Her eye crinkles stopped then. She said, "I'm sorry if you think I've been tough on you, sweetheart. It's been ever so stressful with your dad gone. You can't even imagine."

"It's okay, Gloria," I said because Rowan didn't open his mouth. I think he was pretending she was disappeared, but she was the only one who could do that.

"Well, it's good for us all to be together again, isn't it? Telly's been dying to come home, he told me. Get everything back on track. Right, Telly?"

"It'll be great to talk," he said. He scritched his head.

"Yes, talk. We need to talk."

"So other than butterfly hunting, what's going on, Bids?"

When I said "Not much," Gloria's eyes got small. So I changed my answer. "I mean, lots of stuff. Gloria made the front door nice. Do you like the color?"

"I surely do, Bids. It's a fantastic color."

"I think so too. And me and Rowan saw Darrell fixing his bike. Shar's coming back from her mom's soon. Oh, and I lost Jenny the Head again this morning. Can you believe it?"

"Jenny the what?"

"Jenny the Head. She's my doll, but she don't got no body. She doesn't need a heart, Rowan said, and Gloria found her in the drawer with the toothpaste. I don't know when I put her in there."

"You're always in la-la land, Bids," Gloria said. She patted my head. "Good thing you got such an excellent mom."

"Well, let's hope you can hold on to her this time," Telly said. He patted my knee. "You go through dolls like a river goes through water."

I laughed. Telly laughed too. Maybe everything was going to be okay.

The house was all cleaned up. We never used the table in the dining room, but now it had plates on it. In the middle there were ribs with red sauce. There was broccoli that I hated, but it was covered in orange cheese from the bottle that I loved. There were biscuits and corn with steam coming out and a glass bowl full of potato salad.

"How about we all sit? Before the mess of it gets cold. Or warm, I guess. Depending." Gloria sounded just like a breeze making the curtains shiver. "I've been slaving all afternoon."

I sat next to Rowan. He still didn't say nothing. But I swung my feet back and forth to make some noise. Rowan scritched at a new bit of his map growing on his arm. His islands always started out pink and sore. Then they turned white. That was exciting. To see what shape it was. Once after school last year Rowan took me to the library. Mrs. Spooner pulled out a bunch of geography books for us and we traced some of Rowan's spots. We found out he got a part of Hawaii near his eye. And some place called Baffin Island outside his elbow. Iceland was coming out the back of his neck. Mrs. Spooner smiled a lot at us and said, "You two are most wonderfully inventive!"

Gloria put her hand on her chest. "Isn't this just perfect, Telly? All of us having a family meal together. Like it's supposed to be."

Telly smiled and reached for the ribs. He used a fork instead of his fingers. "God, Glow. Some spread you put out." I couldn't help staring at him. I almost didn't know who he was. His face was nice and brown. His teeth were bits of sun caught in his mouth. Even his shirt had no dirt. I think someone might have used an iron on it. Or maybe it was new too, like Gloria's dress. His fingernails were still black though, like they always were. Parts of him were still Telly.

Gloria plopped potato salad on Rowan's plate. Rowan stabbed at it. The fork's sharp parts made a scrape. I got the shivers.

"Your hair looks good, Glow. That color really suits you."

"You think?" She patted her head. "Sometimes you just see someone and think, I could do that. You get inspired, right?"

"Right about that," he said. He took more ribs.

"So, how's work? Garage is busy, I'll bet."

"Summer always is, Glow. People getting away, wanting their cars tip top." Red sauce was smeared on his chin and strings of rib meat hung down from his fancy teeth. He looked better then. More like himself. "It's an honest day's work."

Rowan coughed, but not a real cough. Then he said to Telly, "Still playing old women?" He sounded mad and his plate was still full.

"What's that, Row?"

"Old women," he said. "Playing old women."

Gloria coughed then. I don't think that was a real cough neither. "More ribs, Telly? We got plenty. A real heap."

"What's he saying, Glow?"

"You heard me. Running your scams." Rowan laughed in a not good way. My heart started to go tak-tak-tak.

"Rowan. Please."

My air stopped coming in. This was turning terrible.

"Why would you say something like that to your dad? You're such a hard worker, Telly. We all know it. You've never let us down. Never. Rowan, you should apologize right now."

Rowan dragged his knife back and forth through the potato salad so it was tic-tac-toe. "You guys were talking about having an honest day and all. Well, I was just being honest too."

Then Telly threw a rib bone down into his plate. "Jesus, Glow. You didn't tell me I was walking into a goddamned trap."

It got dark in that room fast. Like night came and no one noticed.

"It's the age, Telly, darling. You see what I've been dealing with here? He's tetchy all the time."

"Still. No reason for him to be acting so ugly."

"No reason? You can't blame him after everything's gone on. It's going to take some time. Once you're all settled away, things'll get back on track."

"Settled away?"

"Yeah. The drawers're empty. Not like I filled them up with someone else's stuff."

Something jabbed at my leg. Hot and sharp. I yelped and tears came out. Gloria looked at me hard. She touched my arm with one hand and pulled the other one out from underneath the table and put her fork down.

"What is it, sweetheart? What's got you so upset?"

"I got stung. My le—"

"It's Telly, isn't it? Such a relief to have him back." She was nodding and nodding and soon my head was nodding too. "Isn't it, Bids."

"Mm-hmm." I hiccuped and wiped my face. I rubbed the spot on my leg.

"A relief. I know it is. For both of you." She smiled.

Telly sniffed and licked at the red around his mouth. "I can try better. Row? Bids? We can do more. Go for a drive. A bite to eat. Out for a movie. They just built that new cinema over by Stafford's, right, Glow? We could go check it out, if that's okay with everyone."

"'Course it is, Telly." Gloria made a purr. She sounded like a cat nobody owned. "You don't need to say that, but I know it's music to their ears." Then she got shy. "To my ears, too."

"But, Glow?" He cleared his throat. "We need to get a couple things out of the way first."

"Won't be a big deal. Not like you got a lot to bring in. Bag of clothes and your guns."

"That's not what I meant. My boss says you got to stop calling. That's a big part of why I'm here. I figured we could try to be civil about things, for the sake of the kids. I want to make sure you get that message about calling the garage loud and clear."

"What message?"

"You got to put an end to it. He can't change the number, it being a business and all. I mean, that, that makes sense to you, right? He's this close"—Telly squished his thumb and finger together—"to calling the phone company. Reporting you."

"I made cobbler, Telly. Apple and oats. The one you love."

Gloria picked up her fork again. I spread my hands out over my legs.

"That's real nice, Glow, but you got to know, you can't be coming 'round all the time neither. You got the kids here, and you got your own work. At Stafford's? Surely you been missing some shifts, right Glow? Glow, you listening?"

She shook her head. "Oh, Telly. You always make me laugh." Then she looked up. "Darn if I forgot the ice cream."

"I'm not dicking around here. Do you want me to just lay it out? You can't be dropping by. At the garage, when I'm working. And you can't leave shitty notes under my windshield. What're you thinking? They come off like you're threatening me. They do, Glow. Even if you're just joking." He took a big sip of water. The lump in his throat hopped up and down. "And the boy can't neither. Just showing up with no warning. Moping around acting all like—"

Her eyelids fluttered. "Rowan went there? To the garage?"

"Yeah. Yeah, he did."

"When?"

"I don't know. A while back. Beginning of summer? I wasn't going to mention nothing, but I want it all out on the table. He stopped me right in the middle of my work. Dealing with a customer. Did a good job messing up my tool trays." Telly shook his head left and right. "Boss got his eye on me something fierce ever since then. I don't want to lose my job, Glow."

"Asshole." Rowan whispered that, but everyone heard it. Even Chicken. His ears stood up then went right down. He squeezed under the table.

I reached my foot just to touch Rowan's a tiny bit. He nipped me with his toes.

"This don't make no sense," Gloria said.

Telly pushed his plate away. "Sure, I'm speaking plain as day. It's nothing complicated."

"But what about what you said on the phone? Staying for a while. I thought—"

"C'mon, Glow. I meant a supper. An hour, two. See the kids. Toss the Frisbee around. Straighten everything out and get a plan together. It got to happen."

Her eyes went real small again. "Are you kidding me?"

Air got sucked in through his shiny teeth. It was a terrible noise. "I don't got time for this shit, Glow. I'm a busy man."

"Telly, I—"

"Glow? I'm trying here, but I don't need to hear it. We're done. I said what I came to say. I want to see the kids, and you can't stop me."

"Why you—" But before Gloria could open her mouth to holler, he was up and out the door. He jumped in his shiny truck and drove away slow. I could tell he didn't want to get dust all over it.

Gloria stood up. Her face went pink. "Going to Telly's work? Going to Telly's work? What were you thinking?" She was yelling with her face right up in Rowan's. "Over two months I've been trying to get him back on side. And you ruin it all. In one fell swoop."

I peeked at Rowan. He just looked at the wall, but I could see his cheeks were turned pink like Gloria's and his chin was wiggling bad. He wanted to cry. I did, too.

"Rowan didn't mean to go," I whispered. "Maybe he got off at the wrong spot." My mouth was full of sand.

She yelled at me then. "Don't you say one word, miss! You and your butterflies with that nosy Mrs. Spooner."

My middle got a bad pain. I got up and took my plate to the sink. Everything inside my eyes was fuzzed. Gloria turned quiet, and I knew she was thinking what to do and that made my middle hurt even worse. I looked out the window. Even through all the mess in my head I could still see dark clouds over the trees. They were blue and purple and yellow. A sky bruise.

I knew those hurt clouds were coming this way.

"Up," she said to Rowan. He was chewing on a rib bone. He let it fall straight out of his mouth. "Up you get. Nothing but a disgusting slug." Rowan got up. "Do you know what slugs do, Maisy? They slime into your garden after all your hard work. And cowards, they just hide under the leaves and destroy from below. They don't care about your plants. They don't care you need to eat. They don't care your hands are covered in blisters and your back is sunburnt and your eyes are raw from sweat. You agree, Bids?"

I stood in front of the sink. My knees shook. I couldn't make them stay still. Dark was coming so fast I could see the kitchen get shadows. Wind burst through the windows. Hot and rushing like something was chasing it.

"Well, Bids? Don't you agree?"

"I, I—"

"Say it," she said. She was next to me now. "Rowan is a disgusting destructive slug."

I could smell the storm pushing in with the wind.

"Rowan is," I whispered. I tried to get some air. But it was too thick in my nose. "A destructing slug."

"Get in here!" Gloria yelled.

My brother came into the kitchen. He looked down at his new island and scritched it.

There was a loud bang outside. Like a tree cracked right in two. Under the table, Chicken whimpered. He put his paws over his eyes. He didn't like storms.

"Too bad they don't make bait for human slugs." She yanked on the sliding door. The metal screeched. "Then it'd just be you and me, Maisy. Easy street."

Rowan followed her through the door. She didn't even need to say a word. She was going to take him into the woods. She was going to leave him there like she done last time. But when she was halfway across the deck a bright flash went off and rain poured out of the clouds. Buckets of it. I heard her squeal. She stopped and pointed near the two steps that went down to the grass. Rowan went and stood right in that spot. Another blast of light went off, but Rowan didn't budge an inch. Gloria did though. She skipped back inside real fast.

Water dripped off her and she made puddles on the floor. She grabbed a cup towel and wiped at her face. "That was sudden," she said with a gasp. There was black under her eyes because her makeup was all smeared. She reached over the sink and slammed the window shut. "Don't worry, Bids, darling. Everything's going to be okay with Telly. I know him, and he'll be bored with that witch in no time." She moved her head toward Rowan. "As for that one. I just need him out of my sight for a while. I don't know how to get through to him. He can't leave well enough alone."

I put my hand in my pocket. I held the metal in my fingers. *Something terrible is coming.* There was more banging and light outside. Sometimes I couldn't see nothing.

She pushed the little black switch by the door handle and it snapped down, so it was locked. "Got to keep the wolves out," she said. "Right, Bids?"

I nodded, but only a little.

"Now I'm off to get a bath, miss. That rain got me chilled through."

She went up the steps, and there was another thunder crash outside. The light on the ceiling hummed like it was full of beetles. I heard the floor creak upstairs. The pipes creaked and snapped, too. She'd turned on the taps.

When I looked out I could see Rowan through all the lines of water. He was standing still, and his hair was like a helmet. His shirt stretched around his neck and there was nothing on his feet.

Light exploded out of the sky. In the flash I saw Rowan was only bones inside his clothes. He didn't come closer. He didn't put his fists on the door. He didn't try to sneak in or kick nothing. He just looked back at me.

I sniffed. The smell of flowers crept down the stairs. That was Gloria's bubble bath. The water stopped, and I could hear her singing a song.

I put my hand up and pressed it against the door. Rowan wobbled in the rain. I squeezed my eyes tight together. I knew he was hurt inside, but he probably didn't feel it. Same when I sliced my finger on tinfoil. Nothing was there for a while, but later dots of blood dribbled out.

There was an empty thump. When I opened my eyes, Rowan was jumping off the deck. He ran fast like he was flung from a slingshot. Another blast of yellow lit up the sky, and Rowan disappeared into the woods.

ROWAN

I ran. Over the grass. Water splashing around my ankles. I leapt through the scratchy bushes at the edge of our backyard. And then I was surrounded by darkness, thick and heavy on my skin.

I slowed down. An arm bent, my face tucked into my elbow, I swung my other hand around. Patted the trees and branches. Rain rolled from leaf to leaf, striking my head, sliding down my back. The lightning flashed, giving me a snapshot. I crept forward. Step by step.

Keep a straight line. You'll get there.

I lifted my legs up and over imaginary boulders. Moss squished under my feet, then rocks, dead twigs. Scraping me. My skin so cold I could barely feel it. But I was doing it. I was getting away from her. And him, too. I hated them both. How could Telly do that? He was the one who told me not to tell about my stupid bus ride to the garage. And then, when he didn't like my old ladies jab, which was just the truth, he opened his mouth and spilled everything. He was worse than my school counselor. Worse because he was my own father. And what was wrong with going to see him anyway? Even Mrs. Spooner thought it was a good idea.

But Mrs. Spooner didn't know them. Nobody did. Gloria only cared about herself. And Telly was nothing more than a charlatan. A swindler. Who would have guessed he'd con his own son? Make me actually believe he loved me. Well, I wasn't going to fall for that shit again. I was never going back there. Maisy would just have to fend for herself.

Another flash, then sudden darkness. I closed my eyes to hold the image, but everything was unfamiliar. The looming trees, the gnarled branches. I didn't know the way. *Go! Move!* My heart fluttered and panic squeezed the hard lump in my throat. Inside my head, I tried to focus on Carl's voice. *Hey, Magic Boy.* Carl was my friend. I was certain of that. Gloria was wrong; she always said I'd never make friends. But that was before she made that sign and pointed at a tree. Told me not to move. And Carl came along and let me follow him. Didn't ask for a single thing in return, and just invited me to stay. That was friendship.

I tried to keep a straight line. One foot in front of the other. I felt something glide past my leg. Wet and furry. I jumped. An animal? Or moss on a rock? Didn't dare reach down to touch it.

Carl will be there. He was always there. *But what if, this one time, he isn't?* He said he was going to be there until he died, or was reclaimed, was it? But was Carl a reliable person? What if he and Girl took off? Moved to another bridge. What if there was nobody waiting?

What if I'm alone in here?

Another flash. The woods had grown denser. It felt like hours since Gloria had turned me out. Since Maisy had watched me from inside. Fear made my lungs wheeze. I rushed ahead, fingers spread, grasping and tearing. A root grabbed my ankle. I stumbled. Face struck. A stone? A log? I was on all fours now. Pain radiated out from my chin, and my throat swallowed mouthful after mouthful of watery blood. My tongue felt a gap near my bottom lip. Then a small pebble. No. My tooth! I spit it into my hand. Pushed it to the bottom of my back pocket.

Leaves and bark and dirt stuck to my arms and legs. Stuck to my neck. In my hair. I sat back on my heels. Lightning flashed again. Thunder cracked. Rain dropped through the trees, blanketing me. It was drowning me. I was shaking. Could hear clanking inside my head.

What was I thinking, running away? What did I even know about Carl? His mother was a ghost. He acted like he could read the future. He had a nice dog, but he also had three different people chattering inside his skull. He liked to eat food from a package or a can and he thought birds were picking surveillance wires out of trees and every time I saw him his eyes were redder, and his beard was thinner, and he talked more and more about the workers.

Gloria was right. I'd never have friends. Who was Carl? I didn't even know his last name. And of course I didn't know where he actually lived because Carl didn't have a home. Now I was stuck in the black woods without even a pair of sneakers. I could find my way back if I wanted, but I didn't want that either. I hated Gloria. And I hated Telly. And I loved them, too, so much. But no matter how hard I tried, they just wouldn't love me back. Why wouldn't they love me? Why wouldn't they? What was wrong with me?

Then I couldn't stop it. My mouth opened and saliva and blood and sobs barreled out of me in great heaves. I was nothing. I was a stupid kid, with no mom. With no dad. Getting what I deserved. And I didn't even care.

I don't know how long I crouched, shivering in the tarry darkness, my whole jaw throbbing. A pulse inside my bones. But finally the rain became lighter and I could make out small shapes, shadows. When I looked to my left, I saw a faint glow. From a fire? I thought I smelled a thread of sweetness from burning wood. That must be him. That must be where the bridge was.

As I got up and inched forward, my knees were knocking together. The moon was still behind thick clouds, but I followed sounds from the creek. Then I saw the solid blackness of the stones. I pushed through the bushes, and he was there. Under the bridge. Hunched by a fire. Rocking back and forth, a blanket over his back. The rain had finally stopped, and above the gurgling water I could hear Carl humming. Loud and long and tense, like an old generator. He pulled in a raspy breath. Then more humming.

"He's not good," Maisy had said. "I think he might be a wolf."

Icy skin tightened along my spine.

What was I doing? Was it safe to be here? With this stranger?

I edged toward the fire. I was so cold, even my bones were rattling. Carl looked like an enormous animal with its shaggy head lowered. Girl leapt up, snarled. Then Carl lifted his wild mane and blinked. He stood, blanket crumpling at his feet, and I held my breath. The humming hitched in his throat. And stopped.

Girl raced toward me and licked my hand. Carl mumbled, "No, no, he doesn't. Electricity released in the air. You don't, urh, look so good."

When he said that last part, I started crying again. My legs were shaking and my nose was running. Tears dropped off my chin. *You're acting like a baby*, Gloria's voice, a whisper in my mind. But Carl didn't smirk or laugh. Instead his eyebrows knotted together and he twisted the hair in his beard.

"I'm so stupid." I tried to say this, to explain to Carl, but it sounded all jangled. My mouth was swollen. When I tapped it with my thumb, the skin felt like it might burst.

"What's that?"

"Stupid," I tried a second time.

"Stupid," he said back. He shone a flashlight in my face and I lifted my hand to block it. When he clicked off the light he said, "I got it, I do. I got it, Dot." Carl picked up the blanket he'd been using, and came toward me. "Sure, now. Urh. Don't be like that." He shook his head forcefully. "You're wrong, Stan. Without proof there's only doubt. First year, first day. The brightest room in the whole solar system."

Sometimes Carl made no sense at all, but it didn't matter. I don't know why I was so scared when I got there. He was the exact same as he'd been all summer. Peculiar, but welcoming. He put the blanket over my shoulders and it was still warm, and even though my face throbbed, my chest filled with relief. I was with a person who knew me and cared about me and would never, ever leave me outside in lightning.

He nudged me toward the fire. I sat down, wrapped the blanket over my knees. A long time passed before I stopped shaking. The smoke smelled good.

"I thought you were Workers," Carl said. His fingers combed through his hair, worked the twists of metal. Fixing them tighter. "Workers coming to find me. They rang my doorbell once. Stood right on the, the, urh, steps of my house."

I shook my head. There was a low drone inside my skull.

"Hard to tell sometimes. Workers only come in twos, though. Dressed better than you, and I never saw them cry before. They tried to tell me a message out of a book. A message about, urh, a powerful being. Wires, urh, hidden under their coats."

I wished Carl wouldn't talk about people who worked. Everyone worked. There was nothing wrong with that. My stomach started quivering like I was scared. But I couldn't be scared. I was with Carl. I knew Carl. I'd known him for weeks. He was a good person.

I heard plastic crinkling then. "You hungry?" he asked.

"My tooth." I pointed at my mouth and started crying again.

"My tooth," he said.

Flashlight in my face again, and he reached out and pulled down my lip.

"An avulsion injury. You got it, Magic Boy? Teeth decay. Teeth depart. It's the government. They start with a seed and then they cultivate and pull . . ."

I couldn't make out the last bit, but I nodded.

"Give it to me."

I fished in my pocket and handed him the sticky shard. I thought Carl was going to hide it away somewhere inside his coat. Maybe he'd think it was good luck. But he didn't; he went to the creek and bent down. He was a boulder stooped at the edge. He mumbled, "Water will have to do. No milk. Of course I know what I'm doing, Dot. I just. I'm trying to think and do."

He crunched back over the pebbles and knelt beside me. He had the flashlight tucked up into his armpit, and he pulled my lip down again. His fingers were in my mouth. I tasted bitterness, and I closed my eyes. Lips stretched, my jaw shook up and down and I felt him guiding the tooth down into its socket. "Urh. I think it's level there," he said. "Should stick." Then he cupped his hand under my chin so that my mouth stayed closed. Held it there for a moment. Ever so gently.

"It's going to be fine, Magic Boy." He laughed loudly, then cocked his head. "You're right, you're right. Unless I got it the wrong way around."

I ran my tongue over it. I tried not to budge it. I put my head down on my knees. Throbbing moved through my chin, out through my ears. The woods around us glowed when lightning jagged to the north. But it was far away. The storm had ended. Through the trees I thought I saw the moon. Bright and yellow and nearly full.

Carl went back and sat down next to Girl. "Sure, sure. It's okay to tell him that," he said. "It's not confidential." Girl kicked out her legs, moved her body closer to Carl. With her paw, she clawed her toy squirrel toward her. Took its pointed face in her mouth. "He was trying to get currents to move around outside wires. The man. Then the government got, got, got, urh, hold of his research. They shoot it through the air when it's raining. That's the testing phase."

"Oh," I said. I blinked. It sort of made sense, though, but I wasn't sure. It was different from what I'd read in a science book Mrs. Spooner lent me from the library. And it was hard to think about anything with the pain. Part of me felt as though I was drifting. Floating up. I was warm. My eyes closed.

"Strange, though, urh," he said. Carl stood up again, walked back and forth. "Stan? You think that's proof? I don't know, I don't know. He's only one, not two. Like the Workers with their books. Magic Boy did show, show, show, urh, up when they let the electricity out. Flying through the sky. I wonder . . ."

That was the last thing I remembered Carl saying. I followed the sound of his pacing as I was falling asleep.

Curled in a ball by the fire, I dreamt about Gran. When I was little, I lived with Gran. I must have lived with Gloria and Telly before that, when I was a baby, but Gran is the first person I remember. In the dream I could see the two white whiskers poking out of her chin, and her skin smelled like gingersnap cookies. But as I leaned into her she started to smell strange. Like old cheese or fish. Then she was licking me. Her rough pink tongue gliding up my cheek. I shook my head. "Gran," I whispered. "Stop it." She licked me again. She really missed me a lot. *Too bad she's already dead.*

I laughed. Pain shot through my tooth and my eyes opened. At first I didn't know why I was on the ground. Why there was no ceiling above me. Then the memories all rushed back. Gloria. The storm. Running away. Finding Carl. The way he held my chin after he'd fixed my tooth.

Girl was beside me, lapping at my face. I looked around. Gray light filled the space under the bridge. The creek trickled over the rocks and in the distance a morning bird called. My jaw pulsed, and my neck and back were stiff.

But as bad as everything had been last night, morning still arrived.

"Hey, Carl."

"Good," he said. "About time." He twisted a section of his beard and yanked. "You need, need, need, urh, to get up. Get up right away."

MAISY

I didn't mean to, but I fell asleep next to the sliding door in the kitchen. It was me and Chicken and Jenny the Head, and I woke up when Chicken started whining because he needed to go pee. I got up and looked at the black switch, and I saw that it was still snapped down tight. Then I knew Rowan never came home. He never broke open the door and stepped over me and snuck into his bed. I lifted up the lock and let Chicken outside. I went out too, and then tiptoed across the deck and the grass and over to the edge of the woods. The sun was already getting hot but it still looked wet and dark in there. I whispered, "Rowan, you can come out now. You don't need to hide no more. You can come home." But Rowan didn't say nothing back, and my middle went twisty when I remembered about Carl.

I walked back and sat on the deck. I sat in the same spot where Rowan was. Water from the storm went through my shorts, but I didn't care. Chicken finished his business and came and plopped down next to me. He didn't care about the water neither. He was warm, and I pushed in close. Me and Chicken watched the woods together. We waited and waited. I picked all the tiny bits of wet grass off my feet. I pulled some burrs out of Chicken's fur. Then I put my face near his ear. "Rowan's not with Carl. Right, Chicken? He's going to come out of the woods any second." Chicken yawned and closed his eyes.

"What's wrong with you?"

I jumped. Gloria was yelling out from the kitchen.

"Talking to a dog? Get up from there and come inside."

I went into the kitchen. Gloria's hair was puffed and there was still black under her eyes.

"Go wake up your brother. I want him scraping down the porch. All that flaking paint gone."

"He's not home, Gloria."

"What? Up and out already?"

I shook my head.

"That kid spends more time at the library than the bloody librarians."

I shook my head again.

"Well, he better not be up at that old bat's house."

"Mrs. Spooner?"

"You got that right."

"He went into the woods. I saw him last night. I slept with Chicken and the door was locked and he never came back." I closed my mouth then. I couldn't tell about Carl, because I swore on Telly's future grave.

"What?"

I nodded.

"Well, that can't be right. He's got himself poked away somewhere. He's not that senseless."

I followed Gloria upstairs and she opened Rowan's bedroom and looked at his messy bed and all the books spilled on the floor. "Pigsty," she said. Then she went down the stairs and out the front door and across the porch. She went around the side of the house where the clothesline was. The dead bird grave was there, and the basket was full of soggy clothes. "Well, he'll be hanging those up again," she said. "When he comes out from wherever he's hiding." She opened the door of the shed and poked around. I hugged Jenny the Head tight and stayed right behind her. "I don't know where that boy's got to." Then she went back to the front of the house and walked up the driveway to the circle. Muck stuck to her slippers, and she waved at Darrell. He was digging dandelions out of Aunt Erma's lawn, but he stopped when Gloria called out, "You seen Rowan?"

"Nope. Not this morning."

"Early bird today, it seems!" She laughed, and Darrell shrugged. He threw the weeds into a bucket.

She turned around and pinched my chin. "What game's he trying to play with me?"

"No game, Gloria." My mouth was dry and my heart was going tak-tak-tak. Carl was not a game, was he?

"You know where he's got to, miss." Her breath smelled like Chicken's. "I know it."

"I think—I think he ran away."

"If you're lying to Gloria . . ." she said.

That was not a lie.

Then she marched back inside, and I could hear her on the phone. "Thanks ever so much, Mrs. Spooner. First place I thought was the library. You know how much he enjoys it there. You've always been a lovely influence on him." I snuck into the kitchen. She hung up and walked around the kitchen opening cupboard doors and then slamming them closed. When the phone rang again she grabbed it, said, "No? Even checked the bathrooms?" She tapped her foot. "He got into an awful argument with Telly last night. Misses him terribly, I figure that's the root of it. Mm-hmm. Yes, he came to visit, trying to sort things out and all. I'm just worried about Rowan." Then she was biting hard at her mouth. "Yes, I'm sure he's fine. That age, you know. Sure, sure, if he shows up, I'd appreciate it. You're a godsend." She put the phone back again. Hard this time.

Gloria went upstairs, and a long while later she came down with a dress on. It had blue and yellow flowers, and her hair was curled nice. The black was gone off her cheeks and they were turned pink. She made me and her a sandwich. She didn't cut it into a heart like she did sometimes. It was dry but I ate it all. After lunch she washed our plates and all the dirty stuff from last night and told me to broom up the floor. Then when the kitchen was sparkly, she picked up the phone and called Telly.

"He's just gone," she said. "Yes. That's what I said. Since last night."

She used a mean voice. She told him Rowan was so upset after dinner he got some madness in his head. He just up and took off. She said the mess was Telly's fault. He was a useless disaster of a father. Completely worthless. After all the work she'd done to get Rowan on a straight path, he brought on this garbage. "Yep, yep," she said. "You heard me. Surely you can't be that thick."

Gloria put the phone back real gentle. "He's on his way," she said. "He's going to fix everything, Bids."

"That's good," I said. I didn't know if that was true. I reached into my pocket. My little metal piece was still there.

"Now why don't you put that silly doll thing away and go brush the dog."

I put Jenny the Head by the toaster and took Chicken out to the front porch so I could watch for Telly. I combed out Chicken's knots. He always had tons of them. The sun was shining and birds were singing. All the long grass outside was still wet. It was hanging over but soon it'd be dry and it'd stand up again. I looked everywhere, but no Rowan. He wasn't lying down with his mouth and eyes full of rain.

"Maisy-Bids? You listening with both ears?"

Gloria had sneaked up behind me and my heart popped right up in my neck. I dropped Chicken's brush.

"We got to go over things. Talk about last night. You know, before Telly rolls in here and things get all turned around."

Air couldn't get up my nose. But I smiled.

"What show were you and Rowan watching before he ran off?"

"Show?"

She stuck her fingernails in Chicken's fur. "On the television."

"No show, Gloria. I promise. I didn't let him inside."

"It's okay, darling." A real *darling* this time. "Let him inside? What are you on about?"

"But I didn't."

"I don't know what's got into you. Rowan was never outside, Bids. Not in a storm like that. What a thought to have in your head!"

My mouth went open. I scritched my head. Was I remembering wrong?

"No mother would ever allow a child out when there's lightning, Bids. You got a dreadful habit of lying."

"I don't tell lies, Gloria. I don't."

She touched my hair. "Well, not on purpose, sweetheart. But you do dream up crazy ideas. Get all confused."

Gloria was right. Sometimes things got mixed around in my head. And I was always forgetting. Losing my stuff. "Sorry, Gloria. I don't—"

"Good girl. And you don't have to make things up for me. I'm not upset that you and Rowan had a show."

Little lights were zooming around inside my eyes.

"Can you breathe, Bids?"

I tried to breathe. Chicken stood up and shook himself.

"Did Rowan even finish the root beer I gave him?"

I loved root beer. We only had it twice, when Telly took us for burgers. A girl on roller skates clipped a tray onto the window. She gave us root beer in frozen mugs with huge handles. Last night Telly said he'd take me and Rowan out to eat. When Rowan got home, maybe we could have root beer again.

"Are you listening to me? This is important. Real important."

Gloria put her hands on my shoulders. They were warm and heavy.

"Before I went to take my bath. Think hard, Bids. I split the last bottle between you and Rowan. You know I'm generous like that, right?"

I nodded. A lot of times.

"Don't you remember? A cold root beer, and you both snuck an extra show. Even though I said to go straight to bed right after. Don't that sound about right?"

I put my hand on my head. I didn't know.

"You got to get this straight. Don't you want Rowan to come home? If you don't tell this right, Telly'll be thinking the wrong thing. Blaming me. And Rowan won't come back if everyone's angry."

"He might."

"No, he won't." She smiled but her eyes didn't crinkle up the way they do sometimes. "Just think how special it was last night. I was so upset about that disagreement with Telly, I let you and Row have a treat. A show. Sipping away at your sodas."

My mouth watered. I could almost remember the root beer. It was probably real. And it was much nicer than Rowan outside in the rain. Gloria being friendly, not mad. Me and Rowan got squeezed into Telly's soft brown television chair. I had my head on Rowan's shoulder. It was a hard shoulder, but I didn't mind. I remembered the root beer foam tickling my chin. I burped, and Rowan said, "You're a turtle. Not a warthog." We could hear Gloria singing in the bathtub. It was a song about someone being in the kitchen. Rowan whispered straight into my earhole, "Just one more show, Turtle. Come on. She won't know. We'll hear when she pulls the plug."

"Bids? Did you go to bed first?"

Her hands got extra heavy on my shoulders. I closed my eyes and had to think hard. "I fell asleep," I said. But not with Chicken. I was with Rowan. "In the chair."

"Without brushing your teeth, miss?" Her eyebrows were up, but she didn't look angry.

That was a mistake. I forgot to fit it into the story. I looked down at Gloria's feet. Her toenails were painted purple.

"That's okay, darling. And—and when you woke up? Just tell me the truth, Bids." She was talking fast, and when she took her hands away I could see they were all shaky.

"And when I woke up." I thought and thought of a good answer. One that wouldn't make Gloria frown. "When I woke up, he was just gone."

She hugged me. Full and tight. "Oh, you are such a smart little girl. So very clever with details. And an excellent memory! Just like your mother."

It felt good being squeezed by Gloria, but I wanted to cry. Me and Rowan might've watched a show in Telly's chair, but it didn't matter. Rowan still went out the sliding door. I knew he went to find Carl, and I had to keep that secret because I told Rowan I would.

"He'll come back, Maisy. Any minute we'll see him sauntering across that yard like he owns the place."

Then I saw Telly's truck rushing down the middle of the circle. He roared into the yard and he drove right over the grass. His horn honked a bunch of times. Then his door flew open and he exploded into the yard.

"What the hell is going on?" he yelled.

Chicken went and stood behind Gloria, and I went and stood behind Chicken.

"I don't know, Telly. Like I told you on the phone, he just disappeared." She was calm as could be.

"Jesus. That was a rough storm last night. Why would a kid take off in that?"

"Other than him being upset with you? I got no idea. He doesn't have my temperament, that's for sure. How about we go inside. Or do you want the world knowing our business?"

"The world don't care, Glow."

Then Gloria pointed up the driveway, and when I looked I saw Mrs. Spooner out on her front step. She waved. I was going to wave back, but Gloria grabbed my hand and pulled me into the house. Telly followed us as we went to the kitchen. "You think he went out this way?" He touched the sliding doors.

"Certain of it. Had to mop up water this morning."

In spots the door screen was sewed up with black thread. Other spots were just holes. A breeze came in that smelled like clover and wet grass.

He had his back to us. "Were you two at each other again?"

"Theodore Janes. Don't even try to turn this around on me. There wasn't a cross word between us. Was there, Bids?"

I shook my head.

He looked at his watch and tapped it hard. "Which way'd he go?"

"That's the thing. We don't know. Maisy was asleep, right? Tell your dad what happened. About the extra show in Telly's chair?"

When he turned and got close to me, I could see hairs under his nose. They stuck out through his skin. I didn't like his mustache being gone.

"What happened, Maisy?" He touched my shoulder like Gloria had done. But his hand was soft and cold.

"I don't know," I said.

"You're going to have to do better than that, miss." Gloria pointed her finger at me. "We're not joking around. This is serious. Your brother could be lost or hurt."

Telly said, "We're not mad, Bids. We just want to find Row."

I thought about seeing Rowan through the door. I thought about his wet shirt falling off his bones. I thought about the trees far away when the yellow lightning glowed. He ran so fast I don't think he touched the ground. Then when the sky flashed again I saw the woods swallow him in one greedy gulp.

I looked at Gloria. "Please, Bids," she said. All the pictures of Rowan in my head started to go gray. Then the other truth, the nicer truth, was getting colors.

"Gloria was in the bath and we had another show. Rowan said we could."

"Of course he would." Gloria rolled her eyes up.

"We like being in your chair, Telly. We did."

Telly's face went sad. "You can use it anytime you like, Bids."

"And I fell asleep in the chair. Then he wasn't there no more."

"What do you mean, wasn't there no more?"

"When—when I looked out again."

"Looked out?"

I could hear Gloria breathing hard. "Woke up, I mean."

"I carried her up to bed, didn't I, darling. I figured Rowan was already gone to his room. The door was shut. What else was I supposed to think?"

Telly stood up straight. He closed his eyes. He pushed the top of a finger between his eyebrows and pressed hard. "This is unbelievable. Did you ask his friends?"

"Really? That's what you got to say? He don't got no friends, Telly. Other than that Darrell kid he's clinging onto half the time. I mean what kind of seventeen-year-old wants someone Rowan's age glued to him?"

"No one else?"

"Not a soul."

I found a loose thread on my T-shirt and I tugged on it until it snapped. I knew what Gloria said wasn't true. He did have another friend. A friend who lived in the woods.

Gloria shivered. She started to cry. "I'm sorry for acting so rotten, Telly. I'm just—I'm just not myself since you left. There's so much to do all the time, and I can't handle Rowan. He's just out of control."

"Let's not worry about that now, Glow. We just got to find him." Telly hugged her and rubbed at her back. "I don't know where to start. What do I do?"

"Maybe the woods? All summer he's been wandering around in there."

"No kid in their right mind's going in the woods in the dark. Especially the way it was last night."

"That's just it. He's not in his right mind." She started crying harder. She put her face in Telly's chest. "He's not. He misses you so bad."

"Okay, okay. It's been hard, I know. Come on, now. Don't be crying. I'm here, Glow. I'll find him. You can count on Telly, right? I'll find our boy."

Telly went down the hall and out through the front door. He started searching around and calling out. I went behind him to see what he was doing. He got down on his knees. He stuck a stick under the porch and banged it back and forth. Then he went to the side deck and yelled for Rowan. He shone a flashlight under there and shook his head. He went around to the other side and opened the shed like Gloria did. He moved some boxes. Next he went to the potato patch and he looked at the dirt. Nothing was growing so there was nowhere to hide. He walked back and forth over the grass real slow. And then he went into the woods. I couldn't see him no more. Every few minutes I'd hear him hollering or branches breaking or rocks banging. Sometimes he sounded scared. Sometimes he sounded angry.

"Please, Rowan!"

"Goddammit, boy! Show yourself!"

It was a long, long time before Telly came back. He looked like he rolled around in a buttered-up frying pan. His neck and arms were covered with scrapes, and there were lots of red spots from black fly bites. Some of them were scabs of blood.

"Not a single sign," he said. He took the cup towel and wiped his face. "If there was a trace, rain got it washed clear."

"Where'd you go?" Gloria asked.

"All over. Far out as the farms. Behind the school. The playground."

I put my hand in my pocket and felt the piece of metal Carl gave me. The more I squeezed at it, the smaller and smaller it got. "Did you, um, go out to the bridge, Telly?"

"The stone one? Where the old tracks cross over the creek?"

I nodded. Gloria looked at me hard. "Rowan caught tadpoles there once. With Darrell."

"I didn't go in that far." Telly put his hand on top of my head. "Besides, he's not a little boy, Bids. No thirteen-year-old is catching tadpoles."

"Oh," I said.

He went out of the kitchen and was going upstairs. "I'm taking a shower."

"Your soap's still there, Telly."

When he came down again, he was even more red. He drank a big glass of water. We waited and waited. The clock on the wall kept ticking and Rowan still didn't come home. Telly and Gloria walked in circles around the kitchen. Gloria cried more and Telly gave her another hug. He said, "It's going to be okay, Glow. We're in this together." Then when the sky turned orange and crickets started chirping, he picked up the phone and he called the police.

ROWAN

I stretched and yawned. "Get up now," Carl said again. "Before the sun gets too high."

He took my blanket and folded it. He placed it inside a cardboard box on the ground. Then he looped a rope through Girl's collar, and tied it to the trunk of a tree. He gave her a quick scratch behind the ears, and started walking.

"Where're we going?"

"Where're we going?" he said back.

I stayed behind him. We picked our way through shrubs and grass and climbed a steep hill up to the main road. We came out of the woods right behind a sign with swirly letters, *Welcome to the Town of Little Sliding*. The crushed stone poked my feet. They were still bare but at least my shirt was dry. I nudged my tooth with my tongue and it didn't wiggle back and forth. It throbbed, but not as bad.

"You have to see the full day ahead," Carl said. The buttons on his enormous coat were mismatched with the buttonholes, and it made his body appear lopsided. "You can't twist it to serve your own purposes. You don't have maternal rights."

"What did you say?"

"Urh," he mumbled.

I could already tell it was going to be warm, and as we stood on the gravel shoulder, Carl was panting. A couple of times he hacked and spat. "Pardon me," he said.

A silver transport truck barreled past us. Carl waved an arm, but it didn't slow. The horn blared, a long whine that trailed through the air. I felt the blast of wind push me back, then the sharp pull toward the giant wheels. Like suction. I stumbled, but Carl grabbed my arm, yanked me.

"Stand back, Magic Boy. You get flattened and I'll never hear the end of it."

"Yeah," I said. My heart was beating. I could feel it in my face, and I reached up to touch my lip. It was still swollen, but it no longer felt as though it was about to burst.

Another transport truck came around the bend. On its side was a gigantic image of sliced bread. Carl waved both arms this time. I held onto the sign's wooden supports. The metal machine tore past, but then I saw brake lights flicker. It began to slow, hazard lights flashing. "Let's go," Carl said. I hesitated. *Go where?* Carl was already speeding toward it. Where was he going? How far away from home? Were we coming back?

"Hurry up!" he yelled.

I had to stick to my decision. It was time to forget about home. Forget about Gloria and Telly. And—and Maisy. I was with Carl now. We were doing something. Having an adventure. Exactly what sort of adventure I didn't know, but most of me didn't care. Then I realized *all* of me didn't care. I started running. "Hey, wait up!" I called. "Don't leave me behind!" Not too loud, as it still hurt when words vibrated my teeth.

The door kicked open and Carl nudged me forward. I climbed three shallow steps, slid across the sticky gray seat. The driver had thin hair stuck to his forehead and sideburns on the side of his face. Sweat trickled down over his skin, soaked into the collar of a red-and-white checked shirt. He smelled strange, like wet newspapers, although I probably smelled strange too.

When I straightened up in the seat I saw a bunch of photographs taped to the dashboard. Of a young woman. A whole lot of skin. I kept looking left or right, trying not to stare. Carl eased in next to me, and when I glanced up at him, I knew he'd seen the pictures too. He said slowly, "Lots of wholesome trees out my window, Magic Boy." His arm pressed into my shoulder. I felt safe beside him. He was a huge person.

"Howdy," the man driving said as the truck grumbled and popped forward.

"Hi," I managed, but my heart was still beating hard and I twisted my torso away from him. I tried not to look at the photos, to focus on the forest blurring by, but my eyes wanted to wander, settle there. I stared at Carl's pant legs. I didn't understand how they could have a sharp crease. He had the nicest shoes I'd ever seen.

"Where you friends headed?"

"The Stop," Carl said. "Just the, the, urh, The Stop."

"Gotcha."

The man kept taking one hand off the wheel. He stroked his giant silver belt buckle with his thumb. Then a sideways gaze. "Looking rough there, kid. About as worn as a cow's tail in summer."

"I fell and hit a—"

He banged the dashboard. "Is not my business. What youse do with your life. I won't even ask you why you got no shoes on. You see?"

"Urh," Carl said. His guttural grunt sounded annoyed. "Magic Boy was made with no shoes."

"Ain't we all?"

I could hear Carl grumbling. Saying things I couldn't understand. I looked down and sideways. I didn't want to stare, but it was hard. The bottom of the truck driver's blue jeans stopped way above his ankles. Near his knee a compartment had fallen open. Inside a glass bottle full of small white cubes lay on its side. No label. Pills, maybe. The man laughed, picked up the bottle and shook it. "Sleep is for the dead."

"Urh," Carl said. His grunt was even sharper this time.

Then the man banged his knuckle on the dashboard again, right above the photographs. I had to look then. "Got myself a little missy," he said. "That's her right there. Having our first young one, we are. Already put up a swing set in the backyard. Hammered right into the ground."

"Kids like swings." My voice sounded like hands were around my neck.

I counted fast. There were seven snapshots fixed there. The instant kind that slid right out of the camera when you pressed the button. The tape was yellowed and cracked. Not that I really noticed the tape. Instead I stared at the pictures. A lady with dark curly hair, bright red lips. In one she was wearing a pink bra and panties. In another her back was curved and everything on the top was out. And in another she was completely naked on her side. My eyes kept flicking toward the one closest to the man. The lady's head was tilted, she was smiling, and her legs were bent and spread open and her parts were right there.

I swallowed all the water that rushed into my mouth. It seemed like the lady was grinning at me.

"She's really something, ain't she?"

"Urh."

"Sure she could've been one of those model types. I bought her a big set of tits, cost me a bundle, but one of 'em popped. No way to get all that shit out. Ruined her dreams, it did. I felt downright awful about it."

My stomach was curdled and excited and a little bit queasy looking at the photographs. Of the lady he married. Who was at this moment growing a baby, and that baby already owned its own swing set. I put my hands over my lap and stared at my fingernails. They were long and there was dirt and dried blood under them.

Carl was breathing heavily. Grunting and muttering. We seemed to be driving forever. I didn't know what The Stop was, or how far away we were going. On the radio a man sang about missing his girl. I thought of Girl, hoped she wasn't lonely or hadn't gotten free from her leash. Finally, the cab of the truck bounced side to side as we drove over broken pavement and pulled into a gas station. Carl was tugging at the handle before we even stopped.

"Have a good one," the man said, but Carl had already hobbled down the steps.

"Thanks, mister," I said quietly.

"Sure, friend. Anytime."

I slammed the door closed and followed Carl. He went inside the building. Hanging in the window was a poster showing a plate of burgers and a boy with a checkered napkin knotted around his neck. My stomach growled. I hadn't realized how hungry I was.

I found Carl seated on a stool at the counter. A woman in a polka-dot dress and white apron was writing something on a notepad. She stuck the pencil into her hair and smiled wide at Carl. As I got closer I heard her say, "Haven't seen your hairy mug in three weeks, darling. Where you been hiding yourself?"

"Urh," Carl said. He shuffled his feet a bit. His cheeks were greasy, but I thought I saw a flush of pink. "Here and there. Here and there. High security turnouts, so I can't discuss it. We have to keep a cover."

"Don't worry a pinch," she said, a finger to her lips. "I won't tell a soul."

Her name tag said "Marion." She winced when she saw me. "Oh honey. You poor bird. I know just what you want. A milkshake'll fix near anything."

Then I felt something tickling my neck. Hairs from Carl's beard. He was really close to me. "Faulty. The man in the truck was faulty," Carl whispered. "We picked the wrong transportation, Magic Boy. She wants me to tell you real ones are different. Real girls have hairs and rolls and wrinkles. Urh. They're way better."

I nodded, but the heat rushed up my chest and neck and the pulse in my tooth got worse.

Marion brought two milkshakes and a plate of fries.

"Mind your lip," she said.

I took tiny sips and bites and chewed way at the back of my mouth. It tasted so delicious I forgot how much my chin hurt. Out of the corner of my eye I watched Carl eat. It was not what I'd expected. I thought he'd push the fries into his face as fast as he could, but instead he was very particular. Almost thoughtful in the way he took a reasonable mouthful, chewed slowly, and swallowed with a small drink. He didn't slurp or belch. He used a paper serviette to clean his fingers, clean a dot of ketchup off his beard. Standing up, he dropped the serviette over his plate and walked away.

I took a few more bites, and when I swung around on my circular stool, I couldn't find Carl.

My mouth went dry. A ball of fries lodged in my throat. I searched every table, but he was nowhere. Just like that, Carl was gone.

He'd ditched me. He was probably out on the road trying to climb into a new truck. He could be going anywhere. Was he leaving Girl? Would he hurry back there, grab her, and then take off before I could find my way? Was I so bad he couldn't stand to be around me? Had he just used me to steal food? I couldn't pay. Marion would call the police. Squad cars screeching, sirens blaring. They would arrest me. I was filthy and I didn't even have shoes on. They were going to push me into the back of a car and take me right back to Gloria.

I tried to think, to breathe. Going back home. Would that actually be so bad? She probably realized I was gone by now. Maybe she even missed me. Gloria was angry last night, but so was I. Choking on it. I'd bet she was devastated that I'd run away. Wishing she hadn't punished me like that. I could imagine it all, Gloria pacing around wondering where I was. Maisy was probably crying.

I looked at my food. Lines of ketchup crisscrossing my white plate. Drops of melted milkshake on the countertop. My tongue bumped my tooth, and I gasped from the jolt of it. Why was I trying to trick myself? Gloria wasn't upset about me. She wasn't worried. She didn't care if I lived or died.

Everything inside my heart was one big ugly snarly mess.

Marion brushed past me, then stopped, said, "You good, honey? You want me to find your uncle?"

I shook my head. I actually had a real uncle. Gloria's brother, Rick. He used to visit Gran's house, and he constantly complained that she shouldn't have me there. That Gloria was "once again shirking her responsibilities." Gran always hugged me tight and said something nice in my ear. "Never you mind him. He's just grumpy about his sister." After Gloria and Telly took me away from Gran's, I never saw him again. I never saw Gran again either. Except that one time through the window when she came to Pinchkiss Circle. She was standing on the road just in front of our driveway, and Gloria was screaming so Telly went out to talk to her. Gran kept patting her chest, her heart, but Telly wouldn't let her come in. Then she turned around and walked away.

Tears started slipping out of my eyes. I didn't want them doing that; they just started falling. Splashing onto the counter. My face hurt and my stomach felt sick. There was no going forward and no going back. I was stuck.

"Oh, sweetheart," Marion said. "Go on. Have some more shake."

I brought the straw to my lips but couldn't swallow. The thin arm on the clock above her orange hair kept clicking. What was going to happen to me now?

Marion pushed another serviette toward me, tapped the side of her face with her finger. "Here. You got a spot of mayo."

I wiped, but I knew that spot wasn't going to disappear. It was part of my map. Maisy always called it that. What an idiotic idea. It wasn't a map. I wasn't going anywhere. My blotches were probably the reason no one wanted to be around me. Gloria acted as though it was my fault, but Telly took me to the doctor, and he said it was just a condition. Nothing to do with me.

But then Telly left. Gloria kicked me out. And now Carl just walked away. Like I was worth nothing. Zero. Zilch.

"Well, don't you look handsome." Marion was staring over my shoulder.

From somewhere behind me I heard a gruff cough, then a shy "Urh."

A wave of happiness flooded me.

When I turned, Carl was right there. Wide smile. All the shiny streaks of smoke were gone from his face, and the bottom of his beard was trimmed. His fuzzy hair was damp and patted to the side. I could smell soap. Even the buttons on his coat were fixed.

He was still mumbling to himself, but cleaned up, Carl almost looked like a regular man. He could definitely be some boy's uncle. Even some boy's father.

"You acquired your nutrition?" he asked as he put money on the counter.

"Yes, sir," I replied.

"Good, good." He ruffled my hair. "That's my boy."

We went outside. Carl signaled a truck driver headed in the opposite direction. We climbed up into the cab. No weird photos this time. The man told a joke about spilled cutlery and a fork in the road. It wasn't very funny, but I laughed out loud.

"That's my boy."

"That's my boy."

"That's my boy."

ROWAN

When we got back to the camp Girl rushed toward us, yanking on her rope. She sprang up, pawed the air like a pony. I untied her and threw her mangy squirrel in the air. She brought it back to me again and again.

"See, Stan? She trusts Magic Boy," Carl said. "She doesn't trust anyone."

"Except you," I said.

"Urh," he said, and he grinned, rubbed his nose.

The dampness underneath the bridge lifted, and the day was warm and breezy. I could hear bees buzzing and birds chirping. I sat by the creek. Thin green reeds grew up through the water. Mosquitoes hovered among them, and when tiny fish darted up to snap, bubbles remained on the surface. I watched a handful of tadpoles skitter this way and that. Darrell came to mind, and I wondered if he was finished tinkering with his motorcycle. Maybe he'd take me for a ride. Telly used to forbid it, said anything with a motor and two wheels was a deathtrap, but he wasn't around to stop me. Then I remembered my decision. I was gone from Pinchkiss Circle. And I was never going back.

I put my feet in the water. The tadpoles edged closer, but when I wiggled my toes they scattered. I wondered where their mother was. She probably abandoned them after they hatched from their eggs. Maybe even before. Some mothers were like that.

As I rested by the creek, Carl inspected every corner under the bridge. Tapping stones and pulling out pale weeds. He bent and organized the mound of garbage so that it was neat and contained. As he moved from one side of the space to the other, he reached up and ran his palm over the *Almost*.

"Did you paint that?"

"Did you paint that?" he repeated. He stared at me as though my question didn't make sense. Maybe he was insulted. Carl would never destroy property. Do something illegal. I just had that sense.

"Sorry," I said. "Dumb question."

"Urh."

The afternoon passed in a hazy way. I collected twigs and fallen branches for later. I waded in the cool water, washing the dirt off my feet and arms and neck. I discovered a trail of ants and followed them until I located their volcano-shaped nest.

"Don't touch that," Carl said.

"I won't."

Often, I noticed Carl gaping at me. Not in a menacing way exactly, but in an intense way. As though he were studying me. When I stepped from one place to the next, he followed my feet. When I cleaned the grime from my skin, I could tell he was watching my hands. When I spoke, he stared straight at my mouth. A couple of times I heard him talking to Stan. His voice got way louder. "I *am* being logical. I don't believe it." "Not a single live wire on his person." "Always twos. That's the rule. Magnetic force too strong to break."

He paced back and forth and lit one of his brown cigarettes. "You know any other languages, Magic Boy? Foreign languages?"

I stopped blowing on the blade of grass nipped between my thumbs. "No. They try to teach me Spanish in school and stuff, but I'm no good at it."

He mumbled, then his eyes narrowed. "Nothing else? Conspiratorial languages?"

The grass-blade whistle fell onto the surface of the water. It floated away. "I don't get what you mean."

"I don't get what you mean," he said.

I wondered why he repeated my words so often. Maybe he was trying to hear parts of our conversation a second time to understand better. It didn't bother me. He wasn't being mean.

He didn't ask me anything else about foreign languages. Instead he stepped on his cigarette, then brought the squished butt to the trash pile.

Girl bounced over and dropped her stuffed squirrel beside him. Carl plucked it up, and while inspecting it, he must have noticed a hole. He retrieved a small tin from his backpack, and with needle, thread, and squinting eyes, he repaired a tear.

"I can sew too," I said.

"Urh."

"I made my sister a body for her doll. But our dog ate it." I was going to ask him if he remembered Little Fawn, but I stopped. I didn't want to talk about Maisy.

In the slanting afternoon sunlight, sleepiness crept up on me. I put my head down on Carl's folded wool blanket and began to drift. The wool was itchy under my cheek. I saw Carl bringing the mangy squirrel to his mouth, bite away the last of the red thread. Then I was asleep.

I was there and at the same time I was not there. I could hear Carl rummaging around, talking, chuckling. "Altered the, the, the, urh, current. The tipping point is hidden in the node. Expand the truthful verdict. Only birds know everything, they're so high up. Can't see me here, no, can't see me here." Then, behind my closed eyes, I saw thousands of birds drifting overhead. Settling onto wires that rose and fell. The creek sparkled underneath them. Carl said, "You, Henry. You're always grumbling. I can't understand anything you say." Blue dragonflies hovered and the birds pelted toward them, fat bullets, strings of yellow electricity zapping from each wing.

I woke up to Girl yelping. Leaves crunching. Something was tiptoeing through the shrubs. The sunlight had vanished, and shadows filled the space beneath the bridge. I sat up. My heart drummed. A pulsing pain increased in my tooth. My neck ached as I craned to see.

It had to be Gloria or Telly. Maisy must have told them about Carl and they'd decided to come find me. I was surprised to sense a wave of joy welling up inside. Even though Carl was my friend, I had to admit that I missed my house. I missed my bike. I missed having a pair of clean socks or crawling into my bed for a nap. I missed that nail clippers were in the top left drawer and I could use them whenever I needed. I missed Maisy and hanging out with Darrell and Mrs. Spooner waving to me from her front porch. I even missed Shar, Darrell's snotty little cousin, snapping her fingers in my face or grabbing half my Popsicle.

Girl scratched the pebbles with her claws, but she didn't leave Carl's side. The noise got closer and she snapped her jaws. I held my breath, waiting to see Gloria or Telly's worried face emerge through the bushes. But when Girl let out a vicious bark, whatever was behind there bolted away. Branches cracked and leaves tore.

It was just an animal.

As the rest of the afternoon passed, I listened closely. I heard small padding footsteps, a rabbit or a skunk, but no one appeared. Once I thought I heard someone calling my name. It sounded a little like Telly, but I knew my head was only making that up. Playing a moronic game with itself by wishing for something that never existed. I'd been gone almost a full day, and no one was coming to look for me.

MAISY

Telly went to all the wrong spots in the woods. I couldn't stop thinking about it. The right spot was the bridge. Tadpoles didn't matter when there was Carl and Girl and a fire and wieners and a magic deck of cards. My middle felt sick, but I couldn't say nothing because Rowan made me swear. Gloria kept looking at me hard, even when Telly was hugging her. She knew I was keeping a big horrible secret.

I went outside and sat on the front porch. Chicken came out too and sat next to me. From the front step I could see a lot of the circle. I could see Aunt Erma's house where Darrell and Shar lived. Mrs. Murtry lived right next door, but her car wasn't there, so she was gone. At the very top was Mrs. Spooner's house. She might be home or she might be at the library. I tried not to look at the woods. I counted to ten and then looked fast. That gave Rowan time to come out. I did it a bunch of times, but he wasn't playing.

A brown car came into the circle and drove straight down to our driveway. The wheels were moving slow. I jumped up and went inside to the kitchen. "Someone's out there," I said.

"That was fast," Telly said.

There were loud slams, and then I heard the screen door creak. Our happy, happy door was already open, but a person reached in and tapped on it anyway. "Hello? Anybody home?"

I peeked around the corner and saw two tall people standing there. One was a man with a gold badge stuck to his shirt and a shiny gun on his belt. The other man was wearing a blue tie with yellow bits. Not yellow like our door but moon yellow. Telly rushed past me to let them in. He had to tip his head back to see their faces.

"Detective Aiken. And this is Officer Cooper." He shook Telly's hand. "You're having some trouble with your boy?"

"He took off." Telly rubbed his face. "Seems."

The men came into our house. Telly pointed at me and my heart started going, but then he said, "The kitchen's through there." They followed him and then chairs scraped on the floor. The tie man sat down but the policeman was walking around. I stayed in the hallway and held onto Chicken's collar, and when the policeman passed the kitchen doorway he smiled at me. I didn't smile back.

"Your son?"

"Yes, sir. Rowan. Rowan Janes."

"When did you last see Rowan?"

I knew Telly was looking at the gun stuck to the man's hip. He probably wanted to hold it or clean it. Telly loved guns a ton. Lots of nights he put down newspaper on the table and took them apart and brushed them out or greased them up. I didn't like to watch, but Rowan did.

"I— Well, I don't live here no more. We had some bumpy times."

"Bumpy times?" The man took a notepad out of his pocket and opened it up.

"You know. Nothing major, really. I moved out. Stuff changed. The boy's upset with me leaving. Probably just trying to make me upset back."

"Could be, Mr. Janes. How old is your son?"

"Thirteen."

"Thirteen. And he's been out for a while?"

Telly yelled over his shoulder. "Glow? Where are you? Cops are here. They got questions."

Gloria walked past me. Her nose was red and fat. She wiped her face with a balled-up tissue. Chicken pulled at my hand, but I held on good.

"Hello, ma'am," the older one said. "We got a call about your son. Been gone for a while?"

"I thought we had to wait twenty-four hours," Gloria said when she sat down. She kept squeezing the tissue. Squiggly bits of white fell on the table.

"No, ma'am. Not with a minor."

"I didn't know. He's only twelve. A tiny twelve."

"He turned thirteen, Glow."

"Thirteen." She squeaked. "Time's gone crazy. Rushing like that."

"When did you last see him, ma'am?"

She was sniffing a lot. I wanted to squeeze her to stop her being so sad.

"Last night. But—but I thought he'd gone to bed. Was in his room. You know how they never come out at that age."

The man nodded.

"When I came down this morning, the door was wide open."

"What door?"

"Those." Gloria pointed at the sliding doors. The ones I watched Rowan through. But I didn't watch Rowan through. Rowan was not outside.

"You think he went out through those, ma'am?"

"I do," she said. "I do."

"Okay."

"And what a puddle of water on the floor this morning. Everywhere."

The man in the tie scritched his face. "Rainwater, you think?"

She nodded. "From the storm."

"That was quite some rain we had last night. But it calmed down around, around . . ." He looked at the policeman.

"Around midnight, sir. Cleared away completely."

"So, if that was rainwater on your floor, he exited the premises before midnight." He wrote something in his book. Then he looked down at the floor and coughed. "Did you notice anything, Mrs. Janes? Footprints? Any signs someone came into your home?"

"Nothing," she said. She shook her head for a long time. "Other than the dog's. Mud from his paws. I cleaned it up. The water. I shouldn't have done that? I should have left it?" Her voice went funny. She started to cry again. Then she waved at me. "Bids?"

I looked at the floor in front of the door. I had to remember it good. It was wide open this morning. Gloria's hand didn't flick the black switch last night to lock out Rowan. And lock out the wolves. She was upstairs gone to bed. She didn't put Rowan outside. I was sleeping in Telly's chair. I had root beer before and the bubbles tickled my chin. There was a big mess this morning. The water was all spread out and slippery. Chicken made muddy paw prints. Gloria was angry about the floor. But not too angry.

I nodded. My head felt worse and worse. Like my brain was in a radio and the songs weren't playing right. I was trying to push the pictures in there and make them stay. "It was messy. From Chicken. Chicken can be a very bad dog."

I let go of Chicken's collar. He went right over to the man. The man rubbed Chicken's head and Chicken's tail bumped. Then he looked at me and smiled. "I'm sure he can be a very good dog, too."

Gloria hiccuped from all the crying. "I'm beside myself, Mr. Um. Detective. Just out of my mind with worry."

"Has he done this sort of thing before? Gone out overnight?"

Gloria tucked her head down and started crying loud. "No, never." She sounded all sloshy. "He's a wonderful boy. A wonderful son." Telly put his head low too. He was smoothing her back. "What type of child would go out in that weather?"

"I'm sorry," the man said. "I know this is difficult. But it's not uncommon, you know. Teens, especially, like to startle their parents. Keep us on our toes."

"We already searched the house," she said. "Searched the shed, and Telly went through the woods as best he could. No sign."

"Friends? Neighbors? Someone he might want to meet? A girl, maybe? Or people he might seek out if he were upset."

I swallowed. Inside my head I heard Carl whisper *Little Fawn*. Like he was right next to me.

"No. He's not one of those kids with a crowd, let alone a girl. He likes being on his own, mostly. I don't know how to say it. He's not popular. Can't get along and stuff. Besides with his sister. And this boy named Darrell. A really good kid. He's like a mentor to Rowan, like a role model. He's in the house with the motorcycle out front. But I asked him, and he said he hasn't seen him."

"We'll talk to him. Anyone else he might have reached out to?"

"Maybe Mrs. Spooner?" Telly said. "Did you call her, Glow?"

"She hasn't seen him neither."

"Who's Mrs. Spooner?"

"She's his favorite teacher," Telly said. "And during the summer she volunteers at the library. Older lady. First house on the north side when you come into Pinchkiss Circle. Likes Rowan a lot."

"I've never been comfortable with her, if you ask me. The way she dotes on him."

"Glow, seriously. She's nearly sixty-five at least. Lost her husband. Lives alone with some cats. I don't think she can do much harm."

"You never know." She looked at the man with the moon tie. "It just plucked my radar, if you know what I mean."

"I do," the man said. He wrote down more. "We'll talk to her. We'll talk to all your neighbors."

Gloria's eyebrows pushed together again. She was crying more. "It's just—I didn't mean . . . I'm being foolish. I'm sure that lady got nothing to do with it. Telly moved out. Came last night for dinner and didn't stay like we all thought he would. That's what set Rowan off. It's been so hard on the boy."

"You don't got to say that, Glow." Telly's face got red. "Don't you think I'm torn up enough?"

"It's the truth, Telly."

Telly stood up. "I need a smoke." He went out on the porch. The policeman followed him.

Gloria kept talking. "Telly left a month or so before school ended. Moved in with some other woman, right out of the blue. It was quite the blow. To all of us really. Rowan's been acting up since. Just distraught, I suppose. I mean, can you blame him? It's been impossible on me, trying to keep his spirits up and work most days and watch after Maisy."

"I can imagine," he said. The man wrote everything down. "Difficult relationship between the two of them, then?"

"Oh, yes. It wasn't healthy. Pick, pick, pick. That can drive a kid bonkers."

He wrote down some more. Telly's smoke stink came into the house. He was against the screen. The policeman was talking to him and Telly smoked hard. His cheeks were pulled and I could see what he looked like if he was just a skeleton.

Gloria wiggled her hand at me. "Come here, Bids?" I went closer. "Tell this gentleman everything, okay? Exactly what you told me. After the root beer? You know, and the show? I went on up to bed. Just worn out doing home repairs." She picked at specks of yellow paint still on her hands.

"Are you his sister?"

I nodded.

"What's your name?"

"Maisy Anna Gloria Janes," I whispered. My middle squeezed up.

He smiled. I chewed at my lip.

"How old are you, Maisy?"

"Seven," I said.

"I know this is upsetting, but if you can tell me as best as you remember. It sure would help. Do you understand?"

"Yes," I said, but it didn't come out very loud.

"So you were the last one to see your brother last night?"

I nodded again, then shook my head. In my side eye, I saw Gloria frown because I started wrong. Stars were coming out around the man with the tie. I wanted to sit down and lie against Chicken. But I didn't.

"Can you tell me what happened?"

"Yes, tell the man everything. He's here to help, sweetheart."

I knew this time *sweetheart* didn't mean *sweetheart*. My mouth was full of dust. "I was just, um, watching. And then I, I fell asleep."

"Watching what?"

"What show, Maisy?"

"I—it—"

"I remember," Gloria said. "You told me it was outer space something or another. *Jetsons* or was it those blobs that change shape or—"

"Mrs. Janes? It'd be really helpful to let your daughter tell me."

"Oh. Of course. Right."

"Maisy?" He looked at me.

"About animals," I said. I closed my eyes. All the right pictures were there, I just had to line them up and keep them from getting away. And not let any other ones in. None of Rowan on the deck in the rain. None of him running at the woods. None of lightning. None of Carl. Especially none of Carl. "Tigers. A whole lot of them. They were eating squirrels."

"Oh my." Gloria frowned harder. Maybe I'd gotten the animals wrong too.

"Or maybe possums," I said.

"That don't sound like a show for a child. I didn't know."

"Tigers and possums, hey?" the man said. "That's quite the combination." He smiled again and tapped his pen. "Scary."

I looked down at my feet. "No," I said. "Rowan was there. We had root beer. We weren't allowed to watch another show, but we did. Gloria said that's being crafty." Gloria had her mouth moving when I was telling stuff. I watched her mouth real close.

"Crafty, hey? I'm sure your mom isn't bothered by an extra show," the man said.

"Gosh, no." Gloria sounded like a bird feather. I smiled at her.

"What happened then, Maisy?"

"I fell asleep."

"You fell asleep. Okay." He kept on writing. I didn't like that. "Do you know what time you woke up?"

"Uh-uh." I didn't know about the waking up part. I didn't have a picture for that.

"Was the television still on? Was there a white screen? Or some colored bars? A noise that just goes on and on?"

The question was too big and long and I didn't know what to answer. Gloria was looking at me with strong eyes. I started to feel dizzy. I couldn't remember how to get air.

"Or did Rowan turn it off?" Gloria asked.

I nodded, and Gloria nodded, and the brightness came back into my eyes. Then I had an idea. "I thought he was gone to pee."

"Was the door open?"

I chewed more off my lip. A bad taste came in my mouth. Like pennies.

"Just think," he said.

I shook my head.

"That's okay, Maisy. You've done very, very well." Then he said to Gloria, "And you were in bed? Is that correct, ma'am?"

"I said that already."

"Yes, of course. I'm just trying to make sure I have everything right."

"Rowan is gone," she said. "Just gone. We can't find him nowhere."

"I understand, Mrs. Janes. We're going to do everything we can to get your boy back." He made a loop with his hand. His notebook snapped shut. "I'm just going to step outside for a minute. Talk to my officer."

Gloria came and gave me a giant hug. She hugged me so tight it hurt, and I coughed. My back went crack-crack and my eyes closed up.

"You're such a good girl," she whispered. "Such a good, good girl. You told them the whole truth. Perfectly."

MAISY

"We'd like to take a look around," said the man with the tie. He had come back inside. The policeman was with him. They were both looking at Gloria. "If that's okay with you, ma'am. You'd be surprised how many kids just tuck themselves away right inside their own homes."

"Really?"

"Really."

"To make us worry." Her eyes were still big and pink.

"Yes, ma'am. Exactly." The policeman twirled his mustache on his finger. "Where's his bedroom?"

"He's not there," she said. "I told you. We already checked. Telly and me."

Telly was still outside smoking more. He put his hand in his hair. The smoke came out the top of his head and it looked like a tiny chimney.

"Of course you checked," the policeman said. "I understand how upsetting this is, and we're taking it very seriously."

"A second pair of eyes, ma'am. Certainly won't hurt. And to be effective, we need to be very systematic in our approach."

"No, I guess." Gloria walked them around the house. I heard their feet coming through the ceiling upstairs. Quiet steps and then Gloria's stomp, stomp. With my ears I followed them moving around until they came back. "Do you have a downstairs?"

"Basement," Gloria said. She pointed down the hallway.

He walked over and looked at the basement door. "Do you always keep it padlocked?"

"Yes, sir, I most surely do." Gloria put her hands on her hips. "My husband still got some of his guns down there and it's the responsible thing when there's children in the house."

"Good for you," the policeman said. "I wish every parent was as conscientious. Accidents do happen. I've seen it firsthand."

"I can tell you right now he's not down there, but I can open it up."

"Please," he said. "We need to be thorough."

Gloria went upstairs again and stomped back down with a shiny key in her hand. She wiped her forehead. I think she was sweating. Then she unlocked the door and they went down the basement stairs. They were mumbling down there but I couldn't hear. Outside Telly flicked his cigarette away, and then he started patting the yellow paint on the door. He was looking at it real close like he didn't know what it was. Then he looked at the tops of his fingers, but it had to be dry by now.

Gloria and those men came back upstairs. The moon-tie man said, "We'll just check around outside." They both went out the front door and down over the steps. Telly followed. I sneaked behind them.

"Odd, isn't it," the man in the uniform said. "A kid going off in that weather? My guess, he was furious about something."

"If he went off at all," the tie man said.

They were doing the same thing Telly did. They looked under the front porch and the side deck with their flashlights. Telly was watching them and shaking his head. Then one went to the shiny car and talked into a thing on a cord. The other went to the shed, but he poked his head out and chopped the air with his hand. A little bit later a van came down our driveway. It wobbled side to side in the potholes. Then a real police car came with lights, but the lights were turned off. Our driveway was full, and there were lots of extra people outside. Some of them were our neighbors who lived around the circle. Telly was standing there talking to them. "It's the boy," he said. "We don't know where he's got to."

When I sneaked inside again, the tie man was talking to Gloria.

"Mrs. Janes, do you have a recent photo?"

Gloria scritched at her neck. "Not really. My camera broke."

"School photo?"

"Do you know how much those things cost? And they're never no good.

Blinking or scowling. You get the worst of the kid, you really do. I just gave up on them."

She had pictures of me. A bunch on the same sheet. They were in an envelope upstairs.

"Anything at all to help us?"

I tugged at Gloria's sleeve. She bent down. "Yes, Bids?"

"He got a class one," I whispered. Everyone got a group photo for free, and Rowan gave his to me. He said he didn't like seeing himself in a picture.

"Yes, yes. You've got such a memory. Go and grab that, will you, darling?"

I ran up to my room. I found it right away because it was in my night table, hidden under my book Mrs. Spooner gave me for passing the year. Mrs. Spooner didn't have no children, so she was extra nice to me and Rowan. It was not for my grade, she said, but she thought I could do it if I tried a page at a time. I only read a bit of it though. When I knew the dad was going to kill that baby pig with an ax, I folded the page and put it away.

The policeman looked at it. He brought the tiny picture close to his face. He scritched Rowan's face with his fingernail. "Is that a water stain on the print or—or does your son have vitiligo?"

"Viti-what?"

"Loss of pigment. Leaves white blotches on otherwise healthy skin. I have a cousin with the same condition."

"Yes, yes. Something like that. It'll grow back, though. Even out. Just needs to get more fresh air."

"Must be tough on the boy." The end of his mustache went into his mouth. He nibbled at it. "Well, we'll get that information out there. I think we can enlarge this."

"And what was he wearing last?" said the tie man.

"Maisy-Bids? Do you remember?"

What was Rowan wearing? I remembered him outside, water bouncing off him and raindrops pushing down on his hair and his T-shirt and his shorts. He made those shorts from an old pair of blue jeans. In my head I brought him back inside. I dried him off. I put him in Telly's chair and I put the soda in his hand. He took my glass and gave me his because he said I could have the bigger one, like Carl did with Girl and the wiener. That was being nice, Rowan said. And I put my head against his shoulder and laughed. Then I had to squeeze up my eyes because the tiger was eating another squirrel.

"Maisy?" The tie man said my name.

"She does that," Gloria said. "Drifts off."

"That's okay, Maisy. I drift off too sometimes. Can you remember what your brother was wearing?"

"A T-shirt. A white one and it had a donkey on it, kicking out its back legs."

"Well done, Maisy. Anything else?"

"Shorts. His jeans."

He wrote down what I said. "Was he wearing shoes?"

I shook my head. I knew for sure because the rain was hopping all around his bare feet.

"Shoes missing, Mrs. Janes?"

"Not that I can see."

"Okay. This is all useful. It'll help us get a description out."

The phone was ringing a lot, and Gloria was talking and Telly was talking, and then there too many people in our house. Neighbors were coming in and out. In the kitchen, Telly was scooping coffee into mugs. Gloria was right next to him. He gave her a hug and kissed her on her hair. Gloria's face went sort of happy. I heard a shish when he poured water over the powder. "What don't get in their heads, hey?" he said to a policeman.

Chicken was under the kitchen table. He was pretending he was asleep. I could tell he was tricking because he kept opening up one brown eye. And when I went out on the front porch, he followed right behind me. He was missing Rowan, even though his belly was empty and that made him Gloria's dog.

I sat on the top step in the spot with no nails. There was a bunch of people outside, too. It was getting dark already, but a man had papers smoothed out on the front of his car and he was shining a flashlight on them and pointing. Telly came out and started talking to him about going into the woods again. To find Rowan. When I looked where they were pointing, the trees were black and wiggling. If I was brave like Carl said I'd go into the woods, too. I'd find him and Girl, and Rowan would be right there.

Chicken stood up and wagged his tail and blinked his eyes. Gloria was behind me. She sat down next to me.

"Things are going to right themselves with Telly," she said. "I just know it. He hasn't called that woman once, you know."

I nodded and bit my fingernail. There was a tiny sharp piece on my tongue.

Gloria smacked my hand. "I know you got something in your head," she said. She pushed in close to me and put her mouth next to my ear. "I can tell. You're keeping things from me."

My hands went all tingly and my tongue got thick. Rowan made me say it. He made me swear on Telly's future grave. I slid my hand into my pocket and squeezed my little piece of metal.

"You think I don't know every single thought that passes through that little noggin of yours?" Her voice was quiet and slithery. She put her hand on top of my head and bobbled it around. "Why'd you ask Telly if he went out to the bridge?"

I swallowed all the spit and the piece of fingernail.

"If you're lying to Gloria, miss . . ." When she said *miss*, it had a lot of s's.

She was reading my mind and I tried not to think about Carl and Rowan.

"Don't you love your mother?" she whispered. "Don't you love me?"

Even though I tried hard, I couldn't stop stuff squeaking into my brain. I was going to break my promise.

ROWAN

Carl cooked dinner over the fire in his frying pan. Spaghetti and meatballs from a large can. Hand digging inside his coat pocket, he pulled out a plastic bag with two dinner rolls. Marion had given them to him as we were leaving. "You need to finish it all," he said. "Clean your plate. Then brush your, your, urh, teeth. Except the bottom one. Leave that one alone."

I didn't have any trouble cleaning the plate. I shoveled food in past my swollen lip, my loose tooth, and chomped with my molars. Would have licked each drip from the plate, but Carl was following the movements of my spoon. He ate with a fork and knife. Fancy-looking silverware. Drops of liquid landed on his newly trimmed beard, but he was still a polite dinner companion. I tried my best to be the same.

"It's the best ever. Thanks, Carl."

"Thanks, Carl." He put his plate on the ground, his cutlery side by side, fork turned downward. Then he said, "She always wanted to be a mother. She says that. Would take whatever kind she could find."

I knew it was the lady talking inside Carl's head. Dot. One time I asked Carl if they'd told him their names. He said no, but that they didn't complain when he offered suggestions.

"She'd love anything, she would."

"No, she wouldn't. She wouldn't love Gloria." I'd already told him a lot about Gloria. A million shitty things she'd done.

Carl nodded. "Oh yes, she would. Everyone gets stressed, urh, stressed.

Signals get crossed and tangled back and they're just wrong messages she's reading."

Even though it was an odd way to explain it, I sort of understood what he meant. I thought about that for a second. But only a second.

"What about your mother?" I asked. "How long ago did she, um, did she become a ghost?"

I rubbed the last bit of the dinner roll through the tomato sauce and glanced at Carl. But he was mumbling, raking at his beard. Hairs came away and he twitched them loose. The strands went into the fire, and I could smell burning hair.

"You don't have to answer, Carl."

"She's been a ghost since"—he poked the side of his head—"since I killed her, Magic Boy. Killed her."

My hand jerked. I dropped the soggy piece of bread.

"I had to. She was a tracker. Urh. Sending correspondence to the government. Collecting my thoughts and letting them seep into the pipes. Even water from the shower was contaminated."

I swallowed. "Do—do the police know?"

"Do—do the police know?" He peered behind him. "They try to follow me. Government sent Workers to my house with books in their hands, talking about the great power. Jelly, jelly, jellyfish on my doorstep. I could see neural wires inside of them. My mother opened the door. They wanted to sting me."

I put the plate on the ground. Darkness had fallen down around us, the trees and leaves coated in it.

"They trapped me in a white room, Magic Boy. The walls were soft and went on forever. When my mother took me home I didn't take my eyes off her. I told her I was going to kill her. She knew, urh, she knew. She cried and cried and then she said goodbye. She was selfless like that. I had no choice. I had to kill her, but"—he put his hands out in front of him and turned them over—"there is no blood on me."

Air shuttled in and out of the very tip of my lungs. A horsefly landed on my forearm, punctured my skin. I didn't know how to absorb what Carl was telling me. He was rocking back and forth, talking so fast that it was a blur of syllables flooding my ears. Firelight moved over his face. Sections of his beard were thin and his skin looked raw.

I looked at the woods. The darkness was thicker now, and yet I could still run. But which way to go? What if Carl chased me? He was enormous, and I was certainly small.

Girl pawed at his leg and Carl stopped rocking. "She's okay, though. My mother. She likes marigolds best of all. They grow all around her white house. Sometimes I borrow a ride, and I see her. But I don't get close."

"Oh," I whispered. I didn't understand.

He poked his head again. "I just killed her up here. Inside my, my, my, urh, brain. That's the way to do it best, you know. Her heart got broken, but she wasn't hurt."

"Your mother's not dead?"

"Did I say that?"

"Sort of."

"You're all mixed up, Magic Boy. Killing a person doesn't have anything to do with that person being dead. I—I just didn't trust myself."

I closed my eyes and took a deep breath. Blew it out through my mouth. I realized what he meant. Carl's mother was alive and well and living in a white house with marigolds. He was just talking about thoughts. Leaving home. Putting her out of his mind so he could get on with his own life. Live the way he wanted to live. Not actually murdering somebody. Exactly what I was trying to do with Gloria.

I just didn't trust myself.

That last part nagged at me, but I said, "I'm sorry if I upset you, Carl."

"I'm sorry if I upset you, Carl," he said back. He ran his hand over Girl's head.

I smiled. Carl was a good person. He was smelly and grumbly and eccentric, but he was perfectly fine on the inside.

The ground beneath the blanket was bumpy from small stones, but I was warm and dry and my stomach was full of spaghetti and meatballs and bread. Dot told Carl I had to eat an apple, too. He dug one out of his backpack, shined it up, sliced it in half, and gave it to me. It was soft, tasted like a bruise, but I still ate it.

Lying there quietly, I watched the fire dancing, smoke occasionally drifting into my eyes. Carl shaved slices of wood off a stick with a hooked blade.

He was jumbling up words. "That's when the tank got stuck. No one knew. No one knew!" He laughed out loud, and I laughed too.

I closed my eyes. If Carl and I stayed like this I could help out, keeping our camp clean. I could learn to fish further down the creek where it was wider and deeper. I knew a good berry patch, and I knew dandelion leaves were sweet if I got them before the flowers opened. Summer was great under the bridge. But where would we go once the snow came? What about winter boots? And a jacket? I only had shorts and a grimy T-shirt. And what about school? Gloria would probably tell them I'd gone to stay with Uncle Rick, or some imaginary relative. They wouldn't miss me. Well, maybe Mrs. Spooner might, but she'd forget soon enough.

I had just started floating away when I heard a loud crack. My eyes jumped open. Carl heard it too. I saw his head jump back, tilt like a crow's. I sat up. Girl sprang forward, darted toward Carl, put her paw down on top of his shoe. Ears pointed, a low snarl rolled out through her bared teeth.

Then more noises. Strange shrill barking. Coming from deep within a stray dog's throat. A wet strangled sound. Girl continued to snarl but didn't bark back. And as it got closer, I realized the noises weren't coming from a lost dog at all. They were coming from a man.

MAISY

Dogs were barking outside our house. They were hungry barks, but not like Chicken's hungry barks. I saw them through the screen door. A woman was holding three leashes. They looked like the same dog that Darrell and Shar had. That dog escaped a lot, and sometimes he'd run home with a rabbit in his teeth. He'd get blood all over his chin and cheeks. Once I saw Aunt Erma rip the rabbit right out of the dog's mouth. Then she tore off its fur and dropped it in a pot.

Behind me, Gloria was talking to the man in the tie. She yelled at me to come over. "My daughter got something else she needs to tell you."

I saw Telly give the lady with the dogs one of Rowan's T-shirts, and she pushed the T-shirt into their noses. Then I turned around and went next to Gloria. Her fingers dug into my shoulder.

"She got something to share. About Rowan. Company he's been keeping."

The tie man said, "I'm all ears." He grabbed the flappy parts and shook them.

I think I wanted to laugh, but it wouldn't come out.

"Tell the man what you told me. Exactly."

I coughed. My throat was all squeezed up. I had to sit on the floor because my head wanted to float away. My heart was so sad and heavy I thought it was going to fall out. I knew I was a horrible sister.

"Is she okay?" he said to Gloria.

"She's good. Just dramatic." Then she shoved me with her knee. But not hard.

"He said Ca-Carl was nice."

"Who said?"

I licked my lips. They were dry. "Rowan."

"Carl?" He squatted down next to me. "Maisy? Who's Carl?"

Gloria was frowning, shaking her head. "Tell him, miss."

"He lives under the bridge. A man troll. But no goats tromping over. Just me and Rowan." I tried to smile. Maybe he would laugh.

He didn't laugh.

"Can you please tell me a little more about this Carl fellow?"

"Me and Rowan went to visit him. He lives there. Just him and his dog, Girl. She gets to eat the biggest parts. Rowan said that was being nice, not being dumb. He had a big coat and a fire, and the smoke went in my eyes."

My jawbone was hurting. Like I was chewing old gum. Rowan told Carl I was safe. "I'd trust her with my life," he said. But he was wrong. I was a no-good blabber.

"What bridge?" the man said. I looked close at his tie. All the moons had pieces missing. When I was little, I used to think some of the moon had fallen off, but Rowan said it was still there. I just had to look super hard. I had to look in the shadows.

I pointed through the kitchen and out the sliding doors and into the woods.

"Good girl," he said. "That's a wonderful help." His eyes turned into rat eyes. Squished and dark. He stood up and looked at Gloria.

"Filthy homeless beggar sleeping under the old stone bridge," she said. "Luring in kids. Nice, he says. How can my own son be so gullible?"

"It's going to be okay, Mrs. Janes. We'll find him."

"What was he thinking?"

The tie man scritched his chin. "Hard to say, but could be the age, ma'am. They imagine it as an adventure. A few more hours in the woods, cold and hungry, and the charm'll be gone."

He went outside then. He talked to a mustache man on the porch, and came back in. Telly followed behind him.

"You got to be kidding me," Telly said. "What's this, Glow? What's this he's saying?"

"Oh, Telly. I always told Rowan to be careful around those people. Out in the woods of all places. Time and time again. Sure, you said the same yourself.

If you don't got a home, you shouldn't be allowed to wander around. Should be against the law. You can't trust them. You too, Maisy. I told you too."

Her fingers patted my head. Worming through my hair all tickly.

"I never went there," Telly said. He looked white. "When I was out today. I came just shy of it. Reached the creek, but didn't follow it to the bridge. I can't believe it." Gloria had her arm wrapped around his. "We're going to get him back, Glow. I promise you that."

"I know, I know." She was smiling a sad-smile. "I don't know where we went wrong, but we're a team now, Tel. You and me. We got to stick together."

The man with the tie nodded. "We have people on it right away. We're familiar with the bridge. A common spot for vagrants. Especially during summer."

"What if he's not there no more? What if that man took him somewhere?"

"We're setting up for a systematic search at the same time, ma'am. Following a grid to ensure we don't miss a thing. We'll be moving shortly. Your boy could have fallen and hurt himself. With the high temperatures we had today there's risk of dehydration, so we don't have a moment to lose. Door to door is already in progress, in case anyone's seen him. Volunteers are here. Lot of folks offering support. You've got a good neighborhood, Mr. and Mrs. Janes."

"We really do." Gloria sounded wavy.

But I knew she just said a lie. A small lie. She didn't like our neighborhood. Or our neighbors.

There was lots more barking from outside.

"As you can hear, we've got three dogs on site. But with the heavy rain, and now this wind." He stopped.

"What're you doing with dogs?"

"They smell, Glow. Pick up what we can't."

"That's right, Mr. Janes. They'll follow your son's trail, ma'am. His scent. Their handler brought them into the station for a demonstration this afternoon. When the call came in, she was happy to assist. So that's a bit of good fortune."

"I'm sorry if I don't feel fortunate today, Mr. um, Detective Aiken."

"Poor phrasing," he said. "I apologize."

"Those dogs." She pointed her finger out the door. "They're sniffing around my house. Is that his trail?"

"Standard procedure. Nothing to be worried about."

Gloria scritched her head. "Everything's happening so fast."

"Well, if you're right about the rainwater on your floor, your son's been missing between twenty and twenty-four hours."

"Of course I'm right about the rainwater," she said. "Telly?"

"It's okay, Glow. We're all on the same page here."

"Absolutely," the tie man said. "We're doing everything we can, Mrs. Janes."

Telly let go of her. He and the man went outside. On his way, Telly held the door open for Aunt Erma to come in. She came over and hugged me. "I talked to Shar, sweetheart. She wishes she was here." Then she hugged Gloria.

"Erm," Gloria said and started to cry. "He's gone off with a beggar. A homeless beggar."

People kept going in and out of our house. They were making noise and moving around. Outside my bedroom window a big group of men were talking about the woods. How it was easy to get turned around. Or fall over and bang your head. Gloria came upstairs to tuck me into bed.

"Look who I found," she said, and she gave me Jenny the Head.

"Where?" I said. I thought I put her next to the toaster, but I was wrong.

"Stuck behind the cushion in the blue chair."

I held Jenny the Head tight. I must've forgot sitting in that chair. Gloria always told me my remembering was not very good. I had lots of holes and things got mixed up and moved around. "Thank you, Gloria."

"You're welcome, sweetheart."

"He'll come back, Gloria. I just know it." Before Gloria came in, I put the tiny bit of metal under my pillow.

"He will," she said. "Telly will see to that." She bent over the top of my bed and looked out the window. "There they go. They're starting the search. They know where to look now. You did the right thing."

Even though I told on Rowan, my middle didn't hurt so bad no more.

Then she put her hand on my forehead. "You remember, Bids. No one will ever, ever love you as good as I do."

She snapped out the lights and mostly black filled my room. I couldn't see my hand or my nose or my tongue when I stuck it straight out. I thought about that morning after Rowan came home from the woods. After he stole those chocolate bars before school ended and Gloria took him for a walk with the sign. He smelled like wet dirt and smoke. I couldn't tell what was grime and what was his skin map. He let me comb all the sand out of his hair. I even found a tick with a little dot on its back. I showed Rowan and I squished it between my fingernails. He said, "You saved me, Turtle. From a deadly disease."

But I knew that was wrong. I didn't save him. The night before, when Gloria came back from the woods by herself, I didn't worry. Gloria gave me a tomato sandwich made on toast. She told me over and over how much she loved me and she let me take Rowan's big blue book of Stories for Boys that he didn't read no more, but didn't share. A four-leaf clover was hiding in there. She put me in her bed and even let Chicken up. He snored like trees crashing down. It was so snuggly. In my head, I put Rowan in his own bed. He was asleep and happy. After I closed my eyes, I didn't even wake up once.

I had to be a better sister.

Strange voices came in with the breeze. They were far away now, but I thought I could hear Telly. Darrell, too. They were in the woods with the other men, searching and searching. They were calling, "Row! Rowan Janes! Where are you?" I pinched my leg to stay awake. I waited and waited but I never heard him answer back.

ROWAN

Carl got to his feet. The yelping was getting closer and closer. Mixed among the man's yowls was high-pitched giggling. Coming through the darkness. I heard feet trampling sticks. Two people were up on top of the bridge now. Stomping and laughing. Girl kept making that rumbling noise, but she didn't leave Carl's side.

My mouth was dry and my heart hammered. I could feel it in my lower jaw. Carl snapped on his flashlight, aimed it at the side of the bridge. "Stay still, Magic Boy," he whispered. "Workers are at our door."

I curled underneath my blanket. If I didn't move, didn't breathe, maybe they would keep walking along the tracks. They wouldn't check underneath.

No.

I heard them moving down off the tracks. The bushes quivered and then a person with long shaggy hair slid through. At first I thought it was a girl, but then I saw there was nothing inside his unbuttoned shirt. He was holding hands with a second person who followed close behind. She had on overalls and a floppy hat, but her eyes still caught the light.

"Will you lookit," the man said over his shoulder. "Ocupado."

They both burst out laughing. Not like Carl's gentle happy laugh, but a laugh that sliced through the air. It made my hair lift.

"She's wearing a hat," Carl said. "The Worker's wearing a hat."

I slowly sat up. The blanket fell off my shoulders.

"Stan? Yes, they are two. Two."

I gripped the blanket in my fists.

"Hey, man." The man's words sounded as though they were pouring from his nose, stretched thin. "Down with the interrogation lamp, hey, hey now?"

"What's coming?" Carl didn't put the light down.

"Didn't you hear me? You're blinding me here, man."

The beam quivered on the man's face. I knew Carl's arm was shaking. "Urh," he said.

"Come on, friend. I'm asking real nice."

Girl whined, bumped her head into Carl's knee. He flicked off his light. Flames from the low fire still glowed on their faces. They crept closer. The man had his elbows bent, hands up. Like he was ready to catch a ball. Or fight.

"We're lost, man." His head bobbed up and down smoothly. "Strollin' with my lady. Totally fucked up, you got me?"

Carl shook his head. "Beams broken. They're here." He was still gripping the flashlight, but I caught the silvery glint of something in his other hand. His whittling knife, tucked just inside the fold of his coat.

"You know, hard to tell what it's like down here from up on the tracks. But there's some serious space." Then he spoke to me. "Right, buddy? Plenty of room for two more to bunk down?"

Carl bent his head. He was mumbling rapidly, and I was only able to catch parts. ". . . don't know . . . Stan, Stan, systems in place, the Workers . . . No, no. Can't be Magic Boy. He's only one . . . Those signals . . . just circling in the outer orbits . . ." Girl continued to whimper, rubbing her head into Carl's leg. But Carl didn't seem to notice.

The lady stumbled toward Carl, pointed at his knapsack. "You got anything in that? I'm, like, so starved."

I edged closer to Carl, dragging the blanket behind me.

"Back!" Carl yelled at the lady. He drew out the knife, pointed it straight at her chest. "Back! Get back!"

My limbs went numb. Was Carl going to stab her?

Girl showed her teeth then, her gums. Wet snarling, but she still didn't budge from Carl's side.

While the lady froze, the man tiptoed even closer. Hands up, waving. "Calm down. Everyone got to calm the fuck down. We can all be friends, right? Hey, buddy?" He grinned at me. "We can all be friends."

"Get behind me, Magic Boy!"

But I couldn't move.

"I don't like this. I don't like this." Carl jabbed the air with the knife. "Stan. Stan. Stan. Workers. Two. They always come in twos. The concrete and the metal. Breached. No good, no good. It lost its functionality. Stan, you need to help me. I'm found."

"Stop," I whispered to Carl. But the word never came out. I stood up slowly, my legs wobbling. The blanket around my feet.

"Oh, my, god," the lady said. "This guy's, like, nuts for real. I'm totally freaked out."

When Carl's arm shot forward again—"Back!"—the knife flew from his hand. Clattered on the stones. In a flash the man lurched, snatched it up. A blur around me, and the man grabbed my wrist. Tugged me toward him. My back smacked against his chest. With one arm he gripped me around my waist. The other arm pinned my shoulder. I could feel damp heat from his armpit. Then stinging on the side of my neck.

"Eeeeee-sy, now. Eeeee-sy, my little friend."

Girl was barking now, snapping her teeth.

"Better call off your mutt, old man."

Carl kept mumbling. "What should I do, Stan? What should I do?"

My legs were icy rubber.

"They've come to take me. Put me in the white room."

"You heard me, you whacked-out piece of shit." He shuffled me in his arms. I was like a rag doll, responding to each nudge he made. A stream of tears coursed out of my eyes. I could see bubbles of spit around Girl's mouth. She wouldn't stop barking.

"Call off your bitch or I'll cut it."

The lady took off her hat. Her hair rippled over her back. "Lionel. That's not funny."

I stared at the lady. She stared back at me. Carl made a click-click noise in his throat, and Girl went silent. Sat back on her haunches.

"Lionel," she said again. "Let him go."

"Magic Boy!" Carl yelled. "Dissolve yourself."

A cry escaped my lips. I couldn't dissolve myself. I was real. The skin of my neck prickled. My feet and hands and lips were numb. The guy was pressing the blade, harder and harder. It was going to slice through my skin.

Into my artery. I was going to die. I prayed fast. *Please, Gloria. Find me. Tell the man to let me go. I'll be the best boy you can imagine.* One look at her steel face and I knew he would listen. *Telly. Come save me. Please, Telly.* But Telly had a new life now, and he didn't ever want to see me or Maisy or Chicken. Somehow, Telly had managed to do it. To dissolve himself.

I turned my neck a fraction of an inch. It burned, and I whispered, "Let me go. I won't do anything. Honest."

"Lionel!" the lady said. "He's just a little kid. Stupid camping with his dad, or some shit."

A strangled sob fell from my mouth. *Camping with his dad.* I had no dad.

Carl was shaking his head back and forth, yelling, "The Workers! How. How? The white room. My mother will come, Stan! I don't, don't, urh, I don't trust myself!"

"Lionel!" She took a step closer. "Let the kid go."

"Fuck it," he said. Then he laughed that creepy laugh, relaxed his grip. "I was only fucking around with him. Joking. Right, my little friend? I was only just horsing around with you, sure."

He shoved me. I fell forward onto the pebbles. My knees and palms smacked the ground. I touched my neck, the stinging spot. It was slippery. Scrambling up, I rushed toward Carl. Toward Girl. Carl pushed me behind him. "You did it," he said. "You did it, Magic Boy."

Still pointing the knife, the man wiped his nose on his sleeve. "I suggest you and that little runt mosey on out of here."

"Maybe we should go?" the lady said.

I gripped the back of Carl's coat.

"Yeah. And why would we do that?" the man said. "You are one dumb whore."

She put the floppy hat back on. I couldn't see her face anymore.

"You heard me," the man growled. "Get!"

When Carl reached for his backpack the man sang out, "Ah, ah, ah. That's ours now, old man. Thanks for being so hospitable." His eyes squinted. "Now I'm going to count to ten. If you're not gone from my sight I'm going to carve your face so deep your own mother wouldn't know you."

The lady's hat shook back and forth. Maybe underneath there she found it funny. Or maybe she was scared, too.

"One. Two. Three—"

Carl edged away. Girl stayed by his side. "Keep close, Magic Boy. We need to lift off."

"Four, five, six—"

I looked at the backpack, full of his clothes and food and Girl's stuffed squirrel with the deformed face, but the man poked the air with the knife and grinned again.

"It's okay, okay," Carl whispered. "Just involute, Magic Boy. Make yourself invisible like me and Girl. They don't see us. Put extra space between your electrons. They can't see our atoms. We are spinning and spinning."

"Seven!"

"Okay," I whispered. My mouth was like paste. I followed Carl and Girl toward the end of the bridge. Behind us, the woods were black. No moonlight found its way through the dense leaves. The creek gurgled and bubbled as though everything was fine.

"Eight thousand nine hundred and ten-fucking-zero!" He was laughing. Then he howled. And yipped. I heard tin cans crash together. Glass smashing.

"Keep your feet in the water," Carl said. "Don't leave a smell."

Moving carefully on the silt and pebbles and slimy grass, the three of us stayed near the edge of the creek. Stepping back and back and back. Somewhere off in the distance I heard real dogs barking. A chorus of them. This time, though, Girl didn't react at all.

After a long time, Carl stopped. My whole body flumped right into his, and I jumped. "Sorry," I said. "I didn't see you."

Movement of fabric, and Carl flicked on his flashlight. "Not invisible anymore. Urh. If you stay like that too long, you can't come out again."

Cool water rushed over my ankles. The creek had gotten deeper. I stepped onto the bank, sat down on a large rock.

"Where are we going?" I asked.

"Away," he said.

"Away where?"

"Urh. Why do you ask so many questions?"

"Sorry," I said again.

I leaned down and rubbed my feet. Even though they'd been in the water, they felt hot and swollen. The bottoms were tough, but not tough enough for walking so long on rocks and twigs.

Carl came out of the water and stood beside me. Girl was right next to him and shook, droplets pecking my face.

"Did you know them, Magic Boy?"

"What?"

"Did you know those Workers."

"Know them? How would I know them?"

"Did you, did you, urh, did you send out a signal?"

"What? I was almost asleep. You saw me."

"Sure I did, but I can't see what you emit."

Emit? I swallowed. What was he talking about? "I swear, Carl. I never sent out anything. I don't even know how. I never saw them before. And I don't want to see them ever again."

"Urh," he said. "I told you so."

"Told me what?"

"Not you," he said. He twitched his fingers, and I knew he'd pulled out more hairs. "I was figuring things out with Stan."

I looked around. Outside our tiny orb of brightness from Carl's flashlight, there was nothing. Only blankness. But maybe I should try to find my way home. If I kept going in a line, I'd come out of the woods eventually, wouldn't I? Then I could fix everything with Gloria. I could mow the lawn, in those perfect straight lines she liked. Or dig up the garden and plant some beans or some radishes. It wasn't too late. I'd even scrape the old paint off the porch. And the deck, too. Things would be better if I didn't give her a single reason to get upset.

Carl's flashlight sputtered and we were swallowed in heavy black again. I could feel the cool darkness in my nose and sitting on my top lip. Winding its way down my arms, around my fingers. If I left Carl and Girl, I might run into that man and the lady with the stupid hat. Straight into Carl's whittling knife. I touched my neck. The spot was sticky. I couldn't go home now even if I wanted to.

Three bangs against his palm and the flashlight burst back into life. Carl shone it up the length of the creek.

"The Workers might be, urh, tracking us. We best stay close together."

I wanted to reach out and hold onto his coat.

"What are we going to do, Carl?" I said. "Where can we go?" I knew I was asking even more questions, but I couldn't help it. Water pooled in my eyes. I tried to shove the wetness away but Girl trotted over, licked my cheeks.

Carl mumbled. He sounded frustrated. "No, that's right. We can. It's still mine. Once you build something, it'll always be yours. Paper doesn't matter. That's the law."

"Carl?"

"We're going to a secure location, Magic Boy."

He shone the flashlight on my face, then onto my feet. Rummaging in another enormous pocket, he pulled out a roll of gray tape. He walked toward me, and I could hear squelching from his shiny shoes. They were ruined. Bending in front of me, he picked up my left foot, swiped the bottom on his pant leg, then peeled off strips of tape and stuck them to my skin. Over the toes and up around the heel until my foot was a secure clump of silver. Did the same with the other.

"Too tight?"

"No."

When he stood up, he stuck his big hand in my hair. Ruffled it. "I know. I think so," he whispered. Then to me, "You really should float, Magic Boy. That's just common sense. Much easier on your soles."

After he said that, I couldn't help smiling. The weight around my heart fell away. Carl had a plan. Things were going to be all right. "Thank you, Dot," I said. I knew it had come from her.

He and Girl started walking, moving in and out of the creek. "Just to keep them guessing."

"Do you see them?" I'd wanted to ask this for a long time.

"Who?"

"You know." I limped along with my taped feet. Water had oozed in, and with each step my heels made a soft gulp. "Dot," I said. "And the others."

"No. They're not like that." He took a few steps then stopped, whispered, "Sometimes I see Stan though."

"Really? What does he look like?"

"He's vast, Magic Boy. So vast. Dark, dark red in, in, urh, in my sky. And when he's mad, he fills me up and stretches me so thin and he seeps out through all my pores."

Carl sounded afraid, so I said, "It's okay. I get it." I sort of did. Sometimes I felt that way about Gloria.

ROWAN

It seemed like we walked for hours. I thought I was going to collapse. Every part of me was exhausted, and my tooth throbbed. Insects bit my neck then flew into my mouth, a metal taste spreading over my tongue when I crushed them.

Carl did not seem tired at all. He stomped ahead, step after step, swinging his flashlight left to right. Several times he caught a pair of yellow eyes in the glow, low to the ground. The creature would stare, then skitter away.

Eventually the creek grew wider and the bank turned into a tangle of tall grasses and sharp bushes. I knew I was covered in cuts and scratches, and I could feel blood trickling down my legs. More than once when I stepped, my foot met with nothing. A dip in the ground or a space between rocks, covered by leaves. I went down. Cracking against the ground, bones twisting. While Girl halted, Carl kept ambling forward, shoulders hunched. He didn't even notice. It sounded like he was arguing, saying, "No, you've got it wrong this time. Listen to her, listen to her. I can tell, Stan. Urh. Listen to her. Unsubstantiated slanderous allegations."

I tried to breathe slowly. I didn't like it when Carl talked to Stan. His voice always went low and hollow.

Finally the creek spread out, gently tumbling over larger rocks into a lake. As we got closer a line of purple appeared on the horizon, and then a layer of orange slowly pushed up beneath it. As the colors flushed across the water everything was suddenly alive and glittering and magical. I'd never seen anything like it before. I stopped. "Carl. Look!"

Putting his hands out straight, palms facing the water, he said, "Because we're here."

I felt it too. No one owned it. No one could claim it. No one could abandon it or make it disappear. So beautiful and free, the sight of it filled every crack inside of me. Maybe I was even floating a little. Like Dot had suggested.

I looked at Carl and Girl, and even though I was dead tired, I was so happy I'd stayed with them. Carl had protected me back at the camp. Had cared enough to tape up my feet. Girl was right there each time I tumbled. She even licked away my dumb tears.

"Come on," Carl said. "Urh, daylight is coming."

We walked along a narrow path of flattened rock until we came to a dock that jutted out into the lake. A rowboat was tied to a post with a thin stretch of rope. When we stepped onto the dock the dry wood bobbed up and down, water lapping underneath. The rowboat clunked against the dock. Empty sounds. Lulling me. I knelt down, wanted to lie down, but I knew if I did I wouldn't be able to get up again. Reaching over the side, I cupped cold water in my hand, splashed and rubbed my face.

"This is mine," Carl said.

"The dock?"

"All of it. Everything."

He pointed beyond the dock to a small log cottage. Carl strode toward it, then climbed the two steps onto the deck. I followed as quickly as I could, my legs feeling like stumps fused to the ground. I leaned against the wall, watched Carl lift the welcome mat. "Urh," he said. Then one by one he threw over a line of potted plants, flower stems cracking. Next he grabbed a knotted rug off the back of a patio chair and shook it.

"Stolen again. Can't get in. Urh. No, I'm not misinformed. Listen to her. Listen to her." He began pacing in a tight circle, grabbing his beard and tugging.

"Did you check to see if it's unlocked?" I reached out, gripped the knob. Sure enough, when I twisted it the door swung open. "I've got the touch," I said, grinning with relief. Carl's face remained flat.

He peered through the open door, whispered, "What touch? Urh. Exactly what touch are you talking about?"

Inside the cottage he moved slowly, mouth open, inspecting everything. He stuck his nose in the air, sniffed. "It doesn't smell right. They've been in here."

"Who?"

"Who? They have. The Workers. I can tell."

My heart started to beat. Why couldn't he forget about workers? Whatever they were. At least for a little while.

He flicked a switch. Tinkling, then the buzz of an overhead light. The tiny room lit up. Shelves full of books and board games, worn furniture, a pile of nubby blankets, a teapot on a circular table. In the corner a nice-sized television, rabbit ears already tugged out. The walls were covered with photos in frames, hanging crookedly. A big family. I had a feeling the people living there loved each other, and that awareness made me feel heavy inside. I searched through them, but I couldn't find Carl in a single one. Girl went straight for a round cushion on the floor. Turned three times then lay down, settling her head on her paws.

"It'll be good to stay here for a while," I said. I sat on the edge of the couch and slipped my fingers into the taped mess on one foot. I managed to pry it off with a watery slurp. "I think we walked forever."

Carl didn't hear me. He was arguing again. "I can see that. I'm not an imbecile. Stop it. Stop calling me that. Listen to her. Listen to what she says. I told you. All these are wrong. Wrong. Wrong! All of them!" He held up a framed photo of a girl, a fat grub pinched between her fingers, face grimacing. "I don't know these people. I don't know who these people are. They're trying to fool me up. Trap me. Switched everything around, urh. Playing jokes. Not funny, not funny."

"Carl?" I wrenched the gray mound off my other foot. "You all right?"

He put the photo down on the table, turned toward me. Narrowed his eyes. "You look different. I don't recognize you either. I don't."

"It's just me."

"It's just me."

When he repeated my words this time, there was an edge to his tone.

"I washed my face, Carl. In the lake."

"Your color's gone."

"Yeah. Lots of dirt. My spots returned." When I smiled, he didn't smile back. I swallowed. Then I said, "I like it here, Carl. You got a great place."

Those stupid words came out of my mouth even though I knew the cottage belonged to someone else. We had just broken into it.

He lowered his head suddenly. He reminded me of Chicken when Gloria hollered at him. Then Carl's arms jumped up in the air as if his wrists were attached to strings. He yelled out, "Did you hear that?"

I didn't know what to say.

"On the roof. Crawling around."

"Nothing, Carl. It's nice and quiet."

"They're out there. Whispering. Down on all fours. How many? How many?"

He was breathing hard and the sight of his arms flapping made my heart clang in my chest. I'd never seen him do that before.

"Maybe raccoons?" I offered. "Looking for garbage?"

"Urh. Raccoons." Carl sat on the floor right in the middle of the room, and crossed his arms over his body. One hand stuck into his armpit and the other reached up, twisted his beard, and tugged. There was a pale patch of skin along his jaw. It was growing larger. He hummed loudly, and it seemed like a long time passed. My head was nodding forward. Even though my whole body was wired, my brain was trying to sleep.

Then he said, "He's got a headache."

"Who?"

"That man." He pointed to a figurine balanced on the shelf beside him. It looked like an enormous chess piece, but with a human head on top. "Terrible pain. A lot of pressure in his cranium. Urh. Can't get away from it."

I was going to tell Carl it was just cement, or a rock carved up to look like art, but I changed my mind. Instead I said, "That's too bad. No fun if you're bad in the head." Then I realized I'd never seen Carl lie down. Or doze off. Or even close his eyes for more than a blink. "Why don't you get a rest, Carl? My friend Mrs. Spooner always tells me life's easier after a good sleep."

At once he stood up. His arms moved in that weird way again. It looked like he was tapping the air, feeling for invisible things. I pushed my back deeper into the couch.

"What did you say?"

"A rest, Carl. Everyone needs sleep."

He angled his head to the side. I heard his neck joints pop. A gravelly voice climbed out his mouth. It didn't sound like Carl at all. "Why, Magic Boy? Why would you want that?"

Girl was up from the bed, her ears alert. She went to Carl, used her teeth to tug on the hem of his coat. But Carl didn't seem aware she was there.

"I didn't mean anything," I said. "I didn't. It's just, just nice to be here." I pulled my knees up to my chest, hugged my legs.

"Wires in the ceiling. Birds, urh, can't dig them out."

And he took a step backward, ripped a frame off the wall. An old man wearing a party hat, seated in front of a cake full of candles. "I don't know you!" Carl yelled at the photograph. "I don't know who you are!"

Then he threw it, full force, across the small room. Metal crumpled and glass burst from the frame. I opened my mouth but nothing came out. He was standing right in front of the door. I couldn't get around him if I tried. Girl yipped and clawed at Carl's leg, but Carl reached for a second photo, threw that too.

I curled into a ball, put my hands over my head. Pressed my body into the couch as far as I could.

"Trying to fool me," Carl yelled. "I know my rights! I know my rights!"

I heard more smashing sounds. Explosions of glass. Then paper ripping. The flump of a heavy book falling. Plastic crushed into the floor. Girl kept whimpering and whimpering.

When silence finally came and stayed, I didn't get up. I never even opened my eyes. I kept my face against the itchy fabric of the couch, and I don't know how I managed it, but I fell asleep.

MAISY

When I woke up I went to the kitchen and got cereal and milk in my bowl by myself. I stirred it around and around with my spoon, but I only pretended to eat. I thought I'd see Rowan there, but he was still lost. And Jenny the Head was lost again, too. Even though I put the metal in my pocket when I got up, things were getting worse.

The man in the tie was talking to Gloria at the table, and they didn't even notice me sitting at the counter. Today the man's tie had fox faces all over it. Or it could've just been squares. Sometimes my eyes made things up.

Gloria was making coffee. The man waved his hand at her. "Just black, thank you very much." She put it down in front of him. "Should we wait for Mr. Janes?"

"Telly darted home to bring back fresh clothes. He needs to have his things here." She chewed on her thumb for a minute. "So he can stay."

"Okay, then." The man took a loud slurp of his drink. That was rude, but Gloria didn't say nothing. "Well, there's definitely evidence someone's been living under the old stone bridge, Mrs. Janes. We found remains of a fire. Debris. Tin cans, empty bottles, grocery boxes and such."

"Rowan wasn't there?"

"The dogs got a strong hit, so we're confident your son has, in fact, been at the bridge." The man slurped more, and then he wiped his mouth with the back of his hand. Gloria didn't say nothing about that either.

"And you just missed him?"

"It's possible, but we can't say with certainty. Was he there two nights ago? Was he there yesterday? You see, Mrs. Janes, the dogs can only give us a yes or no. We can't get a time frame, unfortunately."

"I see."

"They tracked a path from the bridge to the upper road. Got a strong hit on the sign for Little Sliding. But the scent ends."

"Just ends?" I saw Gloria's mouth fall open, and the part between her eyebrows folded up. I could tell she was scared.

"Yes ma'am. It's possible someone might've picked them up."

"Hitchhiking? They could be miles away by now."

"Or it could've been the heavy rain. We know he was there. And we know he's not there now."

"And that helps?"

I stirred and stirred. The milk turned brown from all the colors in the cereal. When I looked up Gloria's head was shaking back and forth and tears started coming out of her eyes. "That horrible man must've been forcing Rowan. Making him go like that. Threatening him. He's a good boy, Detective Aiken. He wouldn't just . . . do that."

"We're exploring every avenue, ma'am. We've already started a second search. Covering everything. We're going to find your son." He reached down and tugged something out of the bag near his feet. "Mrs. Janes? One of my officers came across this. Nailed onto a tree about halfway between here and the bridge. Does it mean anything to you?" He put a piece of wood on the table. It looked like a sign with marked-up letters. Mostly washed off, but I could still read it. THEIF. It was Gloria's sign because of the chocolate bars. Rowan showed it to me when we were walking back from the bridge that day.

Her head stopped.

"Rowan saw them."

"Saw who?"

Her voice got wiggly. "Some children. I don't know who owned them. Playing cops and robbers out back. Rowan wanted to play too, but those revolting youngsters wouldn't let my son join in." She pulled some more tissues out of the box. She crunched them in her fist. "That part I remember clear as day."

I stirred my cereal again. It was mush now. I made a mistake and that wasn't Rowan's sign. I must've had a dream that got stuck in my head. Or I remembered it upside down. That happened a lot.

"Kids, hey? I figured as much. What with the spelling and all."

Gloria bent her head sideways and looked at the sign. Then she wiped her eyes. "What's going to happen now?"

"As I mentioned, ma'am, we're going to expand the focus of our search. Shift our resources. This Carl, whoever he is, appears to be relocating. We'll have an officer make frequent checks under the bridge, in case your son returns. But we're also going to search roadways, have someone follow along the creek. Bus stations and the train station. There's no guarantee Rowan went with this man, Carl. We'll continue door to door. Canvas stores where they might have bought something. Get word out on the radio, monitor tips that come in. See if we can get a better description on the vagrant"—he looked at me—"and get that information out, along with the photo of Rowan, of course."

"I just don't know what to do. I just can't keep sitting here. I'm—I'm losing my mind."

Gloria stood up and was crying more. I went over and wrapped my arms around her and put my head on her back. My arms slipped into her soft bread sides. I hated seeing her sad. It was the worst thing ever.

"This is the best place for you to be, ma'am. As hard as that is. In case he comes back. In case he calls."

With my ear on her back, I could hear Gloria's insides. They were squirting and thumping and wheezing. As I listened, I felt a pain in my chest. Like someone punched me hard. Right on a rib bone. I knew my middle was hurting because I was so mad at Rowan. For running away into the woods. For letting that terrible Carl grab him up and steal him away on the road in a strange car. For making Gloria cry.

I decided when Rowan came back I was not going to talk to him. I was going to make him disappear for a long, long time.

"Thank you, Maisy-Bids," she said. She twisted round and hugged me too. "You're the only thing keeping me sane."

"Sorry, ma'am. When is your husband due back?"

The clock on the wall was hanging funny. "Soon," she said.

"We thought, perhaps—"

"He'll let me know if Rowan showed up there. But Rowan didn't even know where his dad was staying."

"Do you have other family?"

Gloria blinked a bunch of times. "No. My father's dead. And—and my mother, too." That was Gran that I never met. "I do have a brother. Richard. Rick. But we aren't close. He's just not a good person, not stable, you know what I mean?"

"I do," he said, and he smiled a bit and gulped from his mug. "Family dynamics can be complicated. Especially during times of stress."

"Yeah, that's my brother all right. Ratchets the problem right up, and then blames the fallout on me."

"Is it possible he could have gone there, though?" the man said. "To your brother's?"

"Zero chance. I don't even know myself where he lives no more. Couldn't reach him if I tried."

"We'll check in with him just in case, Mrs. Janes. So we can cross it off our list."

Gloria told him her brother's name and the place he was staying the last time she knew. The man wrote it all down.

"It's important to find people who can offer you some support."

"Telly's giving me support."

"That's good, ma'am. This is a traumatic experience for any parent to go through." He stood up. "I'll be outside, Mrs. Janes. Getting things organized. But I'm going to send in one of our staff. She's a psychologist and I'd like her to chat with Maisy."

Gloria took my hand and squeezed hard. "She don't need that. Talking to someone who shrinks heads. She's doing just fine. Talks to me plenty."

"Sorry. I wasn't clear. We'd like her help to get additional information from Maisy about this Carl individual. She's phenomenal with children. She really is. I thought Maisy'd be more receptive talking to a woman."

"Oh. Oh, in that case."

Then he got up and went outside. I walked behind him, but when the screen went back, I didn't push it open again. I watched him go down the steps and talk to a lady in a brown skirt. She kept nodding, and she had a big envelope in her hands. That was the lady who was going to do something to my head. I pressed my cheek onto the paint. The door didn't feel happy, happy. Even in the sunlight it was cold as an icicle.

Telly's truck drove down the driveway. It was a tight squeeze with the other cars. He jumped out before he was even stopped. Or that was what it looked like.

The man put up his finger to the lady, and went right over to Telly. "Mr. Janes?"

"Yep." His hair was wet. I didn't see any bags of his clothes like Gloria said. Maybe they were in the back.

"I spoke with your wife already about last night's search, but . . ."

"Go on."

"I didn't want to alarm her, but there were signs of a struggle under the bridge."

"What do you mean?"

"Things smashed. Scattered. Garbage strewn about."

"That could be anything. Kids messing around. Animals, even. Or maybe that, that man didn't keep things clean."

"Perhaps," he said. He smoothed his tie. "There were also two individuals there when we arrived. But we weren't able to talk to them."

"Two individuals? What do you mean? Why not?"

"They vacated the premises as we approached. My officers gave chase but weren't able to locate them."

"Rowan? And that bum?"

"At this point we can't say for sure, but we believe one was a female. Based on the voice."

"So he's with a woman now?" Telly rubbed at his eyes. "We know that, right?"

"A female was in the vicinity. But she could have been with this Carl person. Or possibly it's just two people in an unrelated circumstance."

"Then why'd they run?"

"We're trying to locate them. To get an answer to that question."

Telly blew out air. "I can't believe I didn't go out there. Didn't go to the old bridge. I could've found him."

The man put his hand on Telly's shoulder. "We'll continue doing everything we can."

"Thanks, Detective. Thank you."

Then the man went back to the lady. She had on a blouse with a bow by her neck. The man pointed at the door, and the lady looked up and waved at me. I didn't wave back.

"Maisy?" She was on the other side of the screen now. Her face got close to mine. Her eyes and hair were brown, the same as her skirt. Her face looked like Jenny the Head, without the bite marks, though. "I'm Susan," she said. "Can we talk a bit? Detective Aiken says you're a very bright little girl. With an excellent memory. And we'd really love your help to find your big brother."

I nodded.

"Is there a quiet place we can chat about the man you met, Carl? I have photographs." She lifted up the envelope.

I went into the kitchen, and she followed me. We passed Gloria. She was sitting in Telly's television chair staring at the screen. But it was turned off. Maybe she was sleeping with her eyes open. She did that sometimes, so she could still see everything.

The Susan lady sat down. I sat down, too. Her two hands were on the envelope. Her fingernails were full of skin hitches, just like mine, but she didn't hide them the way I did.

"So you and your brother like to explore the woods in the summer, hey?"

Not really. Rowan did. I just followed him by accident. On purpose.

"I used to love that when I was a girl." She picked at the corner of the envelope. "How many times did you meet Carl?"

"Once," I said.

"Under the bridge?"

"Mm-hmm. He was there with Girl."

"Girl? He had a girl with him?"

"His dog. Her name's Girl."

"Dogs are nice." She smiled. Her eyes got even prettier. "What sort of dog?"

I swung my feet under the chair. "Sort of orange or brown. And big. But not fluffy like Chicken. Girl got a whip-around tail. A little bit of her fur on her back sticks up straight and some around her neck is all gone. Sometimes she snap-bites at the flies, but she doesn't catch them. She's a good dog. She wears a rope around her neck with three beads. Carl wears beads too. Kind of. In his beard."

"Wow. Detective Aiken was right. You've got an amazing memory, Maisy."

I shook my head. I don't got a good memory. It was always making things up. Putting the wrong pictures in there, or mixing them around. But I didn't tell her that.

"Is Carl a nice man?"

I looked out through the glass doors. There were so many people on our lawn. Tramping down our grass. I wondered if it would ever stand up again, and I wondered what I should say. If Carl stole Rowan, he was not a nice man. But he was nice to me under the bridge. He was nice to Rowan. He was extra nice to Girl.

"He called me 'Little Fawn,'" I said. "He called Rowan 'Magic Boy.'"

She opened a notepad. Her pen made a scritching sound.

"Did you feel afraid?"

I sucked on my bottom lip.

"Did he ever say or do anything that made you feel uncomfortable, Maisy? Nervous? You know, get that squiggly feeling in your belly."

I shook my head. That was a small lie. Carl did make me feel squiggly in my middle. Real squiggly. But if I told her, Rowan might get hurt. More bad things might happen. I wanted to tell things the best way. It was better to make Carl friendly.

"Can you guess Carl's age?"

"Old," I said.

"Old like me or even older like, um, Detective Aiken?"

I frowned.

"The man who was just here talking to your mom. That's Detective Aiken. He has little foxes on his tie."

I was right. They were foxes. "More old like you," I said. "He's smart, too."

"Smart?"

"Mm-hmm."

"How can you tell?"

"I just can." Because Rowan said it.

"Thank you, Maisy. Do you know what color his hair was?"

"Shiny color. Black and white shiny. And clumpy. And he has a big beard with things in it. Sparkly silvery things." I didn't tell her about the metal piece he put in my hair. I could feel the corner of it sticking my leg through my pocket. "And he laughs a whole lot. Like someone is telling jokes in his ear. His eyes squish up. It made us laugh too. Laughing about nothing. Me and Rowan." I started smiling, even though it was only Rowan that laughed. It sounded better if it was both of us.

"That's a wonderful description, Maisy. Thank you. Sometimes laughter is catchy, isn't it?" She wrote more down. Her notebook was the same kind as the fox-tie man's. "Do you remember what he was wearing?"

"A lot!" I pinched my face to make my smile go away. "He must've been real warm."

"Like?"

"A sweater and a coat and pants and fancy shoes."

"Fancy?"

"Special shoes. Black with little laces." Telly never had shoes like that. He only wore work boots. Or sometimes sneakers. Once before he left he put his sneakers in the washing machine. They slapped around in there like they were fighting. Gloria said with all the grease they'd ruin the dryer. I watched until it stopped. They came out white and clean.

"Great," the lady said. "You're doing wonderfully. Every detail is important, Maisy, and it's going to help us bring your brother home."

I straightened up my back. Gloria always told me to do that. Susan was nice. She was a little bit like Mrs. Spooner, but not all covered in wrinkles and brown spots.

"Can I ask you one more favor? Could you look at some photographs? To see if you can find Carl?" She opened the top of the envelope and pictures came out upside down. She made them into a pile.

"Why do you have photos?" I asked.

"Well, sometimes we take pictures of people so we can remember them later. It doesn't mean they're bad or dangerous. A lot of these people are just a little lost in their heads."

"Lost in their heads?"

"That just means they're having a difficult time."

"Oh," I said.

I began to turn the pictures over. One after the other. There were men with smooth heads. Some had broken teeth and saggy red eyes and bony cheeks. One had a funny blue anchor drawn on his neck. But no Carl. I kept turning the photos over, and I was starting to feel afraid I wasn't going to do my best job for Susan. "It's okay," she said. "Take your time. Look at each one carefully." I looked as hard as I could, but Carl wasn't there. Then, when I flipped almost the last one, there was someone who could be Carl. Maybe. His hair was long and his beard wasn't sparkly and his forehead was sort of dirty. Next to the picture of Carl was another picture. A dressy man with a tie and a white shirt and combed hair and no beard. The eyes looked the same, but that wasn't Carl for sure. Maybe it was his brother.

I tapped my finger on the dirty face. "Him," I said.

She whirled the picture around and shook her head. I knew I made a mistake.

"Are you certain?"

"Mm-hmm." But I wasn't certain at all. I pointed at the other man. "Is that his brother?"

"No, that's him too. In better times, sadly." Then she looked at me and smiled wide with lots of teeth. I knew I didn't make a mistake and I did a good job. I got it right. Carl and the other Carl.

"You are amazing," she said and stood up. "I'll be one sec." She left the kitchen and called out, and then I heard the screen door squeak, and she and the fox-tie man were back. He poked at the photo of Carl. They mumbled to each other and then pointed at other papers. He moved his finger over some words and his lips were moving. Susan smiled at me again. I smiled back. I liked her because she looked like Jenny the Head. I'd probably lose Susan though, if she was mine.

"Mrs. Janes?" the man called. "We need a moment. Could you ask Mr. Janes to come in as well?"

When Gloria and Telly came to the kitchen, he showed them the photo. "His name's Howard Gill. He's a lawyer from the city."

Howard was not Carl?

"A lawyer?" Telly said.

"No longer practicing, obviously. Untreated mental health issues. You can see the physical deterioration between the two snapshots. Once clean cut, and now he's a transient."

"They're both him?" Gloria rubbed at her eyes.

"Yes ma'am."

"He looks like a lunatic. How can someone like that be allowed to walk around? Let alone live in the woods behind my house! How is that safe? Telly?"

Telly stuck his hands in his pockets. "Glow. I don't know what to say."

"I understand your frustration, I do," the man said, "but we're really limited. He has rights as long as he doesn't break the law. As I said, mental struggles."

"Rights!" She frowned. "What type of country don't have a law against that type?"

Susan talked then. "We've some familiarity with him. He's been picked up a couple of times for loitering, trespassing, urinating in a public park. Found in someone's backyard going through trash."

"So, nothing serious?" Telly said. "He's not going to hurt Rowan?"

The fox-tie man coughed. "Well, there was one incident. An assault."

"What?" Telly pulled his hand out of his pocket and put his arm around Gloria.

"Yes, but they refused to press charges. Religious folks, a pair of them, going door to door. Trying to convert people. They went to Howard's house and his mother opened the door, let them in. Mr. Gill did not react well, and after that he spent some time in an institution. But eventually he was released into his mother's care."

Gloria started crying.

"Christ," Telly said. "So he's dangerous?"

"When provoked. And he's delusional, that's for certain. We know his usual haunts, Mr. and Mrs. Janes. We're going to locate him as quickly as possible. Bring him in." He looked down at me and patted my shoulder. "Maisy? We're going to find Carl. I promise you we'll find him."

My head was getting woozy. There was lots of static inside me. I imagined them throwing a net over Carl, or Howard, who might not be Carl. Then Carl-Howard trying to escape, and a policeman shooting him through his back. I could see the black hole right in his middle. And it'd be my fault. I wanted to tell the fox-tie man please not to hurt him when they found him. He made us laugh even though we couldn't hear his jokes. He gave most of his burnt wiener to Girl instead of eating it himself.

Then Susan said, "You've been tremendously helpful, Maisy. You're a very intelligent and brave young lady."

You are not brave . . . but you will be brave. Carl said that when he saw my cards. But Carl was wrong, and I wanted to tell Susan and the fox-tie man. Anyone could point at a picture.

MAISY

After Susan put all the photos back in the envelope, the fox-tie man said, “One quick thing. Channel 6 would like to talk with you. Come out here and do a short piece.”

“What do you mean?” Telly said.

“We want the public’s help. Have them out there with their eyes open, Mr. Janes. Searching for Rowan. Any kind of information, any tip, we want to hear it.” He lifted up his tie and dropped it again. “Her name’s Anita, and she’ll ask you some questions about your boy. We want the public to know who your son is. To care about him.”

Susan smiled. “Tell them what’s in your heart. That you love him and miss him.”

“We can do that. Right, Telly?” Gloria took Telly’s hand.

“Of course we can,” he said.

She squeezed his hand. I could see the white parts.

“All right, then. Sometime this afternoon.”

Then we heard a shout from the backyard and we all went through the sliding doors. Chicken, too. Gloria stood right in the spot where Rowan was in the storm. If he was outside, but he wasn’t. He was having root beer, and that was nicer. A big crowd of people stomped out of the bushes at different spots. They were shaking their heads, and a lot of them were scritching hard at their necks and their arms. They were dressed in shorts and sneakers and T-shirts and hats. Most of them were men. Some of them were ladies, and a couple of teenagers, and Darrell was there again. He was wearing black jeans and a black T-shirt and a spiky belt around his middle. He waved at me, but I sat down and picked at Chicken's fur. Chicken didn't have no burrs. I just pretended.

Two men wearing police clothes came up on the deck. They talked and the fox-tie man nodded. Telly put his hands on his head and kicked air with his feet. "Jesus," he said loud. "I feel like I'm going crazy." A bunch of people got in their cars and drove away slow. Their tires left lines in the muck. Telly hugged Gloria and said, "They're giving up. Already, Glow. Some of them are giving up."

"They're not, Telly."

"Well, I'm going back in."

"Mr. Janes," the fox-tie man said.

"I don't care what you say. I won't stop until I've turned over every leaf in those goddamned woods. I'll call up a few fellows from the garage. They'll come out. We got to try again."

I looked at the trees. Branches were going up and down and making a shush noise. There were lots of dark spots. Rowan could be hiding anywhere. Rowan and Carl and Girl.

Then I heard a terrible loud sound up in the sky. A helicopter was driving overhead. Telly and Gloria pointed at it, but I put my hands over my ears and pushed. It was trying to find Rowan, I knew, but the sound hurt my head. All I could think of was the top of the helicopter swinging around so fast I couldn't even see it. Fast enough to slice me up. Or slice up Rowan if he got too close.

I ran inside and through the kitchen and into the hall. I jumped when I saw Mrs. Spooner. She was standing on the other side of the screen holding a huge plastic plate heaped up with sandwiches on fluffy white bread. They were all cut in fours. I looked quick at the middles. Egg salad and ham and cheese and tuna and some other pink stuff I couldn't guess. My mouth started to water. Rowan would eat all those tuna ones if he could. He loved tuna. He said Gran always made him tuna on toast with melted cheese. Gloria never bought it because she didn't want her kitchen stinking of fish.

I took my hands off my ears because Mrs. Spooner's mouth was moving.

"I said awful racket, isn't it?"

I nodded, but the helicopter was driving away. Getting quiet.

"Might I come in?" She sad-smiled at me.

I looked behind me and couldn't see Gloria. I didn't know if I should open the door. My head was getting floaty.

"Oh, I won't be but a minute. I just want to drop these." The sandwiches. "My arms are near gone."

"Who's that, Maisy?" Gloria called out from the kitchen.

"Mrs. Spooner," I called back.

"Well, let her in." Gloria came into the hallway. "Don't just stand there gawking at the poor woman. Where're your manners?"

My head got even more floaty. I opened the screen door. Mrs. Spooner brushed past me. I could smell her perfume, like the spray can Gloria got once for our bathroom. And I could smell the food.

"Maisy, dear, can you take these? I thought the searchers might want a snack." She put the plate on my arms. "But some of them are leaving already?"

The plate was heavy and dug into my skin.

"Let me," Gloria said. She swooped the sandwiches away and went back to the kitchen.

Mrs. Spooner touched my arm. "How are you doing, Maisy?"

"Good," I said.

She smiled again. "How's your new doll? Jenny, was it?"

"Chicken got hungry and ate her body."

"That's too bad, sweetheart."

"It doesn't matter. She likes being Jenny the Head." I didn't tell Mrs. Spooner she was lost. Gloria told me I wasn't good at looking after her.

"Can I get you a coffee or tea or anything?" Gloria was calling out from the kitchen again, and me and Mrs. Spooner went in.

"No, no. Nothing at all, dear."

"Thank you so much for the sandwiches. Everyone's being so kind."

"Don't even mention it, Gloria. I'll help any way I can. I've been hoping for news?"

Gloria shook her head. "They've done two searches through the woods. Fine-toothed comb, the detective said. And not a single sign." The back of her hand went over her mouth. I heard her sniff.

"I just can't imagine what you're going through. Rowan is such a sweet boy."

"It's all happening so fast. How can they be done in the woods already? He's still in there somewhere. I know he is. Telly's going back in. He's not giving up."

"Telly's a fine man, isn't he?"

Gloria's face got red and twisty. I wished Mrs. Spooner would go back outside. She wasn't helping at all. I was still angry at Rowan, but now it was a scared-angry. What if he broke his legs and was lost in some bushes? What if he fell and got his eyes poked out on some sticks and couldn't find his way? What if Carl was not nice and read out horrible things on his deck of cards and tied Rowan up? What if Girl growled at Rowan and he was frightened and freezing and hungry for a tuna sandwich?

Then different thoughts snuck in and pinched me. What if Carl didn't make him go? What if Rowan was happy now? What if he was eating lots of wieners and sleeping outside under the stars and snuggling up with Girl? What if he didn't miss us at all?

"He'll be back soon," said Mrs. Spooner. "I sense it in my bones. He's such a wonderful child. The brightest boy I've ever had the pleasure of teaching, and I say that without hesitation. Such curiosity. He's bound to be a writer. You've read his stories?" Gloria nodded. "Then you know what a gift he has. Of course you do."

Tears poured out of Gloria's eyes. She bent her head over and they splatted on the plastic covering up the sandwiches.

"Oh, dear," Mrs. Spooner said. Then she saw the THEIF sign on the table. The sign those boys made when they wouldn't let Rowan play with them. They were garbage. Those boys. Mrs. Spooner turned it around with her finger. She looked hard at that sign and then her face went funny.

"That's quite odd," she said. She tapped on the letters.

"What is? What's odd?"

"Oh, nothing. Just reminded me of something, that's all."

When Mrs. Spooner left, I watched her stop in front of the fox-tie man. He was by his car and he squashed a cigarette into the grass. She talked to him. Her hands were moving, and she made a rectangle shape. She talked some more, and I heard her say, "Just concerning, don't you think?" The man made me think of Telly then. All those times when Gloria was telling him things. His head would nod, but his ears and his brain were gone off somewhere else.

Some of Telly's friends came in big trucks. Six of them went in the woods and I watched and watched but seven didn't come out. If night came, and he still wasn't home, that meant Rowan was gone for two whole days.

Telly came inside and wiped his face on a dishtowel. He told Gloria they didn't find him, and he looked right at me without blinking. Like he knew I'd told a lie. At first I didn't know what I lied about, but when he kept saying there was no sign of nobody, I started to worry Carl wasn't real. Maybe there was no one under the bridge. Maybe I pointed at the wrong picture. I knew my mind had too much imagination. It was a giant problem. Gloria told me that all the time.

Then Telly held my shoulders. "You got nothing to worry about, you understand? I know you're worried, but Row's going to be back home in no time at all."

I made a mistake. He wasn't angry at all. He let go of me and ate three ham sandwiches fast.

"We should get cleaned up," Gloria said, and she smoothed down her hair. "All of us. That new dress, okay, Bids? And Telly, a couple of your shirts are still hanging in the closet. The reporter lady'll be here soon, and we're a family, aren't we? So we got to look like a family."

ROWAN

I woke up dripping with sweat. A pile of blankets lay on top of me, a pillow tucked under my head. Near my chin I found a small furry bear, black plastic eyeballs, missing its nose. Carl had covered me up and tucked the blankets around me, just like Gran used to do when I was little.

I expected to see the whole cabin destroyed, but the broken frames were back on the wall, hanging crookedly. The glass had been swept from the floor and rug. Books and torn out pages were piled in the shelves on their sides. Even the board-game boxes had been cobbled back together, fake money sticking out.

Carl had cleaned up everything.

I kicked off the blankets, and my skin erupted in goose bumps. My head throbbed and my eyelashes were weighted with crust. I pulled them apart with my fingernails. When I stood up my neck and my legs ached, like I had the flu. Sunlight slanted over the top of a curtain, and I realized it was late afternoon. I'd been sleeping all day. I noticed the couch had been pulled out from the wall. I leaned over, saw Carl sitting behind there, his forehead on his knees. Girl was lying flat, her chin resting on his shoes. Carl was humming. It was a gritty, sore throat kind of hum that came out in a long stream. Then he sputtered and rapidly sucked in air before starting again.

Girl opened an eye then stretched out a paw. Carl mumbled and grunted and up came his huge head. There were more bits of metal nipped on his beard. He squeezed his swollen eyes together, and when he lifted his hands to rub them I saw that his fingertips and palms were crisscrossed with deep red lines. He was covered in cuts. He must have hurt himself while he was straightening up.

He lowered his hands and opened his eyes. "Magic Boy." His voice was raspy. "The circuits are broken now."

"But your hands, Carl—"

"Urh," he said. "Found the wires. I contained the breach and threw them off our trail. Fixed everything like it was. We're okay now." He wiggled his fingers and winced. "It's secure, Magic Boy. We can stay."

"Carl," I said softly. "Do you want a wet cloth or a Band-Aid?"

He shook his head and his shoulders slumped further. I waited, Girl yawned and resettled, and then the humming returned.

"Carl?" I whispered, but he didn't budge. I looked at his hands again. They looked raw, dried blood in the creases. Water filled my eyes, and I yanked at the collar of my T-shirt and scraped away the tears. After last night, that asshole under the bridge, the panic inside the cottage, I couldn't pretend Carl was okay anymore. He wasn't just a man who lived life his own way. He needed someone to help him. He needed me to be a better friend.

I went to the bathroom, and as I peed I looked out the window. The sun was touching the tops of the trees now, making the water sparkle. Soon it would slip down further and the shadows would thicken inside the woods. I wished I hadn't slept for so long. I decided that tomorrow, as soon as there was daylight, I'd go home. I'd follow the creek until I came to the bridge. From there I knew the way. As soon as I could I'd go see Mrs. Spooner and tell her everything. She'd have the solution. Exactly what to do about Carl. How to help him.

When I came out of the bathroom I realized how hungry I was. There was a dull cramp underneath my ribs, and I went to the kitchen hoping to find food. Sticky tape residue was still left on my feet, so with each step I was picking up dust and hair. Fuzz from the rug. But no shard of glass stuck in my skin. Carl must have gotten it all.

There was an undersized fridge in the tiny kitchen with an opened pack of bologna, a loaf of bread, margarine, and an enormous jar of jam. I tore into the bag of bread, spooned mounds of jam onto a slice, stuffed it in my face. In a cupboard I found a can of peaches. I opened them, and with a fork stabbed the pieces and brought them to my mouth. I barely mashed the chunks with my tongue, just let them slide down to my stomach.

When I had enough, I sat down on a chair. Jogged my knee up and down. I heard a splash, then someone shouting outside, laughing maybe, and all at once I remembered that Carl didn't own the cottage. We'd broken in, and there was still plenty of damage done, even if he'd cleaned everything off the floor. I watched the door. At any minute a person could charge in, arrest me and Carl. We would go to jail. Probably for a long time.

A fishing pole was leaning by the back door. I didn't want to be inside anymore, even if there might be people outside who knew I didn't belong there, so I grabbed it, went out, then sat on the edge of the dock. I dipped my feet into the cool green water. I couldn't see much beyond my white toes, but I knew the water was really deep. There were a number of cottages spaced around the lake. Docks stuck out here and there. Other rowboats tied up, red and green. A bright yellow paddleboat. What appeared to be buckets and rubber boots. No one was around, though, except for a single person gliding in a red canoe far, far away.

I wiggled my toes, counted up the hours. I guessed at the time, figuring Carl and I had been together for forty-three or forty-four hours. Not even two whole days. It felt so much longer, like I'd been away from home for weeks. I wondered what Maisy and Gloria were doing at home. Were they having dinner, or maybe throwing the Frisbee for Chicken? Did they miss me? Were they worried? Would Chicken spin in circles when I made it home?

I pulled out some line and let the hook drop into the water. I didn't know how to throw it further out where the fish were jumping, making bubbles. Casting, I thought it was called, but maybe I could catch something near the dock. If it was big enough, I could cut off the head and scrape out the intestines and fry it in a pan. Carl and I could share it. A meal might make him feel better.

I closed my eyes, and for a moment I forgot that Carl and I were criminals. Thieves, like my sign said, but now plural. Instead I thought about Telly and Dian, what they'd been talking about when I went to the garage to see him. A cottage vacation in the fall. I remembered how excitement shot through me when I imagined Maisy and I going along. Our first actual vacation. The leaves would be turning color. The air would smell sweet and sharp with wood smoke. We'd build puzzles and drink cherry soda until our lips were stained. At the time, I'd really believed that was possible. Until Telly told me to stop coming around. Even though I only came around once.

The sound of dribbling water made me open my eyes. The man in the red canoe was coming closer, silently, except for drips from his paddle when he lifted it. When he was almost beside me he held his oar in the water and the canoe slowed. He was old and tanned, wearing a clean white T-shirt, a wide beige hat with a string hanging down the back. "Quiet evening, hey?" he said.

I swallowed, pushed the hair out of my eyes. "Yeah. Quiet."

"You friends of Bertie's?"

"Bertie's?"

"Marilyn's then."

I realized he was asking about the cottage. Those must be the names of the actual owners. "Oh yeah. Yeah." I nodded. "My dad knows her."

"Figured as much. Bertie's crowd is all button-down types, you know." He smiled, touched the brim of his hat. "Not that there's anything wrong with that. It's good to meet new folks."

I stared into the water, lifted my rod, pretended to check my hook. Black insects skated over the surface, looped around my legs.

"Fish bitin'?"

"I don't think so."

"My grandson pulled out a perch this morning. Close to the dock like you're doing. Not much else, though." He laid his oar across his lap.

"How do you know?"

"Know what, son?"

"If you got one hooked."

"What? You've never caught a fish before?"

He was gaping at my face. Maybe at my split lip, still swollen. But then, with his finger, he patted near his left eye. People often did that when they noticed my spots. Touched their own skin in the same places where the white blotches were growing. To check, maybe. Or to feel if they were still normal. I could feel my cheeks go pink. "No, sir. I haven't."

"Oh, you'll know, son. You'll feel the pull. They don't just sit there, all polite, waiting to be reeled in. They'll fight you for their lives. Like they should, right?" He watched me for a second, then said, "Digging worms, I take it?" He pointed at my T-shirt. There was so much grime that it was hard to make out the picture of the donkey.

"Yeah. Playing around in the woods and stuff."

"That's what summertime's for, isn't it? Getting filthy and you couldn't care less. Don't tell my wife I said that." A wink.

"Yeah."

"Looks like the bugs made a meal out of you, though. Ran out of spray?"

I scratched my neck, and when I looked, my fingernails were filled with brown powder. Dried blood.

"Well, we're just two over, if you and your dad need anything. I'm Jim Russell, and my wife's Jackie." He laughed, tapped his hat again. "Jackie Russell, you know, like those small dogs. No end to her energy. Always in a super mood."

I smiled, but I'd never heard of Jackie Russell dogs. Chicken was a Heinz 57, same as the ketchup. I think Girl was too. I could picture her, though, Mrs. Russell, thin and hyper, running here and there. She probably smelled like ginger cookies, the same as Gran did. I couldn't help imagining myself climbing into the canoe with Mr. Russell, gliding across the water. *Just two over.* Mrs. Russell would be there waiting, and she'd have something cooked. Baked drumsticks, mashed potatoes. Steaming corn on the cob with real butter. She'd make me sit down, pile up a plate. When I was full to bursting, she'd lift the glass dome off a chocolate cake. Rainbow sprinkles all over the top. With a drink of icy milk. She'd say, "He's a growing boy, Jim. See how he packs it away?" She'd hug me to her side, pressing my face into her ribs, and I'd sniff in her cookie smell. Mr. Russell would tell me to go swim myself clean: "Put that dirt back in the lake, son. Where it belongs." And I'd listen. To everything. I could be such a good grandson.

"Anything you need, okay? You just tell your dad."

"My dad?"

"Sure."

Carl. The bubble popped. Worry seeped out around me. The sun had just gone below some clouds, and everything had turned dull and gray. Was Carl out from behind the couch yet? Would he think the intruders were back? Planting wires, or whatever it was they did. Last night I'd listened so hard that I was certain I heard things too. Scraping and moaning. Branches. Or creatures stalking through the darkness. "I will," I said.

"Happy fishin', then."

“Thanks.” As soon as his back was turned I stood up and wound in my line. It snagged, and when I yanked the line snapped, floated up in the air. Rod in hand I walked across the dock, a trail of wet footprints on the weathered boards. Just as I reached the back door of the cottage, Carl opened it. Girl rushed out between his legs and squatted down on the soft grass.

“She really had to go,” I said, and tried to smile.

He nipped strands of his beard between his knuckles. “Who was that man, Magic Boy? Who was that man you were talking to?”

MAISY

Me and Gloria were waiting on the front step when a van came driving down the circle. It was white and big and had "Channel 6" on the side and it had muck, too. It came into our driveway. A lady wearing a pink sweater and pink skirt got out and so did a man with a big camera thing.

"Mrs. Janes?" the lady said. "I'm Anita Cahill. Detective Aiken mentioned we'd drop by? To record an appeal for the news?"

"Yes," Gloria said. She patted her hair.

"Is your husband here as well?"

"Telly's my husband."

"Is he here, Mrs. Janes? To be part of the appeal?"

"Oh, yes. Sorry. He's almost ready."

The lady touched my arm. "You must be Maisy. Detective Aiken told me how helpful you've been. And what a lovely dress."

It was one Gloria bought me from Stafford's. It was mostly blue and had puffy sleeves and tiny squiggles all over it. I wasn't sure if I liked it, and Gloria said she was going to put it straight back in the bag and give it to Shar. But it went in my closet.

"Well, what do you say, miss?" Gloria bumped me.

"Thank you," I said. "I like your, your belt." It was red.

The screen door banged and Telly ran down the stairs. He was buttoning up a blue shirt. "Sorry," he said. His cheeks were pink and shiny. "I was in, you know, searching the woods. And I had to get washed, and, and shave." He squeezed his eyes closed and he was breathing hard. "I mean, I didn't have to. I just—I'm just not used to—"

Gloria rubbed Telly's back. Her shirt was blue too, and it had sparkly beads sewed around the neck. Her eyebrows were fixed with a brown pencil and she had on lipstick.

"I understand. This is as difficult a situation as anyone can face, isn't it? I'm going to ask you a few questions, okay? We'll have a conversation. Please forget about the camera, and just share your thoughts with me."

"What if"—Telly put his hand on his neck—"what if nothing comes out right?"

"Please don't worry, Mr. Janes. We'll edit it at the station. And believe me, our viewers will be very understanding, given the circumstances." She looked at the cameraman. "Should we start?"

Then the man lifted the camera thing up on his shoulder. I didn't like the flashing red light. The lady asked a lot of questions and Telly and Gloria talked about Rowan in a microphone. "He's quiet and gentle," Telly said. "And he's got a dog named Chicken that's always by his side." And Gloria said, "He likes to read a lot. If he's not in school or outside poking around, he's at the library. You can't drag him away from a book." Anita said, "What would you say, Mr. and Mrs. Janes, if you could talk to Rowan right now? What would you tell him?" Telly said, "We love you, Row. We're doing everything we can, and you just got to hold tight. We're going to find you." Gloria started crying and Telly put his arm around her and squeezed her shoulder. "Mrs. Janes?" Anita put the microphone near her mouth. Gloria rubbed her nose and then said, "Rowan? If you're listening, all we want is to have you home. Back with us, with your mom and dad, and your sister. You belong with your family. We're right here, together, waiting for you." She put her face on Telly's shirt and her back shook bad. Telly held my hand, and I put my cheek on his shirt too.

When the man took the camera down the lady said, "You're both so strong. And you too, Maisy. What a horrendous ordeal you're going through. I can't imagine."

People kept saying that. *They can't imagine*. But if they were thinking it, weren't they imagining it too?

"We'll feature it on the six o'clock, and again on the eleven." The lady did a sad-smile, the same as Mrs. Spooner's. "I'm praying it will help get word out."

Then they got in the van and drove away. Gloria took a big breath and said, "I'm going to put together something for us to eat. I won't be a minute. Telly?"

Telly looked at his truck and scritched his head. "Sure, Glow. Sounds good."

I followed Gloria inside. She went to the kitchen and got food out of the fridge and filled up three plates. Rolled-up meat. A slice of tomato on top of lettuce. An ice cream scoop of leftover potato salad and a biscuit jammed full of butter. Chicken was right there. His eyes watched Gloria and his tail banged on the floor.

"Can we take some out for Rowan?"

Gloria frowned. "Oh, Bids. It'll only make us all more sad, won't it? Why don't we just have supper. The three of us."

Telly walked into the kitchen. "What's the harm in it, Glow?"

"You're right." She put another plate on the small kitchen table. "Of course you are."

"Who knows? He might come home right in the middle of eating. Never did miss a meal, did he?"

I sat down and tried to swallow, but the food got stuck in my throat. I could hear Gloria and Telly chewing. The phone rang and Gloria got up to answer it. "No," she said. "Kind of you, but we're just trying to have quiet family time together."

Gloria sat down again and said, "Just Erma. Wondering if I wanted her to pop by for company." She took a long drink of water and said, "But I told her I got you here."

"Yes, you surely do, Glow. We're going to get through this. I just got this sense Rowan'll be home soon."

"You do?"

"I do," he said, and he touched her hand.

Gloria's eyes turned wet, but she didn't cry. "Sometimes it takes a tragedy to put everything right."

Then she was talking about all the stuff she wanted to do. Paint the front porch and fix up the basement and next summer grow more vegetables out back. Maybe even try a few watermelon plants. Aunt Erma got some small ones in her backyard.

"So much to do when Rowan comes home. Right, Telly?"

Telly coughed and smiled at me, and then he put a big spoon of potato salad and a whole roll of ham into his mouth.

ROWAN

Carl looked terrible. His face was puffed, and sections of his chin were hairless and raw. There were smears of blood on his cheeks and nose, probably from his injured hands, which he kept curled against his chest. The sight of him standing in front of me in his oversized coat, his eyes dark and confused, made my chest fill with sadness. But also a tight knot of fear.

"It was just a man, Carl." I remembered what he kept saying about two people together. "He lives by himself around the lake. He asked if I caught a fish."

His eyes narrowed, and I thought he was going to ask me more questions, but instead he whistled softly to call Girl back. We went inside and I dug around in the kitchen again, found a can of noodles in tomato sauce and heated it in a saucepan. I made toast, put slices in the bottom of two bowls, and poured the sloppy orange mess over the top. Carl came into the room, his fingers covered in bandages. "That feels better, hey Carl?" I said, sliding the food toward him across the counter.

"Doesn't hurt," he said.

Carl took only a few bites, then placed the bowl on the floor. Girl trotted over and stuck her snout into it.

"Didn't like it?"

"I did. But Girl likes it too."

She lapped up every drop.

The evening passed quietly. I pulled a thick book out of a pile and sat on the couch. *Mountains of the World.* A bunch of pages were ripped out, but there were still plenty of interesting parts to read. Carl stayed in a plaid armchair in a corner, mumbling. I tried not to listen, but I could hear him arguing a little. Though he was laughing a little, too. Girl sat by his leg, her head balanced on his thigh. He rubbed her head with the back of his hand, stopped mumbling once to say, “You miss your squirrel, don’t you, Girl?”

I flipped through all the pages in the mountain book and got another one. Deserts. Then a third about cats. But they were starting to get dull. I looked at the television, its shiny silver knobs and smooth wooden legs. I waited until Carl was quiet for a moment, then asked, “Can I turn it on?”

He shook his head. “What?”

“The TV.”

“Fine. Fine. It’ll be okay, right? Sure it will. But only for a minute. I know, Stan, but it’s just a box, and I broke the connections last night. Fixed the breach.”

“I don’t have to, Carl. I changed my mind. I’ll just read.”

“No, turn it on, Magic Boy. But after, you need to, urh, break the wires again.” I leaned to the side and saw that the plug was sitting on the floor. “In case it transmits a signal. Sends it out.”

“Thanks,” I said. Carl seemed better. More relaxed, anyway. “I’ll check for a show. Something short.” I missed that, squeezing into Telly’s chair with Maisy. Watching anything.

I plugged the TV back in and yanked out the button near the bottom. The whole screen was fuzz. Switching channels, I saw only hazy figures, heard a kid snicker, a gun fired, car tires screeching. I adjusted the rabbit ears, but static still distorted the screen. I flicked the knob again, saw the jagged shape of a man sitting at a desk. The nighttime news. I was about to switch the television off, but the man said something that made my hand freeze. “. . . still searching for Rowan Janes from Little Sliding. Anita?” I checked the tips of the rabbit ears, pulled them out as far as they would go. Then I struck the side of the television with my fist. The image snapped into view.

There was my yard. Right on the screen in black and white. I could see the corner of our house and the edge of the deck where I’d stood in the lightning storm. Our lawn looked all chewed up. A woman in a skirt was holding a microphone with a number six on it. I crouched down, turned up the volume.

“Police have widened the search today, covering every inch of the extensive wooded area you see behind me. But not a single sign has been found.

We're here with Rowan's family, Gloria and Theodore Janes. And his sister, Maisy." The camera view widened, and my mouth fell open. Gloria, and Telly beside her, holding her hand. Maisy was pressed into Telly's side. Even Chicken was there, asleep in a grassy patch behind them.

"That's about me, Carl," I said, pointing. "They're talking about me. On television!"

"Can you tell us what happened?" the woman asked.

"We— All we know is he was exploring the woods," said Gloria. "That's something he loves to do." She pushed a tissue into her face, looked over at Telly. He wrapped his arm around her. "And the police say he crossed paths with a man in there. He's that way, Rowan is. Always treats people with respect. Would talk to anyone."

I was holding my breath. A low hum came from behind me, but I barely noticed it.

"He's a most wonderful boy," Gloria said. My face got warm. "He's a great big brother to Maisy."

Maisy tucked her chin in. I laughed. She was being just like a turtle.

"He's quiet and gentle," Telly said.

They said other nice things, too. I pushed my hand into my chest. Then the woman asked them what they'd like to say to me if they could. Telly said, "We love you, Row. We're doing everything we can, and you just got to hold tight. We're going to find you." Gloria started crying and then she said, "Rowan? If you're listening, all we want is to have you home. Back with us, with your mom and dad, and your sister. You belong with your family. We're right here, together, waiting for you."

Carl's chair scraped on the floor. Springs groaning.

The lady thanked Gloria, and then the screen flicked over to the man at the desk. He said, "Rowan Janes was last reported seen at the old stone bridge that crosses Slowrun Creek. A resident of Little Sliding, Karen Grace, told police she was taking an evening stroll with her friend, Lionel Horton. The pair happened upon Rowan Janes and an adult male in that vicinity."

The screen flicked again, and then I saw the same lady with the microphone, and a front porch I didn't recognize. The camera moved out and there was a girl standing on the bottom step. An older woman was beside her. Maybe her mother.

The girl looked familiar, and then I knew her. She was the one wearing the floppy hat, with that sick freak who forced me and Carl from our camp. She looked younger than I remembered, cleaner, and I felt a jolt of shame that I hadn't fought back. I touched my throat.

"He was so aggressive," the girl said. "Talking real strange. Lionel and me were just hiking around and having a laugh. Not hurting anyone. I don't even think it was that late. But that guy was really spazzing out."

"Can you define what you mean by 'spazzing out'?" the lady asked.

"Well, he rushed at us with a knife. And he had this ferocious dog. I knew the boy wasn't supposed to be there. We tried to convince him to break free, but I think the man had some type of hold on him. Mental hold."

"What?" I yelled that out.

"So Rowan was not there willingly?" the lady asked.

"No, not at all. We should've tried to save him." The girl looked over her shoulder. "Mom?"

"You didn't know." The mother put her hand on the girl's back. "We're all praying for young Rowan. That he finds his way home."

My mouth was full open now, and my face was pulsing with heat. No longer in a nice way. I could feel Carl behind me, pacing back and forth, but I couldn't tear my eyes from the screen.

The newsman appeared again, rifling through papers on his desk. "Police believe Rowan Janes is being held by this man."

Being held?

That didn't make any sense. Then a photo flashed up. Two men, side by side. One clean and shaven, one bent, dirty, and peering away. I squinted, crawled even closer to the television. A narrow shard of glass jabbed in my palm. I pulled it out and squeezed my thumb over the bleeding puncture. Both men were familiar. Could they be? Yes, they were pictures of Carl.

"His name is Howard Gill," the man said. "Call authorities if you see either Rowan Janes or Howard Gill. Do not approach them. Howard Gill is known to be dangerous."

Who's Howard Gill? He looks exactly like Carl.

"Enough, enough, enough!" Carl screamed. He rushed past me, slammed the knob with his foot. The image collapsed into a white dot and vanished. I scuttled backward.

"They got me, the Workers. Stan said they would. Stan was right all along. Stan knew. Urh. Urh. He tried to warn me. Warn me. Urh. They caught me inside that box."

"Carl," I said. "You got to listen to me. There's nothing real in a tele—"

In one swift move he grabbed the cement man with the headache and, with an awful cry from deep within him, he thrust it at the television. The screen splintered, inside something burst, sparked, and smoke drifted out the front. Carl stomped on the glass then reached behind the TV and tore the plug from the wall.

I pulled up my knees and wrapped my arms around them. With my hands pressed over my ears and my eyes closed, I tried to remember how Chicken had been snoozing in a rectangle of sunlight. And how worried Maisy's face looked. And how Gloria and Telly told the woman with the microphone that they missed me. Gloria was crying. My mother was actually crying. About me.

MAISY

"Do you want to clean your guns, Telly?"

"No, Bids. Don't feel like that now. How about a show? We can wait for the late news to come on."

Telly turned on the TV and sat down in his chair. I squeezed in beside him. A man and a lady were playing a piano and singing funny. Telly laughed. I laughed too, to make Telly happy. I put my head on his shoulder, like I did when me and Rowan watched our show together. Telly put his arm around my back. I forgot how soft and warm he was. I was really tired.

Next thing, Telly was shaking my arm. "Bids? There you are. There you are again."

I opened my eyes.

"Wake up, sleepyhead," he said. He pointed at the TV.

Then I saw me in my dress. Me and Gloria and Telly in front of our house. I already saw it once after supper, and there I was again. My eyes were shut up with the sun. Chicken's eyes were shut up, too. He was pretending to be asleep on the grass, but he kept chomping at the flies. The man at his desk and then Anita all dressed up, and then that girl who saw Rowan with Carl. But she said stuff that didn't sound right. Both times Telly put his hands over my ears for that part.

"Do you think that's true, Telly?" Gloria said. "About the knife and the dog?"

"Could be." He took his arm out from behind my back and rubbed at his face. "I can't think about it."

"But for our part, we did a decent job," Gloria said. "Didn't we?"

"Best we could, Glow. Given the circumstances and all. That sort of thing's not easy for no one."

"I really think it's going to help." She had her elbows on the back of Telly's chair.

"It might. I mean, they got to be somewhere, right? No one just disappears."

I sat up. And then I remembered Jenny the Head. She just disappeared all the time. "Do you think Rowan seen us?"

"I got no idea," Gloria said. "But lots of other people did."

"Lots of people who might notice Rowan out on the street or in a store. Or they might see that man, Bids. And then they'll call the police, and they'll go catch him. That's how this stuff works."

I nodded, but I had a happy squishy feeling in my middle. I bet he did. I bet Rowan saw us and I bet he missed us and I bet he was coming straight home.

"Now up to bed with you, miss."

I slid off Telly's lap and almost stepped right on Chicken. He was sleeping on Telly's feet.

"Goodnight, Telly," I said.

He hugged me tight. "Goodnight, Bids."

Gloria took my hand and we went upstairs to my room. I took off my dress and Gloria hung it in my closet and I tugged on my nightgown with the horse on the front. Gloria put a sheet on me because it was too hot for blankets, and she sat on my bed and smoothed my hair. "Bids? Things are going to get better around here. I'm going to be the best mom. You'll see. The absolute best. No more being bothered by you kids. Getting upset over nothing. I'm going to remember what's important. And me and Telly won't fight no more. We're closer than we've ever been."

I smiled big. That happy squirmy feeling was all over me now. Any second, I knew I'd hear Telly yell out, "Heeyyy!" and Rowan would be home.

She poked some hair behind my ear. "That's all I ever wished for in this world, you know. To have a perfect family. A perfect home." Then she got up and flicked off my light and went out.

I wasn't sleepy at all. I listened to Gloria and Telly talking downstairs.

They were saying stuff, but I couldn't hear what it was, and Gloria laughed, but in a nice way.

Then they were talking loud. Telly said, "I don't know, Glow. I really don't." I wiggled free of the sheet and got out of bed and tiptoed over. The door was open a little bit and I crept out into the dark hallway and peeked over the railing. There was a light on by the front door. Telly sat on the bench putting on his sneakers. He was wearing a cap with a car on the front.

"Where're you going?" Gloria said.

"Home."

"You call that place home?"

"I need to grab a proper rest."

Gloria rubbed her lips together. Sometimes she did that when she was thinking hard. "You can manage that, can you? Getting a rest?"

"C'mon, Glow. Don't be like that. We been through the woods three times. He's not there. Not knowing where he's off to is destroying me."

"I see."

Gloria stood under the light, and I could see her old brown hairs making a line in the yellow.

"I'll be back," he said. "I'm here for you, Glow. I really am. I need an hour. Two at most. It's all a bit complicated, with things. You know?"

He got off the bench and got close to Gloria. Then he kissed her on the lips. For a long time. When he finished it made a smack.

She patted her cheek and coughed. "You can get a rest here, Telly. With me. Up in our bed."

"I—I—"

"I just want things like regular. Us to be a family."

"We are, aren't we? A family?"

"Not if you're leaving."

"Couple of hours, and I'll be back. We got to focus on finding Rowan right now. Not this mess between us. You understand?" He kissed her again. Not as long this time.

"Oh, Telly," she said. "Why did it take this to bring us back together?"

Telly lifted his hat up and pushed it back down. "I got to go. We can talk later, okay?"

"Promise?" she said.

"I just got a lot of balls in the air, Glow, but I swear, I want to be right here when our boy gets home."

The screen door creaked. Telly went out and then I heard his truck grumble and the dirt crunch. I watched Gloria wave and shut the door. Then I heard her say to nobody at all, "I'm doing my best to be patient. I really, really am."

ROWAN

"Why did you turn on the TV?" Carl yelled. "Tell me. Tell me. Why'd you turn it on, Magic Boy?"

"I don't know."

"Tell me. Why'd you turn it on?"

"Carl."

"Why did you turn it on? Tell me why."

"Please. I'm sorry. I shouldn't have done it."

"Why did you turn it on?"

"I don't know."

"I don't know," he repeated.

"I don't, Carl. No reason. I thought it was okay."

"You know. Why did you turn it on?"

"I wasn't thinking, Carl. There was no reason."

He was getting closer and closer.

"Why did you turn it on?"

"I just—I just wanted to watch a sh-shh—"

"What show." His words burst out before mine even finished.

"I don't know. I wanted to check."

"Check what. Urh. Hey, Magic Boy? Check, check? What did you need, urh, to check?"

"What was on?"

"What did you think was on?"

"I don't know. I wasn't thinking. Any show. That's all. Just a show. Something regular." So I could pretend that things were normal. That I had a home.

"You knew I was in there, did, did, urh, didn't you?"

"In where?"

"In the box. You knew they locked me in the box."

"I didn't. I really didn't. You're not in the box, Carl. You're right here with me. We're here. Right? In your cottage."

He didn't seem to hear me.

"Keeping me in there. Restraining me. Collecting my thoughts to destroy me. I'm contained. I'm, I'm, I'm, urh, contained."

"I swear I didn't put you in there, Carl. I swear!"

"Swear, swear. Imagine if I put you in a box. Hey, Magic Boy? How would you like that? Think about it. Locked inside a tiny space and you can't get out. You feel all around your hideaway and there's no door. You can touch the ceiling."

I shook my head.

"Workers come in twos!" he bellowed. "Workers only come in twos. That's an irrefutable fact. Is it? Is it? You called them to the bridge. Them. You sent a signal. You are the exception. You are the exception."

I rolled over, squeezed my eyes closed. I didn't want to be at the cottage anymore. I wanted to be home. With Maisy. With Chicken. With Gloria and Telly.

"Stan is watching!" he screamed. I heard him spit, the splatter hitting the floor. Then the floor rumbled from a smash. The television struck only inches from my head. I slit open one eye. Carl's face was right there. I could smell the oil on his skin. Stale tomato sauce on his breath.

"Stan is watching you now," he whispered.

When I looked at Carl the muscles all over my body began to quiver. I could see Stan. I knew I could. Stan was vast. Red, red, red in Carl's sky. There he was. Seeping out from the inside.

Then Carl said in a strange soft voice, "Let's go for a boat ride, Magic Boy."

"Now? It—it's late, Carl."

"Now. It's late."

I don't think he was echoing me that time.

I stood up. My legs were like jelly.

"Go ahead of me," Carl said.

"Sure, Carl. Sure."

With the brightness from the moon, I managed to walk down to the dock. Behind me I could hear Girl's nails clipping the wood and Carl's feet dragging. As he stepped past me into the rowboat, it rocked back and forth. He pressed the side of the boat to the dock, held it there, steadied it for Girl. Then steadied it for me. When I saw him do that, making things safer, I thought maybe, just maybe, everything would be all right. We were just going to enjoy the water, the view of the bright full moon perched over the trees. Carl did seem calmer. He was like that, his moods flipping one way and then back again.

We sat opposite each other, our knees almost touching, and he rowed us out into the lake. I listened to the oars sliding into the smooth water, lifting, sliding in again. A splash hit Girl in the face, and she shook, her wet ears slapping. Droplets splattered my face, and I cried out. Good-naturedly, though. Or so I hoped.

"Does it hurt your hands, Carl?" The words were sticking in my throat. "Do you want me to row?"

He began to hum. The same low growling hum he'd been making behind the couch. I looked over my shoulder. The dock was getting further and further away.

"Should we turn around, Carl?" The humming just grew louder. "I want to go back. Please. Can we go back?"

But Carl did not stop his mechanical rowing. On and on he went until finally he lifted one of the oars and put it across his lap, his bandaged fingers wrapped around the shaft.

"Carl?"

His left hand slid up to his beard, tugged. Most of the hair along a section of his chin had been yanked out.

"I need to ask you some questions, Magic Boy."

"Sure," I said. The night was warm, but shivers moved up through my back. "You could've asked me back inside. At your cottage."

"No. It's contaminated. Urh. Workers implanted beams on the roof. No one can hear us out here, you know. No one can hear anything."

"O-okay." I swallowed, but my mouth was dry.

Carl turned and watched me through a single inky eye. "You better tell me what you're doing."

"Doing?"

"Stealing from me. Hooked into my currents. Drawing out my intelligence."

"I'm not, Carl. I swear." My teeth started to chatter.

"Yes, you are. It all makes sense now. Stan explained it to me. I should have listened to him when I found you." He shuddered. "Hiding in the woods that night. Showing up after the rain. Thinking you were just a little boy."

"I'm thirteen."

"You could be two hundred. Couldn't you? You could be a thousand."

"But I'm not. No one can be a thousand."

"Liar!" he yelled. "You know what they do in those rooms. The Workers drag you there. Two of them arrived on my doorstep. So friendly. They had a, a, a, urh, book."

"Maybe they were door-to-door people, Carl. Trying to sell you something."

"No. No. They wanted to manage my circuits. Everything is electric. Lightning in the sky." Girl pressed her wet nose into my hand, and Carl yanked her back by the rope collar around her neck. The boat shuddered. "But you know that, know that already, don't you. You know all about the rooms."

"I don't. I promise. I really don't. I don't know anything about any rooms."

"You were sent. I know now, urh, what you're trying to do."

My heart was pumping fast. I watched his fingers pinch at the metal pieces in his beard.

"Please listen to me, Carl." In the distance I could see a light further around the lake. That might be Mr. Russell's place. Jim and Jackie. If Carl didn't stop, I could jump in and swim toward that light. I leaned over and looked into the black water. I pictured it, a forceful dive from the side of the rowboat, swift strokes, strong legs kicking. But then I remembered I couldn't swim.

Carl leaned forward. The boat rocked and water lapped against the sides. Girl whined, pawed at Carl. I felt coldness around my feet. "Are you trying to probe me? Scan me? I saw you outside talking to that man."

"What man?"

"In the water vehicle. Urh. Flying through."

"The canoe? I told you about him. He just wanted to know if I'd caught a fish, Carl. It was nothing. Honest."

"Stan said that man could be your two, but I didn't think. I didn't think correctly."

"He lives in another cottage. Him and his wife. He's Jim. She's named after a dog. I can't remember what it's called. They're just two down." I put my hand on Girl's back. She was warm. Her tail was twitching back and forth through the water at the bottom of the boat. "Two down, Carl. He was nice."

"I know what you were doing. Putting out a message. I managed two years without getting caught. But they fooled me with you. They did. Hide a boy inside the darkness."

"I'm sorry. I'm really, really sorry. I'll just leave, okay?" We were floating inside the line of moonlight. The lake looked enormous, its edges appearing miles away. I looked down into the water again. "Can we go back to shore? Please, Carl? I'll just go. You won't ever see me again. I'll go."

"It's too late," he said. "I'm going to give you one chance. Urh. Tell me who sent you here."

"Please, Carl." I was sobbing. I slid forward, closer to Girl. "Please. I don't know what you're talking about. My name is Rowan Theodore Janes. I live at 17 Pinchkiss Circle. I have a little sister Maisy and a dog named Chicken. My mom's name is Gloria. She stuck me under that stupid sign. Remember? Then I ran away. I made a mistake, Carl. I made a mistake." Tears poured out of my eyes. My whole body was shaking. "I shouldn't have run away. It was really dumb. I didn't think. Then it just went on and on, and I wanted to go back last night, but I was afraid, and maybe I should have just tried. But I want to go back. I want to go home."

"Stop!" he yelled. "Where's your pair? Workers come in twos. Always. Where's your two? Where. Is. Your. Two?"

"I don't have a two." An image of Maisy's face burst into my head then. I could see her leaning over that robin with its broken neck, asking me if we should say a prayer. I told her no one was listening. That it wouldn't make any difference. And the memory of that was like a knife to my stomach. I clasped my hands together. "Please," I whispered through sobs. "Please somebody be listening."

"I'm not going to ask you again Rowan Theodore Janes 17 Pinchkiss Circle."

I saw the light click out at the Russells'. Darkness two down. I stood up. The boat was rocking back and forth. "I'm your friend, Carl. We're friends. I don't want to hurt you. You can go back to the bridge, okay? I'll walk with you. Tonight. That's your home. That's Girl's home. I'll leave. I promise, I promise, I promise. Let me leave."

Carl stood up, too. The boat tilted, and I grabbed for the sides. Water sloshed over the lip. Girl barked, and her claws stabbed my bare foot.

"I can't! I can't! I have to. I won't let him! I won't! Won't take me. Won't take me. Won't take me. Won't take me. Won't take me."

"Carl?"

He screamed, "I don't know who Carl is!"

He lifted the oar. More water sloshed in. I raised my arms. Grabbed around my head. The oar whirred through the air.

A shock of white went through me. Girl barked and barked. My body bent, shoulder smashing the edge of the boat. I struck the surface. Black water wrapped around me. Exploring every crevice. Bubbles exploded from my mouth. I couldn't see. Gulping, gasping, metal on my tongue. I fought. Kicked. Thrashed.

Moonlight above, the shape of Carl peering down at me. His mouth wide open, his head getting smaller and smaller. Girl beside him. Her muzzle snapping the air.

Shhh.

I drifted downward, heavier than I'd ever been before.

Are you there?

Turtle?

I was alone.

Are you listening?

Silence.

I was invisible.

Help me!

MAISY

I ran back to bed and hid under the sheet. Gloria came up the stairs and opened my door, and I knew she was going to hear my woodpecker heart tak-takking like crazy.

"What? You're still awake?" she said, but she didn't sound mad.

"Not tired."

She came over and took a blanket off the bottom of my bed and pushed it tight around me.

"There," she said. "You're like a hot dog in a bun."

"But not a corn dog," I said.

"Never. Corn dogs can't breathe."

I laughed.

"Try to think boring things, Bids. Tell yourself a story to knock you out."

"Can you tell me one?"

"Not now. I want to take a bath. Telly promised he'd be back before I know it."

Then Gloria left, and I heard the splish of water going and the bubbly smell of flowers sneaking through the air. The water stopped. She was singing that song again. The same one she sang when Rowan ran away.

I didn't know what story I should tell. Gloria's favorite was about the wolves in the woods, but that was too scary. I looked down at my hot dog blanket. Not a corn dog. I only had a corn dog one time at Stafford's. That was a good story. A true story, though Gloria said the wolves were true, too.

Telly was supposed to get me and Rowan from school, but he never came, and we stayed on the swings for a long time. All the lights in the school turned off. I think the teachers went home. The other kids and moms went home too. There were leaves on the ground and I was kicking them in the air and they stuck on the fuzzy orange scarf around my neck. It was cold, and it started to get dark, and Rowan took my hand and we walked and walked. We could've walked home, but Rowan said, "I got an idea." So we went the wrong way. We went up by the road that turned into the highway. I hid behind Rowan and he stuck out his thumb like they did on television. A lady in a big brown car stopped and Rowan tugged open the door so I could climb in front. She had hair like gray string, and her enormous belly pressed into the wheel.

The car smelled like a pet store and hairspray, but it wasn't bad. When we got in, she said, "Watch where you plunk your wee asses. Chimp's tucked away in there." That made me laugh. Chimp was her ferret. He was sleeping inside a ripped part of the seat. The pink tip of his nose was poking out, and that was all I got to see of him. This lady sang along to music from her radio. She never said nothing about why we weren't home. Or why Rowan was sticking his thumb out. She just asked us where we were going, and she drove us all the way to the front doors of Stafford's.

Me and Rowan looked in the windows and we could see Gloria pulling shirts out of a cardboard box and slipping hangers down the necks. Then we sneaked inside and hid right in the middle of a circle of sweaters. Some of them were falling off, but that wasn't Gloria's fault. They just had big necks. Gloria kicked the box of clothes near our hiding spot, and we burst out and rushed at her.

"You two wonders!" She yelled that out loud, and her mouth was a huge smile. "Oh, oh, my loves, my loves!" She got on one knee and squeezed us both up in a hug. Other ladies asked who we were, and she told them our names. They patted our heads and cheeks and told Gloria we were adorable. She was lucky. "Blessed," she said. "So, so blessed." I saw Rowan pull his hands inside the sleeves of his sweater. I think he was hiding his spots.

She wasn't finished her work, so she let us sit at the back counter. She even bought us deep-fried corn dogs. Rowan squirted drops of mustard from a yellow bottle but I ate mine with nothing on it. They tasted so good. Rowan grabbed the stick because I was chewing on it. He thought I was going to eat it but I was only pretending.

When she was done her work, Telly came and picked us all up. Gloria never said nothing on the ride home. Telly played his music. He hit all the potholes and me and Rowan popped off our seats. We laughed when our heads bumped the roof. Wind came in the open windows and I could smell smoke and my eyes itched. Even though it was dark I could see the empty trees waving their branches.

The truck turned down our circle, and Gloria pointed her finger at us. "Straight to your rooms, you two. I've had more than enough rigmarole for one night." Maybe she was angry at Telly for leaving us at school. Or maybe she was so happy with our surprise she just got tired. It didn't matter. I never remembered how it ended. I only thought about her smile and what she said when all the other workers at Stafford's were looking at me and Rowan. "I'm blessed," she said. "I'm so, so blessed." We were her wonders. We were her loves.

ROWAN

I didn't fight anymore. I slid down through the water. Dropping and dropping. Stringy weeds brushed my arms and legs. Then a hard fist punched my side. Clawing against my spine. My T-shirt hitched. Caught on something. Tugging. I twisted in the water.

It was Girl. Oh, Girl. I reached through the water, felt her hind legs, tail, and I held on. Her body moving, thrusting force pulling me up and up and I kicked and kicked until I pierced the surface. Broke through.

Hands grabbed my arms. Carl. I was soggy paper. He pulled me over the edge of the rowboat. My T-shirt slipped off, splatted when he threw it. I collapsed onto the bottom of the boat. A hammer banged inside my head. I felt pounding on my back. Then I was rolling over. Weights clamping down on my ribs. I hacked. And gasped. And retched. Hot watery vomit gushing from my mouth, my nose, until my ribs and skull were close to exploding. What was he going to do to me? What? Then there was blackness.

"Stan. It was Stanley!"

Carl was yelling. I opened my eyes. Wet wood against my mouth, against my chest. I was shaking. I closed my eyes again.

"Dot is so angry. We had a verbal, and I broke it. I broke the law we made. Urh. Just stop arguing. Just stop!"

A gentle bump against something solid. My body lurched.

"We're back," he said.

I clawed out. Crumpled on the darkened dock. I couldn't think. I couldn't run away. I wheezed, and stabs of pain came with each cough. I touched the side of my head. Found a massive lump, the middle split open. Warm oozed behind my ear, pooled underneath my cheek. I dragged my fingers through it, brought them to my nose. Smelled metal from the sticky blackness.

Shuffling on the dock. Carl was coming. Stan was coming. They were coming to kill me. Fear stopped my breath. I tried to stand but dizziness knocked me to my knees. More vomit shot into my mouth. I spat it out.

"Stop," I said. I lifted a hand toward him, but I fell backward. "Please. Don't." I was moving, but staying still. I worked my fingers between two boards of wood and held on. Darkness slid over me.

When I opened my eyes, he was standing nearby. A blanket and clothes in his arms. He dropped the clothes, then opened the blanket. I sat up and pain shot through my skull. He covered my shoulders. He dug inside his coat. I felt his bandaged fingers poking at my mouth. I gagged. "It will help," he said. Then two small stones sat on my tongue. He had a bottle in his hand. Twisted the cap, held it out to me. The smell of apples.

"Drink this."

I lifted my face, took a sip, swallowed the pills. Whatever they were. I didn't care. My throat burned.

"Drink more."

"Can't more. Hurts."

"I know, I know, I know. Urh. You need to go. I know. Dot says it. I don't trust myself. I don't." He was crying. I looked at him. Blinked. He kept licking his lips. "Stan," he said. "It was Stanley. He just pushes me and pushes me. Until I can't stop. He's gone, but I don't know when he's coming back."

Carl wasn't going to kill me. Not right now.

"Bad. Bad. Bad things. When I looked at your cards. I wouldn't say. The cards told me bad things were going to happen to you. To stay away. I'm the bad things, Magic Boy. Urh. I'm the bad things."

"You're not bad." Words like scratches.

A shadow pacing by Carl. Girl. Each time she passed him she nudged her head against his knee.

"Henry's mumbling and mumbling. But I can barely hear him over Dot," he said. "Just wailing. She's really upset with Stan." His hands were jumping around. "And with me."

"Tell Dot I'm fine. Doesn't hurt. Was an accident."

"It doesn't hurt. Was an accident. Urh."

I closed my eyes again. Lay down on the dock, shivering. Water lapped somewhere. I listened and listened. The sharp banging in my head faded, still there but a distance away. I think I fell asleep. I don't know how much time passed. When I woke up my stomach retched. But nothing came out.

Carl was beside me. His hulking figure blocked the moonlight. I sat up. Leaned on my arms. I winced. Waited for the blast in my head, but the pain was hollow. The blanket fell away from my bare back and my skin prickled with goose bumps. I picked up a long-sleeved shirt from the pile, eased it over the gash in my head. Poked my shaking arms out through the soft cotton. Put a dark sweater on over that. Then I changed into a pair of dry shorts. Everything was about my size. Maybe the cottage owners had a son.

"I couldn't find anything for your feet," Carl said. He was holding something in his hands, rubbing the edges with his thumb. "So I made these. Better than what you had before." Near my bent knee, he placed what looked like two silvery shoes. Holes punctured near the opening laced with two long thin strips. All made from gray tape. "Urh. Measured when you were resting."

"You didn't have to, Carl," I said. His injured fingers must have stung badly. I eased them on my bare feet and knotted the strips. "They fit."

"Now they won't hurt. When you go home."

When you go home. I was going home. I swallowed. My whole body was full of sadness, but also full of relief. "I really like them." I was telling the truth.

"And this," he said. He handed me a small flashlight. "Found it in there." Head tic toward the cottage. "Don't know, urh, about the battery life."

"Thank you." I stood up on jelly legs. Stared down at my shoes, turned the flashlight over in my hand. My heart was jelly, too.

"Wait." From inside his coat he took out a long yellow box. Peeled a strip of aluminum foil, folded it into a neat triangle, pinched. Tapped his thumb along the edges and twisted corners. "Keep this on your head," he said. "Dot insists. Keep good thoughts in and bad thoughts out."

"Tell her I will. I won't take it off."

Carl lowered his head. "She can hear you just fine, Magic Boy."

I nodded slowly. The foil crinkled around my ears.

"I'm going to miss you. Urh. But Stan doesn't trust you. He, he says you're a Worker who lost your pair. He doesn't care about the laws. Urh.

Won't follow them. It's tangential and arbitrary. He wants to kill you, Magic Boy, but I can't do it that way. No, not that way. Just the same as I did with my mother." He touched his temple. "You need to go now. Before Stan comes back. If he comes back, I can't make him leave."

He hugged me. I was scared and dizzy and sick to my stomach, but I hugged him back. My face pressed into his coat and beard. He smelled like mildew and cloves. I felt his body hiccuping. Tears crept up to the edge of my lids. Even though he'd hit me in the head, I knew there was something good and kind and honest that shone inside him.

"Bye, Carl."

Most of the eeriness had left the dark woods. I was tired and strangely numb, but I wasn't afraid. One foot kept drifting in front of the other. After a long time the creek started to narrow, its banks less crowded with brush and tall grass.

Then came the curve in the water. I was getting closer to the bridge, to my and Carl's old camp. I turned the flashlight off, making steady steps on the sand and pebbles. I had to hurry. Inside my head I could feel a weird pressure growing. Were the pills wearing off already? If the pain came back full force, there was no way I'd make it.

A branch snapped behind me. I flinched when the noise echoed inside my skull. Then I heard a splash as though a flat stone had fallen into the creek. Animals, I told myself. A baby bird falling out of its nest. I refused to be scared.

A dense shadow just ahead, the bridge right in front of me. I stopped. I couldn't see anything at all, but I knew something else was there. I could hear scratching. Like long filthy nails cleaning the inside of a can. That asshole was back, maybe. With the girl I saw on TV. I touched my neck. The cut had dried into a hard scab. I tried to silence my breathing, to push away the growing pounding in my head. My finger was on the flashlight switch, but I didn't slide it up. With my other hand I felt along the ground, plucked up a rock and threw it. Crouched low in case they turned a light in my direction.

An animal lumbered past me. A skunk. Or a possum. Rustling as it moved underneath the brush, pushed through the leaves. When I stood up the ground shifted, but I caught myself. I stepped forward and clicked on my light. The camp was empty except for junk strewn around, glass bottles, most of them broken. A wet mound of blankets, Telly's shirts. Girl's squirrel was sliced up the middle, stuffing falling out. The circle of rocks that outlined Carl's firepit were kicked all over. The whole place smelled like a filthy toilet.

I sat down on a stone. One of Carl's *fine chairs*. The distant pounding was inching nearer. *Whomp. Whomp.* Slowly building. Getting louder and louder. I was so tired and empty and cold. I wished I had more pills to hold back the pain. I slid my hand inside my tinfoil hat. Touched the sticky swollen side of my head.

It was going to be okay. When I reached home, Gloria would give me some medicine. I kept remembering how she was crying on the television. No matter how angry she was the night I left, she would be relieved to see me. And I would be relieved to see her. She was frustrated and made a mistake, and I was an ungrateful kid who ran away. But I was still *her* kid. That counted for something.

But what about Carl? What if I should have stayed with him? Found Mr. Russell, just two down, and asked for help. For a moment, I stopped. I wondered if I should turn back. Go to him before my head got unbearable. But Carl had told me to leave, hadn't he? He told me he didn't trust Stan. He didn't trust himself. And everyone inside of him was fighting about me. If I went back I'd only make that worse. Besides, home was so close. I would sleep until morning. I would go see Mrs. Spooner as soon as I could. Gloria wouldn't understand about Carl. Mrs. Spooner would.

My stomach twisted. I put my forehead to my knees, the foil crinkled, and I tried to breathe. The pressure. How could it be getting worse and worse by the second? When I closed my eyes, weird bursts of light arrived from nowhere. I thought I heard stones crunching behind me, someone walking around, but I couldn't lift my head to check. Blackness washed over me.

I rubbed my eyes. I'd fallen asleep. Or passed out. For a minute? For an hour? It was still dark, but everything looked a lighter color of gray. I slowly got to my feet. My legs wobbled, my mouth was dry, and each throb in my head made my muscles seize.

I flicked on the flashlight. Shone it up on the cement, and the glow lit up *Almost,* painted on the wall.

I have to keep moving. I'm almost home.

I pushed through the bushes. There was no path. I stepped. It was harder to lift my legs, and each time I stumbled I grabbed at the trees. My feet seemed so far away. Was this the right direction?

The pain was suddenly overwhelming. Flashes burst inside my eyes. The side of my head was firing shots through my jaw and eyes and down the bones of my neck. My teeth chattered. My rib cage shook.

Another branch cracked. I was not alone. Maybe it was a bear. Or a wolf. Maybe they weren't all gone. Or even a man hunting around for me. Didn't they say exactly where I went missing on the news? What if there was a reward?

I spun the light around, through the wet, shiny trees. I tried to yell "Who's there?" but the words went somewhere else. I grabbed my head. Pain gnawed through me. One strike after the other. So sharp and violent.

Which way was I facing? My feet dragged over the wet ground. Step after step after step. And then the trees vanished. I was in a yard. My yard? How did I get here? I dropped the flashlight. A thin beam across the grass. I squinted. Another light coming from the house. Behind the sliding doors.

I started crawling across the backyard. I could no longer walk. Something solid was expanding inside my skull. Trying to find its way out. Every bone and joint tingled. Spit pooled under my tongue.

Gloria was in the kitchen. Was that her? A big fluffy bathrobe. It had to be. The pulsing pain hammered out a message inside my head. *Your mother. Loves you. She really. Loves you.*

I edged forward. My brain was splitting open.

Can you see me?

Mom?

Gray washed over me. Inside the haze, I heard something. A cough carried across the vacant yard. Or a gasp. Maybe it was an "urh."

I tried to focus. I saw, I saw, I saw a shadow cutting in front of the glow. Moving past the flashlight? The porch light? A flurry of movement, a sloping outline. Rushing across the grass toward me.

PART TWO

ROWAN

Dark world tilting, falling down. Yard zigzagging under my feet. Grass in my mouth. Lifting, tugging, stumbling. Thick fingers digging into my armpits. Pulling me up, dragging me, lifting me. Seconds. Minutes. Hours? I am moving away.

Where are you taking me?

Stop.

I want to be home.

Stop it. Please stop it.

My head hurts. Hurts bad.

Grunting then, and I'm down on the hard ground. Something cold against my cheek. I curl into a ball, but the stomping, smashing will not leave my skull. I clap my hand on the wall. Damp cement. Am I back under the bridge?

Everything is spinning.

Spinning.

Stop.

It won't slow down.

MAISY

In the middle of the night I woke up. Rain was tapping my window and coming in on my pillow. I got up and closed the window and then I heard Gloria downstairs. She was screaming like crazy. No one was screaming back. I knew she was on the phone to Telly.

"You can't just come and go whenever you want—"

. . .

"—being selfish."

. . .

"Not until we're all back together, you're not."

. . .

"You think there's no consequences?"

Then she stopped and next was an angry slam. Maybe she broke the phone. I hugged my chest but my heart wouldn't slow down.

I waited and waited and maybe I went back to sleep because I didn't hear nothing else. When I opened my eyes again birds were cheeping and orange light was going across my ceiling. I got out of bed and snuck down the hallway. I passed Rowan's room, but his bed was still empty. I tiptoed down the stairs and into the kitchen. Chicken was far back under the table. He was whimpering out a dream, but there was no sign of Gloria. The phone looked okay, but the phone book was on the floor.

I pulled open the sliding doors and went outside. Wind lifted up my hair. The sun was at the top of the trees and the backyard was wet and sparkly. Something extra sparkly was on the grass, but when I went over, it was just tinfoil. A big triangle, enough to cover two roast chickens. We had that once when Telly got his new job at the garage. Rowan wanted all four drumsticks, and when Telly said it was okay, Rowan ripped them off and sucked the bones clean. He could have them again if he came home. I just knew Gloria wouldn't be mad, and she'd say yes.

I wondered if a neighbor brought chickens for us to eat. Maybe. I had to run to catch the tinfoil because wind was getting inside it and pushing it away. I grabbed it up and went back to the kitchen. There was a rabbit casserole from Shar's aunt in the fridge, and a container full of something orangey brown with Mrs. Murtry's name written on a piece of tape. A chicken, too. Just one though. All roasted up brown. But it looked weird and kind of sad because the drumsticks were already gone.

When I woke up again I was under the table with Chicken. I could see lines on Gloria's legs. They were blue and red branches. Her feet were inside pink slippers with a pompom on the top.

Gloria smacked her hand on the table just above my head. It was loud and I jumped. She bent down and frowned at me. "Get out right now! How long have you been under there?"

"Just a little bit," I said.

"And what's that?" She reached down and grabbed the tinfoil. "Where did this come from?"

"The backyard."

"With all we've got going on, people just let their trash go?" She crumpled it into a ball and threw it in the sink. "First thing Telly's going to do when he gets back is put up a fence. I don't care if nobody got one. I won't have garbage blowing all over."

I nodded.

"Now, you need to get out from under there and call him."

I got out quick. When I stood up, my head and arms filled with fuzz. I held onto the edge of a chair. "Telly?" I said.

"Of course, Telly. You know, that man who was supposed to stay here last night? And decided he was just too tired to be with his family?"

I swallowed fast. Gloria told me the numbers and I turned the dial careful. It rang and rang and then a lady answered. I looked at Gloria.

"Ask for Telly," she said. Her face was angry.

"Um. Is Telly there?"

"You're not calling the queen," Gloria said loud. She picked up a spoon and waved it at me. There was jam on the end of it. "Just tell her to put him on."

"She says he's not home, Gloria."

"Home? Thinks that's his *home*, now, does she? Well you tell her to tell him, he got to be at the police station for ten sharp."

"Um. Gloria says Telly got to go to the police for ten sharp."

"And that he'll be bringing us back here. To our *home*. His *real* home."

"And he'll, um, he'll—"

"Be driving us back, I said."

"Be bringing us back."

"And that we don't need to be taking the bus both ways."

"And that we don't—" I stopped talking and chewed at my lip.

"What?"

"She says she can hear you already."

Gloria's mouth squished up like lemon was inside. "Can she now."

"Yes, she can, she says."

"Well you tell that witch Telly finally got his priorities straight. He's moving back here. Just as much said so." She flicked the spoon. The jam flew off and splotched on the wall. "And if she hadn't of broken up this perfectly fine *home*, none of this would've happened. Rowan'd be good and safe."

I held out the phone. "She already hunged up, Gloria."

"What?"

Sparks zipped around behind my eyes. "Do I call back?"

"No, you do not call back." She threw down the spoon. It made a loud crack. "What were you doing, sleeping under the table like that?"

"I, um, don't know."

"Well I won't have it. I don't need a little insomniac. You wandering around all hours. When you go to bed, you stay in your bed."

She pulled the lid off a container of cookies and pushed it across the counter. "Eat," she said. "And get out of that nightgown. Throw it in the trash while you're at it. I can see everything you got right through it."

My face got hot. I looked hard at the cookies. There were flat cookies and squares with cherries and something jiggly and pink. I picked a sticky coconut thing and took a little bite. "Are we going to the police house?"

"They called and said for me to come in."

I dropped the cookie. "They found him. They found Rowan?"

"How do I know?" She looked even more angry. "They would've told me if they did, wouldn't they? What a mess this all is."

I chewed and chewed the coconut.

"We got to take a bus. Don't know why they think every single person's got a car ready at the drop of a hat."

"Am I going?"

"Of course you are. Better for you to learn when you're young how horrible life can be."

Our neighbor Mrs. Murtry saw us waiting at the bus stop. She stopped and me and Gloria got in. Gloria told her we got to go see the police.

"Why didn't you call?" Mrs. Murtry said.

"I didn't want to put no one out."

"You're not putting me out, but you need a car, love. You really do."

"Cars cost money," Gloria said. She folded her arms across her chest.

"They certainly do. But I seen that one Telly's tangled up with driving a brand-new one. Red and shiny as can be. You know where that came from."

Gloria didn't say nothing. But I saw her fingers sticking into her arms. Maybe Mrs. Murtry saw too because she stopped talking about the new car.

"Has there been any word?"

"Nothing. No. Nothing at all."

"Well, that news report should help. I saw it last night. You all did a wonderful job, Gloria. You too, Maisy."

Gloria's fingers stopped poking into her arms. "We did our best. No different from what any other family would do."

"And surely if they want to see you this morning, there's some news. Maybe some leads?"

Gloria sniffed, rubbed her eyes.

"Some *good* news," Mrs. Murtry said. "It's only a matter of time, love. Not like a person can just vanish into thin air!" Then she slowed down in front of a building with two glass doors. "Does Maisy want to wait with me? I've got time. I'll park over there and wait, okay?"

"No. Telly'll be here, too. He'll run us home."

"If you're certain."

"I am, Belinda. He's moving back in with us, where he belongs." Gloria sounded happy again.

"Oh. That's wonderful news."

"We just been so close these past two days. Realizing, I guess. What we had and what we lost. I just got this feeling, once he's home, Rowan's going to walk through my front door."

Mrs. Murtry smiled. "Isn't that always how it works? Good things bring more good things."

Gloria nodded. We got out and Gloria waved at her as she drove away. I waved too.

"What a windbag," Gloria said when she was out of sight. "Going on and on and on about that witch's new car."

Inside, Gloria had to line up at a tall counter and say who she was. I could tell she didn't like it when she had to tell about Rowan disappearing. Her cheeks went all pink. A lady in a black skirt said, "Yes, yes, oh my. I'm so sorry. Just this way. Straight through here." She walked ahead and me and Gloria followed her. We went into a room. There were two chairs and a desk covered in messy piles of papers. The blinds on the window were open and sunlight was shining in. I sneezed two times and Gloria whispered, "Stop it."

The man who was in our house came in. He was wearing the same clothes, but his tie was different. It was blue and covered in question marks.

"Is your husband joining us?" He sat down in his chair.

"Telly's not here?"

"Not yet. We can wait a few minutes."

Gloria took a big deep breath. Her foot tapped.

"No. If you got news, I want to hear it."

"News. Yes," the man said. He went back in his chair. He put his hands on his stomach. "The appeal last night, Mrs. Janes. It really helped. We've already received a number of calls, and . . ." He went back further. His chair creaked. He might tip over. "Can we have, um, Maisy, is it? Can we have her wait outside?"

I looked at Gloria, but her eyes were just zoomed in on the man.

"Is that necessary?" Her voice was all squiggly. It sounded like those waves coming off the road on a hot day. If those waves made a noise.

"I think it's best," he said. "We won't be long. There's a seat just outside my door. Maisy? Would you mind?"

I went outside and sat in a plastic orange chair. There was a table next to me with a plant covered in dust and white dots. The door was still open a tiny bit. I closed my eyes to listen. I wanted to know where Rowan was hiding. I wanted to know when we could bring him home.

"We have Mr. Gill in custody," he said. "As I said we had a number of calls, and one came from the owner of a convenience store. Mr. Gill was there buying some items, and we arrived just as he was leaving. We were able to bring him in. He's cooperating somewhat. Answering questions."

"What did he say?"

"He was with your son. He's confirmed that. And Mr. Gill was wearing a shirt belonging to your husband."

"Telly's shirt?"

"One from work, I suspect. Your husband's name embroidered on the pocket."

"Where on earth would he get Telly's shirt? Was he in my house? In my bedroom?"

"No, ma'am. He claims it was a gift from Rowan."

"A gift. Huh." I could hear Gloria blow out air.

"Mrs. Janes, the shirt supports Gill's claim that there was interaction between him and your son."

"And? What else does this filthy man say?"

"We're still trying to get things straight."

"What does that mean?"

"He indicated that some type of altercation took place, an argument. He said that afterward Rowan drifted off his own way."

"Drifted off?" She sounded mad now. "Who says something like that? Kids don't float away like balloons."

“I understand your frustration.” I heard papers crumpling then. Maybe the man was messing up his desk even more. “I’m just relaying what he’s communicated to us so far. We know he’s spent time with your son. That’s evident.”

“So where is he? Where’s Rowan?”

“Well, we’re taking a three-pronged approach. One, we’re working to determine what happened when they were together. Two, we need to understand the circumstances as to why your son is no longer with Mr. Gill. And number three, as rapidly as possible, we are doing everything we can to locate Rowan.”

“This is just beyond me.” She blew out more air.

“Mrs. Janes?”

I listened but no sound.

“There’s something else.”

Nothing.

“Do you know your son’s blood type?”

And even more nothing.

“If you don’t know it, don’t worry. Most parents don’t remember. Why would they need to?” He coughed. “I’m sure we can track it down with a call to the hospital where he was born. That should be on his file.”

“His file.” Gloria was whispering. “Why?”

“There was blood on Howard Gill’s shirt. A substantial amount, I’m sorry to say.”

“Blood?”

“He hasn’t been able to tell us where it’s from.”

“What? Why can’t he just say?”

“We’re making every effort, Mrs. Janes,” he said, “but you have to understand. Mr. Gill is confused. He struggles with severe mood swings and has, ah, difficulty staying connected to reality.”

“I don’t care if he’s in a bad mood. Or he don’t like reality. Who does?”

The man sneezed. Two times like I did, but Gloria didn’t tell him to stop. Then he said, “Officers are taking him now to collect his clothes from the campsite at the old bridge.”

“Why would you want his clothes?” Her words were all wavy again.

“Potential evidence. And we’ll want to type the blood on the shirt. No stone unturned. Just in case.”

"In case."

They got quiet. I tried to get closer to hear but then a horrible stink filled up my nose. It smelled like rotten eggs. When I looked up, there was Carl. He was walking down the hallway. My heart went wobbly.

Two policemen had their hands under his arms. His big coat was hanging off his shoulders, and I could see a blue shirt with *Telly J.* sewed over a pocket. Carl's hands were pushed together tight because he was wearing handcuffs. I'd seen those before in cartoons. He waved his fingers at me and said, "Hello, Little Fawn." He sad-smiled and I forgot for a second that he stole Rowan and I sad-smiled back.

Then he slowed down right in front of my orange plastic chair and said fast, "I'm sorry I hurt him. Stan was afraid. Urh. He was scared. He pushed me. And I wanted to keep him safe. That's why I did it. To keep Magic Boy safe." He patted brown marks on Telly's shirt. Then he was crying and talking extra fast and wet. "But they took Girl. Took Girl away. Urh. Won't tell me where, until I say. I don't know what to say yet. I don't know what they want. They got my Girl."

One policeman shoved him hard, "Get moving, Gill," and he scuffed his feet down the hallway. He went around the corner. He took most of his smell with him.

I felt shivery cold and my teeth clonked together. I sat on my hands and pulled my arms in close and stared at the plant without blinking. Around the leaves were tiny webs. White bugs crawled around like they had nowhere to go. I tried to follow the bugs as they climbed up and down and not think about Carl or Girl or what that man in the office was saying about blood and Carl's shirt and Rowan being a balloon.

"I can't talk about this anymore. I just can't." Gloria pulled open the door. She said, "Come on, Maisy. Let's go."

The man was behind her. All I could see was the question marks on his tie. It was not nice to wear it. It told me he didn't know where Rowan was. He didn't have no answers at all.

"We're following up on every lead," he said. Gloria dragged me down the hall. I hurried but my shoes were rubbing my heels. "We're not slowing down. And we'll continue questioning him until we get at the truth, Mrs. Janes. The truth. You have my guarantee."

MAISY

"Where have you been?" Gloria jumped off the bench outside the police house. She was yelling at Telly's truck as it got closer. Her arms were flapping. When he stopped, she yanked at the door. "I had to go through that alone, and we've been cooking out here for twenty-five minutes."

"Well I'm here now, aren't I?" He was wearing greasy overalls unzipped down to his middle. I could see his undershirt. "Better late than never."

"Sometimes, Telly, never is better."

Inside my head, I said a prayer. *Dear Gloria, please be nice. Please be nice to Telly.* I remembered what she told Mrs. Murtry. Telly was going to move back in and then Rowan would come home. She had a funny feeling. Gloria's feeling was always right. Mostly always.

Gloria climbed up first. I got in next. She reached across me and pulled the door closed.

"You okay, Bids?" Telly said.

"I'm good," I said.

"Well, let's get you home."

She tugged on his overalls. "Surely you can't be working," she said. "Stafford's isn't after me to come in. Not when my kid's missing. And I doubt the garage is either."

"I was at something else."

"What then?"

He kept his mouth shut, not saying. Just hiding his teeth. All white and fancy.

"Ah," Gloria said. "Looking after stuff for her, was it? That's what you were doing instead of meeting me here. Your own son don't even take priority."

"He does," Telly said. He slapped the steering wheel. He slapped it hard. "Do you think I didn't want to be here? There was an accident out on Wendell's Road. No one was getting through."

"Like I believe that."

"Don't matter if you believe it, Glow. That's the truth." He slapped the wheel again. Even harder. "Just what do you expect from me?"

"Oh, just to be a husband and a father."

"I'm trying. I really am." He wiped his face. "I haven't had a wink of sleep. Can't barely eat."

"Oh, Telly," she whispered. "I didn't mean it. I'm just exhausted. I know you are, too."

Then she told everything the man had said in the room. She said they were going to keep pushing the disgusting bum. I didn't know what that meant. Push him where? I tried not to hear. I let my arm hang outside the window. The wind went through my fingers. It made my hand flip-flop. I watched the fields going by. Some had corn and it was getting tall and green. The leaves made a shushing sound that I liked. Some other fields had fat cows and they pushed their wet noses against the wire fences. I think they were trying to get at the long grass in the gutters when there was lots of other grass all over the place. Dumb cows.

"A lawyer, if you can imagine," Gloria said. "And now he lives under a bridge in the woods. Who in the world would want that for themselves?" Her hands went into fists. "I'll sue them, Telly. If they mess this up. The entire police department. Sue them for every cent they got."

"We'll do it together," he said. "Take a stand. Just like we done before when that truck hit us. We stuck together, and got what we were owed. Remember?" Telly slowed down at the stop signs. He spat out his window. "Rowan belongs to both of us, you know."

Gloria's side was squished into mine. She was shaking bad. Even without taking my eyes off those cows, I could tell. Then I felt Telly's fingers tickle my shoulder. He had his arm wormed around Gloria. He was hugging her. When I peeked, I saw she had her head on his shoulder. She let out a big sigh. "How do people get through this?" she said.

"One minute at a time, Glow. That's all." He kissed her hair. The brown part that was growing out was gone, and it was all yellow again.

Telly wasn't mad no more. Gloria wasn't neither.

He drove into the circle and I saw Shar out on her front step. She was home from visiting with her mom. She waved at me and I waved back.

Telly turned down our driveway. When the truck stopped Gloria said, "Come in, just come in."

"I can't. I mean. Not now. I got to get. I mean, I just can't, Glow."

"We got to talk," she said. "Get this figured out right now. Today. This afternoon."

"My things. Glow. I got to—"

I wasn't trying to look, but I saw Gloria put her hand inside the unzipped part of Telly's overalls.

"Glow. I—"

"Stay awhile," she said. "Get used to being home again. You can take my mind off everything. I need that, Telly." Her hand was on his private parts. I could just tell. She was rubbing up and down. Telly grabbed the wheel. His knuckles went white. He made a weird sound and I knew something shiny and red was springing out of Telly. I saw it when Chicken rubbed at himself with his paw. Whenever Gloria caught him doing that she said, "If only that dog had sense to polish something useful." She'd yell at Chicken. But she wasn't yelling at Telly now.

"Well. It won't hurt no one," he said in a soft way. "No one got to know." He turned off the truck and dropped the keys on the floor. He leaped out and Gloria scooted her legs under the steering wheel and went fast behind him. They ran into the house. The screen door crashed back.

I got out my door and went around to close Telly's door. Then I went up and sat on the step. Behind a piece of wood on the porch, I saw curly yellow hair. I reached and pulled out Jenny the Head. I couldn't remember putting her there. I held her on my lap and patted her. She was so soft. I remembered how dirty she was when me and Rowan found her floating in the ditch. How Rowan cleaned her for me.

Shar came running down the driveway. Her T-shirt was coming up and I could see her bright middle. Her shoe slapped the ground because part of it was broken.

"I'm back!" she said, and her arms hopped up. "I got back this morning." She sat on the step next to me. Shar was like Rowan. She never checked for nails.

"Your hair is nice," I said. Shar had it cut so it looked like the top of a mushroom. "Did you have fun?" I asked. I put Jenny the Head back behind the wood.

"With my mom?"

"Yeah."

"Of course I did. She lets me do whatever I want. Not like Aunt Erma."

"Oh."

"But Aunt Erma said some man tricked Rowan and he ran away. And that the police were all over everywhere. And Darrell was searching too, and you guys were on the TV. Is that true?"

I nodded.

"My best friend's famous." She put her arm around my shoulder. "So, when's he coming back?"

"I don't know. Soon."

"Yeah. Probably soon."

There was creaking behind me. I looked but Gloria's special chair wasn't rocking back and forth by itself.

"Do you hear that?" Shar said, and she laughed.

"What?"

"Your mom."

It wasn't Gloria's chair, it was Gloria. Her bedroom window was open, and she was making sounds like when she tried exercises from a little book that fit in her hand. She bent over and up again and side to side. She counted to ten a bunch of times. Her head got red and her tongue stuck out. Then she smacked her middle and said, "What's the point." She threw the tiny book into the garbage.

Shar laughed again. "They're up there making bacon."

"What?"

"Belly bumping."

"What?"

"Nugging."

I shook my head.

"Never mind. You're too young."

Shar was ten.

"So?" I said.

I closed my eyes. Carl was behind my eyelids, smiling at me.

Sorry I hurt him, Little Fawn. Sorry I did that.

Did what?

Made him drift away.

Drift away where?

I wanted to keep Magic Boy safe.

I could see Rowan the balloon. He was the same color as our happy, happy front door. Carl grabbed the balloon with his big hands and it squeaked and he pushed and pushed. Then it burst.

My eyes sprung open. Gloria and Telly were in the hallway behind the screen.

"May as well take the last of them," he said.

"Your guns?"

"Yeah. Seeing as I'm here."

Then Gloria was roaring. I heard a smash. Maybe glass. Shar ducked her head down. Gloria screamed at Telly to get out of her house.

"Your house?" he yelled back. "It's ours, I'll have you know. Half of every cent is mine!"

"I'll break your skinny neck! One snap, Telly!"

The screen door kicked open. It banged the side of Gloria's special chair. Shar pushed in close to me. Telly was jumping into his overalls and yanking at the zipper, running for his truck. Gloria rushed behind him. I could see almost all of her. Her legs were naked and her hair was stuck out. She was tugging at the ropes on her bathrobe and screaming loud at Telly.

"Going back to that hussy! What about me, Telly? What about everything you said? About coming home?" Yank, yank went the bathrobe ropes.

"I never said nothing."

"No? No?" Gloria sounded like she wasn't sure no more. "What about your son? Your son?"

"Glow! Come on, now! Calm yourself down. I'm doing everything I can. Out there every day. Doing what they tell me—"

"It's your fault. All your fault he went, you know."

"Now, Glow. I don't—"

"And she's too stupid to see it. What a waste of space you are."

Gloria went off the porch. She was in her bare feet. She picked up a rock and flung it right at Telly's head. It just missed. Telly ran and ducked. Gloria's bathrobe came undone and her stuff was hanging out. They were bouncing.

Telly jumped into his truck. "You're freaking wacko!" he yelled out the window. "Freaking crazy."

"Tell her Gloria says thanks." Another rock went in the air. "Taking your lazy ass off my hands." It smacked on the hood. Another one. The red light smashed open. "Lots of 'em way better than you."

Inside the truck I saw his head swinging around. He was trying to find his keys. A rock banged off the roof. Then the truck roared and Telly took off.

"Wow," Shar whispered. "Your mom really, really hates your dad."

I nodded, but I knew what Shar said wasn't true. Gloria didn't hate Telly at all. She loved him more than anything else in the world.

Gloria came back on the step and said real soft, "You saw a little show, Sharlene. No need to spread it to the world. A lot going on is all."

"I won't, Mrs. Janes."

"That's a good girl."

Behind Gloria, Chicken yelped and shoved his snout at the screen. It stretched out where he poked.

"He got to pee," Shar said.

When I opened the door he flew past us and rushed around to the side of the house. Me and Shar followed and caught him pawing at the ground right at the spot with the buried dead bird. I yanked his collar, but he wouldn't budge. He just kept scraping his itchy sides on the cement part of the house. Bits of his fur came off and stuck to the broken plastic vent.

Gloria came around the corner. I was glad her bathrobe was knotted up again. All her private parts were hidden away.

"What's he doing?"

Chicken was still pawing at the dead bird spot. He was barking. I could see feathers.

"Me and Rowan," I whispered. *I wish he was here. I wish he was here.* I tried not to cry. "The bird hit the window."

"Who cares about a bird," she said. She was angry again.

Gloria grabbed Chicken's collar hard. She dragged him over to the front step. Then she tied a rope around him so he couldn't go nowhere.

"I can dig it up," I said. "Make a new grave."

"That you won't. Disgusting. Would you dig up something half rotted, Shar?"

"No," Shar said. "Of course not."

"See? Even Shar's not that dense."

She told Shar to go home and me to wait with Chicken. Then she went behind the shed where Telly took a pile of big rocks when he dug up dirt for potatoes. She started carrying them over, one by one. They were dusty. Gloria wiped her hands on her bathrobe. I could see the smears down her front. She piled the rocks up real high. There was no way he was getting at the bird now.

"Common sense," Gloria yelled at me when she was finished. "Who'd bury something dead right up against the house? All we need now is that dumb dog getting sick. Or even worse, rolling in rot and stinking up the whole place. Do you think, with everything going on, I got time to clean?"

Chicken pulled at the rope and made a low growl in his throat like he was angry too. Or maybe he wanted to chew the bird down because he was starved. Maybe Gloria forgot to feed him.

Gloria turned around and stomped into the house. I went to look. I remembered how, when I asked to say something nice about the bird, Rowan said, "No one's listening." But just in case, I made some wishes. I pulled off some of Chicken's fur still stuck to the cement and blew it into the air. Dog fur was just as good as anything to wish on.

ROWAN

When I open my eyes, I can see pinpricks of yellow up above. Moonlight through the leaves. I blink, and the yellow is gone.

Carl?

Carl, are you there?

Will you let me explain?

I put my hands on the ground. I can hear him. I know he's there. Somewhere close to me. Shuffling around. Grumbling. He is fixing the neat border of stones around his firepit. I can hear Girl, too.

Carl? I know you're afraid.

I'm not a worker.

I just want to go home.

But I can't see. It's too dark.

I try to sit up. Bright shocks of pain rocket through my head, spill into my chest, my legs.

Are you listening?

There's a lady that can help you. Help us. She will, I promise. My neighbor.

She can make things better. Mrs. Spooner. She's nice. Really nice. And she's smart too.

Pain pushes me deeper and deeper.

Carl?

Are you listening?

She can fix everything.

You won't be in trouble.

Girl is barking and barking. She won't stop.

Please. Please be listening to me.

I try not to cry.

I just want to go home.

I reach out my hands, but I can't wipe away the darkness. It covers me and I gulp it down.

MAISY

Gloria was so upset about Telly she was wandering all over the house. She kept going up and down the stairs. I heard them creaking. She was talking to herself, too. "What am I going to do? What am I going to do?"

I sat up in bed and called out, "Gloria?" I hated when she was sad.

She was there in a second. "I thought you were asleep," she said.

"I woke up."

She put her hand on my forehead. "Not feeling well, I know." Then she dug around in the pocket of her bathrobe and pulled out a green bottle and a spoon. She poured out a spoonful and I opened my mouth. "This will fix your head," she said. "Vitamins and sleep medicine."

I swallowed and sneezed.

"Try not to worry. Rowan'll be home soon, darling. And Gloria's going to make everything better with Telly."

She smoothed my hair over and over and a warm feeling went in my arms and legs and up in my head.

When I woke up, it was morning and someone was knocking on our front door. They knocked and knocked but Gloria wasn't answering. I got out of bed and went downstairs. Gloria was snoring in Telly's chair. On the floor was a fork and plate with orange smears on it. I think it was from the rabbit stew Aunt Erma made.

"Gloria?"

"What's happening?" She lifted up her head. Her neck made a lot of rolls. There was greasy stuff around her mouth.

"Someone's at the door?"

"Is it Telly? Is he back?"

My chest hurt. I peeked through the glass. "No," I said. "It's Mrs. Spooner."

Gloria got up from the chair and started going upstairs. "Tell her—tell her to go away," she said in an angry way.

"I can't," I said.

"Well, just tell her whatever you want."

More knocking, and I heard the bathroom door slam. I cracked open the door. Mrs. Spooner was holding a white dish with a glass lid on top. She put the dish in my arms.

"Sorry to make such a racket, but I was certain you were home. And I—I wanted to check on you." She looked behind me, and then she got close and said, "Is everything okay, Maisy?" She still smelled like the squirt can in the bathroom.

I nodded.

"I mean, is everything all right in there?"

I didn't know what she meant. Rowan hadn't come out of his hiding spot. Gloria was sad and angry all the time. Telly told a whole lot of lies about coming home, and he was still living with that lady. "Everything's good," I said.

"Did you know I submitted Rowan's work for a contest? He wrote about a boy spending a night in the woods."

I remembered the THEIF sign. My face got hot. Those boys. It was from those boys that wouldn't let him play. Gloria was upset about that too, them being mean to Rowan.

"I just received a letter this morning saying he won second prize." She sounded cheerful, but her face looked like she stubbed her toe. "Won't that be wonderful news to share when he returns? He's such a special talent."

I nodded. I looked at my feet.

"If you need to talk. About anything at all, darling, please come see me. You know where I live, and most afternoons I'm at the library."

I got woozy in my head. My brain turned into clouds. I could hear Gloria stomping around upstairs.

"You best put that in the fridge," she said. She pointed at the food. Then Mrs. Spooner turned around and walked up the driveway. The dish in my arms got heavier and heavier, but I watched until I couldn't see her no more.

When I went inside, Gloria was coming down the stairs. She had on a polka-dot dress and her hair was combed neat. She was holding her purse.

"I just got to get out of the house, Bids. I got to do something."

I shook my head.

"And I figured, my teeth are so gritty these days, I'm going to go in and get them cleaned."

"At the dentist?" I said.

"No." She looked at herself in the mirror. "I don't got no cavities. I just need to see a hygienic person. I think that's what they're called."

"Oh," I said. I opened my mouth. My heart started going tak-tak-tak.

"Apparently there's an excellent one just across from your father's garage. Belinda's lending me her car, so I won't be late. I had no trouble getting an appointment. They don't seem very busy."

I swallowed. "Can I go to Shar's?"

"Of course you can. Erma already invited you over," she said. "You can play with Sharlene. And I don't want you twiddling your thumbs while you're there." Gloria tied a rope to Chicken's collar and then pushed open the screen door. "You can take him with you and snip the burrs out of his fur."

"Okay," I said.

"That's my good girl. Go and get changed. Erma'll give you breakfast."

I hurried and got out of my nightgown and into a sundress that was bunched up on the floor. Then Gloria walked me and Chicken over to Erma's house. Shar was already gone swimming with Darrell because no one knew I was coming, not even Erma. Erma asked if I wanted to come in, but I stayed on the front porch. Gloria walked next door and got keys from Mrs. Murtry and drove away. I watched, but she forgot to wave. Aunt Erma gave me a grape Popsicle. "It'll be okay, love," she said. "Your mom needs to clear her head."

She gave me tiny scissors to cut all the sticky burrs out of Chicken's fur. Then Aunt Erma gave me a peanut butter sandwich. I waited and waited, and I took the metal bit from Carl out of my pocket and rolled it around in my fingers.

Shar and Darrell finally came home. They were wet and smelled like pond. Shar asked if I wanted to go to her bedroom and play dolls, but I said no because she always made the boy doll wiggle on top of the girl doll to grow babies. I stayed on the step with Chicken.

After a long time, I saw Mrs. Murtry's car coming back into the circle. "She's back," I called out and Aunt Erma came to the door. She dropped her cigarette on the wood. Lines of smoke came off it. Gloria came up the stairs and Chicken wagged his tail.

"How was your drive?" Aunt Erma said.

"Good. I feel a little better."

"I'm glad to hear it."

Gloria didn't say nothing about going to get her teeth shined. Out near Telly's garage.

"I don't know, Erm," Gloria said. "Maybe it was just doing something regular? Since Rowan's been missing, I can't keep hold to anything. One minute I'm angry. One minute I'm broken in two. I don't fit in my own skin."

"Of course you don't."

"I just keep telling myself," she said. "He'll be back any second."

"And he will."

Gloria wiped her eyes. "Thank you for watching Maisy."

"Anything I can do to help. That girl's no trouble. I'd trade her for Shar in a heartbeat." Aunt Erma laughed, but it was a joking laugh, not a mean one.

We walked home. I held Chicken's rope, and Gloria put her arm on my shoulder. "You know, Bids, I learned something important these past couple of months. There's too many bad people in the world. People who'll steal from you. Want to hurt you."

My mouth turned dry.

"Ever since he took off, I've been so shaky. Sometimes I wonder if it's my fault. Sometimes I don't even think any of this is real. I miss him so much, Bids, I feel like someone tore my heart right out."

Then she stopped talking. I heard her gulp air, and I looked up. There was a small blue car in our driveway. And someone was on our front porch, sitting in Gloria's special chair. She had curly grey hair and round glasses and dark under her eyes. I never seen her before.

"What—what do you think you're doing here?"

"It was on the news, Gloria."

"What?"

"About Rowan. I saw you and Telly." Then she smiled at me. "And you must be Maisy."

I went behind Gloria.

"Well, you can turn around and go back where you came from."

The woman stood up. "Why didn't you call me?"

"Why would I?"

"Because I'm your mother?"

When she said that, I had to grab onto the back of Gloria's dress. I felt like someone cut a hole on top of my head and filled me up with cold water.

"Because I care about him, too? You don't own him."

"I damn well do own him. Until he's eighteen, that boy belongs to me."

The lady got up then. "I'm at the motel. I'll be there until Rowan is found. And I want to see him, Gloria. And spend some time with Maisy. Too much time has passed. I should be allowed to do that."

Then she got into her little blue car and drove away. Gloria unlocked the front door with a key.

"Was that Gran?" I whispered.

"It don't matter, Maisy."

"But I thought Gran was dead."

"Dead to me. That's all I ever said about her. She's dead to me."

Then Gloria went inside. I stayed out on the front step. I looked at Gloria's chair where the dead-to-me Gran was sitting. I had a bad feeling in my middle, but I didn't know what it was. It just sat on top of all the other bad feelings. I remember when the school nurse told me to think it was butterflies in there when my middle hurt. But butterflies were too pretty to live in the dark. I think there were spiders and ants and potato bugs and huge centipedes with thousands of feet down there. Nothing I did made them crawl away.

MAISY

The sky turned pink and orange. Some crickets started scritching their legs. Through the open window I could hear Gloria in the kitchen. I went down the steps into the yard and turned to watch the woods. I closed my eyes and counted to ten and I opened them. Still no Rowan. I stayed there and kept trying to give him chances to jump out and surprise me. But he didn't. That game never worked.

A car came straight down the circle to our driveway. Not a little blue car, a black one with blue and red lights flashing, but the siren wasn't going. I knew those lights meant something terrible. It looked like the noisiest thing ever, even though it didn't make no sound at all.

Gloria came outside. She must've heard the car doors slam. The lady with the pictures, Susan, and the man with the funny ties were already on the step. He wasn't wearing a tie this time. I didn't like that.

I went up behind them.

"Mrs. Janes," he said. He nodded his head.

"Hi Maisy," Susan said. I looked at my feet. I didn't want to say nothing to her. I wanted them to get back in the car with the star on the side and disappear. "Detective Aiken wants to talk with your mom. Do you want to show me some of your toys?"

"No, she does not," Gloria said.

"Susan is here to help, Mrs. Janes. I'd suggest that Maisy—"

"My daughter'll be staying right here beside her mother."

Susan smiled at me, but it was a sad-smile. Maybe a bit of a mad-smile.

The man and Susan sat on two old stools on the porch. Gloria sat in her special chair. She was playing with her fingers like she always told me not to do.

The man took a big breath. Maybe he was trying to get calm. He looked behind him. "Should we wait for your husband?"

Gloria shook her head. "You talked to him?"

"We were in touch. Asked him to meet us."

Gloria moved back and forth. She tapped her fingernails on the rocking chair arm. "If he don't care enough to get over here, then I don't want to wait."

"Okay. Okay." The man looked at Gloria. Then at the Susan lady. Then back at Gloria. "Mrs. Janes. We have news."

Her fingers stopped tapping. She reached at me and I inch-wormed closer. She grabbed the back of my dress so tight the buttons pulled apart on the front. My bellybutton was peeking out. The man looked at me like I should find another chair way away somewhere. But Gloria wasn't letting me go.

"News? What sort of news?"

Please good news, I whispered inside my head. I looked at the car. *Please good news*. I wanted Rowan to leap out the back. Jumping-jack arms. Oh! A big surprise. Gloria would be happy again. Chicken would bark and spin in a circle. Rowan would tease him with food and make him dance on his hind legs. We'd have a welcome-home party. Gloria would forget he ever disappeared. We'd forget he made us cry and cry.

Nothing happened. The doors didn't open. The trunk didn't pop up. No one crawled out from the shadow underneath. I leaned as far as I could. No one was hiding behind the car neither. The man rubbed his face up and down with his big hand.

"Not the news we'd hoped for, unfortunately. We're very sorry. We wanted you to hear from us first."

Gloria shook her head again. "I don't understand."

"We've been with Howard Gill nearly around the clock. He finally opened up and decided to do the right thing. Told us what happened. Out at Ansel's Lake."

"Ansel's Lake? But that's miles from here. Rowan's never been to Ansel's Lake."

The man scritched his chin. "They made their way out there. It's about four or five hours of walking. Apparently, Gill used to go there as a child. Parents owned one of those cottages near the water, and they broke into it. We've connected with the current owners." He flipped open his notebook. "Mr. Bert Baxter. They were away but returned once they heard. Gave us access. Howard Gill and your son were there for two nights, as far as we can tell. The interior sustained some damage."

"What does any of that got to do with where Rowan is now?"

"Well. Mrs. Janes. Howard Gill says they fought, that the blood on his shirt is your son's. He told us he believed Rowan wasn't who he said he was. That Rowan was sent to put a tracker in him. Rowan was dangerous, and Howard Gill was afraid. He's a deeply paranoid man."

"Why are you telling me? A grown man, scared of a boy."

"You'll read it in the news coverage, ma'am. I think it's better if you hear it from us first. We've laid charges against Howard Gill."

"What're you talking about?"

"Ma'am. We've charged him with the death of your son."

The words made my ears sting. Stars zoomed around all over.

Gloria let go of my dress and I crouched down. Her hand went on her nose and she squished it in. "What? What? That's not true. I don't want to hear any more. That's nonsense. Rowan is just fine. Telly's going to come here, and we'll get this straightened. He's got to come around." She stood up and I knew she was looking out at the circle for Telly's truck. "He's just got to fix this."

"We have divers out there as we speak, Mrs. Janes. Searching the lake. We'll do everything we can to bring him home to you."

"Bring him home? Bring him home?" Gloria started walking back and forth over the porch. The wood creaked under her feet. "I won't believe it," she said. "I won't believe one word. It's not true. This is just a waste of time."

"He's been very specific in his account, ma'am. Provided a lot of details. We have a witness who confirms he interacted with Rowan. Spoke to him on the dock. Your boy was fishing."

"I mean. Well, that could've been anyone."

"He identified him from his picture, ma'am."

"That still don't mean nothing, Detective. Lots of people look like Rowan."

"Mrs. Janes. We feel confident his memory is accurate. The man, Mr. Jim Russell, said he was immediately suspicious about Rowan. Had a feeling something was off. When he asked him about his father, Rowan told Mr. Russell his dad was a friend of Mrs. Baxter's."

"His dad?"

"We assume he was referring to Howard Gill."

Gloria's head was shaking fast. "That's the lowest thing I ever heard. Of course that's not his father. Of course it's not. I never even met the man."

"It goes to show," Susan said, "that Howard Gill had a considerable controlling influence over Rowan."

"It's going to break Telly's heart to hear that. Just break it."

"Mrs. Janes? There's more. Jim Russell's wife saw two people out in a boat, late that night, just as Howard Gill described. Full moon and all, and she had a clear view. She maintains she heard an altercation. Voices carried over the water. A man was hollering, and she saw two people standing up. Later she claims to have seen the man tying up a boat on his own. A dog was with him, but no one else. Appeared he rowed back by himself."

Susan's mouth was a straight white line.

"Well, why wouldn't someone call that in?"

"Not everyone has phone service around the lake. Maybe she didn't want to get involved. Or maybe she explained it away. Didn't believe her own eyes. People see all kinds of things, ma'am, but just don't think it's worth reporting. And most often they're right." He coughed. "Her husband stopped over in the morning, but no one was there."

The porch was creaking and creaking as she walked.

"This is not the news we wanted to bring you. It truly isn't. Our team of officers has worked very hard. They're distraught over what's happened. They send their condolences, Mrs. Janes. We're very sorry."

"Very, very sorry," Susan said. She held her hands tight. The toes on her shiny shoes were touching each other.

"That man's demented. You can't trust what he says. Things'll be okay. Telly's coming. Everything'll be okay."

"Ma'am, I know this is so hard to accept. He's confessed. Signed a statement. Our officers found a T-shirt at the bottom of a rowboat. There was an image of a donkey on it, consistent with Maisy's description, and it appeared to be bloodied. We're confident the T-shirt is Rowan's. And there was blood and hair on the oar, Mrs. Janes." He rubbed his face again. "We're searching now. Got the best divers out there, I guarantee it."

"So they had a fight. Rowan would've taken off."

"Ma'am."

"Have you checked the bus stations? Is his photo up by the trains? He's run away. I know it. He might've been with that man, but he didn't stay. He's run away. He could be who knows where by now. Far away from Little Sliding. We need to make the search bigger, not turn it into nothing. He didn't drown. That's not what happened. If you don't keep looking, you're not going to find him. You need to search. Telly will say the same thing. You're not taking this seriously and he's just getting further and fur—"

"Ma'am!" He squished his eyes like he had a headache. "We're taking this very seriously, Mrs. Janes. It's not the news we wanted to bring, but we're confident we're on the right path here. Ansel's Lake is a large body of water. We want you to know we won't give up searching. Trying to recover your son."

Then Telly's truck growled and crunched down the driveway. Rocks popped out under his wheels. I could see the busted red light. He jumped out and ran up onto the porch. "What's going on?" he said. He lifted his hat straight up and pulled it back on. It was the same one with the car on it.

"Oh, Telly. Where've you been?"

"Dealing with Dian," he said. "She's had— Well, she hasn't had a good day." He looked hard at Gloria.

"How unfortunate," Gloria said. "But that, that, whatever you call that woman, and what type of day she had should be the last thing on your mind."

"Why? What's happened?"

The man stood up. "Do you want us to—to share things with your husband?"

"No, no. I should tell him. I'll, I'll try."

"What's happened? Glow?"

"They got this terrible idea. But trust me, you won't believe a word of it." Then everything fell out of Gloria's mouth. A huge splat. All the same words that the man without the tie said.

"Jesus." Telly's mouth was wide open now. I could see his new white teeth. "For the love of Jesus."

"It's not true, Telly. We can't stop waiting for him to come back. I promised Maisy. We're going to be a family. Rowan'll come home and we'll be a family again." She grabbed at his arm. "We can't stop searching for our boy. Far and wide, Telly. The police looked at this Carl person, but they never looked nowhere else. We got to stay together on this!"

Telly didn't seem to hear her at all. He rubbed at his face and paced around. Then he pulled his fist back and was going to punch the side of the house. He stopped a tiny bit from the wood. I jumped. He said swear words.

"Mr. Janes," Susan said. "Sir. You need to keep a cool head. Please. I understand your shock and your rage, but your daughter is right here."

She squatted down next to me and touched my shoulder. I twisted away.

"What's going to happen to that bastard? Hey? What's going to happen?" Telly bounced up and down.

"You've got my word. Howard Gill will remain in custody."

"Jesus," Telly said again. "None of this makes no sense to me. What was Row following him for? What put that in his head?"

"He's a teenager, Telly. Acting out. Got no sense of what's dangerous." Gloria shut her eyes. "He needs his father around. We all do."

"He came to the garage. Remember I said, Glow? Wanting to talk to me. But I never—I never. I never gave him no time. Just got rid of him."

"Mr. Janes. No one can predict—"

"Why'd I do that? Why didn't I show him I cared? I loved him, I did. I loved him so, so much. And I didn't do nothing." He was shaking hard all over. Gloria hugged him. "Just too worried about my own shit. That's all I was. Thinking my own shit mattered."

"Oh, Telly," she said. "Oh, Telly. Sit down. Sit down for a minute. I'll get you a drink. We can't give up. We can't. I just don't believe it. I won't."

He took Gloria's special chair. His greasy hands were on his knees. "Glow. C'mon. Listen to yourself. They got his statement. No matter what's going through a man's head, no way he'd lie about killing a child."

Then he started crying. I never seen Telly cry before. His mouth was open and sounds popped out, like old towels getting ripped up. It made my heart go super fast.

Gloria got down in front of him. She put her head in his lap. He patted her hair. Her back was twitching. "Now, now," he said. "We'll get through this. We will. We'll see each other through, Glow."

The man's voice was cotton-ball soft. "We're going to go, Mrs. Janes. Give you all some privacy. I'm certain Channel 2 or Channel 6, once they get wind of what happened, will be trying to get another interview. You're under no obligation to talk to them. Or anyone else, for that matter. Absolutely none. It's your choice."

The man and Susan went down the steps and got in the car. When they drove out of the circle they never turned their lights back on.

"I want you home, Telly. I need you home."

Telly wiped his face hard. "You hear yourself? Is that all you think about?"

"You need to be here, we've got to make a plan."

"He's gone. Gloria. The boy can't swim a single stroke. I—I never taught him." More towels ripping.

"I can't get through this without you."

Telly stood up and bumped Gloria back. "I need to see Dian."

"What? All you got to see is right here. Your wife and your daughter."

"Is that what you got on your mind? Really? Really? Right now? Destroying what's left of my life?"

"I never—"

"Our son is gone, our son is drowned, and you're going to get your goddamned teeth cleaned and telling her all kinds of shit?"

My heart was tak-takking like crazy.

"Telly. I told her what happened. That's all. Listen to me."

"No, I'm not listening to nothing."

"I'm sorry, Telly." She grabbed him. "I'm sorry. Please. I wasn't thinking. I'm not thinking straight. Please, Telly. I'm not."

"I got to go, Glow. I can't, I can't even look at your face right now."

Telly kissed my forehead and said "I love you, Bids," and then he walked away.

"You can't leave," she called out. "I won't let you!"

But he started his truck.

Then she screamed, "She didn't believe me. I told her the truth and that bitch didn't even believe what I said!"

When Telly was driving away I ran around to the side of the house. Chicken was there in the shade. Sniffing and pawing at Gloria's pile of stones on top of the dead bird because she forgot to feed him again. I took the good-luck ball of metal out of my pocket and threw the tiny thing into the pile. Carl lied. Something terrible had happened even though I didn't lose it.

Then I put my face in Chicken's warm fur. Rowan was gone. My brother was gone. I pushed my face into his ribs and I cried and cried. Where was Rowan now? Where was his laugh? And all his ideas and his secrets? What about his skin? The map of islands never got finished. But maybe those white patches weren't islands at all. Maybe he was gone because all his white spots got huge and turned him into a ghost. A beautiful speckly dead ghost.

ROWAN

I roll onto my side, knees bent to my chest. Pull my hands inside the sweater Carl gave me to wear. He made me shoes too. That fit my feet perfectly. He cares. He cared?

Carl?

I need to go home now. Everyone is waiting for me. Expecting me.

"He's a most wonderful boy. He's such a good big brother."

Gloria said that. She misses me.

Don't you remember?

Behind my back, the creek is trickling. A sharp stink of pine needles and turpentine stings my nostrils. Makes me retch.

Are you there?

Can you hear me?

I put my hands on the ground. On the wall of the bridge? Everything is shifting. Am I lying down? Leaning against the bridge? There is nothing to hold. Which way is up?

Carl?

Listen to me. Please.

My head pounds.

Maisy was sad. You saw her too, didn't you? That's my sister. That's Little Fawn.

Telly was holding her hand.

And Gloria was crying. She was crying on TV.

Carl?

Even in the blackness, I know I am alone. I pull the sweater over my bent knees.

Listen! Listen to me!

I want to go home!

No one answers.

I lie still. I am sliding.

MAISY

After the bad fight with Telly, Gloria stayed in bed for a long time. Her hair got shiny and there were crumbs on the blanket. Tiny black ants crawled around. Gloria smacked at them, but most times she let them crawl. Mrs. Spooner and Mrs. Murtry knocked on the door, but Gloria wouldn't get up. Everyone said they were real sad about Rowan, but Gloria told me she didn't want anyone in the house. Sticking their nose in where it didn't belong.

Lots of days went by and then Gloria got a phone call from work. When she hung up she said, "Two girls are off sick. They can't manage without me."

"Do you got to go?" I said.

She did a sigh. "I don't have to. But it'll be good for my head, Bids. To get out of here for a few hours."

She made me go over to Aunt Erma's. It wasn't that bad. Me and Shar watched a movie and played games. It stank, though, because Aunt Erma smoked tons of cigarettes. When she dropped them in a can with a sip of soda in the bottom, they sizzled up. After lunch she heated up cookies for us. I liked them even if they tasted a little bit like cigarette smell.

Shar was winning checkers, and she said, "I can't believe your brother was murdered. Drowned in the lake." I didn't say nothing back. Even though Shar was my best friend, sometimes I didn't like her very much.

"Why don't we go and find him?"

"What?"

"We'll go at night so no one'll catch us," she said. "We could steal a boat and row out and take turns diving down with a flashlight."

I shook my head.

"You don't want to find your own brother? What a scaredy baby."

Then Darrell's door opened. He told Shar to shut up. "That's a stupid idea," he said. "And kind of shitty to even say, Shar."

I wanted to push against Darrell. I wanted to hug him and put my face on his shirt and tell him how good he was.

After she was done work Gloria came and got me, and we walked home. I told her I had fun and I tried to forget what Shar said. But that night it went into my dreams. Me and Shar and Darrell went out to the middle of a big circle of black shiny water, and I dove down first. The flashlight in my hands gave out because water got in, and I knocked it, but it didn't get fixed. I was afraid, but I touched around in the dark and I heard Rowan clear as day telling me, "I'm here, Turtle. I'm right here. Under your nose. Come find me."

I found him, too, with my fingers. I found his hair. Then his neck. Then his arms. But when I tried to yank, handfuls of him came off and I could feel it floating past me, touching me. "Don't give up," he yelled. "I'm here, Turtle!"

Then I woke up crying and choking on pretend water. Gloria rushed in. She gave me an extra spoonful of green medicine because she said it was hard to tell when I might catch a cough.

I didn't dream no more after I swallowed that.

"Just stay in the backyard," Aunt Erma said the next day. "Okay, girls? I'm having the carpets shampooed. And I can't have you tracking in dirt." Then she smiled at me. "I don't mean you, Maisy, sweetheart. I know you'd never do that."

Aunt Erma closed the back door and I heard the roar of a cleaning machine.

"*Not you, sweetheart*," Shar said in a mean way. "*You'd never do that*."

I went over to the sandbox with the fallen-down sides and started digging with a plastic shovel. Gloria was gone to work again. I asked her not to work as long as yesterday but she said it wasn't up to her. "Besides, they're not pushing me. The girls are being real supportive. It helps screw my head on right." I dug some more. I tried to make a castle with the sand, but it kept rolling down the sides.

"I saw Mrs. Spooner's cats poo in there," Shar said.

"Oh," I said, and I put down the shovel.

"It's so lame out here." Shar twisted around.

I picked up a tangled-up rope from the ground. "We could do a skipping contest."

"Hardly. I'm too old for that." Then Shar was flapping her hands all over the place. "I know what we can do," she said. "Let's go see the spot. The exact spot where Rowan was grabbed."

"He wasn't grabbed," I said.

"How d'you know?"

I didn't know. "We're not allowed in there anyway."

"Yeah? Says who?"

"Aunt Erma. She told us to stay in the yard."

"Well my mother said Aunt Erma's not the boss of me, and I shouldn't forget it."

"Well, I don't know how to get there." I'd only ever gone that far in the woods with Rowan.

"I do. Me and Darrell went a bunch of times."

"Really?"

"No, not really. But so what?"

My heart was thumping. "I don't want to go. I want to skip."

"You're just a scaredy cat, scaredy cat." She was singing.

"Am not scared."

"Is too."

"Am not."

"Well I'm going."

Shar opened up the gate and she was stomping down the circle to my house without even looking back. I went behind her, and she kept going down our driveway and across our grass. "Wait up," I said.

"You hurry up."

On the ground, I saw some old squished-up sandwiches with bugs on them. Me and Shar had long skinny shadows. Mine was longer and skinnier than Shar's because Shar's mouth was always full of junk and trash. That was what Gloria said.

I tried not to think about it because Shar was going extra fast. Her broken shoe was flopping. Then she disappeared behind some bushes, and

I ran to catch up. Inside the woods things were humming and buzzing and croaking. Twigs cracked under Shar's big sloppy feet. She was way up ahead. I didn't like being in the woods without Rowan. Everything was trampled down. I kept hurrying, but I couldn't see Shar no more.

"I'm going back!" I yelled.

Then her head popped out from behind a tree. "Scaredy cat!" she yelled back. She called me that a lot.

She stopped and waited. When I got where she was I saw the ground was kicked up and strings of soft green moss were yanked off the trees. Someone had ripped new leaves right from the branches and thrown them down. Maybe it was the searchers looking for Rowan, or some strangers just messing up the woods.

"I bet the bad guy did this," Shar said real loud. She sounded like that helicopter. "What if murderers are still in here?"

"In the woods? I don't think so."

"There could be, Maisy. You don't know everything. A whole bunch of them might be watching us right now."

Me and Shar walked together then. Shar kept slapping my back or my cheek or my arm saying there was a fly on me. I wondered how she saw flies because it was getting harder and harder to see anything. The trees were going gray and fuzzy. And finally we got to the bridge. "Found it," Shar said, like the bridge was something lost. I heard the creek trickling along near us. It was giggling. That sound made me mad. The creek should've shut itself up.

"Come on," Shar said, and she stomped through the bushes.

"Wait," I said, and then gravel crunched behind me. There was a loud crack. A branch whizzed through the air and shook. My heart tried to burst out of my throat and I ran behind Shar. Branches scritched at my legs.

"I heard something."

"What?"

"I don't know. I think it was . . ." *A wolf. I think it was a wolf.*

I couldn't tell Shar that. She'd just laugh.

"The bad guy?"

"I want to go home," I said. It was darker under the bridge than when I came with Rowan. It smelled like pee and there was garbage all over. It wasn't like that when Carl was there.

Shar picked up a stone and threw it in the creek. A frog hopped off a rock and swam underneath some bubbly green scum.

"Do you think he kidnapped him when he was sleeping?"

"No," I said. I was too filled up with sadness to tell Shar anything. *Have a seat in one of these fine chairs, Little Fawn.* It was forever ago when Carl said that.

I saw something shiny and I went over to the burnt-out fire, and there was a big triangle of tinfoil. Just like the one in our backyard. I picked it up.

"What's that?"

"Nothing," I said.

But Shar snatched it out of my hand. "It's a hat." She opened it up and put it on her head. "Who'd make a dumb pirate hat in the woods?" She crumbled it up and threw it into the creek.

It floated for a second and then it went under the water. I wondered if the triangle I found in my backyard was a pirate hat too.

Another branch broke and me and Shar both jumped.

"Maisy," she said in a shivery way. "I'm afraid."

Shar didn't look afraid. She looked excited. The same face she got when she stole stuff. Like the time she found one of those glass machines with a twist knob that gave out candy. It wasn't working and didn't need money and she twisted like mad. She filled up her cheeks and her pockets and the inside of her tucked-in top until candy was dropping out the bottoms of her jeans.

"What if he leaps out and stabs us in the guts?"

"Who leaps out?"

"That man who lives under here."

"He don't live here no more," I said. "The police took him." The police grabbed Carl.

Shar's mouth was hanging open and she was breathing loud. "But what if, Maisy?"

"Carl wouldn't stab us," I said with my teeth locked up. "Carl's nice."

"Nice, she says." Shar started yelling and the sound bounced all around under the bridge. "The bum that drowned my brother is really nice!"

"I didn't say that."

I wanted to cry. I couldn't do that in front of Shar, and I wished she was gone. I wished her dog would find a hole in her backyard and escape under her fence and sniff her out and come chomp right down on her squishy fat. Like he did with those poor rabbits.

When we got out of the woods it was almost dark. Gloria was racing across the grass at us, her yellow hair was standing up. "Maisy! Where did you go? I was calling you! I've been frantic."

"I didn't mean—"

"And you!" Gloria pointed a finger right in Shar's face. "You get yourself home, miss. Erma's gone wild looking for you."

Shar's eyes went big and round and she took off up the driveway like her backside was on fire.

Gloria squeezed my arms. "Are you trying to drive me completely bonkers, Maisy Janes? I get back from work and you've vanished. You know what happened in there. You think because they got that man in jail it's safe to trot around? Well, it isn't. What if there's another one of him? Did you think of that? Or a hundred? Like animals. Like wolves."

I shook my head fast. And swallowed. The crying was still right behind my eyes wanting to explode out.

"Why'd you go in there?"

"Following Shar," I said. I didn't say nothing about the woods or the bridge or the tinfoil hat.

"Last thing I'd be doing is following a twit like Shar."

"I didn't mean to."

"I can't take much more worry," she said. "I'm nearly gone inside."

"I'm sorry, I'm sorry." Tears poured out of my eyes, and she held my wrist and marched me across the grass. When we got inside she told me to sit in a chair and not budge an inch. She even called Telly on the phone.

"Yes, it's me again. Don't you even care where your daughter's been?"

MAISY

The next morning Gloria told me to put on the blue dress I wore when I was on TV. Telly was going to come and get me. "He's taking you out somewhere," she said. "To talk some sense into you." I brushed my teeth and my hair and I went downstairs. Gloria was coming up from the basement. "Hurry up. He'll be here any minute," and she dropped a zipped-up bag by my feet. It sounded like rocks were inside. "You can tell him that's the last of them. Seeing as he cares so much."

"About what?"

"His guns. Now he got no reason to step foot in my house." She pinched my chin and leaned down close. "And did you know? Gloria wants to tell you something. I'm going to do up a surprise down there. Make our basement into an amazing spot when it's finished."

"Really?" I smiled as hard as I could.

"After all we've been through, miss, you bet I'm doing something special. I've got big plans."

I hugged Gloria tight as I could. Then I put on my shoes and picked up the heavy bag and walked to the bottom of the circle. Gloria told me to stand there because she didn't even want Telly coming down her driveway. When I turned around I could see her face in the kitchen window. She was frowning. The truck came, all shiny, and Telly got out. He ran around and opened the other door for me and I climbed in and dragged the bag up on the seat.

When he got back in he said, "What you got there, Miss Maisy?"

"Guns," I said.

"Jesus."

"Gloria said you don't need to set foot inside her house now."

He lifted the bag up by the handles and tucked it behind his seat. "She did, did she? *Her* house."

I sipped at the air. "I don't know. Maybe not. I don't think." It smelled clean in there. A cardboard lemon swung from the mirror.

"Never you mind, Bids. That's between me and your mother. She shouldn't be giving you my guns, is all."

"They weren't very heavy," I said.

Telly drove the truck around and when we came out of the circle he stopped where a lady was standing on the side of the road. She was wearing a frilly dress the color of peaches and the wind lifted it up. Telly got out and the lady slid under the steering wheel and went in the middle.

"Hello, Maisy," she said. "My name's Dian. I'm your dad's friend."

"Don't be shy," Telly said as we drove away.

"Hi," I whispered.

She was in the same spot where Gloria sat that time Telly drove us home from the police place. But she didn't put her hands all inside Telly's clothes like Gloria did.

"Do you want to have brunch?"

I shook my head. I never had a brunch before.

"It's kind of like breakfast and lunch mixed together. You can choose lunch things, you know, burgers or fried chicken or a grilled cheese, or you can have breakfast. Waffles. Sausages. Or both of it together, if that's what you want." Her hands were in her lap now. "It's okay. You don't need to say anything. We're going to have a nice time."

My mouth filled up with spit. I knew that lady was trying to trick me. She was pretending to be nice.

We went to a spot called Barney's Diner. It had red booths and plastic tables and the floor was a black-and-white checkerboard. Telly said, "Go on, Bids. Whatever you want."

A lady in an apron was beside my shoulder with a pencil and notepad. I pointed to the picture of blueberry pancakes and sausages on my placemat. "And that," I said. "Strawberry milkshake."

When the food came, I knew Telly's friend was reading my mind. "Don't worry," she said soft. "If you can't finish it all. I never manage."

The milkshake was good. The pancakes were really good. I burst some of the blueberries between my teeth.

"Yum, hey?" Telly said. He smiled. His teeth were so dazzly. I could see why his friend liked him so much, even though he looked like a stranger to me.

I nodded. "Yum."

"We're going to do this regular, Maise. I promise. You, me, and Dian."

"No reason we shouldn't," she said.

Then his face went red. "I just wish we could have your brother here, too. I wish that. More than anything." His eyes turned watery and he put his fists in them. "Damn," he said and stood up. Then he went to the back of the diner.

"Oh," Dian said. "Your dad's so distraught. I don't know how he's keeping it all together." Then she touched my hand. "And you, Maisy? Are you doing okay? It's such an impossible thing you're all going through. With your brother."

Maybe it was because my stomach was full of warm br-lunch. Or because when she smiled her eyes looked sad. Or because her peachy dress was so pretty. I told her how sweet the milkshake was. And about Gloria sleeping all day when she wasn't at work. I told her about the dead bird me and Rowan buried. And that Shar was my best friend and she said she could swim down and find Rowan. And I told her how much I missed trying to figure out his skin map. And that I kept a little picture of Rowan under my pillow. And how Jenny the Head didn't have a body for her heart, and I kept losing her. And that there were wolves in the woods behind our house. And how Gloria thought Mrs. Spooner watched our house, and her cats used Shar's broken-down sandbox as a litter box. And that I didn't want them to find Rowan in the water because then he could never come home. I was going to tell her about Rowan standing out in the bad storm, but I stopped. Instead I told her about Shar's cousin, Darrell. How he was tall and had an earring and a leather bracelet and a motorcycle and how he told Shar to shut up because she was stupid. The lady giggled a little bit. I knew I said too much about Darrell. I said too much to Dian.

Dian wasn't listening to me no more. She was looking at a man standing next to Telly, who had got back in his seat.

"Tony here's a volunteer fireman," Telly said to her. "I fixed up his car."

"You sure did," he said. He had on a ball cap. It was the same red as the one Rowan always wore. "Gave me a great price, too."

"Just trying to do good," Telly said. The lady bent her head over. She smiled at him.

"I'm sorry, man, about your boy."

Telly took a deep breath. "Yeah, they got that bastard locked up. An institution a hundred miles north. Got to evaluate him, they're saying."

"Figures. Taxpayers' money, when that type should just be taken out and shot."

"Yeah."

"Do society a favor. No loss there."

"That's for sure." Then Telly said to Dian, "Tony's involved with the dive."

"Oh my," she said back. She shook her head.

"Just heading back out there now."

"What's going on?" Telly said. "Can't get a straight answer out of anyone. Why haven't they found him yet?"

The man tapped his hat. "The team's doing their best. I can tell you that, but it's a real mess underwater. Lot of trash down there."

"Trash?"

"Years of people dumping everything under the sun. It piles up. Won't decay."

"Terrible," Dian said.

"Plus, the sediment. Even as careful as we are, once it gets disturbed, it's nearly impossible to see. That lake is sixty-plus feet deep in places."

"Jesus," said Telly.

"And the witness. She's hazy on where she even saw the boat. She couldn't position it in relation to any landmarks, just never took notice. We can't triangulate."

"What do you mean?"

"You know, use some other markers to get a better idea. She just said she saw them out a ways. Wasn't very specific."

Telly rubbed at his face. His eyes went pink again. "What can we expect, Tony? I just want to bring him home, you know? It don't seem right. Not being able to—you know."

The man looked at me then, and they both took a step away. The man talked quiet, but I could still hear.

"Most likely, he'll surface. Could be days, could be weeks. I don't know a delicate way to frame it."

"Just say it, Tony. I'm okay." Telly didn't look okay.

"There are instances on record where the individual never floats up." He put his hand on Telly's shoulder. "You got to be prepared for that."

When I got home, Gloria called me into the kitchen. She was sitting at the table and she had a different dress on. I didn't tell her it looked the exact same as the dress Dian was wearing at br-lunch. The same sweet peachy color. The same little flowers.

Instead I said, "It's nice."

"Nice? Can't you think of anything better to say?"

I looked down.

"Well, I deserve it. Belinda loaned me her car today. I went for a stroll along Faye Street. No reason I can't shop in those snooty little stores. Like everyone else."

"Faye Street? I was there, too."

"I know," Gloria said. "Barney's Diner. You and Telly and that other thing were sitting up front by the big window. Did you know your dad used to take me there? That man has no imagination."

With her foot she pushed out a chair. Then she patted the seat.

"Now, tell me everything. What did she eat?"

I frowned.

"Something greasy, I bet."

"I don't know."

"What do you mean, you don't know? I saw you sitting right across from her."

"Kind of."

"Do you think she's pretty, Bids?"

I shook my head.

"Tell the truth."

I could feel the woodpecker stepping up. His claw dug into my neck and stung my throat. "Not one bit." When I said that, all the food got hard in my middle.

"Gloria's girl." She got closer. "Did she talk to you?"

"A little," I said.

"Did you talk back?"

"No." I looked at Gloria's hair. There was a little line of brown growing behind the yellow again. "I had to eat my food."

"Did he ask about me?"

I nodded.

"What'd you say?"

"I said you were good."

She went back like someone pushed her hard. "Good? You said good? My husband took off and my son is out there somewhere, and they can't even find him, and I'm good?"

I blinked. The kitchen went full of shadows.

"I don't know," I whispered.

"Did you say something else?"

I swallowed. "I said you cried a lot about Rowan."

"Mm." Her mouth closed up. "That's the truth."

"And that you were being a real good mom."

"He asked that?"

"No. I said it. And that I was happy staying with you."

"Tell me." She puffed out a lot of air. "Tell me that man did not ask you that."

My face got hot.

"He did, I know by your look. That bastard asked if you were happy with me. Tell me again, Bids, exactly what he said. Word for word."

Her hands were spread out on the table. She was real close to me. I put my fingertips on my neck to keep the woodpecker from bursting out through my skin. Then I told her and told her the story of br-lunch. Until I got it exactly right.

MAISY

A couple of nights later Aunt Erma and Darrell came over to help Gloria with an outside fire. Shar wasn't allowed because she was still in trouble. Gloria was burning cardboard and a bunch of magazines and old baskets from the shed. Darrell used a hammer to take apart old boxes Telly made. One box had wheels. Darrell tossed the wood in the fire. Sparks went up into the sky. He threw the wheels in too. I watched the rubber bubble and melt.

"You been such a help, Darrell," Gloria said. "I wouldn't even know how to get it started."

"It's easy," he said and laughed. "And it sure gets rid of stuff fast."

"That it does," Gloria said. She picked up some dirty rope and put it on top of the fire. Then she put in a mat that used to say "Welcome."

I crouched where there was no smoke, and stuck a stick into the flames.

"This is good for you. Cleaning out your house. Taking a few shifts at Stafford's." Aunt Erma put her arm around Gloria. "It's not too much for you, is it? They're not expecting too much too soon?"

Gloria twisted and Aunt Erma's arm dropped away. "You know, Telly's wanted to clear out the shed for years. One less thing for him to do."

"Really? If I was you, I'd be tossing his crap right in the middle of it. Whatever he left behind."

Gloria frowned. "Why would I do that?"

"'Cause he took off? 'Cause he's out there messing around? 'Cause it might make you feel the tiniest bit better?"

"He's coming back."

I stopped poking the fire with my stick.

"Since when?" Aunt Erma said.

"I ran into him this morning getting a few groceries. You know, it's funny, I don't usually go all the way out there. But Belinda was nice enough to lend me her car, and—and before I went to work, I just felt like going somewhere different."

"You saw him, what, buying milk?"

"I know. Telly's never been in a supermarket in his life."

"Was *she* there?"

"Oh, she was. Trying to keep him on a short leash, I'll tell you that. And he didn't even look at her, Erm, when he talked to me. Not one glimpse. I could tell he's getting tired of her. Trying to be whatever she thinks he should be. It's just not Telly. He's getting worn out with it. I'm expecting a call any day."

"Well, it'd be good to have him back, wouldn't it? You two need to grieve together. I mean, my heart's broken for both of you."

The fire was starting to get small when a car crunched down the driveway. It stopped in front of our house. The porch light was on and I could see the star on the door. I stood. My heart went up in my neck.

The glow came on inside the car. There were two people inside. One got out. It was the man with the funny ties, but it was too dark to see what one he was wearing.

Gloria went over. "Detective Aiken? Did something happen?"

"Rowan." I whispered it out loud by accident. Darrell must've heard me. He reached down and he held my hand. My cheeks got hot.

"I don't want you to be alarmed, ma'am." The man shook his head. "This is not pertaining to Rowan."

"Well, what is it then?"

"Mrs. Janes." He wiped his nose. "We've had a complaint. Normally I'd have one of my officers handle this sort of issue, but I thought to drop by myself. Sort this out."

"Complaint? Sort out what?"

"Your ex-husband has some concerns."

Gloria did a snort. "I don't have an ex-husband, Detective. I have a husband. He just don't live here right now."

"Well, your estranged husband."

Aunt Erma took some steps closer to Gloria, but Gloria waved her hand and Aunt Erma stopped. "What's Telly been saying?"

"That you're harassing him. And harassing his lady friend."

"His laaay-dy friend." She made a little laugh. "That's what he's calling it?"

The man frowned and he took a notebook from his pocket. He opened it up. "Seems you've been calling his work nonstop. Owner had to go through the expense of having his number changed. And frequently trespassing at his place of employment. Leaving threatening notes in and on his truck. Threatening messages under the windshield wipers of his girlfriend's car, and engaging the dental services of his girlfriend pretending to be a customer in order to make slanderous statements. Making slanderous statements to his friends. Making slanderous statements to customers as they approach the business. Following them while they run errands or have lunch." He looked up from his notebook. "Do you want me to go on?"

Gloria shook her head. "I got no idea what you're talking about."

"None of this sounds familiar?"

"No, sir. Not one bit. You know what my day is? Worrying to death over my son, spending too much time at my own work, and trying to look after my daughter. If that witch said all that, she needs her head examined. She's jealous whenever Telly and I have a moment. And believe me, we've had plenty. Maybe you should get that Susan lady to talk to her."

The man scritched his head with the top of his pen. "Mrs. Janes, I know you're going through a whole lot right now, and I'm here as a courtesy. But you need to know, if you're engaged in any of these activities I mentioned, that *is* harassment. There are laws against it. You need to leave them alone."

Gloria looked at him for a long time. Then she said, "I'm not doing nothing, Detective Aiken. I barely got time to get milk."

He turned around and opened his car door. Before he got in he said, "I'd suggest you put that fire out. Wind's picking up."

Then they drove away. Darrell let go of my hand. He got the hose and squirted water in the middle of the fire. It made a sissing sound. "Come on, Darrell," Aunt Erma said. "We best get on home." Gloria went over to the fire and crouched down. She picked up a handful of wet ashes and squeezed them hard. Drops of dirty water dripped out of her fist.

MAISY

On the weekend the man came back. He and the same policeman got out of the car with the star on the side, and Gloria rushed out through our happy, happy yellow door.

"Not more complaints! I haven't even left—"

"No, ma'am," the man said. Today his tie was just black. "We've come to give you an update on the recovery efforts."

"Recovery efforts?" Gloria said. "When it should be search efforts. You should be searching instead of splashing around in some lake. You're not trying to find my son." She folded her arms over her chest.

The man looked at the police officer and said, "Our men have been working day and night, but after some consultation, the dive team has suspended the search."

"I told you he's not in there."

"Ma'am. The conditions are too difficult. We're truly sorry. We wanted nothing more than to bring your boy home to you."

Gloria sat in her rocking chair. She put her hands on her knees. "Where's Telly? Is he coming? You need to tell him about this. He needs to know you decided to give up."

The man looked at the police officer again. "He's been informed. We've spoken with him already."

"Already? So he's not coming over? I need to talk to him."

"I don't believe so, Mrs. Janes. And I wouldn't advise you try to get in touch, given our conversation a few nights ago. If he wants to contact you, he knows where you are."

"I need to tell Telly it's all lies. Until someone puts his body right in my arms, I won't believe it. I'm not giving up hope on my family, even though you police people already have. How can you?"

"Mrs. Janes—"

"Go!" she yelled. Tears went down her face, and she pointed her finger. "You've done nothing to help. Get off my step."

"Of course," the man said. "We'll respect your privacy."

Gloria pulled me on her lap and squeezed me for a long time. Her back was shaking bad. "What am I going to do now, Bids? What am I going to do?" I leaned on her shoulder and closed my eyes. In my head I could see the men swimming around and around until they climbed out of the water and went home. Rowan always was the best at hide-and-seek. Even when he was dead.

ROWAN

I am under the bridge. I float away. I am under the bridge. I float away.

Let me go home. Please let me go home.

Footsteps come closer, then stop. A soft snap. Of wood? Of metal? A breeze across my face.

Carl said it before. Stan is watching you. Stan is watching you now.

I can feel him standing over me. Staring down at me. I swallow. My mouth is so dry.

I slide my hand up, cover my head. My hair is crusted. Tin foil hat is gone. Carl made it because Dot insisted. To keep good thoughts in.

Carl?

I peer through slit eyes. But there is only darkness. A constant wind drones and clicks.

I want to keep the good thoughts in. I do.

And then I can hear Gloria. She is still talking on TV.

"All we want is to have you home. Back with us."

See? Everyone misses me.

My face rests against the wall of the bridge.

Gloria looks straight at the camera, then. There is a rectangle of light behind her. "You shouldn't have run away, Rowan."

I know. I know. I'm sorry.

Carl? You need to let me go home. You need to help me.

I shift my head. Stabs of pain bring it down. The ground smooth under my hands. Like thick plastic.

Light flickers. A flashlight in my face? Sunlight?

Turn it off. Turn it off.

Foggy blackness again.

I smell food. My stomach tightens, and I retch.

Carl?

Maisy was so afraid of you, but I explained.

You're not a bad person, you're not.

She thought you were a wolf.

I swallow again.

Are you a wolf?

Echoing layers of laughter.

Carl is laughing.

Stan is laughing.

Dot is laughing.

Somewhere among this is Gloria's bubbly laughter. The kind that makes her stomach shake. I can imagine her. Arms open, waiting to hug me.

"Everything is going to work out. You'll see. Me and Telly'll make sure of it."

Gloria?

My mind is going crazy.

I need to go home.

Carl? I'm going. I'm leaving.

"Coming home?"

Gloria is laughing her happy laugh again. Full of relief.

I'm going to try.

I know you miss me, Gloria.

I sit up again. Too much pressure behind my eyes. I squeeze my head. Pain rocks through me. The plastic covering buckles, cracks open. I reach my hands out, stretch my fingers over, under. Trying to hold on.

But I fall inside.

MAISY

"This is boring," Shar said. She sat on the counter hitting the cupboard with her heels. "I'm so bored."

Gloria was gone to work again, and then Aunt Erma had to leave, so Darrell was watching me and Shar. But he was in his room with the door closed, like always. I pretended I didn't hear Shar. I lifted up a book and covered my face. Aunt Erma bought it for Shar but Shar didn't want to read it. She said it was a baby book, but it was about a boy with freckles who made juice to get them gone.

"I got an idea," Shar said.

"What."

She dropped off the counter and came close to me.

"Let's go talk to Rowan."

When she said his name my lips and fingers got fuzz. "Don't say that," I whispered.

"I'm not joking." She stuck her finger out and tapped me hard on the forehead. "Darrell's got this board. You can talk to dead people. You know, ghosts or whatever."

Steam was puffing up behind her. Darrell had cooked us hot dogs for supper. He cut them all up on a plate with ketchup, and me and Shar stuck our forks in them. We smeared the ketchup all around and laughed. But the hot dog water was still boiling. He forgot to turn it off. The window behind it was gone foggy.

"I don't want to," I said.

"What a wimp."

"We're not allowed to touch his stuff."

"Darrell says I can."

"No he don't."

"You're scared." Shar was wearing a pink puppy sweatshirt. Some of the puppy was flaking off, and now it only had three legs.

"Am not scared."

"Don't you want to talk to Rowan?"

I shook my head.

"I mean if it was my brother, I'd want to talk to him. Right, Darrell?"

Darrell was standing in the doorway.

"I'm not your brother. And I wouldn't want to talk to a little shit like you."

Shar laughed loud. "Yes, you would. You'd want to know if I was good."

"Okay, fine," I said. I dropped the book on the table. "Nothing'll happen."

"You'll see." Then she said to Darrell, "Can we go get the board?"

He picked at his earring. "Uh. Yeah. Sure." He went over and turned off the hot dog water. "But don't go poking around in my space."

Darrell's room was dark. Stuff was everywhere. Crumpled-up papers and lumps of clothes and plates with food still on them. Their dog lived out in the yard now in a small gray house so he couldn't help clean up. There was a red pillowcase stuck onto the wall with thumbtacks. Maybe there was a window behind it. It smelled like old milk in there. Not horrible. A little bit like Rowan's room. I kept Rowan's pillow hidden in my closet and sniffed it sometimes. But only when I really needed to though. I didn't want to use it all up.

On the night table, Shar found a tiny glass with stripes. Then she put a wooden game on the floor and turned the glass upside down on it.

"Can we play in here?" I asked.

"He don't care," Shar said. "He's gone to the toilet. Sometimes he's in there for an hour."

Me and Shar squatted down on the carpet. The board was all scritched up, but I could still see letters and numbers and *goodbye* on the bottom. Then Shar put two fingers on top of the glass. I reached out my hand but she said, "You don't got to touch it. Just me."

"Anyone there?" Shar asked. The glass didn't move. "Does anybody want to say something?" Still nothing happened.

I didn't like this, but I didn't want to go. "Maybe there's no one around," I said.

"Don't be dumb, Maisy. There's always someone around." Then she said to me, "Go on. You say something."

I swallowed. "Hello?" All I could do was whisper.

The glass started sliding. Slow. Up to P. Then faster to E. Then real quick to A, and R. It stopped on L.

"Did you see that?" Shar said. "I wasn't moving it. I swear I wasn't."

"What did it say?"

"Pearl."

"Like pearls?" I asked. "A necklace?"

"I think that's her name. Go on. Ask her a question."

I didn't want to.

"Do it before she leaves, Maisy." Shar stuck her elbow in my ribs. "Do you think she got all day?"

"Hi Pearl," I said. It was weird talking to nothing. "I'm Maisy Janes."

Shar snorted. "You're such an idiot," she said. "Pearl don't care who you are." Then she put her nose almost on the board. She yelled, "Is Rowan there? We want to talk to Rowan."

The glass scraped over the wood. W. All the way over to A. Then back to T. It started going fast all over the place. My eyes couldn't follow the letters.

"I think it's broken," I said.

"No it's not. She said she's watching him."

"What?"

"Pearl said she's watching Rowan."

Then it was spinning around. E then Y. The glass looked like it was flying away from Shar's fingers.

"Eyes," Shar said. "Do ghosts got eyes?"

My heart was tak-takking even faster. The glass started moving again, scrape, scrape, scrape. I saw what it spelled that time.

"Bitch." Shar slapped her leg with her other hand. "Good thing Aunt Erma's not here. Pearl's got a dirty mouth."

"You should stop moving it."

"Who says I'm moving it?"

"It can't move by itself."

"It can if there's ghosts."

My hands were wet and my throat hurt. The hot dog chunks were hard in my middle. "I don't want to play no more."

"This is fun, Maisy." Shar got closer to the board again. "I said we want to talk to Rowan. Pearl. Get Rowan."

The glass didn't move.

"Now!" screamed Shar.

Then slowly it scraped over to W.

Shar called out the letters. "W-A-T-E-R. Oh my god. Water. She's talking about Rowan. Being in the water. Drowned. Did you hear that, Maisy? Pearl knows how he died. This is real!"

Shar called out more letters. "C-O-L-D. He's cold. That means he's cold."

I crunched up my knees. I tried not to listen.

"Wait, it's moving again. B-O-X. Did the man put him in a box?"

"I want to stop," I said.

Shar yelled again, "Put Rowan on!" Then she spelled, "N-O-T." And, "H-E-R-E."

"Stop, Shar."

"Well, where is he?" More scritching. "H-I-D-I-N-G." Shar screamed, "Oh my god! Does he have a message for Maisy? His sister's right here!" Shar scraped the glass all over the board. I watched close and it didn't stop on any letters. Then it flew off the bottom right through goodbye.

"You were pushing it, Shar. I saw you."

Shar looked at me and her finger made a cross on her chest. "I swear, Maisy. I swear on your life, I wasn't trying to move it. I was just helping it go where it wanted to go."

"Then what did she say?"

"Help him," Shar said.

"What?"

"She said, Help him!"

Even though Shar was laughing and said I should see the look on my own face, the hair on my skin went straight up.

MAISY

I ran out of Darrell's bedroom. Shar ran after me.

"Boo-hoo-hoo." Shar sang it a bunch of times. "If you think it's sucky here, then get out. Go home, you crybaby."

"I'm not supposed to." I wasn't even crying.

Shar pointed at her plastic watch. "Your mother should've been back hours ago. What does she think this is? A motel?"

I shook my head. Her mother wasn't there neither. Her mother was far, far away. Her mother yanked her hair and broke her arm and bumped her mouth so two of her teeth went gray. That was why she lived with Erma and only visited her mom in the summer. "But really," Gloria told me. "She's just at her grandmother's. I doubt her mother's even there."

"Maybe she missed the bus," I said. "Or it was late."

"Yeah, right. I saw her drive off in Mrs. Murtry's car."

I looked at the door. I wanted Aunt Erma to walk in and smack Shar. Smack her right in the head. I wished I had a different best friend instead of just Shar.

"Well? What did I say?" She had her hands on her hips. "We don't got to babysit you forever. We don't want you here."

I grabbed my bag and I grabbed Shar's book, too. She didn't want it. Darrell came out of the bathroom then. He kept turning his skull earring around and his whole ear was red and puffed up. "What's going on?" he asked.

"I'm going home."

"Your mom's back?"

I didn't answer. I opened the door and went outside on the front porch and looked at the bottom of the circle. Nighttime was all around our house. I wished Gloria would be there, but Mrs. Murtry's car was still gone. I looked up to the top of the circle. Mrs. Spooner's car was gone, too. I ran down the stairs.

"Hey!" Darrell called out. "What happened? Was it Shar? You got to ignore her, Maisy. She's an asshole."

I stomped along the side of the circle near the ditches until I got to our driveway. With the streetlamp gone out, our house looked extra empty. Only some of the moon was shining, and it was hard to see, but I went closer. Beside the house the woods were just a big wall of black, and I couldn't stop thinking about the wolves living in there. My heart popped up when I saw a man sitting on our porch. He was skinny with a tiny, tiny head and his arms sticking straight out. He rocked back and forth and I was going to run back to Shar's but I didn't want to talk to Pearl about Rowan because it was horrible and how can you help someone who was already dead? And then I saw the man was just the shadow of Gloria's chair.

Tears came out of my eyes. My cheeks were stinging.

I checked the front door and the sliding doors. They were locked up tight, but the shed was open. Inside was so dark. None of the moon could get in the dirty window. I felt Rowan's old bike. I knew it was his because there were plastic things clipped on the rusty spokes. When Rowan rode his bike they made a click-click sound. I pushed down next to the front wheel and bumped my head hard on a block of wood. I cried loud but no one came. Something made a loud clap. I think it was a mousetrap, but it didn't catch the mouse because I could hear it behind me tearing at paper.

I waited and waited and Gloria did not come home. It wasn't cold, but my teeth were chattering. I put my head on my knees and closed my eyes. I didn't care if a wolf snuck out of the woods and stole me. I hated Shar. She was ugly and mean. Inside and out. Mrs. Spooner said we should ignore people like that, but I couldn't. Gloria made me go to her house. Aunt Erma said she was like my big sister. She was the worst big sister. Rowan would hate her, too. He'd punch her in the stomach if he knew what she did. He'd kick out her rotten teeth. I missed Rowan. I missed Rowan so much.

I curled up as tight as I could. Then I felt something furry shoving against my face. A wolf! My eyes popped open, and then I saw Chicken. I hugged him. He was so warm. But how did he get in here? How did he get outside our house? Maybe Gloria was finally back.

Chicken stuck his head behind the bicycle wheel and pulled out Rowan's soccer ball. It was gone soft and he bit into it. He was snuffing and drooling and shaking his head and he was going to make it burst. I stood up and when the fuzz went away I chased and chased his jumpy body all over the grass. He ran around to the back of the house and I followed him and stopped by the back door. It was open a little bit. No one ever went in that way. It didn't even have steps. Chicken hopped right off the ground and disappeared inside. Gloria must've forgot to close the door. She kept doing that lately, leaving the milk out or not flushing the toilet. "I'm just so damn tired," she said.

I climbed up after Chicken. It was extra dark inside. "You bad thing!" I yelled into the hallway. But Chicken wasn't listening. Chicken was gone. I crept forward. My heart thumped inside my ears. I felt along the wall and went into the kitchen. I flicked the switch and the big rectangle light on the ceiling buzzed on. The kitchen was empty and strange. Like it was still my house, but other people might live there. On the counter there was an empty can of beans and an open bag of bread with some slices spilled out. There were two plates next to the bread, but they didn't look like our plates. Maybe Mrs. Spooner brought something on them.

Chicken started barking. It sounded like he was under me, but that was impossible. I took off my shoes and went back into the hallway. I turned on another light. Then I saw a weird thing I didn't see before. The door to the basement was open, too. Not much, but enough for Chicken to squeeze his skinny fur body through. I looked at that door. I wasn't sure what to do. What if Gloria found Chicken bouncing around in there with a wet ball and making a mess? What if I went down and saw the surprise she was working on? She'd know. Even if I didn't touch a thing.

I opened up the door. It was all black down there. I couldn't even see the bottom stairs. There was a breeze and a loud hairdryer sound coming up from below. On my tiptoes, I went one step at a time. I held onto the rail. The more down I went, the louder the whish got. Cold and dark went on my face. It smelled bad. Maybe Chicken had an accident. When I got to the bottom I reached through the air and pulled the string. I had my eyes shut tight, but I still wanted the light turned on.

I took another step, but my toe hit something hard. I yelped and both my eyes went open in a mistake. I didn't mean to spy, but then my eyes got ideas of their own. When I looked around I couldn't find the big surprise. There was just an old black couch and a closet jammed up with winter coats. There was a pile of red and blue plastic milk crates, and sitting on the floor next to those was the hugest fan I ever saw. It was making that bad whish sound.

Chicken kept barking. I crept around just a tiny bit. I thought I'd see something good. I didn't understand what Gloria was doing. Where was the surprise? Maybe I made a mistake. Maybe I made it all up in my head. I did that too much and it always made Gloria mad. My middle felt heavier and heavier and the lump on my head hurt.

I felt it. It was like a tiny egg under my hair. The same kind of eggs that were in cartoons. Then I knew why everything looked funny. I was having a dream. A strange funny kind of scary dream. I had to just keep going until it was done.

I found the ball behind the milk crates. It was gross and slimy and had green grass stuck in the slime. I picked it up with my hands. It seemed real, but I knew it wasn't.

Chicken was beside the bathroom door. The fan was right next to him. His fur was ruffling all over. He barked, and each bark made his paws leap off the ground. With his nose, he pushed away a blanket that was folded against the door. Then I saw rags stuck in the gap. He was scritching them with his claws and they came out. I think they were some of Telly's old T-shirts, but they didn't say *Telly J.* They didn't say nothing.

There was a little spot between the door and the cement. Chicken whined and whined.

"Come here," I said. "It's okay." I don't know if he heard me because the fan was so loud. I smoothed his fur. I let him lick my face. His dirty spit didn't bother me because none of it was real.

Then I saw a lock on the door. It was shiny gold. The metal bar it was attached to was screwed in, but parts of the screws were still sticking out. Whoever did that didn't do a good job. I pinned the ball under my arm. I touched the lock. I touched the door. Then I reached for the handle.

A mouse on the floor. All skittery. Right by my foot. I jumped like Chicken did when he barked.

Then I squished up my eyes because it wasn't a mouse. It was a worm. My mouth opened to scream but nothing came out. Then two worms. Wiggling. Giant and dirty, slugging on the ground.

I swallowed mouthfuls of air. I got a tiny bit closer. My head was full of cloud and turning into a purple storm. They weren't worms. They were fingers. Just the tops. Filthy like Carl's were, and they reached and stretched. They were chewed and scabby. Coming out from under the bathroom door.

Chicken scritched at them. I thought I heard, I thought I heard—

I dropped the slimy ball. It bounced and bounced. Far away. Stars sparkled around my face. My head got hollow. The dream changed so quick. It was the worst thing ever. Then my air was gone. I was falling into a hole. Glitter and zigzags. Then black and black and black.

ROWAN

"You're still sleeping?"

Am I?

"You need to stay awake."

The sun never comes up. And all I want to do is dream. Dream about home.

Gloria stares down at me. Her face is worried.

You were crying on TV.

"I told them. I told them you're lost."

Watch out for Carl. He's coming back. Any second.

"Oh no he's not. That man can't hurt me."

He might. But he's not bad, Gloria. Like Maisy thinks. He's made mistakes. He can't trust himself.

"Can't he?"

No.

"You're sort of trapped here, aren't you?"

I'm just under the bridge.

"They already looked. You're not there."

What? Where am I?

"You drowned. In the lake."

Can you come pull me out?

"That's Telly's decision. He's still angry. We're talking about it, but it's up to him."

I'll be better this time.

"Yes, you will."

I just want to get home.

"Soon you'll be walking out of those woods with a hell of a story."

A hell of a story.

I can do that.

Gloria?

"What?"

You don't need to cry anymore. I know you miss me, but I'm not far. I'm not far away at all.

I stand up, rest against the cement wall. Darkness coats me, but Gloria said I need to stay awake. Everything is rocking, and I can feel my body swinging back and forth. Nothing under my feet. And then I'm a little boy in the playground. The memory floats in front of me in full color. I'm seated on a slab of wood and Gloria is pushing me so hard, the ropes buckle each time she shoves my back. I feel her fingertips jabbing into my spine. When I cry out for her to stop, I'm swinging too high, she yells, "You're having fun! This is fun!" Then the ropes slip from my hands and I speed through the air, slam into the ground. A guttural belch from my lungs.

She walks over to where I've fallen and kneels down. I wait for her to help me, but instead, she stares at me as though she's confused. I grab at her dress with both hands and through my tears, I say, "You're my mommy!" I don't know why those words rush out of my mouth. It's a stupid thing to say.

Her head goes back, like she's stunned. She speaks in a low voice. "No, I'm not. I'm a stranger."

"You're my mommy!"

She tugs her dress from my grip. "I'm not. I'm a stranger."

The grin will come any second, I tell myself. Any second. But it doesn't.

My tears stop, and sickness fills my chest. "Mom?"

"I'm not your mom," she whispers right in my ear. I heard her slowly inhale. "You. Don't. Know. Me."

"I do."

"How?" She tilts her head and smiles.

"I—I just do."

"Well you're wrong." Her voice is different. Low and growling. She stares at me. "I've never met you before. You weird little thing. I don't have the faintest clue who you are."

"But."

She stands up and takes a step back. I look down at my feet. Just beyond my toes there might as well be a crevice a mile deep. Fear floods me. Cold and prickly, it swirls straight down through my core. Metal blades through that most tender part of me.

My shoulders are shaking, and when my tears turn to sobs, the look on her face shifts. Leaning close to me, her eyes wide, mouth slightly open, corners curled up. She is curious, and she is delighted.

Only a game. A dumb game. Playing like she does. Acting like I'm not even there.

Why did I remember that?

I should have just laughed.

It's going to be okay. She isn't angry anymore. I saw her crying on TV.

"All we want is to have you home."

Home.

Gloria is like that. She always turns things around. She's never made me disappear forever.

MAISY

I opened my eyes and Gloria was sitting on my bed with her face wrinkled up. She smoothed my blanket. Her eyes were pink. She had a ball of tissue scrunched in her hand. She'd been crying, and my insides dropped down.

"I was so worried," she said. "Can you fathom coming home from work and having no idea where you were?"

I shook my head.

"I looked everywhere, Bids. Frantic. I was about to call the police."

My throat went small. I couldn't swallow.

"You can't keep doing that to me. Going in the woods and then, and then hiding in the shed. Very last place I looked. Sleeping like a baby. Chicken trapped in there with you. Whimpering up a storm."

"Chicken?"

"Licking your face so hard I'm surprised you don't got a welt."

"In the shed?"

"Yes, oh yes. In the shed. Pinched right between a muddy shovel and a basket of old rags. A bucket of nails just about fell on your beautiful head."

It was a bad, bad dream. She ruffled my hair.

"Can you imagine my shock?" She pushed the tissues into her nose. "Why on earth would you leave Erma's?"

I sat up and the sparkles came again. They zoomed all around Gloria's head like tiny fireflies.

"You can tell me, I won't be mad."

"I had to leave."

"What?"

"Shar told me to. To go home."

"You listening to Shar again?" Gloria made her teeth clang. "How can she be ten years old and such a little bitch already?"

Then I remembered what Pearl said. About watching Rowan. My mouth turned dry and my head fell back a bit. I couldn't tell Gloria about me and Shar trying to talk to him.

Gloria put her hand on my chest. "You got to take in more air, Bids. You got lungs for a reason."

"Sorry."

"Don't be sorry. Just tell me what happened."

I was in the shed, not the basement. Dreaming and dreaming of milk crates and Chicken's ruffly fur and no surprise and dirty finger worms under a door. So strange and scary. They wanted to touch me.

"The door was locked so I went in the shed. Chicken got in there, too. He was after Rowan's ball."

"Yes, and?"

"He got the ball and I didn't want him to explode it. I chased him all around the grass and into the hou—"

"The house was locked up, sweetheart. I must have left Chicken outside without a drop of water. I don't know where my mind is these days. And then to find the two of you in the shed. You don't know my relief."

I closed my eyes for a second. "I fell asleep in there."

"That's quite a bump you got on your head."

I nodded and touched the little egg. Gloria picked up my arm and bent it. She poked at my ribs and tapped where my heart was. She put her hands on my hair and felt all over. She made me count her fingers. One. Three. Two.

"You'll be fine, says Dr. Gloria."

I nodded again.

"Do you want to say something to me?"

"I didn't mean it."

"That's okay, darling." It was a real *darling*. "I'll just be having a talk with Erma, that's all. If she can't be there to keep half an eye on you, after all I been through, what's the point of her?"

More tears came out of my eyes. They jumped off my cheeks and landed on my nightgown.

"There, there, now, Bids. Gloria doesn't know what all the fuss is about." She slid her arms around my back and hugged me up tight. Her shirt smelled like nighttime. Then she let go. She patted at my pillow and smiled. Then behind her back she pulled Jenny the Head.

"You found her!"

"I did."

"Thank you. I didn't know where I lost her to."

"She was in with the laundry, Bids. Honestly, you can't keep track of nothing."

I held Jenny the Head. I sniffed her hair.

"But I'm not mad, though. I can't be mad, darling. Want to know why?"

I nodded.

"I borrowed Mrs. Murtry's car again and took a lovely drive. Belinda's such a kind lady, she didn't mind at all. And it was wonderful, Bids. Really great to clear my head. I played some radio and had the windows down. Air rushed in and it all smelled so fresh." Gloria reached for the bottle full of syrup. "I don't think I've been that calm in a long, long time. It made me feel full up inside. Doing something just for me." She poured green into my nighttime spoon. Then put it in my mouth. "Every drop," she said. "Down the hatch."

I swallowed. I could feel it spreading across my ribs. All that green was good for me. It tasted like mint. Not peppermint but that other kind. I sneezed twice.

"You were so late," I told her.

"I'm sorry if you thought that. I really am." She put the cap back on the bottle, grabbed my hand. "We're like two halves of a snap, Bids. Sometimes apart, but meant to stay together."

I smiled some more.

"I'm the most important person in your life, you know. No matter what."

"I know," I whispered.

"Tell me you love me best."

"I love you, Gloria. I do." Tears came out again. I couldn't keep them inside. I loved Gloria so much it made me shake.

"There," she said. "There. Time to sleep."

Gloria turned off the light and went away, but I wouldn't close my eyes. I kept thinking about Pearl. I had a feeling she was hanging around in the dark. I bet she followed me home. She went through the walls and came into my bedroom. She could be floating right over my bed. I reached up my hands but there was nothing in the air.

I read a ghost book once. Some ghosts said stupid ghost stuff. Some ghosts were mean. But some were nice. Rowan would be a nice ghost. I knew that for sure. But I was afraid to talk to him. A cold shiver went up my back. I pulled up my blanket. My mind was full of strings. There were lots of ends sticking out. I didn't want to pull at nothing. My head wanted to think, but I wouldn't let it. I stopped it. I stopped it hard.

Soon the green cough vitamin medicine sneaked up into my head. It made me feel warm and heavy and good. The egg didn't hurt no more and I had to close my eyes.

MAISY

"I haven't the faintest what this is about!"

Gloria's yelling woke me up. I went to the top of the stairs and peeked over. The door was open and sunshine was coming in and a policeman was standing there. It was not the man with the funny ties but the man with the blue pants and blue shirt. The one with the gun on his belt.

"Now, Officer Cooper, this can't be another complaint. Not with all I'm going through."

"I'm just doing my job, ma'am."

"What's he saying?"

The man opened up his notebook. "Mr. Janes states he and his wife saw—"

"His wife?"

He put his notebook closer to his face. "Sorry, ma'am. He and his girlfriend saw you trespassing on their property yesterday evening, and Ms. Jenkins states she saw you outside the bedroom window of their bungalow, watching her undress."

"What? That's the last thing I'd want to see. That witch undress."

"And when Mr. Janes went to investigate he discovered damage to the vinyl siding of his home."

"Damage. There was no damage."

"Cut marks, he said. He claims you made stab holes in the siding with a sharp instrument like a screwdriver or a knife."

"So a raccoon scratches up his house and frightens that—that thing, and you come see me?"

"Vinyl siding's pretty tough, ma'am. I had it installed on my own house two years ago."

"Telly thinks this is funny, I bet. This is all some kind of joke."

"No, ma'am. He doesn't see it as a joke. He sees it as escalating behavior, and we're taking it seriously."

"You are, are you?" Gloria laughed a big laugh. "Well, that certainly means a lot. Your Detective Aiken said the same thing when my son got taken. I believe you even said it yourself."

"Ma'am," he said. He shook his head back and forth. "I can't comment on that."

"I told you already, I took the bus for a few groceries and then was home with my daughter. You can ask her yourself. She's upstairs with a stomach bug, but I can drag the poor girl down here if that's what you want." I put my hand on my middle. I never knew, but now it felt a little bit sick. It did. "Is that what you want, Officer?"

I scooted over on the step so no one could see me.

"She's quite certain it was you, Mrs. Janes. They both are. And we've had a look at the side of his house. There's evidence of vandalism."

"If you look at my driveway, Officer Cooper, you'll discover no car is parked around here. I don't got a car. I don't drive a car. I never had the privilege of even owning a car."

"Mrs. Janes—"

"You know what type of person sees someone who's not there? An airhead. A flaky airhead. That woman is unstable. She's one of those vengeful and vindictive types, stealing other women's husbands. Have you considered that possibility?"

My middle was gurgling and squirting.

The man didn't say nothing for a minute. Then he said, "We need you to come down. Make a formal statement."

"You want me to leave my sick child and go to the police station?"

"Exactly, ma'am. You'll have to arrange some care."

I heard Gloria snort. "This is laughable. Completely laughable. You know that, right? That woman is deeply troubled. She's been attacking me since the day she met Telly. Trying to pollute my daughter's mind. Driving around the circle at all hours, going slow in front of my house. Threatened, she is, because Telly's getting bored of her."

"Did you file a report?"

"No. I just rise above it all. But how much patience am I expected to have?"

He put his hand on his belt. His gun wiggled. "Do you have someone to watch your daughter, Mrs. Janes?"

"Oh for god's sakes," Gloria huffed. "My neighbor's here. Erma. In the kitchen. She'll stay."

I leaned over and peeked into the kitchen. It was empty.

"Good," he said. "My partner and I'll be waiting in the car. We'd really like to resolve this, Mrs. Janes. In a friendly way."

I watched Gloria close the door. She was talking but I couldn't hear what she was saying. My heart slapped my chest and I put my face on the cold wall. My stomach bug was really bad. Maybe I was going to throw up. When I heard her coming close to the stairs I scrambled back to my bed.

"Maisy! You don't move, you hear me? Not one toe leaves this room." She closed my curtains and everything went gray. "What foolishness I got to deal with. I swear Telly got himself mixed up with a screwball nutcase this time."

I curled up under the covers. "Gloria, my middle hurts."

"No, it don't."

"I got the stomach bug."

"Don't be a dimwit. You're perfectly fine." She picked up the green syrup bottle. Then she put it back down again.

"Oh," I said.

"I won't be gone long. You can read or draw or whatever it is you do to waste your time."

I sat up. I felt better. "Did Mrs. Murtry's car get broken?"

Gloria stopped and looked at me hard. "Belinda's car? What do you mean?"

"You took it last night."

"What?"

"You went for a drive, remember? It made you happy. With the windows open and the music."

Gloria smiled. She smoothed my hair. "Oh, Bids. You were so turned around last night, so I won't get too upset about your lies. It's an awful, awful habit you got. I honestly don't know how you can make such stuff up."

I heard Gloria slam the front door. I looked out my window and she got in the brown car with the star on the side. When they drove away I saw her face was all scrunched. She looked like a fish in old water. The car went to the top of the circle and then it disappeared.

Then noise started. Tap, tap, tap. Tap, tap, tap. I heard a clicking coming into my room through the wall. There was a leaky pipe. Water dripping.

Or maybe it wasn't water.

I squeezed my eyes together to keep out some ideas. My awful, awful habit. I tried to take big breaths.

Then I tried to find Jenny the Head, but she was lost again. Sometimes I thought she was magic. I reached under my bed and pulled out Rowan's book of *Stories for Boys*. Gloria let me have it. It had colorful pictures. I think Gran gave it to him when he lived with her. I didn't like to think about Gran. Gloria said she was dead, but I knew she was on our front porch and Gloria was talking to her. I even heard Gran's voice.

I squeezed my eyes shut again.

My middle growled. My throat hurt, too. I opened the bottle and took a tiny sip of the green vitamins. It was hard to read the book because my head was making the words skip all over. My imagination kept doing something bad. My awful habit wouldn't stop. I kept remembering those fingers in the basement. But I wasn't even in the basement. I only went to the shed and hit my head and fell asleep with Chicken.

I put the book down. I took another tiny sip of the green vitamins.

It was okay to get out of bed. "Not one toe," Gloria said. I think she said it but maybe I made that up too. My head was so cloudy. It was full of ideas and bits of a terrible movie. The fingers were sneaking out from under the door of Telly's bathroom. Chicken was there too. He was whining like crazy. I didn't see no surprise.

I pushed my head back into my pillow. I wanted to taste more of the vitamins. But I didn't think I should.

Gloria said, "Not one toe." I didn't know what that meant. I had a lot of toes. I looked out the window again. There was nobody in the circle. I pushed back my covers and put on my bathrobe. My middle growled again. She probably meant I could get something to eat. "Not one toe" was allowed to go outside. I wasn't allowed to go into the backyard. Or go into the woods. I shouldn't go into the shed. Or back to Shar's.

The hallway was quiet. I tried to go to the stairs but my feet walked into Gloria's room instead. I looked at Gloria's night table for a long time and then I pulled open the top drawer. It had magazines and candy bars, but no key. Then I looked in Telly's night table. Just pennies and nickels and a blue bottle with a ship on it. I looked under Gloria's bed. Then in her closet. There was a small box almost falling off the shelf. I brought a chair over and lifted it down and put it on her bed. I took off the lid and there were more bottles of green vitamins inside and some folded-up papers maybe from the bank. And there was a key. I knew it was the key for the basement. Maybe if I checked for the fingers and they weren't there then the movie would fly out of my head. Some of the lies would be gone. Then when Gloria read my mind, she'd see better things.

I picked up the key. When I reached the basement door I stuck the key in the lock and turned. Chicken bumped at my legs. The lock clicked and opened up. I took it off the metal loop. Chicken barked and my heart jumped and banged so loud I couldn't even hear. I turned the doorknob. I pulled the door. Chicken rushed down the steps. I could hear his long claws on the wood.

I looked out through the window next to the happy, happy door. I could see the circle. There were no police cars. No Gloria. No Darrell or Shar or Aunt Erma or Mrs. Murtry or Mrs. Spooner.

I could sneak down into the basement. And nobody was there to catch me.

ROWAN

Sunlight is shining on my face. Just over my eyelids. But it isn't warm. I stretch out my hand. My fingers knock something damp and hard. I pick up a smooth rock. But when I open my eyes, it's not a rock at all. It's a white plastic puck. There are thin slits on the top and the bottom. I bring it to my face and smell the sharp stench of an artificial forest.

My head throbs, but I'm able to sit up. I lean my back against the bridge. I blink. But there is another cement wall. And another. Dizziness is making the walls spin. I blink again. When did Carl get a sink? Then I see a toilet. Water gurgles down inside of it. On the ceiling a single yellow bulb glows. Beside that, a bathroom fan drones and clicks.

"Carl?" The word is only a whisper. "Carl? Are you there?"

White bowls sit on the floor beside me. Brown caked to the sides. Carl has brought me beans? The sweet smell makes me retch, but nothing comes up.

Beside the toilet my gray-tape shoes sit side by side, covered in tiny sticks and fragments of dead leaves. We'd come all the way back to the lake. I must have walked, but I couldn't remember a single step. Carl had put me in the bathroom. I was probably bleeding. Throwing up inside the cottage.

I look up at a vent near the ceiling. There was a window before. Wasn't there? I had glanced out at the lake while I used the toilet. I was certain I'd seen the water.

I tried to stand up, but my legs wouldn't hold me.

"Hello?"

Slow drumming inside my head. Wasn't there flower wallpaper before? How can a window vanish?

I rub my eyes. Colors pop and burst out of nowhere and won't stop. Then I notice something. A corner of paper poking out between the cement wall and the cabinet. I reach forward and with my fingernails, tug it out. A magazine slaps onto the floor. *Gun Digest.* I pull it closer and look at the sticker near the bottom.

I rub my eyes again. My head is making things up.

I lift it close to my face.

No, the name and address hasn't changed.

Mr. Theodore Janes. 17 Pinchkiss Circle.

The magazine belongs to Telly.

I look at the door. At the walls. At the ceiling. The sink. The toilet.

And it hits me. Almost knocks me backward. I hold my aching head. Too much piling in at once.

I want to go home.

You are home.

MAISY

It was dark down there. I listened hard but all I could hear was a windy sound. A breeze went on my ankles. I stepped down and kept my eyes open big, but only black got in. The dark was so thick it was hard to breathe. On the bottom step I pulled the string and the light came on.

I saw a box full of cans on the floor. That might be different, but the black couch was the same and the cupboards were still open with the winter coats inside. The same huge fan was still on the floor, and Chicken raced right past me to the bathroom door. Like he did last time. His long fur whipped all around from the fan. I took more steps. Chicken had pushed away a blanket and now he was pawing at the bottom of the door. He got something white out from there. I think it was one of Telly's old T-shirts. I blinked a lot. My mouth and legs and arms were full of static.

Everything was weird because it was already all in my mind. It was the exact movie I saw last night.

I swallowed.

I didn't want to get too close. Chicken barked and the fan whished, but I still heard something from behind the door. It was someone laughing or someone crying. My skin got goose bumps. "Chicken!" it said. "Hey, Chicken. Hey!"

Then, in the tiny, tiny space under the door, the dirty fingers pushed out. I pinched my arm real hard. Tears came in my eyes. I could feel the hurt. Feel it a lot.

Those fingers were real.

And I knew who owned them.

I stopped breathing. I sat down on the floor. All my body went cold. This wasn't my awful habit. I found Rowan. I found him. He wasn't grabbed from under the bridge, or stuck in the trash on the bottom of the lake. He was hiding in our house. My middle felt sick and excited.

Chicken pawed and licked the fingers. He spun in circles and pawed at them again. I didn't understand how Rowan could be hiding there all this time. How could nobody know?

I lay down and I moved my face up close to the door. There was black stuff on the other side. I couldn't see in. He sounded far away like there was wind in there, too. A noisy wind.

I reached out and touched his fingers. They were cold and dry. They got yanked back inside. I tapped on the door. "Rowan," I said. "It's me."

I thought I heard "Turtle," but it was real quiet.

"Rowan? Are you in there?" I looked at the lock. It was a different color. But almost the same as the one upstairs. "I'll get Gloria," I said. "She'll help."

There was a thump. "No!"

I jumped. Above the whishing fan a sound came down over the stairs.

A car door slamming.

Gloria was home.

Rowan tapped more on the door. It wasn't very hard. I pushed my ear in. I think he said, "Don't tell her. Don't."

Why wouldn't I tell Gloria? A shiver went all the way from my teeth to my toes. I raced up the steps from the basement and through the hall and up the other stairs. I tripped on my bathrobe. My knees hit. But I got up again and hurried. I ran into her room and put the key back and threw the box into the back of her closet. I shoved the chair away. Then I ran into my room and jumped on my bed.

I heard her stomping over the porch. "Wasting my time," she growled. "Lies from a sicko woman." Then she came inside and slammed that door, too. As soon as I heard her throw off her shoes I got up and started to go down the stairs. I smiled as hard as I could.

"Hi Gloria."

She looked up at me. I think she was mad. "You stayed in your room, miss?" My face got hot. Gloria made a clicking sound. "You were out of your room?"

I nodded. I couldn't tell a lie. She'd just look inside my mind and know what I did.

"Come down here," she said.

I went to the bottom stair and I wrapped my arms around the rail.

"Tell me exactly what you were doing."

"I—I watched a show." That was kind of true. I was watching a show in my head.

"What were you watching?"

"Cartoons?"

She looked at my chest. "Must've been some awful cartoons. You're out of breath."

When I looked I could see my nightgown shaking from my heart. Then in the corner of my eye, I saw Chicken. He used his snout to push open the door so he could get out of the basement. The lock was hanging open on the hook.

Gloria saw him, too. And she saw the lock. She looked at me and her eyes were small and angry. "You've been sneaky," she said. "You've been a very sneaky little girl."

Everything went drifty. I slid down onto the stair. I hugged the railing tight. I could hear Gloria but she seemed a long ways away. I started to cry.

"Don't think you can pass out on me, miss.

"Do I not do enough for you?

"Do you think this is what I want to come home to? More nonsense from you?

"Do I not have enough on my plate?

"You just want to pile it on."

Her finger pushed in my nose and the back of my head hit the railing. "Pile it on, pile it on. Hurt Gloria. Is that your idea of fun?

"You been so sneaky. Just lie and sneak. Lie and sneak. That's all you do. A sneaky little thing.

"How can I trust you?

"You're not a little kid no more. Grown-ups make decisions and it's none of your business. You hear me? You don't got to know why things happen. You're too young and too stupid. Stupider than Shar. But there you go. Sticking your big fat nose in. Skulking around. I always knew you were like that. A sneaky little spy. You get that from Telly's side. It's disgusting. I'm completely disgusted in you. A sneaky dirty spy. There's nothing worse in this whole world."

Her hands were flying around in front of my face.

"Do you want them to take you away? Enormous men are going to show up on our doorstep and you will be gone, Maisy. Do you get that? Gloria can't do a single thing about it. Gone, gone, gone. They'd probably toss you in a filthy jail somewhere. With all the other sneaky nasty little girls no one can stand. Can't mind their own beeswax. Is that what you want?"

My mouth was open. No air was coming in.

"You're not saying a word, but I hear you good and plenty. You want to be gone. And I won't stop them, you know that? Even if I could, I won't lift a finger. They can cart you off and do what they want."

I put my head on the wall. I was in so much trouble. More trouble than I ever was before. "Not one toe," she said when she left. I was supposed to stay in my room. Rowan was in the basement. That wasn't a good thing. Gloria knew he was there. She wanted him disappeared forever. Now she was going to disappear me, too.

"Do you get me, miss? Everything I've done was to protect you, and now those men are just waiting. Right around the corner."

I nodded.

"All I got to do is open the door and wave my pinkie finger."

I nodded again.

"So you better keep away from that little idiot down there."

I nodded again.

"And if you want to stay under this roof, you won't tell a single solitary soul."

MAISY

Through my bedroom window I could hear Chicken snoring on the front step and Darrell's motorcycle roar and pop. Shar was skipping rope in front of her house, and she must've been singing loud because I could hear that, too. "And how many big boys will I kiss? One, two, three . . ." She never got past three.

I wanted to go skipping with Shar, but I wasn't allowed out. After I found Rowan in the basement, Gloria sent me to my room and said she didn't want to see my sneaky spy face for the rest of my life. I pulled Rowan's pillow out of my closet and cried into it until my nose was stuffed and my eyes were so fat I couldn't even see.

A long, long time went by. Chicken barked and the screen door creaked when Gloria let him inside. Then Aunt Erma called Shar in for dinner. Finally, Gloria came into my bedroom. She brought me a peanut butter sandwich and it was cut in the shape of a heart. She sat on my bed and blew out a lot of air.

"Bids," she said. She sounded sad.

I tried not to cry again. Everything inside me was full of holes. Like when Chicken took Jenny the Head's oatmeal body and chomped Jenny's heart up.

She put the plate on my lap. "You should eat something."

I took the sandwich and I tried to smile. It didn't taste too good. The bread was dry and stuck in my throat.

"You probably thought I was being rough earlier today."

I chewed and nodded.

"I'm sorry you could think such a thing. But you need to trust Gloria."

I nodded again.

She got real close to me. Her eyebrows were turned yellow now, too, and it looked like they weren't there at all. "You got to understand, Bids. That's not Rowan in the basement," she said. "I know you think it is, but it's not. So you can put that silly idea out of your head right now."

I looked at her through my chubby eyes. I didn't know what she meant. I pinched my arm when I was in the basement. I knew it was real.

"He came back, Bids, but he was different. Not normal. I didn't know what to do." She looked at her fingernails. They were painted a peachy color. "I just thought I'd give him a while. Keep him safe and sound, you know? I didn't want him arrested and thrown in jail. Or some hospital for lunatics. I was trying to do the right thing."

I took another bite of my sandwich, but my cheeks were filling up.

"Telly was supposed to come home. To help me figure things out."

I chewed and chewed.

"I can tell you're still confused." She touched my arm. "Imagine Chicken, okay?"

"Okay," I whispered. Crumbs flew out of my mouth.

"And I let him out to do his business. Simple as can be, right? But when he comes back, he's this vicious wolf. Gone mad up here." She tapped her hair. "And he's run off and torn up everyone's gardens. What could I do? If the dog catcher caught him he'd put that choke chain around Chicken's neck and throw him in the back of his van. We'd never see him again."

I lifted up the sandwich, but I couldn't take another bite.

"He's like an animal down there. It's so frightening, Bids. Not Rowan at all. I mean, your brother did some terrible stuff when he was gone off. Really terrible things I can't begin to try and explain. I'm fixing everything, but let me tell you, it's not straightforward in the least." She frowned. "I thought Telly would help, but that man messed it all up. And then that idiot tramp goes and tells everyone he's drowned Rowan. Out in some stupid lake. Which was a lie of course, but how could I tell anyone? And after that, it got to be such a tangle. It was only supposed to be a couple of days until me and Telly got settled. Now that boy's turned worse instead of better. I'm stretched to my limit. But because I'm Gloria, I'm not giving up." She squeezed my hand hard. "I'm still trying to straighten everything out. Do you understand now?"

I still didn't know. Rowan was a wolf? He didn't sound like a wolf. He sounded like Rowan. He called me Turtle. But he was knocking on the door. He wouldn't stop. A wolf might do that if it was angry.

"You're thinking about that man who told all the lies?"

I pushed the food into one cheek. I wiggled my arm away from hers. "Carl?" He put Rowan in the lake. But Rowan wasn't in the lake. Or maybe he was and he didn't stay in the lake.

"Carl." Gloria made a snort. "Doesn't matter what he calls himself, he was a wolf. A nasty wolf. You listen to me real careful, Bids. That animal is exactly where he deserves to be. Even better than he deserves, if I tell the truth. And you know Gloria always tells the truth."

I nodded.

"He hurt Rowan beyond what you can imagine." She patted her chest with her hand. "I can't even get the words out. None of this would be happening if that Carl man had stayed away. If Rowan had stayed away from him."

She was talking fast. I couldn't hear it all. "Well?" she said. "You understand?"

"I do," I said.

"Good girl. You have to trust me, Bids. Gloria only wants what's best for you. To look after you. That's the truth, right?"

"That's the truth," I whispered. The sandwich was a big stone in my middle.

"It's important you do everything I say. You have to listen to me. It won't be much longer. I've just got that feeling." She put both of her hands over her heart. "Telly called just now and wants to meet for a dinner. Don't that sound lovely?"

I sniffed. "When?"

"Soon, I think. He didn't say. But that can only mean one thing, right? Good news."

"Good news."

She smoothed my hair. "Don't you worry, Bids. If you don't misbehave again, those . . . Well, you know, they won't drive over and take you. Of course I can't be certain, sweetheart, but I don't think so. Okay?"

Tears started coming out again. I couldn't stop them. I could just see the men standing at our happy, happy door. They would be tall and angry and they would grab my arms and my legs and they would throw me in a dark trunk of a car. They'd probably grab Jenny the Head, too. Then we'd disappear forever. It'd be cold and wet and smelly. No one would find us. Me and Jenny the Head would be like Rowan. All disappeared. He wasn't on the bottom of the lake, though. He was a wolf in the basement. Maybe I'd turn into a wolf too. Instead of a turtle. Jenny the Head would stay the same.

"Do you trust me, Bids?"

I nodded.

"Who do you love the best?"

"You."

"Say it."

"I love you best, Gloria." And I did. Inside my heart it was mostly Gloria in there. A tiny, tiny, tiny secret bit for Aunt Erma. None for Telly because he didn't help Gloria. Or Dian, even though she was nice. I didn't know how much was for Rowan. If any. He was so bad he wasn't even Rowan no more. Carl killed him dead. But in a different way. Maybe he was on the bottom of the lake and he mostly died and he crawled out and came home. He was probably dripping and rotting and falling apart. Like in my dreams when Shar and Darrell rowed me out. He could be that way. He could. I didn't know.

Later there was a knock on our door. I was in the kitchen because Gloria let me out of my room. My legs went funny. I thought it was the men coming for me, but when Gloria answered it was only Shar. Gloria told her I was sick.

"Caught a cold," Gloria said. "Can't keep enough tissues in the house." I put my hand on my head. It was warm. I was probably going to start sneezing any second. Then she called out to me. "Bids! You got company."

When I went to the door Darrell was there too. He had a black T-shirt and jean shorts and black boots with laces. His ear was still red.

"Hi," I said. I rubbed my nose. "I got a cold."

Gloria put her arm around my shoulder and pulled me in. She was warm and soft.

"Yech," Shar said. "You better not snot all over me."

Darrell bumped her. "Don't be a dick, Shar. Say what you got to say."

Her eyes rolled around. "Aunt Erma told me I got to say sorry." She tapped her foot and stuck out her lip. "So, there. Sorry. I said it."

Darrell smacked her in the head. "There's something seriously wrong with you." Then he looked at me. "We're sorry, Maisy. For the board and everything. Shar was just joking around."

"For what?" Gloria said. She took her hand off my shoulder. "What board?"

Darrell coughed. "Um. They—they were just being bored, Mrs. Janes. Then Shar got rude and told Maisy to get home."

"She said that, did she?"

Shar pulled her lip in.

"Well, Maisy won't be needing to go over there no more. I'm going to have to stop my shifts at Stafford's until I figure things out. And you can tell that to your mother, Darrell. Exactly what I said."

Shar took a big step back. Darrell scritched his head. "I'll let her know, Mrs. Janes. And I'm sorry she took off. I came to check on her, I did."

"What do you mean?"

"Followed her down to your house."

"You were here?"

"Yeah. I knocked on the door for ages, and then I saw lights go on inside, so I figured she was okay if she was home."

He smiled at me. My insides got a tiny bit warm. I looked at Darrell's arms and I could see his muscles. I bet he was strong. He wouldn't be scared of a wolf. Maybe if he went down to the basement he could open the door and wrestle Rowan out. I smiled back at him and tugged on Gloria's sleeve, but Gloria started to close the door.

"I don't got nothing to say to you, Sharlene. I hope I don't see you coming back here for a very long time."

Shar's mouth dropped open and I saw her two gray teeth.

"But thank you, Darrell. I appreciate you trying to look out for Maisy. She got to go back to bed now."

Click. Our yellow door was closed. I could hear Shar and Darrell stomping down the steps. Darrell told Shar she was a real bonehead. Shar didn't say nothing back.

Gloria locked the door. "I really wish that didn't happen."

"What?"

"People. Coming onto my property like they got a right. Thumping on my door. Busybodies, nosing around. I hate that. I really, really do. Puts a lot of pressure on me."

I frowned and nodded.

"And you," she said. "Don't even think about it."

"Huh?"

"Don't 'huh' me, miss." She grabbed my hand and squeezed until my knuckles crunched together. "Don't think I don't notice what you're doing. I can see you making goo-goo eyes at Erma's son. Why don't you go up and kiss him right on the mouth? You scared? Is that it? Yeah. You're scared. Well, you look like a real simpleton, you know that?"

My cheeks got warm.

"Maisy Janes. You answer me. Do you know how stupid you look?"

I nodded.

"Say it."

"I look stupid," I whispered.

"That's my girl." She stopped squeezing my hand. "You listen to Gloria and you'll grow up decent. Not like some moony-faced ninny, tripping over her own feet."

I looked at Chicken, but he went and lied down in front of the basement door.

"And that dog is ridiculous," she said. "Old and ridiculous."

That night in bed I heard the tapping again. I knew it was Rowan down there. It made my middle feel worse. What if he got out? What if he was sad, too? Could a wolf be sad? What if he stopped being bad and Gloria didn't know? If I was brave, I would go down there and check. But I wasn't brave. My head was full of ideas and they raced around and crashed into each other. It made me fuzzy and sick to hold it in.

Gloria came in my room and heard the noise. "Nothing normal acts like that. No one would say otherwise." Then she told me I had to turn off my brain. I had to put all my bad thoughts in a huge box and shut the lid down tight. "That's what regular folks do," she said. "When they got troubles in their life." I wondered if Gloria did that too. I wondered if the basement bathroom was her box. She kept the lid on tight and didn't see Rowan no more.

She gave me an extra giant spoon of green cough vitamins, but I still couldn't sleep. The tapping wouldn't stop and my box wasn't working. I tried to put Rowan in there. I tried to sit on the box in my head, but the lid kept popping off. And when I looked in Rowan wasn't a horrible wolf at all.

He was waving at me and smiling. "Hello, Turtle," he said.

ROWAN

Gloria came. And Gloria went. Every time she brought beans I tried to talk to her, pleaded, but she just kept saying, "Like I said, Telly has to choose. When he wants you out, you'll be out." I didn't understand what I'd done wrong. I know I ran away, but couldn't I just apologize?

For hours and hours I tapped the pipe that ran along the corner and disappeared into the ceiling. Willing Maisy to come back. Why wouldn't she let me out? Was she angry too?

I waited and waited and sang and counted and swore and dozed and dreamt and woke and waited and waited and sang and swore and slept and dreamt and waited and watched, but nothing changed. The room did not dissolve around me. I did not find myself in my bed upstairs. I did not discover Maisy's face smiling at me, delighted I was home. I did not feel my fingers tangled in Chicken's warm fur.

The cement stayed cement.

It seemed Gloria hadn't been there in a while, but I couldn't be certain. I just knew my stomach had an acidic emptiness. Cramps pierced my intestines. I noticed the smooth edges of my shinbone, my ribs. My muscles quivered when I tried to stand up to get a drink. Though I tried not to stand up very often.

I saw movement in the corner of my eye. I leaned over and squinted. A tiny blur of color skidded over the linoleum and slowed in the shadow behind the toilet. A centipede. He was still, silent, but as I slid forward I could see his two antennae moving in the air. He was sensing. My invisible antennae were moving, too. Ever so slightly.

Before, if I'd seen this in the shed, I would have stomped. But now I realized how neat this rust-colored creature was. His skinny legs all moved in perfect unison. A flurry of energy. I wondered about his life. Where did he come from? Did he have a family? Was he just trying to get away from them all? Did he sleep during the winter? Did his legs ever get tired, or did he just ignore the hurt and get on with it?

I bet he ignored it. And just kept going forward.

"Hello there, little friend," I whispered. I stayed very still. I hoped he would move closer. My insides filled up with want. I hoped he would know how badly I needed him to take a single coordinated step in my direction. He was the first living thing I'd seen in forever. Gloria didn't count.

"What's it like out?

"Is it still summer?

"I'm happy you're here."

The antennae flickered. He was listening. He was listening to me.

"Where did you come from?

"Can you sneak upstairs and see if Maisy is okay?

"Can you tell someone I'm here?"

Then the lights snapped out. Darkness shrank around my face, my skin. I couldn't see him anymore, but I knew he was still there. The room did not seem as empty as it had before. He was probably thinking about all my questions. I might have overwhelmed him, but I couldn't help it. I moved my fingers around in the blackness. Delicately touching the walls, the floor, the cold porcelain of the toilet. I couldn't find him.

Next time I woke, the lights were on again. That was how Gloria did it, flicking the switch outside the door. No pattern to when or why. My centipede was near the yellow base of the toilet. His feathery legs were pulled inward. He wasn't moving. He looked much, much smaller. I knew he was dead.

I hadn't cried at all. But I cried then.

MAISY

Gloria did what she said. She stopped going to work at Stafford's. They told her they didn't mind because of what she went through, and now she could spend some time at home. All day long she watched me. If I went outside she watched me through the window or the sliding doors. If I read a book, she watched me from Telly's chair. She even waited outside the bathroom when I was going. Seeing her there when I opened the door made me jump.

"People're going to wonder, Bids, why you're always so twitchy. Worse than a rabbit. Like you got bugs under your skin. You need to know Gloria's got everything under control."

One morning, Gloria told me to go into the basement for a can of tomatoes. She said being afraid was silly and there was no reason for it. She stood at the top of the steps and I went down the steps fast and yanked the string for the light bulb. The fan made its noise, so I couldn't hear Rowan. My legs wiggled. I found the tomatoes and raced back up.

"Good girl," she said. "Now that wasn't so hard, was it?"

After I ate lunch I had to go get a dish. Square and glass. She didn't watch this time. I couldn't find it, so I had to poke around. Rowan still didn't make no sound.

Before dinner, I went to get some beans. I found a can in the box at the bottom of the stairs. I took it out, but I stayed there. I closed my eyes and listened as hard as I could. I think I heard noises from behind the bathroom door. Maybe Rowan was singing. Or maybe he was growling. Like a wolf. Shakes went up my back. I ran up the stairs.

"See? I got full trust in you, Bids." She hugged me when I gave her the can. "And you got to have full trust in me. He's not going to hurt you. I won't let him. You're Gloria's girl!"

She opened the can and poured the beans in a bowl. She took them down to the basement, not even warmed up. When she came back up the phone started ringing, and Gloria let out a sigh and said, "It better not be work. We agreed." She answered it, and I knew she was talking to Telly because her face got shiny and her eyes got shiny and she kept trying to make her hair go smooth.

"Of course," she said. "That works perfect for me. I can make it happen. That's what Gloria does." She put the phone down and smiled big. "This is all so rushed." She used her hand for a fan. "So rushed. He don't give a girl much time to primp!"

"What do you mean?"

"He wants to meet. Your dad. In two hours. Dinner, I think. Maybe dinner." She pinched my chin. "Can you manage with a bowl of cereal, Bids?"

"Okay," I said.

"I don't want to leave you alone, but I don't got much choice. Watch TV, get a snack. Go to bed at a reasonable time, darling!" Her arms were waving around. Then she stopped. "If anyone knocks on that door, you do not open it. You hear me? You never know who it could be."

I nodded. I knew. It could be a man in a car.

It was almost dark when she left. She was wearing her new peachy dress and her hair was done in fat yellow curls. Through the screen door, I watched her walk to the top of the circle. The lights from the bus came and went. Then she was gone.

I took the rope off Chicken. Gloria kept him tied to a chair so he couldn't go wherever he liked, even though he only went to the basement door. He scritched and scritched. He barked at me. Then he flumped down next to it. I went and patted him. I sat down next to the door too. I made a tiny bark.

I stayed by the basement door with Chicken for a long, long time. He puffed out air. I puffed out air, too.

"Are you old and reeee-dicalus?" I asked him. He lifted up his big head and licked my face.

My stomach growled. I started thinking about beans. They were in the basement. I could open a can and eat them. I could go down there real quiet and get the can and come back up. The same as I did for Gloria. That would be okay. That was listening. That was doing what she said to do.

"Can I get some beans?" Chicken licked my face again.

"Okay," I said.

I got the key from the same box in Gloria's closet. She didn't even change the hiding spot. I stuck the key in the basement-door lock. It opened. Chicken got up and his tail was wagging hard but I closed the door behind me so he wouldn't sneak down. I went fast down the stairs and grabbed the string and yanked. Light burst on. The beans were in the box, and I picked up a can and held it in my hand. I could hear noises from behind Rowan's door. My throat got tight. The can was cold. I squeezed it. I had to go back upstairs, but my feet went forward. My feet weren't good listeners. They went closer to the door.

The fan was turned off, and I could hear him. He was scritching at something. I bet he had claws.

I tapped one finger on the door. That finger wasn't a good listener neither.

"Turtle?"

I didn't say nothing.

"Turtle? Is that you?"

Two loud thumps came on the door. My feet took some big steps back until I was far away.

"Let me out, Turtle."

It felt like spikes went in my middle. I shouldn't have come down. What if Gloria came home? What if she told a man and he came to take me? What if Rowan exploded out of that room and—and. But I couldn't think of what he'd do.

"Let me out," he cried.

But you're a wolf.

"You can do this. Stick your neck out, Turtle."

But you don't sound like a wolf.

"Are you still there? Hello? Hello?"

I held my breath. I think I heard him crying. My arms and legs got spikes too. I dropped the can of beans and it rolled away.

"I'm your brother," he said. Then he screamed out so sharp, "I am your brother!"

But Gloria says. Gloria says you're a wolf.

When she got home, Gloria came in my room and put the spoon of green cough vitamins in my mouth. My middle was still shaking but she couldn't see. She pulled up my sheet. She smoothed it down and kissed me on the forehead.

"Me and your dad had a wonderful meal tonight."

"Was it good?"

"Yep. Real good. We had burgers and fries. Nothing fancy, but I've never asked for fancy." She smoothed her finger over her mouth. There was still some peachy lipstick there.

"Oh," I said.

"We talked, Bids. Really had a good talk. I could tell we connected. I helped him figure stuff out. Made him see what's what." She clapped her hands and laughed loud. "After all this time, he's finally, finally seeing my side of things. It's going to be okay." She pinched my cheek. But not hard. "I wanted you to know. He's coming back and we're going to figure out everything."

"Okay." I laughed too. Gloria had twinkly eyes because Telly was moving home. He'd know what to do. He'd fix things.

"I knew he'd be back. I've been watching him, you know? Him and her at their house. Leaving all their lights on at night. Curtains wide open. Easy enough to see everything, Bids. And I could tell, I could just tell, he was almost out of his mind. Numb with her. I mean, what could he have ever seen in some stick of a woman who cleans gunk off teeth? Poor Telly." She chewed her lip and smiled. "I know that man better than he knows himself. And me and him? Things like the two of us don't unravel so easy. Not with that history, they don't." She shook her head back and forth. Her skin looked peachy, too. "Oh, Bids. I just knew. I just knew."

ROWAN

I don't know how many days I'd been in there, but the throbbing in my head was lessening. I was still sore, but when I tapped my tooth with my tongue, it seemed stronger. The wiggle was gone. Maybe that was a good sign. It could be a good sign. Things might be okay. Just like Dot had said. I couldn't give up. I had to keep trying.

I got up and leaned against the sink. Cupping warm water from the tap, I dampened my hair. Pushed it over to the side. I reached under the shirt and sweater and tried to rinse the stench from my armpits. Inside my chest, I felt the thinnest thread of hope. I stared at my face, which now seemed unfamiliar to me. My brain could not connect my eyes with my nose and my mouth. All the parts were separate. Would Gloria even recognize me?

Then she was outside the door, humming a song and fiddling with the lock. I sat back down and put my head on the cold linoleum, but I couldn't see past the bunched-up fabric. The door creaked open. I could smell more beans. While the thought of beans made me sick, my stomach ached and growled.

"Gloria," I whispered. A dry croak. "Has Telly decided?"

She nodded. "He will."

"Really? Can I say something?" This was my one chance of the day to explain. I had to do it right.

She didn't answer.

I stood up again, gripped the edge of the counter. "Gloria? I'm sorry for everything I've done. I'm sorry I ran away. I really am. I'm sorry I made you worry or if you were scared or if I was too much trouble and that's why Telly left in the first place. I realize everything now. I've been doing a lot of good thinking. I really have, and I figured it all out. I've caused enough problems, and from now on, I'm going to be perfect. You can count on that. It's a promise."

She glanced at me then, and I tried to smile.

"Your dirty friend," she said, "had quite a lot to say. Made a real mess of things."

"You mean Carl?"

"Telly's head is muddled with it all, but it's going to be straightened out soon. You can't imagine the aggravation I've had over it. With this mess."

"What mess? What did he do?"

"Oh, he did plenty. But the worst of it? He killed you."

"What?"

"Apparently, you're dead."

"I'm dead?"

She tilted her head. "Are you? Are you dead?"

For a split second I wasn't sure.

"Well, you're as good as dead. But I'm going to bring you back to life. Soon."

"I don't get it."

Her eyes were wide, and her face was shiny.

"You're going to stay right here, mister, and when Telly gets home, we'll figure out the story. Like I already said."

My legs were weak and wobbly, but my heart punched in my chest. "What story? What are you talking about?"

"You'll know when you need to know." She dropped the beans on the floor. Cold brown liquid spattered my legs. "We had a lovely dinner last night."

"All of you? You guys had dinner together?" *Without me?* The sadness inside me vanished. Beneath it, a glassy spray of anger. "How long am I stuck down here? How long!"

She was so calm when she said, "Are you thick? How many times do I got to repeat myself? Until Telly says so."

I leaned toward her, "When I get out of here, I'm going to tell everyone. Tell everyone what you did."

"You think?"

"You'll be screwed, Gloria."

She opened her mouth, started to laugh, and at that moment I shoved the door forward. It struck her lip. She yelped, grabbed her face. I stumbled past her. Climbed over the peeling leather couch. My heart was beating hard and blackness crowded my vision. Gasping, I scrambled toward the stairs. My legs were lead, but I could do it. I could make it. Once I got outside, I'd run. Up the driveway and into the circle. I'd run to Darrell's. Run to Mrs. Spooner's house. I'd scream and yell and someone would hear me or see me with my arms swinging around like crazy. Someone would help.

My foot caught on a box of cans. I tripped. Flew forward. My bony ribcage struck an empty toolbox. Then a slippery vice grip on my ankle. Dragging me back. I cried, "Maisy! Maaaiseeeee!"

Her hand clamped over my mouth and she lifted me right off the ground, her arm a noose around my waist. She carried me, effortlessly. I kicked backwards, but my weak legs only met air. She threw me into the bathroom again. When I hit the floor, pain shot up through my spine.

"Please, Gloria. I didn't mean that. I'll say whatever you want. I'll say anything." Her lips were pulled apart and I could see her gums. "I won't say a word. I promise. I won't say anything. Please just let me out. Please." Tears poured from my eyes. Muscles shaking.

With her foot she hooked the bowl of beans. A flick of her toes, the bowl skidded out of the bathroom, flipped, the contents covered the back of the couch.

"Please."

Her dark form filled the entire doorframe. "You stupid, stupid boy." Then she closed the door and locked it.

A dull ache filled my head and my chest. The lights would not turn off. The whirring fan would not slow down. Water would not sit and wait inside the toilet. The dead centipede in the corner would not stick out its thin legs, balance on pin toes, and crawl toward me.

My skull grew woozy with flatness. With dullness. With sameness.

But most of all. With loneliness.

I pulled my arms inside the shirt Carl had given me. I closed my eyes and hugged my chest. I no longer knew where I began or where I ended.

I couldn't feel my boundaries. I was cement and I was sink and I was tape shoes and I was curling linoleum and I was pine-scented wisp of nothing.

Whenever I was awake I leaned against the black pipe in the corner and tapped and tapped. Made up a code and spelled out *I'm sorry, I'm sorry, I'm sorry, I'm sorry.*

No one answered. No one understood.

MAISY

The next day Gloria was just like Chicken. For hours she went from the kitchen to the front door. She kept picking up the phone and listening and putting it back down. "Just making sure it works," she said. Telly was going to call any minute. Then she went to the door again. She looked out the window. "This homecoming needs to be planned out. What with, you know, downstairs and all." She pointed her thumb at the basement door. "I told him he had to call. I really hope he doesn't just show up."

He didn't just show up.

For dinner she cooked a big breakfast. "Why not?" she said. "We don't have to follow any rules." She fried eggs and sausages. She made toast. The smell went everywhere. I wondered if it went through the floor and into the basement. Maybe Rowan could smell it too.

It made me think of the place I went with Telly and Dian. Barney's Diner. "Is this like br-lunch?" I asked.

Her eyes got small. "What would you ever know about brunch?"

I shook my head fast. "Nothing."

"Brunch is not a proper meal. Only lazy people use that word. People who can sleep in and don't got to work." She put a plate in front of me. It was piled up with a lot of food. "This is a proper meal."

Gloria sat down and hummed as she ate. "You don't recognize that tune, do you?" I shook my head again but she didn't see. She was looking at the spoon from her coffee. It was in front of her face. She smoothed her hair.

"I had quite the voice when I was young, Bids. Full of talent. They said I could've gone professional."

"That's nice," I said.

"Nice?" She dropped the spoon and it made a loud noise. I jumped. "Is that the best you can do?" My heart started to beat fast. "Honestly," Gloria said. "The conversation in this house just makes my head spin. It's so bland. Why can't you say something interesting or insightful?"

I looked down at my sausages. All I could think of was Carl. He would break the wieners in half and give the big parts to Girl. That was being nice, Rowan said. *Nice.*

Gloria smacked the table. "Are you in there? Why don't you talk, hey? I can't figure out what goes on in that thick little skull of yours."

I swallowed. I couldn't think of no words.

"Nothing. That's what I'd say. Nothing goes on."

She poked me between my eyes with her finger. My head popped back. Then she got up and went to the phone again. She checked the front door. She yanked up the curtain and pulled it back down. Outside there were only long lines of sunlight getting smaller and smaller.

"Why isn't he calling? He promised he would. First thing. I don't get it. I just don't get it. That witch isn't making it easy on him. I'd bet this house that's the problem."

Gloria was braiding my hair but she put the wrong bit under another bit and it turned out bad. She stuck her fingers in and tugged hard. Some of my hair got knotted up in her fingers.

"I can't manage a thing today." She threw the comb in the sink. "Not even your frizzy mess."

She was angry because Telly didn't call last night. And he didn't call this morning neither.

"I hate all this waiting."

I didn't know what to say, so I slid off the bathroom counter.

"That's the problem with Telly. He don't want to hurt no one's feelings."

Then, through the open window, I heard pebbles crunching. The sound of a motor. Gloria busted out of the bathroom and ran down the stairs.

"That can't be Telly," she said. "I told him he had to call. Insisted on it."

I raced behind her.

She didn't go to the door. She went to the kitchen sink and lifted up the curtain. I climbed on the stool so I could see out too. Telly's truck wasn't there, but a different one was. It was white and dirty with a sticker on the side. But I couldn't read what it said. A man got out. He had no hair and had sunglasses on, and the front of his T-shirt looked dirty too. He was holding an envelope. Gloria dropped the curtain, but we could still peek out. The man was on our porch and we couldn't see him no more, and then he knocked on the door. My eyes got sparkles and stars. He was coming for me.

Sobs burst out. "I didn't tell nobody, Gloria. I didn't."

"Will you be quiet?" Gloria whispered. Some of her spit hit my face. "It's probably some weirdo. A kid dies and that gets some sickos excited."

He knocked again. Harder this time.

"They want to see where it all happened. Like a damn tourist attraction. That's their thrill."

I tried to clamp down my sobs. My chest was shaking bad.

He knocked again. So loud it had to hurt his knuckles.

"Well," Gloria said. She wiped her hands across her cheeks. "I'm not going to be a sheep in my own home. I refuse."

She yanked open the front door.

"You got no right to be on my front porch, sir," she said.

"Gloria Janes?"

"That's me."

"This is for you." He pushed the envelope at her and she took it.

"What is it?"

"Explains itself." Then he turned around and said, "As for your porch, you might look into painting it. Before all the wood rots." He went back in his truck. It backed out of our driveway and looped around and drove away.

Gloria slammed the door. "Who does he think he is? Talking to me like that."

I took some big breaths. My heart slowed down. I was glad he was gone. Gloria was glad too I think, but she wasn't smiling. She went back to the kitchen and sat down at the table and ripped the envelope. There was lots of paper inside.

"This don't make no sense," she said. "It don't make no sense."

"What, Gloria?"

"It's from Telly."

"He's coming back?"

She wiped some wet off her mouth. "No, no. No. He didn't understand me. Not one pinch. We had such a lovely dinner. Everything was figured out. Now these papers. These. He—he wants to make things official."

"Like getting married?"

"God help me." She threw the papers on the table. "How dense can you get? We're already married, you idiot." Then she crunched up the papers in her fist. "This pile of trash says he wants to get divorced."

Gloria got up and stomped around the kitchen. Chicken was right behind her. She was mumbling. "He didn't understand a single word I said. He wasn't even listening." She went back to the table. She smoothed out one of the pages in her fist. She talked slow. "Disso-what? Diss-olu of marital. Dissolution of marital assets? What does that mean?"

I burped. I didn't feel good inside.

"Oh my god," she said. "Oh my god!" She slammed the paper on the counter.

I looked at Gloria. I opened my mouth. Clouds in my head got thick and dark. I couldn't see through them.

"Your father. Your bastard father! He's going to sell my house."

MAISY

After those papers came, me and Gloria didn't go out for a lot of days. She told me chicken pox was coming. I wasn't itchy, but she said, "I got a sixth sense about these things."

I stayed in my pajamas and Gloria banged around the house. She talked loud but she didn't talk to me. She said, "I bought this. Out of my hard-earned dollars. He never had a cent, not one red cent, and now he wants to take it away?"

She rubbed her head a lot. I saw her put her hands on the wall like she wanted to know if it was cold. Sometimes she went outside by herself and walked around and around the circle. Aunt Erma and Mrs. Murtry and Mrs. Spooner came out and waved at her. She didn't wave back. She just stopped by the red fire thing near the bus stop and didn't move.

Then she sat in the kitchen. She chewed on the back of her wrist. She tapped her fingers for hours and hours. "Where does that moron think we're going to go?"

She didn't even tie Chicken up no more. All day he slept by the basement door. He pushed his nose into the bottom and whined.

"Well, he can think again. We're not going nowhere."

One night I heard Gloria crying in the bathroom. She was sniffing and hiccuping. I pushed open the door. It creaked. "Gloria?" I whispered.

She was squirting toothpaste on her brush. A blue blob went in the sink. "Get out, Maisy. Just get out."

"Don't worry. It's going to be okay." That was what Mrs. Spooner always said.

"Okay? Okay? How did I grow something so dumb?" She brushed at her teeth. I could hear it scritching. She still talked. "How's it going to be okay? Telly's gone. I faced it. I have. There's no way to turn it around. Ever since he left, I done all I could. But I lost, you know that? I lost the fight. Every single ounce of goodness in my life is gone." She kept brushing hard. The white foamy bubbles turned bright pink and rolled down her chin. "And now there's no way out."

I got a hard pain in my middle. I went to my room and climbed in my closet. Dirty clothes were on the floor. I forgot to put them in the basket. Jenny the Head was there, too. She was hiding in the corner. I hugged her. Her hair smelled old like rainwater in the ditch. I curled up and closed my eyes. I thought about Rowan catching Jenny as she swam by. He washed her hair. He sewed her up a body and stuffed it with oatmeal. That was a nice day.

The next afternoon we walked to the library. Gloria told me to stay in a chair and not budge an inch. Then she went upstairs. She walked all around the shelves and she sat at a desk with a pile of heavy books. She opened one up and scritched her head.

Sun was coming in the big windows. The library was always bright and warm. I swung my feet back and forth. Mrs. Spooner was behind her desk. She stamped little cards. When she saw me she stood up and came over.

"I've missed having you here," she said.

I nodded.

"Feeling better?"

I chewed on my fingernail.

"I just noticed your mom. Up in the reference section. Doing some serious research?"

I nodded. I hoped Mrs. Spooner didn't get too close. Gloria said my chicken pox could pop out any minute.

"She doesn't seem quite herself, Maisy. I hope everything's okay?"

I pushed my hand under my leg. I nipped as hard as I could to stop me crying. My chin was shaking bad.

"Don't worry," she said, and she sat down next to me. "I'm sure she'll be fine. Grief is like that, sweetheart. Sometimes it settles for a while, and then a fresh wave can hit you. With no warning at all."

I was having a fresh wave. It was cold and stung bad.

"He's still here. You understand that, right?"

My woodpecker heart went right up my throat. Did Mrs. Spooner know Rowan was an angry wolf in the basement? I squished up my eyes to see her good. I looked at the stairs. Gloria was still sitting at the table. She licked her finger and turned some pages. I whispered to Mrs. Spooner, "Do you know where he is?"

"Of course I do."

I opened my mouth. But no air came in. Everything was going fuzzy. She tapped me on the chest. "Your brother will always be right there. In your heart."

Then I couldn't keep it in. My new fresh wave had got too big. I started crying because I was so sad, and I couldn't tell Mrs. Spooner the truth. I couldn't tell her that since I found Rowan in the basement I was worried all the time. I worried about Gloria and I worried about Rowan, and I worried a man was coming and I worried that no one was coming at all.

Gloria's head flew up. She slammed the book closed and stomped down the stairs.

"Oh," Mrs. Spooner said. "Oh, I didn't mean to upset you. There's something I wanted you to have." She gave me a paper. It had Rowan's name on it with FINALIST on the bottom. "That was the writing contest your brother won, remember? He won second prize? They sent the certificate. I thought you'd like to have it."

More crying rushed out, and my whole head was hot and hurting. Gloria was in front of me like a big shadow. "Why're you making such a fuss, miss?"

"Oh, dear. That was me," Mrs. Spooner said. She smiled at Gloria. "I was trying to make her feel better, but I did a rotten job of it."

"Well, you needn't've bothered."

Mrs. Spooner's mouth went open and Gloria grabbed my wrist. She yanked me out the door.

"Something off about a woman," she said when we got to the road, "who wastes so much energy on everyone else's kids and never put a single thought into having her own."

All the way home the wind tried to steal Rowan's paper. But I wouldn't let it go.

ROWAN

"Telly finally made his decision." Gloria stood in the doorway of the bathroom. Her yellow hair was sticking up and she had rings of makeup under her eyes. "He's not coming home."

There was no bowl in her hand. No spoon. "I can come out then?" I whispered.

"He's not coming home," she said again. Her voice was flat, and she didn't look down at me when she spoke. I could see the powdered underside of her chin. "I wanted you to know. So you understand."

"What . . . understand what?"

"So you understand why."

"Gloria?"

"I told him everything. I did. I told him everything and it didn't matter."

"Did you tell him what I said? That I didn't mean it?"

"I tried so hard. To fight for our family. For you and Maisy. But he has a new life now. A better life. Telly's happy."

"How—"

"He's happy without me, and without Maisy, and without you. He told me he doesn't care."

"About us?"

"Everything's his fault. I want you to understand that too. I never asked for this. He pushed me too far. All I wanted was to be together. Like we were."

"Gloria. Just—just listen."

"And now it's my turn. My turn to make a decision."

"Can I please come out? I prom—"

"It's my turn to be happy."

MAISY

The next morning Gloria's smile was back. She put on the blue top she wore on the news. She told me to do that, too. Put on my dress. She wore earrings and a necklace. She put some shoes and clothes into a garbage bag and threw them in the shed. Then she filled up a box with some plates and a tall lady made of glass and a bowl covered in orange polka dots. "It's good to be organized, Bids. Get some things out of the way."

All afternoon she hummed and smiled and hugged me. "I think those nasty chicken pox skipped right by you," she said. "That's certainly good news."

I nodded.

At night she cooked pork chops and mashed potatoes and corn from a can. She told me to wear my shoes like we were at a fancy restaurant because we were having a special meal. Just the two of us. "That's what's left, Bids. You and me. Me and you." Then she squeezed up her eyes. "Maybe you should put on that sweater I bought you last spring from Stafford's. The lacy one?"

I did.

The pork chops tasted good.

"I know I've been off living in my own head lately," Gloria said.

She laughed a bubbly laugh. I laughed the same. Her face was so shiny.

"Sometimes life throws a good old curveball at you, don't it? I had to think on it. Think hard about what to do. The whole messy thing with Telly and—and you know."

I spooned up my mashed potato and pushed it into the corn. The corn stuck on and I ate it fast. There was a lot left on the counter. She was going to bring it down to Rowan. I knew that for sure. She might even bring him up. Her eyes were dazzly. Something good was going to happen. Something great. I thought of the nurse from school. This time I really did have butterflies in my stomach.

"But as I always say, once you make a decision, the hard part's over. You just got to stick to it. Follow through. Even if it's tough."

I looked at Gloria. She was still smiling, but not at me. She was smiling into the air. Like there was a ghost standing behind me. I looked at her plate. She wasn't eating her food. She just moved it around. It was a mess. I swallowed, and the potato stuck in my neck. The butterflies stopped flying around. They all fell down and they felt heavy and thick and their wings and legs were moving. I put down my fork.

"Gloria? You're not hungry?"

"I've been thinking a lot about that young man. Shar's cousin. What's his name?"

I didn't feel good no more. She told me to kiss him on the mouth. I didn't want to say his name, but I whispered, "Darrell."

"How he came and helped us with that fire. I mean, Erma was there too, but she just stood around. Darrell really helped. Such a small kindness, you know, but it sure meant a lot to me. Our little house cleaning."

I could hear the thump, thump of Chicken's tail hitting the floor. He was next to Gloria's shoes.

"That worked really well, didn't it, Bids? Job done."

The shed got clean. All the boxes and rope and welcome mat and old wood turned black and then to nothing. The wind blew away the dirty ashes.

"Telly ruined everything. You need to understand. When you look back on this night and wonder. I tried really hard to fix things. Gloria gave it her all."

I nodded. But she was still smiling at the invisible ghost. Then she got up. She picked up her plate and turned it. The food dumped right on the floor. It splatted all over. Even up on the wall. She never done that before.

"Oh," I said. "Was that an accident?" She didn't answer. Chicken rushed over and gulped at it fast.

Gloria took my plate, too, and put them both in the sink. Mine still had stuff on it. But she didn't get mad about the waste. She poured a giant glass of water and left it on the counter. I waited for her to drink it, but she didn't.

"Gloria?"

"You know, I haven't told you enough, Bids. Of course I should've trusted you from the start. About the little situation in the basement."

I shook my head. I didn't understand.

"It's time, well, to let sleeping dogs lie."

I looked at Chicken. He was like a vacuum cleaner, sucking up corn off the floor. He crunched a bone. Sharp parts stuck out of his mouth.

"Chicken's awake," I said.

"Chicken's a good dog, isn't he?" She turned the stove on. Maybe she was going to make a dessert. "Every single day I think about how Rowan used to be. And what he became. It truly breaks my heart."

Gloria was talking strange. The woodpecker got up in my neck. It was pecking me harder than it ever did before. Tak-tak-tak. Tak-tak-tak. Tak-tak-tak.

"It's been the hardest thing to accept. I thought for sure I could fix him. I wanted to keep him close. Turn him back into the old Rowan. So he wasn't a wolf no more. But I needed Telly's help to do that. Telly's help. And I didn't get it, Bids. I didn't get no help at all. And Rowan, he's gone. I can't even recognize him no more. Just more and more vicious. And it's not safe trying to keep him. He's a danger. And a menace. And no one can help him. No one. I should never've tried it. Gloria really overestimated herself this time, didn't she?" She laughed a little, but the bubbles were gone. "And now I'm broken inside, and I just, I just tell myself he never came home at all. He's sleeping on the bottom of the lake. He's down there, Bids. Like Telly said. And no matter how much we try to hope and think and imagine, we can't pull him up. Our Rowan. We've got to do that. It's easier to tell ourselves he died, Bids. He drowned, okay? Or his ghost'll never find no peace. It'll be tormented."

His ghost?

"You need to do that. Accept that he died. Your brother drowned, Bids. I couldn't save him. I tried so hard."

My eyes were getting fuzzy. My middle was full of nails. Chicken licked the floor over and over.

"The police did nothing right. From the get-go. I'm going to bring a lawsuit, I am. Take what I'm owed. They need to be held responsible. Maybe I'll save some other family from the misery I experienced. That's a noble goal."

Gloria took the dirty potato pot. She put in some oil. She kept pouring it in. *Glug, glug, glug.* Then she opened another bottle of it. And then another until the pot was full.

"What are you making, Gloria?" I tried to say it loud. But I don't think she heard me.

"Telly never should've left, Bids. Your dad. He really did belong here. In my house. *My* house. You can't imagine how hard I worked to get this place, and all the while Telly learning how to tinker with cars. And he thinks he can take it away."

She smiled again. But it wasn't a happy smile this time. Or a sad-smile. I didn't know what kind of smile it was.

"I can call Telly? I can ask him to come home, Gloria."

"Oh, Bids. He's made up his mind. I got to accept that, too. There's a vicious wolf in our basement, and Rowan is drowned, and Telly's not coming back. He was never coming back. He just played Gloria for a fool."

A bad smell started. Smoke came out of the pot. Gloria put on an oven mitt.

"So now you and me are going to start fresh. Just totally fresh, Bids. Maybe we'll find a little house in a new town. Some place real beautiful. After all we've been through, we deserve that. Don't you think?"

"I don't want a new town, Gloria." My head was so confused. What was in the basement? I knew it was Rowan. He called me Turtle. *Even if he's a wolf, he's still here.* "I like Pinchkiss Circle. I like Little Sliding."

"No, you don't. You just think you do. You're too young. You don't know nothing."

There was a lot of smoke now. The kitchen had a horrible stink.

"You need to trust me, Bids. Do you trust me? We can't tell anyone what we were imagining. Our bad ideas about the basement. Believing we could fix something so wrong. They'd think we went crazy. You and me. We'd be pulled apart. When all we were doing was trying to hold things together. Trying to make life back like it was."

I wanted to cry but I started to cough.

"Do you trust me?" She sounded mad.

"I trust you."

"Okay," she said. "Just do what I say, and everything'll be fine."

Then orange blasted from the pot.

I leapt up from my seat. Chicken barked and barked.

Gloria stepped back real fast. “Get ready!” she yelled. She grabbed the water glass and threw it into the pot.

Wind ripped in my ears. Fire shot up to the ceiling. Angry orange fingers went everywhere. Tearing and eating.

Hot stung my face. I screamed. The curtain was gone. Then Rowan’s FINALIST paper. I saw Jenny the Head. She was hiding on the windowsill. Her hair turned to fire and her face crumpled down to her eyeballs. I couldn’t reach her.

“Go, go, go!” Gloria grabbed my hand. “Run, Bids, run!”

We ran down the hall and out the happy, happy yellow door. Chicken ran out with us. I was coughing bad. Gloria was coughing, too. I tried to get air. I looked at our house. The sky was gray and then part of it was black from smoke and fire climbing out the windows. Tears slipped out of my eyes. They slid down over my cheeks, and Gloria wiped them away. She still had her oven mitt on.

MAISY

Our house was burning. Fire was eating up the floors and walls. But none of it was real. I couldn't think. I had to push it down. I had to put it inside the box and stomp on it. Gloria told me to jump up and down on the box. I tied it up tight with a skipping rope. *Don't let it out. Don't let it out.* I couldn't let it out. *Just look at the ashes flying up into the sky. How pretty they are!*

"Things'll be okay, Bids," Gloria said. She shook me. "We're doing what needed to be done. You got to trust me."

The oven mitt dropped off Gloria's hand. She kicked it far over the grass. Then she held my arm. My teeth chomped together. I couldn't stop shaking. Chicken was shaking, too. He tugged and whimpered, but Gloria wouldn't let him go. I heard glass smashing. Orange climbed out the kitchen window, and it almost got up to the roof. The colors were all over Gloria's face. Inside Gloria's eyes.

This was the worst dream. I was so scared I couldn't even cry. I couldn't even pinch my leg because what if it hurt? That would make it real. Then the box would fly open. I'd have to. I'd have to see inside.

Then Mrs. Spooner and Darrell were there. I didn't even see them coming. Darrell ran right around the house and yelled out at Gloria. "Mrs. Janes! Your hose is gone!"

"Stay back!" Gloria yelled. "Water's all turned off."

Darrell put his hands up in the air. "The whole thing's going to burn to the ground!"

"Oh dear god." Mrs. Spooner was in her bathrobe. "I called. I did. The moment I saw the smoke. I called."

"Called?" Gloria's teeth were closed up.

"The fire department." She put her hands on her face. "Is there anything I can do? Take Maisy to my place?"

Gloria squeezed my hand and it hurt bad. "Maisy'll stay right here with me," she said. "Because *I'm* her mother."

Mrs. Spooner took her hands off her face. "Oh, dear. I didn't mean . . ."

Gloria showed Mrs. Spooner her back. Then Aunt Erma and Shar ran down the driveway. "Gloria! What on earth?"

Gloria started crying. Aunt Erma hugged her and rubbed her arms. Gloria let go of me, but didn't let go of Chicken. He was pulling harder and growling and barking. "Oh, Erm. Grease fire," she said. "Caught the curtains. I couldn't get it out. Nearest hydrant is right at the top of the circle."

"Jesus. It is, isn't it?"

"Worst thing in the world, putting water on it. I'm such an idiot! That place is a tinderbox."

"Now's not the time to beat yourself up. You're lucky you and Maisy got out safe." She frowned. "What you two haven't been through this year. Too much for anyone."

Shar pushed in next to me. Her eyes were big. But she wasn't scared. "That's so cool," she whispered in my ear.

It was summery warm out, but my insides were ice cubes.

There was screeching. Two fire trucks were coming and lots of red lights were flashing. They drove straight down the driveway. Men in brown overalls leaped off the truck before it stopped. They had helmets on.

"Whose house?" the man yelled.

"Mine," Gloria said. He came right over. Gloria put her hand on her head. She said, "I must look a fright."

"You're alive, ma'am. That's what matters." He looked at the house. "Is everyone out? You're all accounted for?"

"Yes," she said. "Everyone's out."

He smiled at me, but the woodpecker was stuck in my neck, tak-tak-takking so hard my head was going up and down. *Everyone's out. Everyone's out.* Gloria said that. That meant everyone was out. *You need to trust me.*

I had to trust her. I had to keep the skipping rope tied tight. I had to keep the lid stuck on the box.

"Are you absolutely certain?"

Gloria puffed out air, and when she reached her arm around me she let go of Chicken's collar. "Yes, I am. It's just me and my daughter and that dog." Chicken was racing at the house. Gloria slapped her leg. "Chicken! Get back here!"

"Ma'am. Nearest hydrant is some distance away. Is there a creek or pond close? Any water source?"

"There's nothing. Slowrun Creek is all the way in the woods. And my outside water's turned off because Maisy was playing with the hose too much."

Her words got wavy. I couldn't remember playing with the hose.

"Okay, ma'am. Okay. I understand. A tank's on its way, but it's a fierce burn. There's no wind, so at present there's no danger to surrounding properties." He pointed his glove at the house. Then he pointed at the trees. To the same spot where they'd swallowed up Rowan. "You're far enough away from the woods, so that's not a concern."

"Okay." She patted her hair again.

"Until the tank gets here, we're going to try to control it as best we can."

Another fireman put a blanket on me and one on Gloria. "Just let it go," she said.

"I'm sorry, ma'am?"

"Burn itself out. There's no point trying to save it. The place is destroyed. Not like there's anything of value in there."

He scritched his head. "We're going to do everything we can."

"Yeah." Gloria laughed, but it wasn't a friendly laugh. "I heard that before." Then she yelled, "Chicken! Get away from there."

I watched Chicken. He was glued to the side of the house. He was back at that same spot, digging his claws at the cement. He pawed away the pile of rocks Gloria had put there over the dead bird. Then he scritched off a square piece of plastic on the vent. With his snout pushed in, he pulled stuffing out of the vent with his teeth. It looked like old grocery bags or T-shirts. He was whining and circling like he had a bellyache from the pork chop bones. They were sharp and pointy, but he chewed them down.

"Chickennnnnn!" Gloria screamed at him.

He barked and barked.

My head was full of cotton.

The blanket fireman said, “He’ll be fine, ma’am. He’ll know when to move. Animals have an instinctual fear of fire.”

Smacking at her leg, she kept yelling. “Chicken. C’mon. Get over here!”

But he wouldn’t listen. He must’ve made her disappear. He banged the rocks with his paws. He poked his nose into a hole in the house. I knew what he smelled. I couldn’t pretend. My fingers pinched my leg. My leg hurt. It really hurt. That vent went like a snake into the basement.

Into the basement bathroom.

Where the wolf was hiding.

The lid on my box was rattling and bumping. I couldn’t look at Chicken. I squeezed my eyes shut.

But I couldn’t keep at it.

I knew he was down there.

I knew.

I knew.

I knew.

I knew.

I knew.

ROWAN

I dreamt I was underneath the bridge, the coolness coating my spotted skin, a new island coming out near my left elbow. Carl handed me segment after segment of an orange. Girl trotted over to lick me beneath my lip, and I smelled the sweet smell from Carl's fire.

The sweet smell from Carl's fire.

My eyes flicked open. In the darkness of that box, I could taste it. Only a faint, sour thread, but there it was on my tongue. I sneezed, sniffed again. It didn't fade back into my dream.

Smoke.

I stood up slowly. My legs were rubber. I felt along the wall, sniffed toward the vent. I sniffed by the toilet and pushed my head into the sink near the drain. Nothing. I stretched up near the fan. I couldn't catch a clear strand of it. I hunched down on the floor and poked out the T-shirts. The blanket on the other side was missing. Air pulled inward. The biting sting of something burning.

The hairs on the back of my neck lifted up. My heart thumped and I could feel the pulse in the tips of my fingers. It didn't make sense. The smoke didn't smell like Carl's fire. Or smell like burning wood or dead leaves or even old tires. It stank like the time I put a plastic bowl on the hot stove.

My chest got tighter and tighter.

The fan above me stopped whirring. Silence wasn't hiding underneath it though. Footsteps. Outside. Stomping past. Yelling, maybe. It had to be Gloria.

She was running around the house. Or else my brain was creating things. Maybe there was no smoke. Maybe I was going crazy.

I could be going crazy.

How could I not be going crazy?

I was going crazy.

That made sense. Crazy.

Does crazy ever make sense?

I told myself there was no smoke. There was only cement and linoleum and blackness and beans and gray-tape shoes and a vent that my fingers couldn't reach.

I held the edge of the sink. I climbed up onto the toilet and slowly lifted my hands toward the ceiling. My head wobbled on my neck. I lowered my hands. Waited, then tried again. It was warmer up there. Much warmer.

Why would the ceiling be warm?

What would cause the ceiling to get—

Awareness cut through me like a stick to my back. I tumbled off the toilet. My knees buckled. The house was on fire. That was the smoke. That was the heat. That was the commotion outside.

I hit the door, but my arms were so tired it was hard to lift them. "I'm in here! I'm in here!" My yell was barely a whisper.

There was scraping near the vent. I tried to yell again. I heard the faintest clanking, like rocks banging together. "Hey! Hey!" Scratching. Someone was scratching at the vent.

Then barking. Chicken was barking. I could hear him! *Chicken!* "Chicken!" I cried as loudly as I could. "It's me, boy! I'm in here!"

I screamed, but my voice just dissolved inside my throat. Then the scratching and the barking stopped. Chicken had gone away.

I sat back against the wall. The burning smell was growing stronger. It stung my nostrils. Clung to my throat. No one was rushing down the stairs. No one was opening the lock and pulling me out. No one was hurrying me to fresh air and safety.

Where was Maisy? I knew she wasn't upstairs. I knew she was beside Gloria, wherever they were. Why wasn't she helping me? How could she leave me here? So many times I'd told her and told her to stick her head out.

Then I remembered. I'd left her first. I'd run off to be with Carl, and she'd been all alone with Gloria. That was my answer right there. Gloria could say whatever she wanted over and over and over again. To turn Maisy against me. And Maisy was doing the same to me as I'd done. I'd stopped thinking about her, missing her. I stopped caring.

The smell seeped in. I yanked off the sweater Carl had given me. Soaked it in the sink. Threw it near the bottom of the door. Water sopped everywhere. I sat back near the pipe. I tapped and tapped frantically. I tried to breathe. To calm myself down. But the smoke was getting stronger. I began to cough.

And cough.

And cough.

Tears poured from my eyes. I curled into a ball, clamped the hem of the sweater over my mouth and nose.

I wasn't going to thrash and kick and fight like I did in Ansel's Lake. I knew what was coming.

I was trapped.

Gloria and Telly and Maisy and Mrs. Spooner and Darrell and Erma and Carl and Chicken and Girl were on the outside.

To them, I no longer existed.

Maybe I never existed at all.

MAISY

Chicken spun in circles.

"Are you sure everyone's accounted for, ma'am?" the fireman said. "Do you have another pet?"

"There's nothing in there. The place is empty."

Then he yelled out, "Can someone grab that dog?"

Another fireman went to catch him, but Chicken took off. He ran around the house and up onto the front porch and clawed and clawed and clawed at the screen until he made a rip. He jammed his head through. Then his body flip-flopped through the hole. Our happy, happy door was already open and he was gone. He was inside.

"Hey!" the fireman yelled out again. "Didn't I tell you to grab it?"

"Oh god, oh god." Gloria was making loud noises. She was wobbling back and forth like Shar's blow-up punch clown. She talked to herself. "What're you going to do, Gloria. Hey, hey? What are you going to do now?"

"Don't worry, ma'am. Everything's going to be fine."

I watched the door. I watched the fire. Smoke and curly orange ribbons came out my bedroom window. I watched the men. They kept looking at the circle, but the water truck didn't come. I looked at the tumbled-down pile of rocks. Then I remembered the little ball of metal Carl nipped in my hair. It was still in there. Inside the pile.

Terrible, terrible stuff is coming.

Terrible stuff was here.

Gloria squeezed my wrist tight. My hand tingled. Dust and smoke stung in my eyes. Chicken was gone. Chicken was gone to get Rowan. Whispers came into my head, *Maise, Maise, Maaaiseeeey.*

Then I heard Carl say, "You are not brave. But you will be brave."

The skipping rope snapped. The lid burst off the box.

I breathed fast. He was a wolf. Rowan was a wolf. I looked at the woods. The creek was in there. Carl and the bridge. Fresh air. He ran through the bushes, and he was laughing. Rowan was happy in the woods with Carl. He was happy in the outside.

Then I understood. A wolf didn't belong in a box. A wolf was supposed to be free in the forest. A hurt wolf would be angry. A trapped wolf would be sad.

Then I felt a hot burn right in my middle. There was wolf in me too. It was a tiny wolf. It was a scared wolf. But it was still a wolf.

I snapped my wrist out of Gloria's hand and I ran, a skipping stone, over the driveway, fast like a train, and I did not fall, I did not fall, and Darrell didn't catch me, and I was up those stairs, and I turned, and Gloria was shaking her fists, and her face was mad and full of orange fire shine, and Mrs. Spooner had her hands over her mouth, and Shar was smiling and jumping, and the fireman screamed "Stop that kid!" and I knew I'd never get back in Gloria's heart, she would slap it closed, and then I'd be gone, taken by those men, no one would want me, no one, no one, no one, sneaky useless spy sneak, and Gloria was growling like crazy and inside Chicken was growling like crazy too, but in a different way, a brave way, and I emptied my head and made a small wolf howl, it felt good to make a howl, and I rushed into the oven of dark clouds, and I closed up my eyes and my mouth and I did not breathe, and I waved my hands and gray still leaked up my nose holes, sunburn on my throat and my skin, coughing, the key in Gloria's closet, up the stairs and too far away, but maybe it will be open, maybe she forgot, fingers crossed, monster arms out through the cloud, tumbling where I knew, then Chicken against my leg, whining, but my turtle head was out, I felt the flat bits of metal, the screws, burning, Chicken was scritching and scritching, the lock, the lock, be open, be open. I pulled on it, my hand got small around it. Both ends trapped inside, and my fingers screamed.

I took a breath. My chest squeezed up and I got on my knees. My hand was burning. Chicken pawed my hair. The hot was on top of me. It shoved and shoved. A heavy blanket. Chicken bit at my dress and my lacy sweater and tugged. Something crashed and clanked. Big people yelling. Maybe Gloria.

Then I felt strange. Nice strange. Like the trick Rowan showed me before he was gone. He made me stand in a doorway and push the backs of my hands into the sides. I did it as hard as I could. Then, after I let my arms down, they went up by themselves. I knew if they weren't stuck on they would've floated away.

Wind moved around me. I was rushing somewhere. But I couldn't stay no more. The lid was off. I twirled down inside the box. There we were. Me and Rowan. One big wolf and one tiny wolf. But still two wolves together.

PART THREE

ROWAN

He came to see me at Gran's house. He said his name was Detective Aiken, and we went into the living room and closed the glass doors. The carpet was bouncy under my feet and the cushions were soft. I noticed things like that now. I sat in a rose-colored chair. Gran peered in through the door. The detective saw her and shook his head ever so slightly. Gran stepped back.

"How are you doing, Rowan?"

That was a big question. How was I doing? I'd spent six nights in the hospital being treated for a concussion, malnourishment, and smoke inhalation. My grandmother, who had *not* died after all, visited me every day. When I was released she brought me to her house, back to the same room I'd stayed in when I was a little boy.

Besides that? I'd been eating tons, watching a lot of television, and sleeping in as long as I wanted. Sometimes when I woke up, though, it took me a while before I realized where I was. Before I recognized the pillow under my cheek or the sun on my skin through the clean window. With my eyes still closed my fingers would reach out to tap the cement wall, and when I found nothing, a hollow threat would arrive in my body. As though, outside of that confined place, the security of limits had vanished. The sensation of being locked in was still locked inside of me. I didn't know how to find the door that would let me get out. To get past it.

"Okay," I said. "I'm good."

"I'm glad to hear it. And your sister?"

Maisy had to stay in the hospital longer as she had damage to the tissues in her throat and lungs as well as burns on her hand. I was excited to see her, but when she did come home with Gran she barely looked at me. Wouldn't say a word. Every time I came into a room she'd slip out. "Remember she's only little," Gran told me. "It's been an ordeal for her too." She told me Maisy had rushed into our burning house. They found her unconscious by the door to the basement.

I kept thinking about that. I couldn't stop myself from imagining what it was like. Over and over again. Chicken barking and circling. Maisy's yanking at the lock. Gloria screaming in the background when she couldn't stop the firemen from rushing in. Swooping Maisy off the floor. Smashing off the lock and hurrying down the stairs. Breaking down my door. Finding me in the dark bathroom, pressed into the corner, gasping.

Thank you, Turtle. Thank you for sticking your head out.

"Rowan?"

"Yeah," I said. "She's good, too."

Detective Aiken cleared his throat. "So you're adjusting all right?"

"Sure," I said. I ran my finger over the white island growing on my lower arm. There was a main mass and a northern peninsula. I wanted to show Maisy so we could guess what island was forming.

"You look healthy."

I shrugged.

"I know you answered many of our questions in the hospital." He adjusted his tie. It was navy and covered in small red apples. I thought it might be better suited to a teacher than a detective. "But I'd like to confirm some things you said. Get a clear understanding of who was involved."

"Who?"

"Yes."

"My mother," I said.

"Yes."

I tried to tell him what I remembered. Standing outside in the storm. Lightning zinging just overhead. Running away to the bridge. Girl. The two losers who tumbled down the embankment, and the one who held the knife to my neck. The cottage. The late-night boat ride. Dot's tinfoil hat to keep good thoughts in and bad thoughts out. Stumbling home through the woods and the pressure building in my skull until I couldn't stand or see. My confusion in the backyard. How Gloria must have grabbed me and hid me away. How I thought it was—

I stopped. "Not Carl, mister. It had nothing to do with Carl. I mean, Howard Gill."

"We understand that, Rowan." He leaned forward, squinted. "Mr. and Mrs. Baxter, the folks who owned the cottage, are not pressing charges for the damage. Mr. Gill has already been released."

"Good," I said. "He didn't force me. I went with him. I don't even know if he thought I was real."

"If it's any consolation, he did receive treatment while he was in care."

"So he's better?"

"I can't comment on that, but what Mr. Gill has—what Carl has, it's a complicated illness, Rowan."

"Yeah," I said. "I figured."

Detective Aiken reached into his pocket and pulled out a notepad. He flipped it open. "Your mother's not being cooperative with our investigation, but to be frank, we don't need it. We have enough. We still have questions, though, about the extent of your father's involvement. Your mother said they were a team, every step of the way, but your father claims to have had zero awareness."

"Oh."

"But I want to hear from you, Rowan. Did your dad know you were locked in that basement bathroom?"

My heart sank inside my chest. I stared at the arm of the chair. If I stroked it with my finger, the fabric changed. Recorded my movement. Then I could smooth it over again. Make the mark vanish.

"Rowan?"

I swallowed. Gloria's voice slipped inside my head.

"That's Telly's decision. He's still angry. We're talking about it, but it's up to him.

"Telly has to choose. When he wants you out, you'll be out.

"You're going to stay right here . . . Telly and I . . . we'll figure out the story.

"I told him everything. I did. I told him everything and it didn't matter.

"He has a new life now. A better life.

"He doesn't care."

He doesn't care.

I scratched my new spot. I knew the answer. Telly might not have spoken, but he still said plenty.

"Rowan? I know how hard this is, but we want to get at the truth."

"Yes," I said. "He knew I was down there. They were trying to teach me a lesson. Both of them decided on it and talked about it. Gloria and Telly. Telly and Gloria. They may seem like they're apart, Detective Aiken, but their minds are always together."

The detective blinked. Then he took a big breath and blew it out. I tapped the rose fabric, smoothed it, tapped it again.

"In all my years," the detective said, "I've never come across anything like this. It's—it's . . . I can't imagine a person who—" He put his notebook back in his pocket. "Thank you, Rowan. You're a courageous young man."

I nodded, but it wasn't a matter of courage. When those words had come out of my mouth it was the first time I felt strong. As though something solid was clinging to the shell that surrounded me. It would stick there and spread out. A thickening layer. Maybe I would stop dreaming about the basement. Stop dreaming about Gloria and Telly's plan to get rid of me. Maybe, someday, I would forget.

The detective asked a couple more questions. I told him everything I could remember. Then I saw Gran's gray hair in the corner of the glass door again. Next her worried face. She knocked gently. Chicken was beside her. He pawed at the doorknob, and when the door swung open he rushed in, sat on my feet. Chicken was my dog now. One hundred percent.

"Your grandmother's right. We've spoken enough for today. I appreciate how much you're helping us, Rowan. It's not easy."

It wasn't hard, either. Doing this. Being here with Maisy and Gran. It wasn't hard at all.

MAISY

"Gloria always gave me medicine, too."

"Did she?"

"It was green with vitamins because I could get a cough."

"Well, this is pink with no vitamins. But the doctor said it will help your lungs get all better." Gran put a spoonful in my mouth.

Gran's place was different from home. It was too warm and had soft carpet and smelled like flowers, same as Mrs. Spooner's. She let me sleep in Uncle Rick's blue room because Uncle Rick lived far away. Rowan was in the room next to mine. Chicken didn't have a corner downstairs, so sometimes he slept in with Rowan and sometimes he slept in with me. Gran said he didn't play favorites.

Gloria's old bedroom was at the end of the hall. Gran kept that door closed, but when I peeked inside there was striped wallpaper and a huge bed with a top part, and a little white table with a mirror, and a whole shelf of dolls.

Gran caught me being sneaky, but she didn't get mad. She put her hand on my shoulder and said, real soft, "Don't know why I kept them after your mom took off. Silly, really. Trying to hold onto better times."

I nodded.

"Your mother was such a beautiful child." Gran took a big breath. "Maybe I never told her often enough." Then she put her other hand on her cheek. "Or maybe I told her too much."

She let me go in and pick out a doll. I found one that looked just like

Jenny the Head, but she had a real body and arms and legs that moved. I liked that she had a place for her heart.

"Hey, Turtle, what's her name?" Rowan was standing at the door.

"Little Jenny," I said, and then I went out of Gloria's room and into Uncle Rick's. I closed the door.

I couldn't look at Rowan. Gran said he wanted to be friends, but he had to be angry about what I did. I didn't let him out. I kept Gloria's secret while he nearly burned up in the basement. My middle hurt so bad when I thought about it, and I thought about it all the time. That lady, Susan, came to see me at the hospital, and she said I saved his life, but I didn't believe her. The firemen saved Rowan. I couldn't even open the lock.

Gran came into Uncle Rick's room. She had an envelope in her hand.

"It's from someone named Sharlene? Was she your friend back in Little Sliding?"

I nodded, and Gran gave me the letter. When she closed the door I tore open the envelope. The paper inside was purple with a kitten and string on the bottom.

"Dear Maisy," it said. "When are you coming back? Your house is all black, but Aunt Erma won't let me go over. She makes it so boring here. Everyone at school wants to know what happened and what you did. Aunt Erma told Mrs. Murtry the cops caught your mom getting on the bus that night. She was trying to run away. Is that true? Mrs. Murtry's mad she ever let your mom use her car." I read as fast as I could. She told me to write her back and "tell her the whole story" so she could explain it to the girls. "They won't stop asking! They think I should know everything cuz I'm your best friend!"

There was a tiny note on the bottom of the page from Darrell. He said he hoped I was doing okay. He drew a smiley face with two little horns. So that was nice, but I still crumpled up the letter. I liked the one Rowan got from Mrs. Spooner a lot more. He left it on the kitchen counter and I could read almost all the words. She kept saying she was sorry, again and again. She said she knew something was wrong when she saw that sign with THEIF painted on it. "In the pit of my stomach, I knew." She was "riddled with guilt" because she never did nothing. Never pushed. Then she said she prayed Rowan would never experience another moment of suffering in his entire life. He was a gifted writer, and she hoped he'd always keep his creative spirit. Those were her wishes for him. I read it twice, and even though I didn't understand everything she meant, I knew for sure she didn't mention me at all.

"So?" Gran said when I went downstairs. "Do you want some fancy paper to write her back?"

"No," I said. "No, thank you."

Then Rowan was next to me, and it was hard to breathe.

"Hey, look what I found in the attic." He was holding a shoebox. "Uncle Rick's old toys. Plastic boats."

Gran laughed. "Don't I throw anything away?"

"You're too old to play with boats," I said.

"Says who? Let's go put them in the pond."

I shook my head. I didn't want to go outside with Rowan.

"Yes, go on, Maisy," Gran said. She was wearing an apron and holding a wooden spoon in her hand. It was covered in chocolate.

"Do I got to?"

"Yes, you do. It's a beautiful day, and the doctor says you need fresh air."

Rowan took the shoebox full of toys and we went out the back door. Gran had a big backyard with a tall fence all around it. We went to the bottom of the yard and Rowan opened up a gate. There was a path behind it, and woods, too.

"I don't want to go in there."

Rowan took my hand and tugged me. "You can't be afraid of everything, Maisy."

The gate clicked shut behind us.

Some of the trees had sharp needles, but the other ones were tall and leafy with white trunks. When I looked up I saw some of the leaves were turned yellow. The woods felt kind of sleepy and quiet. I still didn't like it.

"Guess what?" Rowan said. "I made a buddy yesterday."

"How?" I said.

"One of Gran's friends. She has a grandson. We grabbed burgers, and his little sister happened to come along. And guess what? She's the same age as you."

"Oh." I kicked some pebbles, and dust came up.

"I bet you'd like her. And don't worry, she's the exact opposite of Shar." Rowan smiled. "Would be good to have a friend for when you start school."

"We're going to school here?"

"Of course we are." He bumped me on the head, but not hard. "We missed a few weeks, but it'll be okay. And we'll be in the same school, Turtle, if anyone bugs you. It goes all the way to grade twelve."

"Oh," I said again.

We walked along a wide path. It turned through the woods and at the end there was a small pond. Soft grass went all the way around it, and lily pads floated on the top. It wasn't very deep and I could see all the way to the bottom.

"There's glass in there." I pointed at the water. "Broken bottles."

"Who cares, Turtle? We're not getting in."

Rowan found a stick on the ground and he went over and poked the trunk on one of the trees with needles. Then he came back and scraped shiny gunk onto the back of the boats.

"Now watch."

He squatted down and I squatted down next to him, and one by one he put the boats in the water. They rushed away and rainbow lines spread out behind them.

"Nice," I said.

"Yeah. Nice is just the right word."

A branch cracked behind us. I jumped and twisted to see.

"It's just the woods, Maisy," he said, and he put his hand over my shoulder.

I looked at the boats. They were still going.

"And besides, you're brave, remember?"

I'm not brave, I whispered in my head.

"Yes, you are," he said and squeezed my arm.

I put my face against Rowan's shirt. My middle got a tiny bit warm.

ROWAN

I had to argue with Gran about it, and even though she was uncomfortable with my idea, she finally gave in. We didn't tell Maisy. I knew she'd never want to go, but I didn't want her to be afraid the entire time I was gone. It was better if I did this by myself.

We dropped Maisy off at one of Gran's neighbors and then drove onto the highway. It seemed like forever before I saw the sign *Welcome to the Town of Little Sliding*. When Gran turned onto Pinchkiss Circle I looked at where our house once stood. All I could see was a black scar. We crunched down the gravel driveway until Gran stopped the car on the grass. She shut off the engine and we both got out. Gran drew in a breath, put her hand to her mouth. I just stood there.

With the exception of the red brick fireplace, our house was just a bunch of darkened stubs. The ground was littered with charred wood and ash and shards of exploded glass. Posts were hammered into the earth, and caution tape was tied in a rectangle around it all. A bright yellow bulldozer sat next to it. I guess someone was going to demolish what remained. Crush the walls of the basement. Eventually, a new house might rise up. Maybe new children would live there. A fluffy yellow dog with a full belly. A mother and father who were kind.

I took a step forward, but Gran touched my arm. "Don't," she said. She pointed at the security tape. "It's not safe."

I knew she wasn't only talking about the ground beneath my feet. She also meant the memories. Of being trapped. Of being starved. Of nearly being burned alive by the ones who were supposed to love me best. Those memories weren't safe.

I looked out over the backyard. The trees behind the burned-out house were bright and alive and full of orange and red leaves.

"I'll be back," I said to Gran.

"And I'll be waiting right here." She reached out and touched my fingers. "Try not to be disappointed. Keep your expectations at bay."

I took my time walking through the woods. I touched the moss hanging from the trees. A short distance ahead, I watched a rabbit hop into a clearing. It paused for a moment and wiggled its ears. Crouching down, I noticed a rust-colored centipede tucked inside a groove on a fallen log. So many feathery legs. I took care to step over it. The air was fresh and cool, and when I closed my eyes I could hear the rustling wind pulling at the leaves and the electric hum of insects hiding in the canopy.

After a while I reached the bridge. I pushed through the bushes that blocked the archway this side of the creek. A low fire burned. A man sat beside it, long gray beard, hood covering his face. He drove a stick into the flames.

I stepped toward him. "Carl?"

He glanced up at me. Not Carl. His face was skeletal and his mouth was a dark hole. "Leave off," he yelled. "Leave off!"

I stepped back. My stomach seized. Not with fear, but with something else. Almost hunger. Or maybe emptiness, which wasn't quite the same thing. What was I thinking? The whole idea was pointless. After everything that had happened to him, why would Carl ever come back? But still, I'd had to check. Just in case he was there. In case he was waiting.

A nip on my neck, and I slapped away a mosquito. I looked at my palm—a dot of wings and legs and blood marked the middle. I wiped it on my jeans. "Sorry," I said to the man by the fire. "I'm not here to bother you. I was hoping to find my—to find my friend." The man grumbled and stabbed the fire again.

I was about to turn when I saw someone else squat down near the cement wall. An enormous rounded back covered by a familiar heavy coat that was dragging on the ground.

"Carl?"

"Urh." The hulking mass shifted, but he didn't turn his head. When I went closer, I could see it was him. His hands were digging through a pile of garbage. Cans and plastic wrappers and chicken bones and greasy boxes and newspapers and curled-up magazines.

Above him, I noticed the graffiti was still there. *Almost.*

"It's me, Carl," I said.

"It's me, Carl," he repeated.

"Yes, me." I wanted him to look over. I wanted him to recognize me. To hear him call me Magic Boy.

He mumbled something.

"Carl?" When he stood up, his shoulders were stooped. His head hung down toward his chest at an angle, as though it was too heavy for his neck. He wouldn't meet my eye.

"No, no. You've got to. It's not, urh, a big transitory period." He scratched his beard. "When the birds come. Too many feathers and sometimes they get wet. Don't have the exact documents, urh, for domestic flights."

None of what he said made sense. "Where's Girl?" I interrupted.

He froze then, patted his leg once, twice, but nothing came running toward him. "Gone. Gone. Government took her. When they took me. After I killed that boy." He tapped the side of his head with his finger. Left a streak of something red. "Didn't listen to me when I said the truth. Had to send him away. Keep him from getting harmed. Stan didn't trust him." He rubbed his pink eyes. "And then they turned me out. She wasn't in the sunshine. Wasn't snapping at the flies. Didn't, didn't, didn't, urh, give her back when they turned me out, too. Don't deserve her, they said. Don't deserve her. All the metal bars and the fleas in the mattress and hair in the plastic glass of milk they gave me. And I don't deserve her. Put her down, put her down. Government put her down."

My throat got tight.

He knotted his swollen fingers, pushed them into his chest. "No protection from the Workers. No one, urh, watching out. Gone. Gone."

Tears pooled in my eyes. "I'm sorry, Carl. Girl was a good dog."

The man by the fire threw something heavy in among the flames. Sparks flew up. "Leave off!" he yelled again. "No-good bugger. Leave off, will you."

The dull ache in my stomach spread. My skin was warm, but inside I was cold. Girl was gone. How could they take away the one thing that made him feel safe? Guarded him? Called him back when his mind traveled too far toward darkness? He seemed so much worse than he was before. Rambling and twitching his fingers. Blinking like there was salt in his eyes.

So much had happened to me, but so much had happened to Carl, too.

"I—I just came to see if you were here," I said. "To say hello."

"To say hello."

"Yeah. I didn't mean to upset you. I'm going to go now, okay, Carl?"

"Go." He sat on the rocks, legs crossed, and wiped his hand underneath his nose. "Urh. Do you want to see your cards?"

"If it's okay," I said. I sat opposite him. *In one of these fine chairs.* "That'd be great."

He dug his handkerchief out of his pocket and smoothed it on the ground. Then from another pocket he retrieved the cards. They were the same old ones. Faded and bent, the image of a woman in a flowing dress on the back. I chewed my lip. They'd destroyed his dog, but saved his deck of cards.

"Urh," he said. He shuffled the pack, held it out to me, and I tapped it three times with my pointer finger. Then he began snapping cards down in a row. Four, then five.

"What do they say, Carl?"

Gently, he touched each card with his finger. He didn't hide them as he'd done before. "Bright times. Bright, bright, urh, bright times."

"For me?"

"They say you're going to be okay." For a single moment, he looked me straight in the eye. Shy and uncertain. "You're going to be okay. Now."

Carl plucked up the cards and tucked them away in a pocket. Then he stood up, turned his massive back to me, continued digging through the mound of trash. He found a can and shook it into his palm. Something plopped into his hand and he put it in his mouth. I stood there, waiting.

"Thanks," I said, but he didn't answer. "Carl?" He kept picking through the garbage. I don't think he heard me. "Bye, Carl. Goodbye."

I turned around and walked through the woods toward Gran. All I could think about was Carl's last word. *Now.* It might have meant absolutely nothing, or it might have meant that somewhere deep inside of him, he knew me.

I lowered my head. That was all I wanted, really. The same thing as most everyone else. To be out in the open. To be regarded. To be seen.

MAISY

"She's still claiming some legal right," Gran told Dr. Westerly. "I don't think I have a choice."

I was waiting outside Dr. Westerly's office, but the door was open just a bit. I visited her two times every week. Susan called Gran before I started school and told Gran it was a good idea. The first couple of visits I didn't like it, but Dr. Westerly already taught me some things. I learned how to "read my middle." That way I knew when I was getting upset, and I could do things to calm down. She also made me talk to "the girl from Pinchkiss Circle." At first I thought it was dumb, but the more I talked to that girl, the more I talked back. It was a big surprise when I told myself I was scared all the time. I got even more scared when it was just me and Gloria, and Rowan was gone and Telly was gone. Then I was scared every single second. Dr. Westerly said being afraid made my heart go fast and my head go sparkly. "But now that we know, Maisy, we can figure out ways to make things better."

"Well," she said to Gran. "The only approach we can take right now is to try and prepare her."

"How do you prepare a small child to visit jail?"

Jail?

"If we can help her understand what to expect—"

"How on earth could we do that?"

"Go through the process. Discuss different scenar—"

"Listen. My daughter's not a good woman, Dr. Westerly. I've tried and tried to figure it out, but I haven't the faintest clue why. I don't know where I went wrong."

"Mrs.—"

"I mean, how could I raise such a shallow, vengeful, destructive person?"

Dr. Westerly didn't answer for a minute. Then she said, "But she's still a person, isn't she? We need to help Maisy realize that. Her mother is a person. A very flawed person, granted. One who's done terrible, terrible things, but still just a person." I heard some papers moving around. "I think we'll discover Maisy is much stronger than we think."

I closed my eyes and put my hand on my throat. My heart was going tak-tak-tak. That old woodpecker was back in there, making a lot of noise in my neck.

A police lady opened a metal door to a big room. Another girl walked right past me, but my feet didn't want to move. The room had too many people talking and laughing and smoking and having snacks. It had tables and chairs and those machines with jelly beans and gumballs inside. There was a high-up counter and two police people stood on the other side of it. They were frowning like Shar always did when she was bored.

The lady put her hand on my shoulder. "You need to go in, sweetheart, else the door might close on us." She said it in a friendly way. "I'll help you find your mom, okay?"

I took a step.

"My daughter!"

I blinked. Then I saw her. Gloria was rushing across the room to me. Her sneakers squeaked on the shiny floor. Her hair was shorter and turned back to brown and her face was covered in powder. She was wearing blue-green pants and a blue-green sweatshirt, just like all the other ladies who lived there.

"My daughter!" she said again.

"That your mom?" the lady said.

Before I could nod Gloria said "I sure am," and she grabbed my hand and pulled me over to a table. I sat on one of the chairs. She sat next to me. "Aren't you a sight for sore eyes," she said. "What took you so long?"

I chewed my lip.

"I'm sure I already know the answer. You'd come see me first thing if you had a choice."

My teeth pulled off some skin, and a bad taste went on my tongue.

"Well, no matter. You're here now. You're here with Gloria."

I nodded and looked around the room. There was someone in blue-green at almost every table. One wall was big windows and the other walls were yellow like our happy, happy door. I wondered if Gloria noticed, and if she liked the color or if it made her sad.

A lady passed our table and slapped it hard. I jumped and so did the black plastic ashtray that was in front of me. The lady had a heart tattoo on her arm that was jabbed through with a sword and pretend blood drops were falling out.

"That your girl?" the lady said. "She's just gorgeous."

Gloria slid some of my hair behind my ear with her fingernail. When she touched me I tried not to move. "Don't I know it," she said. "She's the spit of me."

"No joke there, Glory." Then the lady went to another table and a man in a blue coat got up and hugged her. He had a cigarette inside his mouth and it wiggled up and down when he talked.

"Glory. Isn't that lovely?" Gloria said. "That's what they were calling me, from the first day. Just to boost me up. They know I don't belong here."

I don't belong here.

I squeezed my hands together. "Oh," I said. I sounded like a squeaking mouse, but Gloria laughed.

"Of course you're nervous, darling. You and me never could tolerate hubbub, could we? Always enjoyed peace and quiet." She shrugged. "But. You adjust."

I nodded again. She reached over and held onto my hand. Her skin was warm, and around my mouth went tingly and my fingers felt strange. I checked my middle. Dr. Westerly told me when I started to feel shaky, I should listen to my lungs. Make sure they were getting air all the way in the bottom. I took a deep breath through my nose, like we practiced, and blew it out through my mouth.

"Have you been getting my letters?"

I glanced at my sneakers. Gran let me pick them out myself.

"You haven't! I can't believe it. Do you know I've written you every single day? Trying to explain so you'll understand."

I shook my head. I tried Dr. Westerly's trick again, but it wasn't working.

"That woman!" She let go of my hand and went back in the plastic chair. "Always interfering. What does she think? Stealing my letters is going to change something? You're here, aren't you? She probably tried to stop it, but I know my rights. It's piss in her eye."

I took more slow breaths and I tried to stay very, very still. When we drove to the jail Gran told me over and over Gloria was a regular person. She couldn't hurt me or read my mind. We weren't attached by strings. "If she pushes, you don't have to bend."

When Gloria talked again, her voice was quiet. "I tried to hate you, you know. I really did. For what you did to me. How could you destroy me like that? But being separated from a daughter does something to a mother, Bids." No one had called me Bids in a long time. "Of course you don't understand, but it makes things all clear. These months being stuck in here, I've changed my mind and I've changed myself. People can do that when they got a lot of muscle upstairs." She pointed at her forehead.

I chewed my lip some more. Maybe Gloria had changed. She was right. People could do that. People could be better. Dr. Westerly even said so. Maybe she felt bad about everything. About what she did to Rowan. Or maybe she was confused when it happened and thought she was doing something right. Some parts of it were still fuzzy. Maybe those parts were just a dream. I wasn't sure.

"I decided you're going to come see me every week. We'll iron this out in person. Knit you and me back together. Like we used to be."

I swallowed and nodded. My eyes were burning, and I kept blinking. The lady at the next table was crying. She was smoking and picking at a dot of black on her cheek. It wasn't coming off.

"You listening to me? Or is that stranger so interesting you can't tear yourself away? Maybe you should go sit over there with her. You seem to like her so much better."

My leg bobbed up and down. "I'm sorry, Gloria."

She touched my cheek with her finger. "That's okay, darling. I'd just like to spend this time together. Me and you. Tell you everything that's going on."

"I'm sorry," I said again.

"I already got a lot of friends, Bids. I keep busy. Sometimes I'm in the laundry, and sometimes I help in the kitchen. We got a garden. I've been going to church. Don't miss a week." She smiled. "And I've also met someone special. Well, not met exactly. Yet!" She rolled her eyes, but in a nice way. "I got a letter the first week I was here. And I took a chance and wrote him back. And so it goes. I can't tell you how wonderful it is to have someone I can rely on. Who believes in me and supports me." My hand was in hers again. I didn't know how it got there. "His name's Timothy. Isn't that a handsome name? We're already making plans—you know, once all this annoyance gets sorted?"

Gloria giggled. She seemed so happy. I didn't know if I was happy for her. But if I was, was that okay? I had to remember to ask Dr. Westerly.

"You drift off again?"

I shook my head.

"'Cause I got something important to say." She coughed. "I'm sorry if your growing up hasn't been perfect. I'm sorry you think wrong things the way you do. I'm sorry my own daughter can hold such a repulsive grudge against me." She folded her arms across her chest. "There. I made a proper apology. I hope you see fit to accept it."

I looked her in the eyes. Just for a second. I wanted to say something, but my mind was all muddy. Nothing would come out.

"Oh, Bids. It's not fair, you know." She squeezed my shoulder and shook it a bit. "Every single thing I've ever done is with the best intentions. Will you look at me again?" I looked at her again. "You see, I didn't mean for any of that to happen. I honestly didn't. There was so much commotion, wasn't there? I thought once your brother got to a better place, a safer place, you know, inside his messed-up brain, things'd be fine. And then the grease fire. That was so unexpected, wasn't it? Who could've imagined? Not me, for one."

I looked down at my hand. My eyes were still burning and all those dirty cigarette smells were going up my nose. My heart was going fast, and my head skipped right back to when I was in that smoke. I couldn't see. I couldn't breathe. I felt the lock, but I couldn't open it. It was so hot and it burned and I had to let it go.

"And how's that brother of yours doing?"

"Good," I whispered.

"Good? That's all you got to say?"

"I don't know." He went to a movie with his friends, and a girl named Melody. She had long brown hair and wore a tam and a sweater. Gran made a joke and Rowan's face got red.

"Well he always was a tough one to handle. But I have to tell you." She put her elbows on the table and put her chin in her hands. "What he did gave me great pleasure. Still does. Can you let him know?"

I opened my mouth. I didn't understand.

Then she leaned close to me and talked real quiet. "That stuff about Telly. What he said. Of course I confirmed every word to the authorities. Believe me, I had my story straight, and they didn't need much more. I think about it all the time, and my whole inside fills right up with delight." Gloria laughed. "Once this confusion is straightened out, I'll be out enjoying life and Telly'll still be paying for what he done." I tried to swallow the lump in my throat. "I'm so glad your brother told the truth. Tell Rowan to come visit. The past is the past is the past, and he's still mine after all."

I nodded, but I knew that was a lie. Dr. Westerly told me no person owned another person. Not even Gloria.

"You don't talk much, do you? Even less than you used to."

I blinked and blinked. My eyes were burning from the cigarettes and my ears rang from all the noise. Everyone was talking and laughing and crying all at once. I didn't like it there.

"No wonder you look so dazed. That woman you're living with is bland beyond. Not a creative bone in her body." Gloria rolled her eyes again, but not in a nice way this time. "When I get out, we'll spend time together. You won't fritter away another second of your life being bored. I can promise you that. We'll do things we used to do. Me and you."

Gloria spun the ashtray around. There was white coating on the inside and some of it flew out on the table. I could smell the dirt.

"Bids?"

"Mm?"

"You know it was just a terrible, regretful accident, right? My heart is just broken. Completely broken. And I'm paying the price, aren't I? I mean, look at me." She grabbed her hair and patted her dusty cheeks. "I'm paying for everyone's guilt. Yours included. The entire damn community's, if you ask me. Everyone let me down."

My heart was hammering on my throat. I tried to remember my lungs. They were squeezed up. But not with sadness this time. There was something else there. Hot and stuck and twisting up through my middle. Like one of Chicken's burrs.

A bell rang and all the ladies stood up. I stood up, too.

"I'm allowed a hug, you know."

She pulled me into her arms. "I'll always be your mother, darling. And you'll always be my daughter." Her clothes were stiff, and she squeezed me hard. "Tell me you love me best."

I love you best. I love you best.

"Let me hear you say it, Bids."

I opened my mouth. The words were right there, spinning around in my head, ready to gush out. But when I listened close, like Dr. Westerly taught me, I knew they didn't sound like me. I knew those words weren't mine.

Most nights I dreamt about Rowan falling in the water, but after I went to visit jail, I dreamt about Gloria. I watched her tumbling into a lake, and she made a huge splash. I peeked over and saw her sinking and sinking. Her white face and white hands turned the sick color of weeds as she went down. She was looking at me and bubbles zipped up from nowhere. I jumped and swam to her. I tugged at her clothes and her hair to turn her around. She hugged me around my middle and squeezed me while my legs kicked and my hands scooped. I tried hard, but I couldn't swim through the water. Then I felt it. She was so heavy. And I wasn't going higher up, I was going down. I wriggled free and floated to the surface. Two arms reached out for me. I saw a perfect island spot. They were Rowan's arms, and they grabbed my wrists and pulled me into the boat.

When I woke up, I thought about my dream. I would have to remember it, so I could tell Dr. Westerly. How I looked back into the black water and she was gone. I didn't feel nervous or scared, even though, in my head, that was the first time I done that.

I let Gloria disappear.

ACKNOWLEDGMENTS

I would like to thank the Toronto Arts Council for supporting this project. I would also like to thank my agent, Hilary McMahon, of Westwood Creative Artists. Not only does she offer expert guidance and a bottomless well of enthusiasm, she and her colleagues work tirelessly in support of writers and writing. I am grateful to be under those wings. When I shared the book with my first readers, Aniko Biber and Tania Madden, I was (as always) apprehensive. Their kind words and thoughtful suggestions brought the book to a stronger place. Finally, a heartfelt thank-you to my editor, Lara Hinchberger, at Penguin Random House Canada. She saw the worth in my characters and their experiences, and her insight was truly extraordinary. With her careful direction, I was able to fully discover the story I wanted to tell.